Other books by Fred Patten

Best in Show: Fifteen Years of Outstanding Furry Fiction (2003)
Reprinted as:
Furry! The World's Best Anthropomorphic Fiction! (2006)

Watching Anime, Reading Manga:
25 Years of Essays and Reviews (2004)

Already Among Us; An Anthropomorphic Anthology (2012)

The Ursa Major Awards Anthology

A Tenth Anniversary Celebration

Edited by Fred Patten

The Ursa Major Awards Anthology
A Tenth Anniversary Celebration

Production copyright FurPlanet Productions © 2012

Cover artwork copyright © 2012 by Teagan Gavet and Tess Garman www.furaffinity.net/user/blotch

Published by FurPlanet Productions
Dallas, Texas
www.FurPlanet.com

ISBN 978-1-61450-052-0

Printed in the United States of America
First Edition Trade Paperback June 2012

Dedicated to:

My fellow members of the ALAA committee for their ten years (or however long it has been since they joined) of volunteer work in administering the Awards each year; and to those others who have helped behind the scenes in getting our UMA website up and keeping it running; those who have helped publicize the Awards at fan conventions and elsewhere; those who have donated financially towards the Awards' upkeep; and so on:

Thank you!

Special thanks to:

FuzzWolf and Teiran of FurPlanet Productions, for agreeing that there should be a tenth anniversary UMA short fiction anthology.

The Tai-Pan Literary & Arts Project, for its encouragement and permission in reprinting Kristin E. H. Fontaine's and C. D. Woodbury's story.

Jeff Eddy and Tim Susman of Sofawolf Press, the original publisher of M. C. A Hogarth's and Samuel C. Conway's stories, for providing electronic files of those stories' illustrations.

And Blotch for their amazing cover painting.

Table of Contents

Introduction

Fred Patten

Awards!

Everything had an award. In general society, there were the Oscars for movies, the Emmys for television, the Tonys for Broadway theater, the Grammys for music, the Clios for advertising, and the Annies for animation, just to name the best-known. In literature, there were the Anthonys and the Edgars for mysteries, the Spurs for Westerns, and the Ritas for romance fiction. For comic books, there were the Eisners and the Harveys.

The general "speculative fiction" field was especially prolific, with the Hugos and the Nebulas for science fiction & fantasy, the World Fantasy Awards (popularly called the Lovecrafts for its trophy, a cartoon bust of H.P.L.) for fantasy, and the Bram Stoker Awards for horror. There were one or more awards for Australian, Canadian, Finnish, French, German, Hungarian, Israeli (in Hebrew), Japanese, Russian, Spanish (published in Spain; it could be in Basque, Catalan, Galician, or Spanish), or other national science fiction. There were awards for s-f art. There were specialized annual awards for the best s-f by a first-published author, for the best gay/lesbian/bisexual s-f, for the best Libertarian s-f, for s-f poetry, for alternate-history s-f, for s-f by a female author, for s-f featuring vampires, and more.

There were different kinds of awards. Some were voted on by the members of a popular convention. Some were voted on by the members of a society, such as the Mystery Writers of America. Some were juried awards. But they were all prestigious.

But there was no award for Anthropomorphic, or Furry, fiction!

The furry fandom coalesced out of the s-f and comic book fandoms in the late 1970s or early '80s, depending on whom you ask. There were undeniable self-published Furry comic books by 1981 (*Ismet #1*, May 1981, by Greg Wadsworth; *Teenage Mutant Ninja Turtles #1*, May 1984, by Kevin Eastman & Peter Laird; *Albedo: Anthropomorphics #1*, June 1984, by Steven A. Gallacci), Furry parties at s-f and comic-book conventions by 1986 – they were what gave the new fandom its popular name – and the ConFurence, the first all-Furry convention, in Southern California in January 1989. The first Furry fanzine, *FurVersion* (by Kyim Granger) was started in May 1987 and lasted for 21 issues to November 1990. By the late 1990s there were or had been many Furry fanzines/small-press literary magazines, usually lasting for only a few issues but all publishing fiction. *Alternate Realms. The Ever-Changing Palace. Fang, Claw & Steel. Fantastic Furry Stories. FUR Plus. Fur Visions. FurryPhile. Mythagoras. PawPrints Fanzine. South Fur Lands. Steam Victorian. Tales of the Tai-Pan Universe. Touch. Yarf! Zoomorphica.*

I read them all. And as time passed and the total number of issues of Furry magazines grew, and as the number of awards in s-f and comics fandom grew – the Endeavour Awards, for the best s-f by an author living in the Pacific Northwest, were launched at Portland, Oregon s-f fandom's annual Orycon in 1996; and as the number of annual Furry conventions grew – ConiFur Northwest in Seattle began in 1998; Further Confusion in northern California in 1999 – I began to feel the lack of any Furry award ever more keenly. I began to complain about this frequently at Furry conventions, and the response was usually along the lines of, "Well, Fred, if you feel that strongly about it, why don't you do something about it yourself?"

Finally, in 2000, it happened. Darrel Exline, who had just taken over as Chairman of the ConFurences, said that he would authorize an annual Furry award if I would organize it. So I joined the regular ConFurence organizing group in late 2000 as the lead of its Special Awards Committee, with Rod O'Riley and Kay Shapero as the rest of our committee, for ConFurence 12, in April 19-22, 2001.

We started out with four special awards. "2001 begins a new century. The theme of ConFurence 12, in April 2001, is "Funny Animals at the Movies". As part of this theme, The ConFurence Group would like to invite 'morph fans everywhere to join in voting to select:

The Best Anthropomorphic Motion Pictures and TV Series of the 20th Century! This Award will consist of a special trophy in four categories:

Best Motion Picture (Live Action)
Best Motion Picture (Animation)
Best TV Series (Live Action)
Best TV Series (Animation)

The years of coverage are 1901 to 2000. Please help select the best anthropomorphic motion pictures and TV productions of the past hundred years." Fans "everywhere" were invited to vote, but ballots were only sent out to the preregistered members of ConFurence 12. The winners were:

Motion Picture (Live Action) – *Who Framed Roger Rabbit?*
Motion Picture (Animated) – *Fantasia*
TV Series (Live Action) – *The Muppet Show*
TV Series (Animated) – *Animaniacs*

The first runners-up were, respectively, *The Muppet Movie, My Neighbor Totoro, Beauty and the Beast*, and *Rocky and His Friends/The Bullwinkle Show*. The winners received a trophy designed by David Bliss.

The special awards were very popular, so with ConFurence 13, or Confurence 2002 as Exline renamed it (over Committee objections), the awards were converted into the familiar annual awards in, originally, nine categories. But first, we had to choose a name for the annual awards.

This was not easy. First, after suggestions for a name were solicited, we got recommendations to name it after the recommender's favorite anthropomorphic character. The Bugs' or Bugs Bunnys. The Donalds. The Felixes. The Hazels or Fivers (from *Watership Down*). The Kimbas. The Pogos. The Robins or Robin Hoods (after the 1973 Disney animated character). The Wileys. The objection to all of these was that they were copyrighted characters. We had a Horrible Example in anime fandom to work from. In 1995 the new AnimEast convention announced that it was creating the annual Tezuka Awards, honoring Osamu Tezuka (1928-1989), the creator of Astro Boy and Kimba the White Lion, for excellence in anime. In the first place, there had already been a biennial Tezuka Awards in Japan since 1971. Second and more importantly, the Tezuka estate objected strenuously that it controlled the use of Tezuka's name and it did not give its permission. It was agreed that the new anthropomorphics award should not use the name of any copyrighted character. Even if we got permission, that permission could be withdrawn in the future, forcing us to rename the award.

Second, Darrel Exline tried to impose a name on the awards by fiat as head of the Confurence. He wanted to name them the Golden Bear Awards, after the golden bear mascot of the University of California, Berkley, his alma mater. There was unanimous objection to this because the Golden Bear Awards is the well-known name of the Best Film award of the Berlin International Film Festival (Berlinale), awarded annually since 1951 and almost certainly copyrighted. Exline did not feel that this mattered, but he gave in to the argument that there would undoubtedly be a legal challenge if we tried to use the same name.

This did get us thinking about bears, however. When the Ursa Major was proposed, the Great Bear, after the famous constellation, and a search did not turn up any preexisting award of that name, it was adopted.

So the annual Ursa Major Awards were up and running. The first Awards, for the best anthropomorphic literature and art of 2001, were presented at Confurence 2002, on April 26-28, 2002. The rules were the same as before; anyone could request a ballot, but the awards were only publicized to the Confurence's preregistered members. The winners received a certificate drawn by that Confurence's Artist Guest of Honor, Roz Gibson.

The second annual awards were run like the first. Confurence 2003's winners received a certificate drawn by that year's Artist Guest of Honor, Roy D. Pounds, II. But a serious problem had become evident. The Ursa Major Awards were intended to be for all of Furry fandom, and international in scope. Instead, hardly anyone outside of the Confurences' attendees had ever heard of them. Worse, even among those who had heard of them, the perception was that they were for Confurence attendees only. If you weren't a Confurence attendee, it was widely felt, you had no reason to have any interest in the Ursa Majors.

We – the three members of the Confurence's Awards Committee – conferred seriously about how to expand the awards beyond the Confurences. We decided that it was impossible as long as the Ursa Majors remained closely linked to the Confurences. The solution was to disassociate the Ursa Majors from the Confurences, to establish an independent administrative committee, and to persuade other Furry conventions – preferably, a different one each year to emphasize that the awards were meant for all of Furry fandom – to host their annual presentations. To our happy surprise, Darrel Exline gave this proposal his complete support instead of trying to keep the awards owned by the Confurence. Nobody knew that he had decided to end the Confurences, until he made the surprise announcement at Confurence 2004 that it would be the last one. By that time the three of us had already renamed ourselves the Anthropomorphic Literature and Arts Association, invited other prominent fans outside of Southern California to join the ALAA (Chakat Goldfur/Bernard Doove of Melbourne, Australia, PeterCat/ Peter Kappesser of the Anthrocon Committee, and Gene Breshears of Seattle Furry fandom were among the first to accept), begun to strongly solicit nominations and voting throughout Furry fandom, obtained an official and permanent Ursa Major logo drawing from Ontario artist Heather Bruton, and gotten that year's Canadian Anthro and Cartooning Expo (C-ACE) in Ottawa to host the 2004 presentations.

Later, the ALAA invited all of the major Furry conventions to appoint a representative to the administrative committee, so today the ALAA consists of fifteen members representing Furry annual conventions around the world, including the largest, Pittsburgh's Anthrocon, and the farthest, Melbourne's MiDFur.

Now it is 2012, ten years after the first Ursa Major presentations at Confurence 2002 in April of that year. There have been ten annual Ursa Major presentations, at C-ACE, at the Anthrocon then in Philadelphia, at Rocket City Fur Meet in Huntsville, Alabama, at CaliFur back in Southern California, at Morphicon in Columbus, Ohio, at All Fur Fun in Spokane, and at FA: United in New Jersey. Other conventions have volunteered, but we want a Furry convention in the late April to early July time period to keep the delay between tallying the votes and presenting the awards from being too great.

One category that has been steady throughout the ten years has been Best Anthropomorphic Short Fiction. This anthology is a bit different from most award anthologies which present only the winners. The Short Fiction winners for 2001 through 2005 are all here, but the awards for 2006 through 2010 have all been won by Kyell Gold. It was felt that presenting five stories by Kyell Gold would be too much concentrated Gold, so we present only three of his stories; and to keep the anthology from being too short, we have filled it out with other final-ballot tales from those ten years.

The Ursa Major Awards have always been a popular-vote award, controlled by the Furry fans who nominate and vote each year. The administrators get complaints every year of, "How could you allow XXXXX to qualify as anthropomorphic fiction?", or, "How could you fail to put XXXXX onto the final ballot?" It all depends on those who nominate and vote. I doubt that I'm giving away any big confidence when I say that most of the ALAA committee members were supporting *Fantastic Mr. Fox* or one of the other 2009 Best Motion Picture finalists that featured genuinely anthropomorphic characters instead of the big blue aliens of *Avatar*. But *Avatar* is what the fans voted for. Vox populi, vox dei.

And now, as of 2012, there are two Furry awards: the Ursa Major Awards, a popular-vote award open to all Furry fans internationally, and the brand-new Cóyotl Awards, a juried award organized and voted on by the members of the Furry Writers' Guild. The first Cóyotl Awards will be presented at Rainfurrest 2012, in Seattle on September 27-30, 2012. Welcome, brothers!

Brock Hoagland introduced Perissa, his teenage leopardess assassin, in Tales of Perissa *(United Publications, July 2001), a collection of her first five adventures. A* Book 2, *with stories six through eleven, followed in December 2004. "Beneath the Crystal Sea" is the fourth adventure. There are at least five more stories still unpublished.*

The Tales of Perissa *are frank pastiches of Robert E. Howard's Conan the Barbarian stories, set during the Cimmerian warrior's period as a young street thief. Perissa's setting is the "before recorded history" brawling independent seaport city-state of Goedus, "City of Ten Thousand Sails", full of nobles, rich merchants, sorcerers, thieves, and penniless beggars. Goedus is ruled by clever Prince Kalinides and unofficially run by the Assassins Guild. Perissa, nineteen years old, is a new member of the Assassins Guild, still in the general pool of bravos but anxious to make a reputation so she will be requested by name for the higher-priced assassinations. At this point Perissa is still a lone "wolf" (to stretch the metaphor) and has not yet acquired her inseparable companion of the later stories, the chipmunk slave-girl Maelith.*

Beneath the Crystal Sea

Brock Hoagland

Perissa scanned the employment offers posted on the Assassins Guild's notice board. They solicited the deaths of prominent citizens at ridiculously low fees, sought bravos to act as guards on expeditions searching for legendary treasures (wages to be paid in shares of the treasure, naturally) and other such dubious commissions. One even brazenly solicited the assassination of Prince Kalinides. Idly, the pretty, blonde leopardess of nineteen wondered if the Guildmaster would inform the Prince of it or merely assign someone to remove the madman as a favor to Goedus's ruler. Of course everyone, especially the potential victim, knew the Guild would slay Kalinides for the right price. So far no one was willing to meet the equally well known, fabulous sum. The Guild did not seriously consider any of these, but posted them nevertheless for any member desperate enough to accept them.

Perissa was desperate. As a new member she had not yet established a reputation that would have clients asking for her by name, nor was she given choice assignments by the Guild. She brushed a speck of dirt from her silk shirt, then critically examined her satin trousers and tooled leather boots to ensure that they were clean. Somehow the fees she had earned over the past few months, riches though they had seemed to her at the time, had slipped through her fingers. She had been forced to take her meals in the Guild's dining hall of late and was remiss with the rent on her apartment. Granted, her landlord was as yet too much in fear of her profession to broach the subject to her, but the time would come when he would throw her out. And the Grandmaster Assassin would not allow her to slay the fellow over a just debt. She toyed with one of her small gold earrings, its tiny emerald a match for her eyes. If only for once she had not had her usual bad luck at dice.

Another hungry bravo came to stand beside her and scan the board. Nige was a wolf whose fur had lately grayed even more and who wore an almost perpetual expression compounded of wistfulness and worry. Fast approaching the point where age would force him to quit, he had naught put aside to save him from a small room in the guild house for his retirement. He had been unlucky in his commissions, never getting the formidable one fraught with peril whereby he could make a name for himself that would garner the big money assignments. He took down the notice seeking the death of one of the city's nobles with a mere pittance for recompense.

The bravo girl bit back the acid comment that she had been considering it and had been here first. He needed any fee too badly. Besides, she had not yet reached the point where she'd undertake the hazardous slaying of a noble for so little. She smiled at him. "Good Fortune attend you, Nige."

"Thankee, Perissa. May the Lady-Bitch favor ye as well." His broad country accent was quite different from her clipped city tones. "Mayhaps this be the chance I've been seeking. Wilt ye share a cup o' wine with me afterwards to celebrate my success?"

"Aye, gladly, that and more." Her warm response left no doubt as to what the more entailed.

"Ah, lass, ye be kind to an old male. With such a delightful prospect awaiting me, how can I fail?" His face when he left was happier than anyone could recall seeing for a long time.

Perissa had not made the offer out of kindness; as did the rest of her comrades, she had a genuine affection for Nige. In that respect at least he had been fortunate. But the problem of her flat purse still had not been solved. None of the remainder of these laughable offers was worth considering. She decided to pay the Assignments Office a visit on the off-chance she could wheedle a commission even though it was not likely her name had come to the top of the strictly maintained rotation whereby general assignments were handed out. The more difficult, and thus more lucrative, ones were saved for the more experienced guild members.

"Is there aught for me?" she asked a wolverine clerk behind his desk.

"Mistress Ismara may have something," he replied, pursing his lips. "She has said that any of our more comely wenches who stop by are to see her. I think the client wants more than murder!"

"If he wants that, 'twill be by my choice. This is the Assassins Guild, not the Courtesans."

The Mistress of Assignments was a tall, handsome ewe, her brown hair highlighted with a few streaks of silver, her figure kept taut and trim with exercise. Her species had been a great asset during her active career—no one expected a sheep to be an assassin. While every assassin was trained in a variety of ways to kill, each specialized in one or two. Perissa specialized in the sword, taking advantage of a leopard's speed and the new methods made possible with the introduction of a lighter-style rapier a decade ago. Ismara was the Guild's leading poisoner with scores of deaths to her credit.

Her company was a handsome fox in his mid-thirties with shoulder-length russet hair. His clothes were of costly fabrics and impeccable tailoring, but had seen long, hard use and were carefully mended. His pose of studied casualness as he sprawled in a chair, one leg negligently thrown over an armrest, gave him a dashing air, as he well knew. He was not all poise, though. His tall, compactly muscled frame radiated an unmistakable air of confidence and authority. He would rise to any occasion and none would question his commands. Perissa noted that despite his careless show nothing would hinder him from gaining his feet and drawing his rapier in an instant.

He sized her up in turn, lingering especially over her pert breasts. Not large, they were nicely shaped and his face showed his appreciation. He spent almost as long evaluating the manner in which she wore the rapier on her right side. Turning to the Mistress of Assignments, he said, "Aye, she'll do."

"Sit down, Perissa," Ismara told her. "Connal has an intriguing commission to proffer."

Connal! The blonde bravo girl stared at one of the most renowned males in the western reaches of the Tirabaedo Sea and the surrounding lands. Younger son of a powerful noble family in Goedus, he had inherited little upon his father's death. Rumor had it that his brother had cheated him of most of his due. He had become an adventurer and won several fortunes through risky trading ventures, smuggling and treasure hunting. Some said that he did not scruple to turn his vessel, the Sea Falcon, to outright piracy. However, they said so admiringly. Goedusians esteemed anyone who had a knack for accumulating wealth and they almost revered one who could do so outside the law without being caught. He had also lost every one of his fortunes through gambling, lavish living and cutting a wide swath through the ladies, spending freely upon the courtesan who was his mistress for the while.

"Which is?" Perissa inquired.

Connal answered. "I was engaged in a, ah, trading venture—" in which the customs collectors would no doubt be interested "—and was upon the Crystal Sea when I perchanced to glance over the side. Imagine my astonishment when I beheld the Sunken Tower!"

The Sunken Tower of the Crystal Sea! Perissa made a face. It was one of the most persistent of the legendary treasures no one was ever able to locate. "And you plan to return and recover the treasure."

"Of a certainty. It does no good at the bottom of the sea."

"Why did you not dive for it at once?"

" 'Tis too deep for that without special preparations. I returned to Goedus for that purpose. And I cannot entirely trust my crew around such riches. After all, should I meet with an accident their share would be doubled. I need someone I can depend upon without question should mutiny rear its ugly head. Thus an assassin; only they are guaranteed honest."

"How will you locate it again? Many are the tales of sailors who espied it once, but could not find it again however long they searched, even when their ship put about immediately."

"I have the spot marked."

Ismara's curiosity was piqued. "How does one mark the featureless sea?"

"There is a way," he replied smiling and would say no more upon the subject.

"Are quelling a mutiny and safeguarding your life all for which I'll be called upon?"

"Nay, let's say your duties are whatever is needful to gain and keep the treasure."

The leopardess asked the question whose answer she dreaded. "What remuneration do you offer for my services?"

"My crew receives shares amounting to half. What say you to a quarter of my share?"

The typical recompense offered for chasing a will-o'-the-wisp. Well, she'd have naught to do with that. She believed in gold, not legends. "A quarter of a half of nothing, belike. Nay, I want a surety. Pay the Guild's rate for daily service and I'll accompany you over the wide world pursuing legends."

"We'll not reach the Crystal Sea in less than a month with another to return and you want a half-thael for each day! Ismara, I implore you, reason with this unreasonable wench!"

"The fee an assassin accepts for special services is entirely up to him or her."

"Yet she demands a small fortune and may do naught to earn it!"

"And I may waste my time for naught if I agree to your terms!" Perissa retorted.

"You cannot expect to win a treasure without some risk, even the risk of empty hands!" He spoke passionately in a voice whose mellifluous timbre must have swayed many to his views. "Accept my terms and you may win hundreds of thaels!"

"He has a cognizant argument, Perissa," the ewe intervened. "You've the Guild's interests to consider as well as your own."

"Mistress, all I ask is that the Guild's fixed rate be honored. Indeed, I have no right to ask less."

"Not if it means we lose heavily. I think it worth the gamble in this instance; Connal has a certain repute in this regard. Do not forget, he looted the Elephant's Graveyard and found the Eye of Emmaris, equally legendary hoards. I release you from requiring Guild rates and urge you to strike a bargain."

"As you wish, Mistress." Perissa turned back to Connal. "Though I'll not hazard all. A quarter-thael a day if there's no treasure and four apiece for any incidental slayings."

The fox threw his hands up in exasperation. "Again the wench seeks guaranteed gold! Half the adventure in a treasure hunt is the uncertainty!"

"I must side with her now," said the Mistress of Assignments. "And lest you recover some barnacle-encrusted trash and claim it the treasure sought, she must have the option of choosing which she'll take as her payment."

"Agreed, but she must hazard a toss of life's dice there. She must choose on the spot, rather than after the Guild Treasurer has had an opportunity to evaluate our find. She must risk that the treasure not look a treasure and that she may lose thereby."

"The Guild finds that an acceptable risk. Perissa?"

"Agreed." Short of funds, she would have accepted almost any guaranteed fee. "When do we sail?"

"On the morrow with the receding tide. Be aboard by the sun's zenith. Ask any dockside loafer and he can direct you to the Sea Falcon's berth." He got to his feet, bowed with a flourish to each in turn and departed.

"Mistress, Connal is famed for more than his skill in seeking out treasures. You think he can be trusted?"

"He'll not attempt your death; in that regard he is trustworthy. He will try trickery, however. Be on your guard when you make your choice!"

"That I will." She arose to take her leave.

"Oh, Perissa." Turning, she saw Ismara smiling archly. "'Tis said that Connal is welcome amongst the courtesans even when his gold is gone. Mayhaps you can discover why!"

If true, it would not be the least of his legendary accomplishments. Even in Goedus there was no more mercenary a group than its beautiful and skilled whores.

"Aye, mayhaps I can. He is a handsome and engaging devil!"

* * *

Ships from over the known world, and some from parts unknown, thronged the renowned harbor of the City of Ten Thousand Sails. Red-walled Altkreit, island Mahz, far Talleron and age-haunted Ulan-Tor all had vessels there. Lines of longshorefurs loaded and unloaded ships while suspicious custom collectors checked cargo manifests and occasionally ordered a crate opened to verify that the contents did indeed agree with the label. Some captains appeared to be afflicted with a strange nervous disorder as this went on. Confusion reigned at the docks where newly arrived ships were tied-up. Merchants' agents tried to beat custom officials aboard for a private word with captains while whenever the officers turned their backs, sailors attempted to slip onto the dock and do business with the sharks come to fleece those too eager from weeks at sea to seek out better prices elsewhere. Buyers of the trinkets seamen acquired in foreign realms or made to while away long hours aboard ship provided the wherewithal for a brisk trade with vendors of strong drink or spicy foods much different from bland and monotonous ship's fare. The liveliest traffic was with courtesans of the lower sorts.

Perissa stood on the broad stone quay, examining the Sea Falcon where it lay tied fast to one of the multitudinous docks. Although she had never been to sea, no one could grow up in Goedus and not be a fair judge of ships. A small black ship lying low in the water, its lean lines and sharply raked twin masts with their lateen sails bespoke its speed and ease of handling. Not a vessel for carrying bulk cargoes, it was instead ideally suited for trading precious goods in dangerous waters, smuggling or with an abnormally large crew going on the account.

Picking up her bundle of spare weapons and clothes, she walked to the foot of the short gangplank. An ill favored, leering otter with teeth yellow where they were not missing, regarded her from where he leaned on the rail above. "Inform your captain that Perissa has arrived."

The watch spat and replied insolently, "Tell'm yerself. I'm no messenger boy fer his doxy."

The leopardess briefly weighed possible reactions. Someone in the crew was certain to test her and she'd have to react swiftly and decisively to let them know that she would not tolerate undue familiarity or hazing. Yet this was a small matter and she decided to ignore it. There was no sense so quickly making an enemy over so little. Boarding, she started towards where Connal directed the handful of otters, beavers and squirrels in their preparations for sea. Her rump was pinched, hard. She spun about, dagger in hand as if by magic and slashed across the back of the offending fingers. The otter cried out and clutched his bleeding digits.

Work stopped, faces turned towards them and Connal was at their side. "What happened?" he asked grimly.

"Inform this dung heap that I'm hired as assassin, not ship's whore."

The sailor was ill at ease, shifty eyes unable to meet his captain's foreboding glare. "Honest, Cap'n, all I did was give her a little pinch. What's she expect when she wears trousers that cling to her arse like that? By all the gods, I swear I meant no harm by it."

"But I mean harm by it. My arse is mine alone and no male may lay hand on it without my leave. Do so again and you'll pull your hand back short of fingers!"

"Get your gear and get off," Connal ordered. "You knew I was expecting a bravo and that it'd be a wench. Only a fool would take liberties with such unless he knew beforehand that they'd be well received. And I'll not have a fool aboard." The unfortunate opened his mouth to protest, took another look at his captain's unyielding face, and left to get his things.

"The rest of you get back to work! The tide departs soon and so do we!" He turned to Perissa with a smile and slight bow. "My apologies for that boor's behavior. If you'd like, I'll show you to your cabin now."

The cabin was surprisingly large for a small vessel and luxuriously appointed with a thick carpet, rich hangings on either side of the broad stern window and a table with several chairs. With its fur coverlet and silk pillows, the wide bed was not one for sleeping in alone and she guessed that in port he rarely did so. "This looks to be the captain's cabin."

"The Sea Falcon is a small vessel with no room for passenger quarters. This is the only one suitable for a member of the fair sex."

"And the captain, I take it, will also be here?"

The fox grinned winningly. "You cannot expect him to give up his own cabin, can you? The only other one we have is much smaller and will be shared by the mate and our other passenger. I'd not dream of telling them that they must give it up to you and bunk with the crew. And bunking with the crew or sleeping in the hold are your only options other than here."

He was an engaging rogue, handsome and self-assured. She tossed her bundle on the bed and returned his smile. "At least you're giving me the options. This suits me just fine."

Back on deck, Connal was soon pacing about in barely controlled agitation. He would stride to the dockside rail and glare up and down the quay, then it was over to the opposite side where he'd stare fixedly at the water below to see if any of the garbage floating there had begun drifting out on a receding tide. She heard him mutter, "If he causes us to miss the tide, I'll have his guts for a fish line and bait my hook with his liver." Then it was back to dockside to search the crowds with a baleful eye. The crew prudently avoided him in this black mood. He had taken to absent-mindedly drumming his fingers on the railing before his scowl suddenly disappeared and he exclaimed, "At last!"

Perissa examined the crowds in her turn, searching for the one Connal had been awaiting. The brown bear was easily spotted as he towered above all others along the waterfront, nearly seven feet tall with thews to match. A large chest was negligently balanced upon one broad shoulder, steadied by a huge hand. The other hand firmly gripped the arm of an elderly raccoon, more than half dragging him along, heedless of how he must hurry to keep up and equally heedless of his stumbles. The raccoon's difficulties were seemingly not all the result of a vain attempt to match his companion's longer paces. The bear wore typical seaman's garb of leather vest and trousers while the raccoon's tattered robe indicated a professional male fallen upon hard times.

The bear dragged his captive onto the ship. "Here he be, Captain."

Connal glared murderously at the raccoon. The latter tugged at his garment, ineffectually trying to straighten it. The purple staining the fur about his lips bespoke one overly fond of wine. His matted hair and clothes were dirty and his smell was enough to keep the bravo girl at a discreet distance. His attempt at an engaging smile on his befuddled face made him appear even more foolish. "Greetings, Connal. As you can perceive, I've arrived in good time for sailing."

"Only because I sent Tiroc to fetch you. Did you drink it all up or did you manage to purchase some of the items we'll need with the gold I gave you?"

With the unsteady, offended dignity of a drunkard wrongly accused, the old raccoon drew himself up and gestured towards the chest. " 'Tis all in there. I bought my apparatus afore I ever bought the first drop of wine."

"That's something at least."

"Ah, you wouldn't perchance have a swallow or two, would you? This great lout wouldn't even let me finish the goblet I had before me and it was paid for at that!" He was plainly outraged at the shameful waste.

Connal regarded him in disgust. "Get him below and into a bunk, Tiroc. He'll be of no use until he's sober and the palsies have passed.

Luckily it'll be some days yet afore he'll be needed." He rounded on the other crewmen. "What are you standing about for, useless as the nipples on your chests? Cast off and make sail! A treasure beckons!" Cheering, the crew ran to their duties.

Perissa joined Connal at the tiller. "Of what use to us is that drunkard?"

"Ryemart will be invaluable; without him we couldn't succeed." Seeing her skeptical look, he said, "Let not his present condition deceive you. Afore he became overly fond of wine he was one of the leading sorcerers in Goedus. Sober, his skills are yet undiminished and he'll not get a drop of drink until the treasure is in our grasp."

The Sea Falcon entered the Crystal Sea through the narrow break in the isthmus otherwise separating it from the Tirabaedo Sea. The zephyr caught by their sails was just sufficient to glide them across the crystalline ripples. Perissa leaned over a rail, observing the waters over which they sailed. Like the rest, she had adopted less and less clothing as they had sailed south and the heat had grown and now wore only a shirt. She knew the crew was stealing glances at her backside where her garment barely covered her rump and smiled at the thought. They could look all they wanted; only their captain could touch.

It had been an enjoyable voyage for her thus far. She had no duties to perform and could pass the hours as she pleased, almost as if on a holiday she'd never had. Connal made an excellent partner for fencing practice, one who could present her with the challenge she loved. Almost as challenging was letting him win most of the time without realizing she deliberately lost. It was as much to conceal her true skill from the potential foes the crew represented as to assuage his ego. And his reputation as a lover was certainly justified. He was artful, as concerned for her pleasure as his and imaginative. He was also very thorough—his tongue had been everywhere across her body.

Breaking off her reverie, the leopardess returned her attention to the water. Although the shallow sea was as much as twenty fathoms and more deep in places, it was as clear as fine glass, enabling her to discover its ill-hidden secrets. The near invisibility of the water made it easy to fantasize that their vessel was one of the air gliding above the surface of an alien world. Here, too, were deserts of clean, white sands, low mountain ranges of coral and thick forests of seaweed waving in the gentle breezes of the sea's currents. Yet it was a world almost totally devoid of earth-bound fauna, making up for that lack in its multitudes of aerial creatures. Huge schools of fish, some holding thousands of members and the least holding scores, swam through the forests and mountains and across the deserts.

With the bottom everywhere visible, one could certainly see the Sunken Tower if sailing above it. But where to look? The waters were vast as well as shallow and clear. A lifetime could be spent searching and the tower still not be found. How did Connal propose to locate it again? She did not see how he could have marked the spot; as far as she could determine one stretch of water was identical to any other.

"Ryemart!" the captain shouted for the sorcerer. "On deck! 'Tis time you earned your keep!"

Straightening, Perissa turned about. Perhaps some questions were about to be answered, amongst them what black thaumaturgy Ryemart had been engaged in last night. She had awoke just past midnight, preternaturally keen senses arousing her at the sound of faint, unearthly noises through the thin wall separating his cabin from that she shared with Connal. Leaving her lover asleep, she had armed herself and investigated. From behind his door she had heard him speak in an arcane tongue, a tone she had not heard in his voice previously—strong, confident and commanding. A second voice had answered in the same tongue, a voice sunk in a soul-searing anguish of the spirit. Her fur had fluffed up and her lips had drawn back in a warning snarl at the despair and torment lading that voice. From the crack beneath the door issued a charnel house stench that had her gagging.

Deciding that whatever went on in there was best left undisturbed, she had returned to the captain's quarters. She had opened the stern window and stood there inhaling deep draughts of clean air, the salt tang suddenly sweet perfume, flushing the sickening odor from her lungs. Unable to compose herself for sleep again, she had spent the night sitting on the window bench, her legs curled beneath her and an arm resting upon the window sash. The hilt of her drawn rapier had never been as much as a foot from her ready left hand. This morning Connal had smiled maddeningly and refused to enlighten her.

Ryemart arrived on deck dressed in a robe newer and cleaner and richer than any she had seen him wear previously, although still showing signs of mending. His hair and fur were washed and combed. He bore a staff atop which sat a beaver's skull new enough for scraps of scalp and fur to cling to it still. She grudgingly admitted that he looked as competent as Connal had claimed.

"Well?" Connal demanded, fists on hips and legs braced apart as if in readiness for battle.

"Swear it, murderer." The skull's lower jaw moved as it spoke in the doomed tones of the night. "Swear that you will grant me rest."

The crew drew back and exclaimed in dread, even Tiroc the bear mate showing the same signs of fear and loathing. The leopardess, too, had no liking for being involved however slightly with necromancy.

"You've my pledge. Pilot us to the tower and you'll be laid to rest."

"East," it groaned. "Sail east."

"Come about! Lively there!" roared Connal.

A squirrel muttered, " 'Tis bad luck, following the dead. Likely he'll lure us onto a reef and have us joining him."

Seeing them hesitate and their fear grow, their captain addressed them scornfully, "You knew Faxx was the key to finding the tower again. How did you believe it would be done if not by using him as our guide? Would you abandon a treasure because you feared someone more than two months dead?"

The bravo girl sighed and drew her rapier. She'd been engaged to back her employer in any confrontation with his crew, no matter the odds. Quelling a mutiny was certainly part of her duties. She moved to his side, her steel reinforcing his words.

"Now come about!"

"You heard the captain! Jump to it or ye'll feel the weight o' my fist landing on yer empty noggins!" Tiroc was the first to decide. His example combined with the potent threat made up the minds of the remainder; they rushed for their stations.

"How did you arrange for our guide?" Perissa asked Connal.

"That's how I marked the spot. When we were sailing these waters on an earlier voyage, I chanced to glance over the side and espied the Sunken Tower. I knew we'd be past afore we could drop sail and we'd not come across it again. Legends tell of those who have beheld it once and never again no matter how long they searched. As you may or may not know, a murder victim has an especial affinity for the place where he met his violent end. No sooner thought than done. I whipped out my dagger and plunged it into the heart of the male beside me. With Ryemart's magic and Faxx's skull I knew the tower could be located anew." He grinned at his quick-wittedness.

She arched an eyebrow inquiringly. "Did the rest of your crew not take it ill that you should murder one of their number?"

"Fortune the Lady was smiling. My victim was the least valuable and least liked male aboard. He was a surly sort and always bickering with the others. The crew had no objection to his death, especially after I explained why I'd done the deed."

"Fortune indeed. The Lady-Bitch appears to smile upon you most times."

"That's because I know how to make a female happy."

"Aye, I can attest to that!" she laughed.

They sailed at the direction of the skull for several hours. Although they did not balk again, the crew continued uneasy, mostly due to the skull rarely being silent. In between issuing sailing instructions, it bewailed its fate, lamenting the agonies suffered by the dead denied peace and informing them of the pale shadow-life they could expect after they'd met their ends. Its groaning tones were as nerve-racking as its subject matter. Perissa sourly reflected that it was singularly loquacious for one of the so-called silent dead. Connal finally grew irked and swore at it, vowing that if it did not keep its teeth together except when giving directions, it'd never be granted peace. If bones could sulk, the skull did so.

Eventually it spoke again. "Close. We're very close. Hurry or we'll sail past it."

"Down sails!" Connal snapped. "We'll use oars the rest of the way. To the bow, Perissa, and sing out when you spy it. Everyone else, take to the sweeps!"

The crew, including captain and sorcerer, took up oars while the leopardess acted as lookout. The Sea Falcon crept slowly across the crystalline waters, rising and falling oars propelling it as if it were a titanic water insect and they its legs. They were crawling along the edge of a reef, outlying coral pinnacles and gently swaying seaweed fronds making a tangle of growth in which the sunken tower could remain hidden for centuries. When it appeared suddenly she almost missed it. One moment all she saw was coral and weeds, then the next moment the tower was there below. Constructed of a translucent stone that rendered it next to invisible, it could be seen only from a few dozen feet away. No wonder it was glimpsed for a second and never found again no matter how long the search.

"Hi, here 'tis!"

"Stop oars! Let go the anchor!" The crew abandoned the oars without bothering to ship them and scrambled madly to the side for a look. Connal himself, with Perissa's aid, had to drop the hook.

The crew were jostling one another for the best viewpoint and babbling excitedly. "We've found it! We'll all be rich as kings!" "Gold enough to fill a hundred chests!" "Pearls big as your fist and of the finest luster in all the hues imaginable!" "Bigger yet! I've it on good authority from a cousin who bespoke a savant who read it from a tattered and ancient parchment from just after the time the tower sank!"

"Connal!" a doom-laden voice moaned. "Your oath! Give me release!"

The huge mate's temper flared. "I'll give you release, you croaking crow!" The bear wrenched the skull from the staff and hurled it far from the ship.

It shrieked as it flew out over the sea. "Curse you for your treachery! Curse you and all your fellows! I curse you to—!" It struck the water and sank before it could say more.

"Since he did not complete the curse, we've naught to worry about," the sorcerer reassured them. "Unfinished, it cannot take effect."

"Can you fulfill our pledge to him regardless?" Connal inquired.

"Alas, nay. I require at least part of his remains and now we've none."

"A pity, but he brought it upon himself. Faxx always was unlucky and overly verbose. If he'd kept silent this would not have happened. Conversely, if he'd been concise he'd have completed his curse and would have his revenge."

"Aye," Perissa said with heavy irony, "'Tis a real pity he blathered so."

"Come away from there!" Connal shouted to the crew. "We've work to do; the treasure won't raise itself! Ryemart, ready your other spell. Tiroc, drop a line overboard that we can use as a guide and for hoisting the treasure. Perissa, Yoran, you'll be coming with me."

"And where might that be?"

He grinned. "We'll be diving for the treasure."

The bravo girl was no happier than the otter chosen. "Why us? I'm a poor swimmer and can scarce hold my breath!" The only places for swimming a slum dweller had in Goedus were in the river and harbor filled with garbage and sewage only partially removed by the receding tides. And none were so insane as to actually use them. Since the Guild had only taught her the rudiments, she liked no water deeper than that in a bath.

"Yoran is the best swimmer aboard and you've been naught save a passenger thus far. 'Tis time you earned your pay! You need not concern yourself with holding your breath; Ryemart will deal with that."

Still unhappy, she felt that her commission's vague terms left her no recourse to argument. "Then I' best go make my preparations."

When Perissa emerged from the cabin later she was totally naked, unless one counted as clothing the scarf knotted about her head to keep her hair out of her eyes or the dagger in its sheath strapped to a thigh. She would not have drawn more than glances in the public baths where more voluptuous figures than her average one would be on display; however, this was not a bathhouse and they were weeks at sea. The crew leered at her, drinking in the sight of her slender figure with its lovely, ample breasts and long, lithe legs.

Connal chuckled. "We'd best get you over the side afore my crew riots. Can you not spare another scarf to tie about your loins?" He and Yoran wore brief cloths about theirs.

"I'll not ruin my clothing with a soak in seawater." With her funds in a sorry state she could not afford to replace any of her garments. After all, every one was silk, including the scarf she did wear. She'd not ruin a second one. "Bad enough my sword and dagger must put up with it; at least they'll be partly protected by the oiling I've given them. Now where is this magic that'll enable us to hold our breaths as long as need be?"

He gestured to where the sorcerer sat cross-legged on the deck, staring at a basin between his knees and muttering. "Not hold our breaths, but actually breathe underwater!"

Perissa went to stand over the old raccoon, scowling down at him. The basin was filled with water and contained three tiny fish.

"As I understand it," Connal continued, "Each fish represents one of us and so long as the spell remains in force, it'll enable us to breathe water as do the fish."

"'Tis singularly unimpressive for so puissant a thaumaturgy."

Ryemart glared up at her. Connal had not allowed him to touch so much as a drop of wine since they'd sailed and he no longer bore a resemblance to the wine-soaked wreck who had boarded weeks earlier. Now he looked as if he might indeed be a competent magician. "This sorcery is not maintained without difficulty, wench," he growled. "Cease dawdling and dive after the treasure."

"Just be certain you do maintain it. I want not to attempt breathing water without its aid."

Connal handed her a pair of wide leather cuffs to which leaden weights were fastened. "Put these about your ankles; they'll overcome your buoyancy and take you straight to the bottom." The otter chosen and he already wore similar ones.

Perissa reluctantly buckled on the weights, concerned that they might work too well at taking her to the bottom. "You go first."

"Is it me or Ryemart's spell you find it so difficult to trust? No matter, I'll gladly lead the way on our grand adventure!" The fox leaped upon the rail, gallantly saluted them with his sword then stepped off, disappearing with a splash.

The bravo girl gestured at Yoran with her rapier, certain that if she left him behind he would neglect to join them. "Now you."

He appeared to briefly consider the support he would receive from his fellows if he should refuse, took another look at her determined face and went over the side. Perissa followed immediately after.

She quickly sank the fifty or so feet, coming to rest on the tower's flat roof where Connal and Yoran awaited. The infamous rogue grinned at her, apparently breathing with ease, the otter grimly holding his breath. She wanted none of that. Should the spell be worthless, she wanted as much time as she could manage to get the weights off. She took a slight, cautious inhalation. There was no sudden, strangling sensation followed by a surge of panic. Connal's grin grew even wider. She breathed out, then in, deeply. There was a feeling of heaviness in her chest, but other than that it was identical to air. After that she ignored the medium and breathed normally.

An otter could hold his breath for a long time, but not forever. Yoran lost control. Dropping his cutlass, he tried to make for the surface, but Perissa and Connal interposed their swords. Given no alternative, he finally gave in. Face tight with barely suppressed terror, he started breathing. When after a few seconds he realized that he was in no danger of drowning an expression of relief comical in its intensity broke over his features.

Connal beckoned imperiously and they followed to where a narrow flight of stairs led down into the tower. Perissa reflected that that proved the tower had been built on land and later sunk, swimmers having no need for steps. He started down with the bravo girl then the sailor trailing.

The weights about their ankles held their feet down, leaving them upright, so they could walk in a parody of the fashion they would on land. The resistance of the water enforced an exaggerated slowness upon their motions. Fortunately, the water's crystal clarity and the tower's numerous windows admitted sufficient light for their vision, although as they went deeper it gradually grew dimmer and their surroundings took on a faint greenish cast.

''Tis like floating or walking in a dream,' Perissa thought. She would step out, then settle to the step below slow as a dandelion puff falling. In fact, it was too slow. They soon found the best way to progress was by jumping forward over several steps at once and gradually falling to another.

The first floor down was without so much as a clue as to what its purpose had been before the land subsided and the tower sank a millennium ago, barren other than for fish. Their schools swam through the building, darting in and out windows, flying up to the ceiling and spiraling down in streams that almost brushed the floor before spiraling up again, eddies constantly breaking off, briefly going their own way, then curving back to rejoin the main stream. The three moved through living rainbows of blue, green, yellow, red, orange and most especially flashing silver, an ever-changing kaleidoscope. It seemed they could reach out and touch them, but try and the rainbows would swirl away in ever-restless clouds. The only treasure here were the living gems that would quickly die and fade if taken back to their world. Down they went.

The second floor was equally devoid of aught. Perissa saw her companions' faces were as dashed as she felt. Only one floor remained wherein any possible treasure might be found.

Their last hope excited their curiosity and avarice at once. Even after ten centuries it bore signs of occupation, almost as if someone lived there yet. A stone table bore a comb made from the backbone and ribs of a fish and a bronze hand mirror, its handle verdigris while its polished surface was still clean and reflective. Near one wall was a most unusual bed—a huge clamshell, seven feet across, the upper valve forming a partial canopy over the lower. Strung across the opening between the two was a seaweed net, most strands green while others of reddish-brown were woven through them, forming an abstract pattern. Intrigued, they made their dream walkers' way to it. The net was in good repair, a division in it allowing entrance to the bed and the bottom shell was filled with clean, white sand raked smooth. It seemed impossible for it to have remained thus undisturbed for a thousand years, yet what else could explain it? No fish would have a bed and besides, here alone the schools of fish were absent.

Fascinated by the mystery, they failed to note the long tentacle that emerged from behind the clam and snaked towards them. For the first vital second that Perissa felt it curl around her, she thought that the sailor beside her was taking liberties. Then she realized that no otter's arm felt so cold and boneless. Glancing down, she discovered to her horror the true nature of the embrace. Too late she attempted to propel herself upwards and free. The instant before the tentacle had tightened about her hips.

Connal and Yoran stared aghast at the sight of her in the monstrous embrace and at the sight of more writhing tentacles reaching around and over the shell for them. The sailor stared transfixed in terror too long and a ropy limb snaked about his neck and squeezed. Panicking, he dropped the cutlass that he might have used to cut himself free. Grabbing the tentacle, he vainly tried pitting his strength against the monster's. The tentacle contracted, choking him.

Connal had acted quicker, violently kicking himself upwards. The tentacle groping for him managed to snare only a single leg. He reacted at once, slashing it with his sword, a cloud of blood quickly spreading through the water. Yet it would not release him and continued dragging him towards whatever lurked behind the clam while another reached for him.

Lifted above the shell, Perissa discovered the creature that lay in wait. It was a kraken, albeit an infant one. Even so, its body was as large as an animal ox and an evil intelligence gleamed malevolently in its saucer-like eyes. She silently cursed the water hampering her. Earlier, the slow, languorous motions to which it had limited them had given their adventure a dream-like quality. Now the dream had become a nightmare, one where no matter how fast you ran you could not escape the horror gaining on you. In this case, no matter how vigorously she sliced at the tentacles with the few inches of her blade back of the point that were sharpened, the water's viscosity robbed her efforts of their power and she could not cut through them. The best she could do was fend off others, leaving her no chance of dealing with the one around her hips relentlessly drawing her towards the huge, savage, parrot-like beak that would crush her limbs and rend her flesh.

Yoran had been quickly strangled and now his lifeless body dangled with swollen tongue protruding from a distorted face.

Connal found the water every bit as hampering as the blonde-haired leopardess and he mentally damned it with curses even viler than hers. The kraken's tough hide added to his difficulties and aside from his first, powerful slash he could inflict no more than shallow cuts and seeming pinpricks. They must strike for its only vulnerable point but she was closer than he and must do the deed.

Perissa saw him signaling frantically, pointing at his eye then at the monster's. She nodded. It took all her courage and determination to steel her nerves and allow herself to be carried unresisting towards that terrible mouth. Try as she might, she couldn't keep from imagining the feel of that horny beak around a leg and the sudden burst of agony as it crunched through as effortlessly as she could bite through a chicken bone. 'At least it isn't a rat,' she thought relieved, then grinned at the incongruity of her relief. Just before she reached the mouth, she espied the scattered and broken bones of a previous victim. A land fur's skull, arms and rib cage associated with the tailbones of a huge fish solved the mystery of the clamshell bed. One of the rare merfolk had lived here and had died when the kraken arrived.

Closer and closer she was pulled towards the beak awaiting her, a beak that opened and snapped as if already chopping her into pieces, short mouth tentacles waving, ready to feed her bit by bit into the maw waiting to gobble her down. She drew her legs up lest a foot be sliced off. A bare second before the beak had her, her arm shot forward and a foot of steel stabbed through an eye and pierced the brain. Ichor spurted. Another second and she drove her blade into the other evil orb. The kraken exploded into a frenzied spasm of whipping and contracting limbs. She was in danger of being crushed or dashed against a wall. Desperately she sawed at the tentacle prisoning her.

The initial spasm had hurled Connal away, freeing him. He hurried to her aid with the long, slow, gliding steps the water forced. He plunged into the writhing mass, wrapped an arm and legs about the tentacle holding her and sawed at it opposite to where she was cutting. He clung with difficulty to the violently thrashing limb, just as both had trouble retaining their swords as they sliced through it. Both were aided more by the gradually subsiding throes than by their own efforts. At last she was freed from the lifeless monster with no more hurt than a double row of circular bruises about her midsection, sore, but not serious.

The kraken's dying agonies had further crushed and scattered the bones she had spotted so no sense could any longer be made of them. Its throes had also revealed a brass chest tarnished with age. The Treasure of the Sunken Tower was not just a legend after all! The victors grinned at one another and haled it forth from the corner where it had lain hidden for centuries.

It would be impossible to know who had the idea first if in fact they did not think it simultaneously. Still aroused from their battle and near brush with death, heated blood pounding in their veins, it quickly became arousal of a different sort. Words as unnecessary as they were impossible, by mutual consent they let fall the chest and turned to the clamshell. Parting the net, they entered the bed.

It was like making love on a cloud, the buoyant water lifting them up whilst the lead weights around their ankles gave them an anchor point. Entwined to keep from drifting apart, they kissed, lips meeting and opening, their tongues dueling back and forth from mouth to mouth. From nights spent sharing their bed and bodies, each knew what most pleased the other and so sent hands and mouths roaming and caressing. When both were ready they rearranged themselves and joined. They moved together in a leisurely rhythm, their hands still wandering and stroking, slowly climbing the mountain of ecstasy. Nearing the peak, they moved faster and faster until they sprinted the remaining distance. On the summit at last they were as one, together with the gods, briefly mingling their souls as they mingled their fluids. It took them almost as long to descend as they remained intertwined, still kissing and caressing.

It was while they lay thus that Perissa discovered the bed's previous occupant had not slept there alone. Turning her head, she saw they were being spied upon through a window. The bones she'd seen had been heavy, those of a mermale, and now his paramour watched them. She was lovely with the upper body of a seal as slender and supple as an eel, the nipples of her small breasts coral pink and her light green hair a floating nimbus about her head. Her tail was her true glory, its scales iridescent with all the hues of the rainbow and ending in a widespread fan of delicate membrane. For several seconds they stared at one another, the girl of land and the girl of sea, then with a flick of her magnificent tail, the mermaid was gone. The bravo girl decided to keep her a secret to herself, her memory like a rare and exquisite butterfly that a collector was loath to share with his fellows lest the fragile wings be damaged from too much handling.

Finally she and Connal parted to return to their world of air, though neither would ever forget their enchanted lovemaking beneath the Crystal Sea.

Back on the tower's roof they tied the line around the chest and signaled for it to be raised. Awaiting the rope's lowering for them, they bent to unfasten the weights about their ankles. Between one breath and the next Perissa found that she could no longer breathe water. The spell was broken! Looking to Connal, she saw that it was the same for him.

Quickly, grimly, fighting down a feeling of suffocation, they tore the weights off. When she made to shoot straight for the surface, he grabbed her arm and shook his head, pointing to the ship's stern. His meaning was clear. With the very real possibility that they had been betrayed, they should enter where they would not be seen.

They swam to the stern, hampered by swords they could not abandon. Luckily, the Sea Falcon was built with an overhanging stern. They clung to the rudder, hidden from the view of any above, sucking in deep, refreshing draughts of air, more to be savored than the finest wine.

A window opened. "They're not back here. They must have drowned."

"They might be beneath the stern."

"Would you like to jump in and see? Nay? I thought not. Let's get back on deck; Tiroc wants to sail as quick as we can."

"Lock the window first. That way should they somehow yet live, they'll not gain entry through here."

Perissa and Connal waited a full minute and more, giving the pair ample time to leave before they climbed the rudder to stern windows recessed just sufficiently to give them a precarious perch. "Have you anything with which to pick the lock?" he asked.

In common with many assassins' weapons her rapier was more than it appeared. She pressed a seemingly decorative stud on its guard and pulled a lock pick from its hidden recess.

"A versatile sword you have there," he remarked.

"Aye, it has its uses." Lock picking was naturally taught by the Guild. They were through the window and in the cabin within moments. "How should we go about this?"

"I think just have at them. There's only six."

"Six? I count seven."

"Nay, whatever happened concerning his spell, Ryemart'll not have betrayed us."

Perissa kept her doubts of that to herself, readying her miniature crossbow. While thus engaged, her eye fell upon her tortoise shell comb where it lay, inlaid with silver and garnets. She tossed it out the window. Perchance the finder would know it as her gift to her. He regarded her quizzically, but said nothing.

They cautiously opened the cabin door and peered out onto the deck. The crew was gathered around the chest, the muscular mate straining to break its hasp with a pry bar. Ryemart lay sprawled on the deck, the bowl that was the centerpiece of his spell overturned. Mayhaps there was something to Connal's contention that the sorcerer had been loyal.

It was a longish shot, but one within her capabilities. She took careful aim and caressed the trigger. Set for a delicate pull, it fired almost as quick as the thought came. A squirrel staggered a step, then pitched forward. Before his dumbfounded fellows could comprehend what the small, feathered shaft in his back portended, Perissa and Connal were halfway to them.

Tiroc regained his wits first. "Look to your lives! The captain and his bitch are upon us!"

The sailors' first mistake had been to abandon the watch set against the two before being certain that they were dead. Their second was to think that just because she was female, Perissa was the less dangerous, completely forgetting her calling. Two rounded on her as the other three faced Connal.

One of her opponents hurled a dagger hard and true at her. Her blade knocked it aside with ease, her battle grin wider than usual at the chance to show off her phenomenal reflexes. They were disconcerted, although whether by her obvious joy of battle or the display of her speed, perhaps they could not say themselves and both were dead before they could make up their minds.

The bravo girl was almost at the point of crossing swords with them when a flick of her wrist sent her dagger plunging into the abdomen of her squirrel foe. Both had expected her swordplay to be of the usual sort, rapier and dagger together, and so she had taken them completely by surprise. Her target collapsed, curling about the mortal agony in his belly, screaming.

The beaver barely had time to get his guard up before she was upon him like a whirlwind of steel. She ascertained at once that he was an indifferent swordsfur, no match for her, nor was his cutlass a match for her rapier. Bored, wanting some sort of challenge to demonstrate her skill, she dispatched him with a supremely difficult thrust into his open mouth. She finished the one holding her dagger for her, then spun to see how Connal was faring.

He was hard pressed to keep his life from the three who sought it. He did so by attacking, his blade a whirling, darting serpent of steel striking at them, keeping them off balance. The outcome was never in doubt, though. Soon or late he would make a mistake or they would wear him down and he would die. Even now he was forced to retreat, small step by reluctant step.

She watched only a moment before stepping in, engaging an otter's attention. Connal used the distraction to leave the last crew otter writhing on the deck, bright gouts of blood spurting from a throat grinning red.

"Have you finished your dance with the other two so quickly?" he inquired. "They must have been a sorry pair."

"Aye, they knew not the first thing concerning a lady's entertainment, so I dismissed them. Mayhaps they'll find a less demanding wench in Death's halls!"

Her latest foe was better than her last. The otter at least knew some rudiments of scientific fencing though he relied mainly on muscle, wielding his cutlass like a meat clever while using his dagger to ward off her rapier's scalpel-like precision. It struck her fancy to give him a lesson in swordplay. She showed him how he should attack, in a dozen heartbeats slipping past his defense half as many times, attacking in a different spot with a different ploy each time.

"You gods-cursed slut!" he cried. He launched a desperate assault, slashing and chopping at her, all science fled as fear took control and he strove to overbear her with sheer fury and muscle.

Shaking her head in mock disappointment at his lost finesse, Perissa made her opportunity with a feint. Her rapier was not there to be blocked by his dagger. Instead it shifted its aim and shot forward, needle point splitting his heart.

She turned as Tiroc staggered back from the steel piercing his side. He sat down heavily, his hands trying to staunch the spreading crimson stain.

"You were overlong in finishing," she commented idly.

"Unlike the dolts with whom you dealt, he had some skill. His only virtue it seems since loyalty was lacking."

"Are you going to leave me thus or are ye going to finish the deed?" The bear spat a bright pink froth of lung blood along with his words.

"And why should we give you the mercy of swift death after you tried drowning us?" his captain scowled at him.

Tiroc turned pleading eyes on the bravo girl. "Wilt ye do it then?"

"Nay, I feel much as he. Furthermore, I'd wager you put the rest up to it."

"Then curse ye both! Which of ye is it that gave the other the pox?" Perissa listened pityingly; he had no imagination whatsoever. Connal's face grew dark. "I warrant it was ye, Connal, I know ye've had it afore! I only wish I could live to see it eat away at—" He broke off and his head flew back with a snapping sound as Connal stepped forward and delivered a powerful kick beneath his chin that broke his neck.

"Ah, he was cleverer than I'd thought. He knew how to provoke me into killing him quickly." He turned to find her sword's point scant inches from his manhood.

"Have you the pox? I swear if you've given it to me, I'll cut it off so you'll never give it to another!"

"Nay, rest assured I'm clean! 'Twas long ago when I was a mere youth! So soon as I realized I had it, I sought out a sorcerer and had it spelled away. I've taken care to be free ever since."

The leopardess searched his face for a lie. A moment passed. Her furious countenance grew calm and her blade no longer threatened. "Aye, I suppose such could happen, especially to a careless youth."

"I'm happy you decided to believe me. A male's as unarmed as he can get without that sword!"

"I'd surely not want that in your case. I'd be loath to forgo your skilled swordplay!"

"You'd not regret the loss near as much as I! Now we'd best see if Ryemart is slain or merely senseless."

Kneeling, they examined him for sign of injury. His slack features were those of one unconscious, not dead. Perissa stiffened, her eyes becoming as hard and cold as green ice. Beside him lay a brown bottle, the smell from its spilled contents revealing the nature of the foul deed done to him.

"Dead drunk! Swilling wine whilst leaving us to drink a sea! Soon 'twill be dead in truth!" she hissed, readying her strangling cord. She slapped his face. "Wake up, sot, so you can feel yourself choking as I did on the water you left me to try and breathe!"

"Nay, stay your hand; 'tis a weakness beyond his control. I share the blame with him. If I'd given him a cup each day rather than naught he might have resisted the temptation."

"He could have been content with just a swallow or two. There was no need to drink himself senseless!"

"It may have been drugged."

"You sound as if he were an old and dear friend for whom one makes allowances," she said accusingly.

"He is." The fox regarded him sadly. "In my younger days he was my father's resident sorcerer. He fought long and hard before a demon thirst we can scarce imagine bested him and he was thrown out. He it was who took me in when my brother inherited all and I was left penniless. I owe him much."

Perissa was scarcely mollified by his explanation. Her own besotted parents' maltreatment of her and her siblings left her with a loathing for drunkards and contempt for their failings. Then she brightened. There was yet the treasure. Mayhaps it would prove as fabulous as legendary hoards were always said to be. "Oh, let the sot sleep it off in peace. Let's examine our prize."

"Aye, and settle the reckoning of your fee."

With the pry bar his crew had been using, Connal broke the corroded hasp fastening the chest. Both bent closer to catch the first gleam of gold and sparkle of jewels. He threw back the lid.

Perissa sucked in her breath. And spat. "Coral!"

"What constitutes treasure differs for different peoples," he remarked philosophically. Taking several pieces, he turned them over, peering closely at them. "The workmanship's superb at least. With my crew dead there's no need to split it with them. The quarter you're due should run to fifty thaels or more."

"Run the race less swiftly; let me see those." She examined them critically. The artistry was masterful, the rings, beads and pendants carved with intricate designs evoking the sea. However, coral jewelry was inexpensive stuff no matter how skillfully crafted. Of that she was a good judge since it was all she could afford for many years.

She tossed them back into the chest except for a ring that struck her fancy. In the form of an octopus, its arms curled around in a wavy pattern to form the band. It would make an excellent memento, conjuring memories of the kraken as it did. "This is all I claim from there. I think the whole would run to fifty thaels or less. I'm due more than a quarter of that for these incidental slayings alone if I choose the set fee and I do."

"I think it may fetch more than you realize. I'd advise taking your share of it." Connal was quite sincere.

The bravo girl regarded him in amusement. She knew the trick of lying sincerely from when she'd begged on the streets as a child. "Nay, I want the pay of which I'm certain."

"As you wish." He shrugged, then grinned. "No harm in trying."

* * *

"It was some hours afore that besotted wizard came around and I'm happy to say he suffered a most appalling headache well into the next day. 'Twas a hard and slow voyage back with just three of us to work the ship and only one a seaman, but as you can perceive, return we did," Perissa concluded the account of her adventure.

She looked very different from the tired and bedraggled leopardess who had left the ship earlier that day with a satisfyingly heavy purse after Connal had paid her the nearly thirty thaels she was due. She had availed herself of the luxury of a lingering soak in a steaming tub in one of the better bathhouses and followed it with a massage from her attendant (female since a bath and massage were all she desired) prior to presenting herself at the guild house.

"A kraken and four slain. A most remarkable achievement for one years your senior. What a pity the vaunted treasure proved so paltry," Ismara remarked. " 'Tis well you insisted upon having the option to choose a set fee instead."

The girl basked in the approval of her superior. "What's befallen whilst I've been away?"

"Nige slew Lord Kuris."

"Oh, well done for him!"

"Aye, but luck never attended him and so it was again. He was caught by the guards. They spoke of the battle for days—no dragon defending its hoard could have surpassed his ferocity. He slew or grievously wounded a half-dozen and held the rest at bay. They finally called for crossbows to shoot him down."

"Too bad! Oh, too bad! I'll miss him." Perissa felt genuine regret at the news.

"So will we all."

Journeyfur Alwys, a thin and fussy impala from the guild treasury, contemplated the stacks of shiny yellow coins before him. "I could wish you'd returned with more after a commission lasting more than two months. Still, I suppose it would have been worse if you'd heeded his urging to take a portion of the purported treasure."

"I nearly forgot. There is a small additional return," Perissa said jauntily. She pulled off the coral ring and tossed it to him. "Evaluate that and tell me how much silver I owe the Guild for its half."

A first casual perusal quickly became an intense scrutiny. The impala turned it over slowly, studying its every aspect. "Were there others similar to this?" he inquired quietly.

"How mean you?"

"Were many engraved with maritime motifs, especially waves and octopi?"

"Aye, all as far as I saw." She felt a sickening premonition of disaster.

"Perissa, those are the most common themes of the long-vanished island empire of Vocca. Collectors of antiquities pay well for its art objects. It will take every thael you earned on this commission to pay the Guild's share of this ring. That chest was worth thousands."

Her stricken face quickly became one of anger, lips drawn back to show her fangs and a growl issuing from deep in her throat. "That diseased son of an unnatural coupling between a rat and a toad! I'll have his cods for this!" She sprang to her feet and rushed from the room.

* * *

"Connal, you dung-eating serpent, where are you? You owe me my fair share or that measly thing between your legs you call a sword!" Perissa shouted as she rushed up the Sea Falcon's gangplank.

Her way was suddenly blocked by a very large, young bull gripping a quarterstaff as only one experienced in its use did. "Easy, wench! What business have you here?"

Her reach for her sword was halted by the appearance of three more bulls, equally large, beside the first. The grizzled one leveled a crossbow at her. Her hand dropped to her side.

"As my son so politely asked, state your business," the elder said.

Perissa forced herself to reply calmly. " 'Tis a private matter between Connal and myself, if you'd be so good as to inform him I'm here."

"Cap'n Connal? A strange one, he. He'd not been back an hour afore he hired my sons and me to guard his ship and took passage on the next ship to leave port."

The bull and his sons listened to the leopardess admiringly. Even on the docks they'd rarely heard anyone curse so long and imaginatively without a single repetition.

Every wizard and witch has a familiar, traditionally a small pet animal. From medieval times up almost to the present (almost?), the presence of a rat or a cat in the home of an elderly lone woman has been assumed to prove that she is a witch, getting orders through the "familiar" from Satan. Many a fantasy has a familiar, often a sarcastic wise-guy cat, as a supporting character to a wizard or witch protagonist.

See A Night in the Lonesome October *by Roger Zelazny (William Morrow/AvoNova, August 1993) for a rare exception in which the story is told from the familiars' point of view. Or the British* The Stone Cage *by Nicholas Stuart Gray (Dennis Dobson, December 1963), but that has undeservedly been out of print for decades. There is also "Familiars" by Michael H. Payne, which not only introduces an unusual animal as the familiar/protagonist, but has a couple more surprises as well. "Familiars" is the first of Payne's five (so far) tales of Cluny, the sorceress squirrel.*

Familiars

Michael H. Payne

The stink of Crocker's fear hit Cluny like an acorn dropped from the top of an oak tree, made her tail jitter and her claws dig into the desk top. She forced them loose. "All right, Crocker. I'm breaking the link now."

Kneeling on the carpet across the room, Crocker nodded, his eyes fixed on the ball of blue fire spinning between his hands. With a quick prayer, Cluny lowered herself to all fours and backed away along the desk, her fur prickling as she mentally stretched the link between them till she felt it pop.

Immediately, sparks began crackling through the fireball. "Hold on," she breathed, but he was already trembling, sweat now visible on his forehead. "Hold on, you little-"

The ball exploded, fire engulfing his hands, and Cluny leaped to the floor. "Idiot!" She scrambled toward him, pushed her power into his, and water congealed around his arms, the flame dousing and the healing spells they'd set up rushing into place. "You're not feeling the flow!"

"Tell me about it." Crocker fell back onto his calves, ran a wet hand through his hair. "You snap our link, and I don't feel anything."

"Oh, come on." She glared up at him. "You do healings and make light and work doubling magic, so don't tell me-"

"Sure, small stuff." He waved an arm, drops spattering Cluny's fur. "But I can't even evoke a chapter one fireball, and with finals next week..." He sighed, his chubby face lost in the evening shadows coming through the dorm room curtains. "The magisters are gonna kick me outta Huxley for sure. You'd better request a transfer to another novice."

Stomach tightening, Cluny turned away. "I have. Every week all semester."

"You have?" The shuffle of his robes made her ears fold back. "Then... then why hasn't someone asked you to-?"

"Because I'm a squirrel!" She whirled back. "Never mind that I've memorized the whole freshman spell book! I'm not a cat or an owl or a fox, so forget it! And the magisters say I don't have the right attitude to be a familiar, that I'm not deferential enough!" She bunched her paws into fists and scowled up at him. "They only assigned me to you, I'll bet, so I'd get sick of nursing you along and drop out!"

Crocker rubbed his ear. "Actually, I requested you. After we met during orientation week."

"What?" A vague memory, Crocker talking to her at one of the mixers for maybe two minutes. "You...requested...?"

"Yeah." He gave another sigh and shook more water from his sleeves. "Well, if you're stuck with me, I guess we'd better try this again."

Staring another second—he'd requested her?—Cluny shook her head to clear it, scurried across the floor, and jumped back onto the desk beside his book. "Well, since the textbook way isn't working for you..." She closed it with a thump and tapped the cover. "How about you make some light, just a little in your hand. You won't need me for that, right?"

Silence, then a bubble of light began to grow ahead of her, the room brightening, Crocker's eyes narrow and fixed on the glowing ball in the air above his palm.

"That's it." Her whiskers didn't twitch, so he wasn't using her power. "Now, can you make it bigger?"

"Sure." He blew on it, and the ball pulsed into a good handful of light. "Just like...blowing up a balloon,...only with light." His eyes darted up from it. "Now what?"

"Now?" She rubbed her whiskers. Evocation was mostly a mental discipline, so maybe she could get him to... "Picture fire in your mind, lots and lots of fire." She spread her claws. "Then just blow that into the ball instead of light."

A puff of his fear wafted against her whiskers. "It's easy," she said, trying to keep her voice calm. "Focus on the fire in your mind. Then blow just like you did before."

Several blinks, and he nodded, his eyes narrowing even more. He took a deep, shaking breath, puffed his cheeks...

And Cluny's whiskers sprang straight out, Crocker's spell grabbing her power and sucking it in. She tried to snap the link, but the light in his hand exploded into a huge pillar of fire, knocking her back into the wall before she could do anything. "Who dares?!" a voice thundered, and Cluny looked up from where she was sprawled to see the pillar flowing into a fiery female humanoid figure, hair like lava around her broad shoulders, eyes fiercer than the sun at midday.

An ifrit. High Clan, too, Cluny was sure, with those-

"I haven't got all day!" the ifrit roared. She swirled around to fix on Crocker, groaning as he pushed himself up from the floor in front of the closet. "You! Human! Why have you disrupted my schedule?!"

Crocker's eyes widened as his head tipped back, his mouth dropping open. "Well?!" the ifrit shouted.

The briefest of seconds, and Cluny leaped from the desk, rushed across to stand in front of Crocker, bowed down all the way to the carpet. "Uhh, forgive us, spirit, we meant no disrespect. We were just-"

"Talking animals?! I haven't got time for this!" A hand like a burning tree branch slammed into Cluny, knocked her sideways into the tangle of blankets on Crocker's bed. "You will learn the error of your ways, human!" Cluny heard, and she clawed her way free just in time to see the ifrit grab Crocker from the floor. "You will await me in my realm! Upon my return, I will deal with you properly!"

Flames burst from the ifrit's other hand, hit the wall, and spiraled open to a blast furnace beyond; a smile sharp as lightning bolts, and she flicked her claws, Crocker flying into the furnace, his eyes still wide with terror. The whole room flashed, and the creature was gone, Cluny blinking, the fiery hole in the wall beginning to wheel shut.

Half a heartbeat she hesitated; then she leaped for the hole, tucked and rolled and smashed right into the flames, roaring over her, tumbling her headlong into boiling liquid pain, her mouth opening to scream-

And relief surged through her, the breath she drew cool and damp. A moment to get her paws under her, and she rose to find herself standing in a pit of molten rock, the lava sloughing off the water coating her, her charred fur growing back as she watched.

The spell, the dousing and healing one she and Crocker had set up in case fireball practice got out of hand. Yes, her fur prickled under its watery coating, his power drawing on hers, so their link was intact. But where was he?

Squinting against the blazing whites and reds, she could see that the lava pool she stood in was surrounded by walls of magma. She poked at the stuff, steam hissing from her claw, and frowned. Like glowing red pudding, nothing to dig into, no way she could climb out.

Unless, if this really was molten rock... She cleared her mind, concentrated on the flow of her power, focused her thoughts on the cold spells from chapter six of Crocker's textbook. Maybe she could firm it up a bit.

The motions and phrases came easily, and she felt her watery coating get colder and colder. The viscous ground began to seize up beneath her, and when she pressed her paws into the glow ahead, the lava crackled, turned gray and craggy. It still jiggled, but it wasn't much worse than the half-dead trees she'd played in growing up. A quick scramble, and she dug her paws into more of the magma, solidifying under her touch and letting her climb higher.

At least the water spell told her Crocker was still alive, and he'd have the same protection as long as their link didn't break. Unless he'd sunk into the magma: he sure didn't know the chapter six cold spells.

"Idiot." Her breath coming faster now with the effort of holding the cold spell in place, she reached the crest of the flow, grabbed it, froze it, pulled herself up, and looked down to see water, a lake lapping against the molten rock walls.

And bobbing out in the middle, his dark curly hair and chubby face unmistakable even through the curtains of steam. "Crocker?" she called.

"Cluny!" He sloshed around and started swimming toward her. "Where are we? What was that thing? How did we-?"

"You summoned a High Clan ifrit, you idiot!" She struggled to keep on her paws, the magma pushing against her cold spell and against the water rising in the-

Rising? Cluny squinted, saw the lake was expanding up the sides of the pit, felt it draw on her power every time it sloshed higher.

"It's our watery healing spell." Crocker had paddled to just below her, the water bringing him closer and closer. "I used some doubling magic on it, figured I could swim in water easier than lava, and now, well, now I can't get it to stop." He was almost level with her now, the water lapping at her paws, steam geysering up even as ice formed around them. Crocker stared at it. "How...how are you doing that?"

"Chapter six cold spell." She tried to back away, but she was already at the top of the lava flow.

"What?" Crocker blinked up at her. "But...you're a familiar. You can't cast spells."

The water topped the ridge then, rushed past Cluny into the pit she'd just climbed out of. Quickly she cut the cold spell and jumped forward to Crocker's shoulder. "What I can't do, Crocker, is swim."

"Uh oh," she heard him say, then the current pulled them over and sucked them down. Water in her nose, eyes, ears, Cluny dug her claws into Crocker's hair, his shoulders swinging beneath her. She had to get out, had to breathe, had to-

She grabbed the flow of Crocker's power, added it to her own, let their combined force roar into her mind. Directing it downward, she smashed at the water, hot air rushing past her whiskers, her stomach yawing; she pushed her face away from Crocker's hair, gasped for breath, and saw Crocker looking down, his eyes wide and staring. She followed his gaze, the lake spreading below, several dozen empty yards between his feet and the water. "We're flying?" he whispered.

"Can't be." The power burning through her made her pant. "Flying's not...till sophomore year. I haven't learned-"

"What's going on here?!" a huge voice thundered around them, and Cluny's stomach clenched, light exploding to reveal the ifrit, her eyes blazing down over the lava field. "Who put all this water on my magma?!" Her gaze snapped up, an even greater heat slapping against Cluny. "You again??"

"Uhh..." Crocker swallowed so convulsively, Cluny could feel it. "I...I'm real sorry about that, but-"

"I will not have this!" The ifrit loomed through the mists, grabbed Crocker with one clawed hand. "I should have done this to you the first time!" She blazed brighter and hotter than before; then darkness crashed in, and Cluny felt herself falling. She still had hold of Crocker, though, so when they hit the flagstones, he took the brunt of it.

Flagstones? She raised her head and blinked as a flood of firelight showed her the main quad of Huxley College.

"Gollantz!" The fire towered into the shouting ifrit. "Gollantz, get out here!"

A dark puff of cloud, and Master Gollantz appeared. He blinked at the ifrit, then bowed. "Your Majesty, it's an honor to have the Ranee of the Ifriti grace our-"

"Never mind that!" Everything spun, and Cluny found herself dangling from Crocker's neck as the ifrit thrust them into the face of the school's Magister Magistrorum. "This is one of yours, isn't it??"

"Uhh, yes, Ranee." Master Gollantz cleared his throat, his glare making Cluny's hackles rise. "I believe he is."

The world shook again, Cluny jumping away and landing on her paws this time when Crocker thudded to the ground. "He summoned me, Gollantz!" the ifrit bellowed. "In absolute defiance of the agreements you have with the elemental houses!"

"Ranee, I am shocked." Master Gollantz bowed once again to the ifrit. "Rest assured: he will be dealt with."

The ifrit flared up into a huge gout of fire. "See that he is!" And with a burst that Cluny saw even through her clenched eyelids, the creature vanished.

Things got very quiet then, and when Cluny opened her eyes, she saw Master Gollantz, his arms folded, standing above Crocker. "One thing, Crocker," the magister said quietly, but his voice bit at Cluny's ears. Crocker's eyes shot open, and he scrambled to his feet, his robe charred and stained, his face sooty, his hair dripping, his mouth opening.

But Master Gollantz held up a hand. "Just tell me how my lowest ranking novice summoned the Queen of the Ifriti?"

"Uhh..." was all Crocker managed to say.

Cluny scurried forward, grabbed the back of Crocker's robe, climbed up to his shoulder. "It's my fault, sir." She bowed, then straightened to meet Master Gollantz's glare. "Crocker's been having trouble with fireballs, so I, well, I was trying to find another way for him to approach the spell."

"You?" Master Gollantz's brow wrinkled. "A familiar designing a course of study for a student of wizardry?"

Cluny's mouth went dry, but Crocker spoke up. "I'm barely a student, sir. And Cluny's sure not just a familiar."

Master Gollantz's brow wrinkled even further, and Cluny tried to think of something to say. But Crocker went on, his eyes moving back and forth between the ground and Master Gollantz. "See, sir, at the first mixer during orientation week, well, all the other novices and familiars were laughing and talking, and I...I knew I was a fraud, knew I shouldn't be here no matter what the tests said. And then, bam!"

He turned his head toward Cluny, a big smile on his face. "I saw Cluny sitting in the corner all by herself, and the flow of her power, it was like... like I was seeing the sun for the first time. I'd never really felt magic before I saw her, and, well, I knew the only way I was gonna get through Huxley was with her as my familiar."

She blinked at him, the moment rushing back: her frustration that night when the novices wouldn't do more than glance at her and smirk; the sudden wonderful tingle at her whiskers; the short chubby human crossing the room, a goofy grin on his face. All the trouble he'd been since, she'd forgotten how...how right she'd suddenly felt.

"I'm really sorry, Cluny." Crocker swallowed and looked away. "You deserve a real wizard to be partnered with, not an idiot like me." His eyes flitted toward Master Gollantz. "So please don't blame her, sir. She was only trying to help me."

Silence fell, Cluny's throat too tight to speak, until Master Gollantz blew out a breath. "I can see that you are both determined to make my life difficult."

"Sir?" Cluny and Crocker both said, Cluny's ears folding.

Master Gollantz pointed a long finger at Crocker. "Your familiar will accompany you to all your regular classes from this moment on, Novice.

Your record will show that you are a remedial case who cannot function without the constant boost that a familiar provides."

Crocker swallowed and nodded. Master Gollantz's finger didn't move. "Further, you will accompany your familiar to all her classes. Your record will show that this is a punishment designed to teach you the vital difference between what a familiar does and what a wizard does."

"Sir?" Crocker's jaw dropped. "But...I can't handle that many classes! How'll I-?"

"Shut up, Crocker." Cluny covered his mouth with a paw and looked across at Master Gollantz. "So, in effect, sir, I'll be taking the wizard classes while Crocker here learns to be a familiar."

"Nonsense." Master Gollantz scowled. "The record will show that this is Novice Crocker's punishment. And if I hear even a whisper on this campus about animal wizards and human familiars, you two will be cleaning bathrooms till graduation: I'll be your advisor from now on, by the way." He stroked his beard. "I find myself becoming interested in you."

Cluny nodded, a thrill sparking her fur. "Of course, sir." She leaned back and whispered into Crocker's ear, "I'll explain when we get back to the room."

Crocker opened his mouth, blinked, closed his mouth, nodded, and started across the quad toward the dorms.

"Novices?" Master Gollantz's voice made Crocker stop and turn, Cluny blinking at the old wizard still standing with his arms folded. "Where do you think you're going?"

"Uhh..." Cluny looked at Crocker, then crooked a claw over her shoulder. "To sleep, sir?"

Master Gollantz pressed his fingertips together. "I rather think you'll be accompanying me to the realm of the Ifriti Ranee; there's still the matter of your actual punishment, after all." He nodded. "You will perform one task of the Ranee's choosing, and I'll be along to make sure you don't make any more of a mess of things than you already have."

"Back..." Crocker's eyes went wide. "Back to...all that lava and everything?"

Master Gollantz nodded again, and Cluny patted the side of Crocker's head. "Don't worry." She drew a breath, felt their joined power flowing through her. "I think we can handle just about anything right now."

M. C. A. Hogarth, a lifelong author and artist, has been writing the adventures of Alysha Forrest, a 'morphic galactic starship commander, for publication in fanzines since 1996. But the character predates that. Hogarth, then Maggie de Alarcon, had first created Alysha in juvenile cartoon stories, then during adolescence turned her into a romantic feline. Starting in 1996, "influenced by the galactic civilizations of such authors as Larry Niven and C. J. Cherryh", she made Alysha into a cat-human woman in a 25th century star-spanning society composed mostly of the descendents of bioengineered animal-human hybrids. Alysha is a Karaka'An, a furred and tailed digitigrade felinoid. Other "Pelted" peoples who each have their own interstellar planets are wolf-human hybrids, fox-humans, tiger-humans, and so on. The pure humans are considered superior, especially by themselves, in this civilization. Hogarth rewrote seven early stories into a novel, Alysha's Fall (Cornwuff Press, September 2000), telling of Alysha's beginnings as a solitary cadet, doing what she has to in order to survive as one of the prejudiced-against Pelted amidst the human-favored Academe students on Terracentrus.

By the time of "In the Line of Duty", published in 2003, Alysha has successfully entered the Fleet and become a First Commander (a junior officer) in a United Alliance starship. As the story describes, the Alliance consists of many Pelted peoples and humans working together. But they aren't the only civilization in this galaxy…

In the
Line of Duty

M.C.A. Hogarth

458-30 BA

Standing waist-deep in warm water, First Commander Alysha Forrest of the UAV Scattersky watched as six of the alien Platies swam in a circle around her hips. She offered her hand and felt Neon rub velvety skin against her fingers. No one quite understood how the Platies fit their sapience into their flat oval bodies; like the round and fuzzy Flitzbe, no one even understood what the Platies wanted of the Alliance. But many ships carried several Platies in their water environments anyway, and Alysha found their brilliant colors and the ripple of their skins calming.

Calm was what she needed.

A slight splash heralded the arrival of the Scattersky's Naysha lieutenant, one of the ship's navigators. Eyes the size of Alysha's fists gazed at her through the surface of the water, and then the Naysha rose far enough to give Alysha a view of her hands.

"Blood in the water," the Naysha signed, the pearly webbing between her fingers glistening.

Alysha nodded, agreeing with the sentiment. Though Kaymah could hear and understood Universal, she signed out of courtesy, and to keep up her fluency. "We're approaching the distress call's origin," she replied. "Soon we'll know."

Kaymah grinned. "Water-friends say there will be much to do. They hear great noise."

Alysha's brows lifted. She glanced at the rippling Platies. Communication had been the basis of the Platy civilization, as far as any Alliance scientist could tell. They used the dense soup of their oceans to speak over impossibly long distances through means not wholly understood. Observation had proven that the Platies had spatial and subtle senses that didn't correlate well to those of creatures descended from humans. Only the Naysha, the experimental near-mermaid species created by the most brilliant human genetic engineer of the time, reliably bridged the gap between the minds of the Platies and those who walked on land.

"Great noise, ah?" Alysha said. She used one hand to stroke one of the aliens named Brown Burnoose for the cape-like pattern on its back, then brought her fingers back into view. Naysha Sign turned into a pidgin with only one hand. "I'll keep that in mind." She paused. "Do they understand me, Kaymah? Do you think?"

"More than others," Kaymah signed. She shrugged. "You try. You sit in the water with them. They like you."

Alysha nodded, then started as the telegem inside her ear chimed. She flicked an ear to activate it.

"Forrest here," she said aloud.

"To the bridge, Forrest."

"Aye, sir," Alysha said, pulling herself out of the water. She briskly toweled off her lower body all the way to her digitigrade feet and slipped her uniform tunic over the stretchsuit.

"Good luck," Kaymah signed. "We'll await news!"

"Thank you," Alysha signed hurriedly, and ran for the nearest lift.

* * *

Alysha stared at the red line leading toward the gas giant and the hulking ship that fell so gracefully, so inexorably down it. Her hand flexed on the back of the captain's chair, but she did not speak. Only her gray ears twitched, the light blinking on the pale gold hoops threaded through them.

For once, cheerful Captain Maurbery wasn't laughing. She couldn't blame him.

"This is where the distress call led us."

"We don't appear to have much time, sir."

The Tam-illee man rubbed his chin, his much larger brown ears straining forward. He didn't look as much like a fox as Alysha looked like a cat, but they shared their humanoid faces and ancestry in common. "No. They were planning to use the giant to aerobrake, but their navigation computer malfunctioned and they don't have the power to get off their current course."

Alysha glanced at the notes in the upper left hand 'corner' of the two-story holographic display and frowned. "They're too massy for us to haul them."

"And too fragile for us to push," Maurbery finished. "We have to evacuate them and let the ship go."

"Captain, they're answering our comm request."

"Put them through, Lieutenant."

Alysha turned her attention to the display as the vessel's trajectory was replaced with the face of a troubled human man who floated just in range of the pick-up.

"This is Headmaster Dan Hawkins of the freighter UAV Alalbama... Christ, are we glad to see you people!"

"Captain Maurbery of the UAV Scattersky. It seems we're just in time to break up your party, Headmaster," Maurbery said, grinning.

"Well, the weather was gonna get a bit hot for our comfort anyway, sir," the human answered, managing a wan smile in return. "Can you help us?"

"Are your pads operational?"

"I'm afraid they aren't, Captain."

Alysha's ear flicked down at the sound of the soft and very volatile curse that escaped her captain. She said nothing and watched the human on the display. The lines around his eyes had deepened into pale creases that hadn't seen the sun that had tanned his face. His silvered beard bordered a strong chin. He didn't appear to blink often, and his obvious apprehension only intensified an already intense hazel stare.

"We're going to have to send a shuttle to get you out, then. Are you suited, Headmaster?"

From her careful scrutiny of his face, Alysha knew the answer before the human spoke.

"I'm afraid we don't have enough for everyone, sir. We've got fifteen people and twelve suits."

"We'll send some over, then. Herd your men into one place, Hawkins and we'll get them out."

"Right away, Captain. Hawkins out."

Maurbery cursed again, louder. Alysha glanced down at him, privately sharing the sentiment. "Rescue operations are not supposed to be on a time-table with half the equipment missing!"

Alysha spoke, her alto low. "I'll have a team on it immediately. Anything else, sir?"

Maurbery managed one of his trademark chuckles, though the lines around his eyes belied his weariness. "Thank you for keeping me sane, Forrest."

"That's my job, sir," Alysha said with a smile before heading off the bridge.

* * *

Half a mark later Alysha paid out the umbilical that attached the docking clamp on her leg to the Recurve class shuttle. She was leading the two members of the team who had followed her extravehicular; the other two sat inside the shuttle, maintaining its position relative to the falling cargo ship. They'd already padded the suits into the pressurized compartment that held the small crew of the Alalbama. If only pads could create their tunnels from the receiving end as well as the initiating end, they wouldn't be Outside… but there was no use wishing.

"Barnard, Flait, you hear me?"

"Clear as a summer day," came a saucy female voice over her telegem. That would be Meri Flait, the Aeran woman. Alysha had watched from the corner of her eye as the Aeran had tucked her long ears back before sealing on her suit; she hadn't envied Meri the task. Braiding her own black hair for the helmet had been inconvenience enough.

"I hear you, Commander," chimed in Barnard, the Hinichi wolfine. Alysha glanced his way as he swam slowly into the corner of her vision.

"All right, people. You know the plan. We're going to go find these people, attach the extra umbilical outside their door and shepherd them to the shuttle . . . and then we're going to go home and enjoy a nice shower and twelve hours of sleep."

"Aye-aye, sir!" Flait chirped.

"I'm already dreaming of a shower," Barnard muttered, his long-suffering tone communicating his facial expression as clearly as if she could see it.

Alysha grinned. "Let's get it done, then. And watch the tails."

"We're there, sir."

Alysha jetted after them, pleased at their enthusiasm. She was unnaturally aware of her own breathing, her ribcage rising and falling against the memory material that sealed the thin skin of the short-lapse EVA softsuit to her body. . . . her very small body. The enormity of the starscape threatened her with its majesty, and she let her eyes rise up the solid wall of the gas giant, a whirling mass of brown, blood-black crimson and cream that obscured most of her field of vision. The stars that managed to win past the giant's influence were tiny opals, constant in their light. That lack of fluctuation had gratified Alysha when she'd done her first extravehicular maneuvers. It was comforting to find in a world of constant gradation something that held to its course, unwavering.

The Alalbama herself was no small thing. She easily out-stripped the Scattersky in sheer mass, but while the Fleet battlecruiser was a study in purposeful, almost predatory curves, the cargo ship was a collection of vast spindles and containers, strung together with precariously thin cranes and cables. She looked incredibly fragile, coasting toward the gaseous monstrosity that had captured her.

Fully ninety-five percent of the Alalbama's compartments were de-pressurized; the last five comprised her crew quarters. As a Blackspace class freighter, Alalbama wasn't meant for hauling cargo that required air.

Coasting toward the bulb where the fifteen members of the Alalbama crew had reported they'd gathered, Alysha used her telegem to consult a better sensor suite than the one built into her suit.

"Jason, are you still reading the heat signatures in that bulb?"

"Absolutely," came the crisp reply from the Tam-illee ensign she'd left at the shuttle's science station. "No doubting that one, sir. They're waiting for you just as they said."

"Good," Alysha replied. "Flait, you have the extra cable?"

The shape of the Aeran female dove past her, trailing two lines like a fish with exotic white fins. Flait made light contact with the exterior of the bulb, then walked carefully on her magnetic boots to the airlock. She bent and arranged the umbilical, then stood in sharp relief against the darkness of the gas giant and waved her hands triumphantly.

Alysha chuckled and sailed after her. "We're behind you. Jason, give me a line into the Alalbama."

"Patching you through, sir."

"Alalbama, can you hear me?"

"Loud and clear!" The headmaster's voice held an undisguised note of relief.

Alysha slowed herself as the ship rose to meet her feet. "Headmaster Hawkins, this is First Commander Alysha Forrest. Did you receive the suits?"

"Absolutely. They're working fine."

Alysha nodded to herself, then gently touched down on the hull. The magnetic pads in her digitigrade boots activated without incident and she straightened, walking over to join Flait. "My people and I are just outside the airlock with the umbilical. Please proceed through the airlock one at a time and we will guide you to the shuttle."

"On our way, Forrest."

Alysha studied the airlock. Its lights flickered from green to red, then to green again as the thick door slid back. The first of the Alalbama's crew stepped out of the airlock and hesitantly drifted out. "Flait?"

"On it, sir." The Aeran female detached herself from the skin of the ship and met the swimming civilian. Alysha watched in satisfaction as the Aeran ushered him up the cable to the shuttle's airlock. Barnard took the next and the evacuation proceeded smoothly. Alysha directed the procedure from just above the airlock on the Alalbama, informing the headmaster when to send the next crew member through.

It could be that it was just another routine rescue operation and an hour from now she'd be done with the captain's debrief and in her quarters, enjoying hot coffee and a warm shower. Alysha flicked her ear, then said, "Jason?"

"Aye, sir."

"What's the estimated time before this thing goes down?"

"About an hour."

Alysha nodded and returned to her task. When Flait took the fourteenth up the cable, the First Commander said, "I'll take the last one." Cheers accompanied her to the airlock until she toggled the inside line.

"Headmaster, shall we?"

"First Commander... I would very much like to go."

Something in his tone unnerved her. "Mr. Hawkins?"

"Would you mind coming in here, ma'am?"

Ignoring the civilian title, Alysha flicked her ear to switch the telegem pasted inside to the shuttle channel. "Jason, I'm going in to talk to the Headmaster."

"Sir?"

"I shouldn't be long."

He didn't argue. Alysha keyed back to the Alalbama's channel and said, "I'm outside, Mr. Hawkins."

She waited for the lock to cycle and the door to open, then unscrewed her umbilical and attached it to the hull before stepping inside. A few moments later found her inside the pressurized compartment, obviously an antechamber meant as an EVA landing. The bright light reflected too strongly against the flat white walls.

The headmaster was seated in a white chair, his helmet on his knee and his head in his hands. When she entered he glanced up, and his expression stopped her at the threshold. Alysha unlocked her helmet and tucked it beneath an arm.

"First Commander, I don't know how to say this, but . . . there are other people on this ship."

A fine sweat broke from her skin, but she remained composed. "Other people."

"I didn't find out until a few days ago. There was an accident when the things were being mounted." The human grimaced, but she didn't miss the anger that flared in his hazel gaze. "One of ours was smuggling. On my ship. Refugees from the Chatcaavan Empire. I can't say I blame him for doing it, but he never consulted me, and now that he's dead I don't know where they are. They're somewhere on the spindles."

"You've searched the pressurized areas," Alysha said, just to hear it from his mouth. The chill that had seized her spine was only deepening.

"Yes."

"That means they're in cryogenic storage, in some container in the depressurized areas," Alysha said. She refused to let the information phase her in front of the already demoralized human.

"Yes," Hawkins said.

They stared directly at one another, then Alysha flicked her telegem to the shuttle channel. "Jason."

"Sir?"

"Tell Flait to meet Headmaster Hawkins at the airlock and escort him back to the shuttle."

"Done, sir."

Alysha lifted her chin, then slowly inclined her head to the human.

He looked away, then locked his helmet on and walked to the airlock. A few minutes later, he was gone.

Alysha collapsed into the chair he'd vacated. It was still warm.

That Hawkins had admitted to the refugees amazed her. Without sufficient evidence to prove his claim that another crew member had been smuggling, it would be far too easy for him to be pinned with responsibility for the crime... yet he had not been able to leave them behind. Common decency did not always overrule fear and the survival instinct in every reasoning being, and she could not help but respect the human for his moral fortitude, particularly when faced with the messy politics involved in running illegal aliens.

Which did not change the fact that she, Maurbery, and the Scattersky were now in an untenable position.

Lifting a head that seemed far heavier than its crown of black braids, Alysha flicked on the telegem. "Jason, get me Maurbery on a secure channel."

"Aye, sir."

Her heart beat twice before the Tam-illee captain said, "Forrest? What's going on? Why are you still in there?"

Alysha paused, choosing her words carefully. "Captain, we have a situation."

"A what? Dammit, Forrest, we don't have time for situations."

"Sir, there's live cargo on board."

Absolute silence across a comm-line wasn't entirely possible, even with Alliance technology. Alysha closed her eyes and listened to the almost inaudible crackle of the universe's background radiation. Her back ached.

"Give me the full story, now, Commander."

"One of their crew was smuggling refugees. They're in cryogenic suspension and hanging somewhere on one of the spindles. Hawkins didn't know where."

"On one of the spindles? Exposed to space? To any passing meteorite or piece of space dust that wanted to burrow through the shields?"

Alysha grimaced. "We can only assume that they're loaded somewhere near the protected sides of the ship. Sir, we can't tow it. If we break it apart, we risk killing them until we know where they are. And we can't push it for the same reason. We've got to get search parties out here."

"We've got half an hour before that thing sinks too low to get anyone safely away, Forrest. I don't think that's enough time."

The statement hung between them. Alysha bared her teeth in the solitude of the silent white room. "Sir, we can't leave them there. We're Fleet."

A pause. Then: "Fifteen minutes, Forrest. Fifteen minutes, and no more. Use the shuttle you've already got. And when I tell you to jump you'd better be out of there or I'll have your guts for garters. Do you understand me?"

"Absolutely," Alysha said, already screwing her helmet back on and stepping into the airlock.

"Yeah, well, Iley speed, damn you."

Alysha grinned and replied, "Forrest out, sir." She switched channels immediately as the airlock cycled open. "Jason! I need you to scan for additional life signs through the spindles, particularly ones that look slow or dim. Anything that looks suspicious. And give me a report on the areas of this hulk that would be best protected from wayward encounters with free-floaters."

"On it, sir." His puzzlement was obvious, but she'd successfully communicated the urgency in her voice. "It looks like the best places within the shields are only a few minutes down the hull from the pressurized compartments."

"It's my lucky day," Alysha said. She detached herself from the hull and reconnected the umbilical, then jetted down the axis of the ship. "Keep scanning for those signs, please."

"I'm not reading anything, sir."

"Just keep looking."

"Yes, sir."

The ghostly pallor of the ship as it flowed beneath her sent renewed chills down her spine. The spindles and their mounted containers were haphazardly attached to the ship; smaller racks descended into recesses so dark she could only barely see the stars at their ends, while others thrust out at ungainly angles against the gas giant's unstable backdrop. The enormity of her task finally struck her as she passed hundreds and hundreds of cargo containers, each of them big enough for at least four people. Some of them were large enough to sleep forty.

Alysha coasted to a halt beside one of the windmill arms, each of its containers the size of rail cars. "Jason? I could use some data about now."

"Sir, I'm looking all over, but I can't find a thing. I can't even make anything up with these readings."

Were they all dead? Or was it just bad luck that the shuttle couldn't pick out the faint pulse of cryogenic sleepers? Alysha glanced over the edge of the ship and noticed how immediate, how malevolent the gas giant appeared. Was it closer? Or was that her imagination?

Alysha took a breath and choose a random corridor, then dove down it. She employed her suit sensors as the containers flashed past her in the stark chiaroscuro of space. She tasked herself to patience, to calm thought, and gave each as thorough an examination as she could. She was halfway down the corridor when Jason interrupted.

"Sir, we've got a burst from the Scattersky. Maurbery says you need to head back in two minutes."

"Two minutes is not enough," Alysha said, not allowing the conversation to distract her from her scrutiny of the current container. Calm, like the Platies in water. "Tell him I need more time."

Jason sounded uncertain. "Sir, I don't think…"

"I need more time, Ensign! Forrest out!"

Cutting off the link left her alone with the sound of her own swift breathing and the pain in her clenched gut. There was no question that she should obey orders, that there was no way a single person could canvas the entire cargo ship in time. No sensors, no matter how modern, could pick out the life signs of sleepers in close proximity to something as loud as a gas giant. But something in her couldn't give up. Alysha swam down the corridor, gritting her teeth.

Her telegem flared back to life. "Dammit, Forrest, don't play games with me!"

"Sir, I can't let it go."

"You'll do what I tell you to, and you'll do it immediately or I'll have them reel you back in by that umbilical!"

"Just a few more minutes, sir! Please."

The pause before Maurbery's reply gave her time to slip through the gap created by an empty spindle into the next row. She waded up through it, hauling the cable behind her.

"Alysha, listen to me. You can't do it. No one could. We found out too late. There's no use dying with them."

It was so reasoned, his voice so understanding that she almost gave in. "I'll be up in a few more minutes, Captain."

"You'll be up now. I'm calling back the umbilical."

The tug at her leg was unmistakable. Startled, Alysha stared at it as it began to drag her back. Then, with a calm she almost couldn't believe of herself, she reached down and unscrewed it. The tension in the cable vibrated through her wrist until the end popped off the dock in her suit and spun away. She spared it only a moment's glance as it vanished, then redoubled her efforts.

"Forrest!"

The thunder in his voice would have made her regret her action had she not been so intent on her goal.

Softer then, "Curse you to the last level of Hell, Alysha. You'd better know what you're doing."

"I hope so too," Alysha murmured, staring at the vast collection of cargo containers. She struggled for calm, but the only answer that rose from her still center was that she should give up. Only an esper could possibly find the sleepers in time. And even then they couldn't give her reliable directions to the containers.

Unless they understood those things instinctively.

"Jason!" Alysha exclaimed. "Get someone into the water with Kaymah and the Platies. Fast! Tell them I need to find some sleepers."

"Aye, sir," the ensign said, voice trembling.

Her heart fluttered as she waited, and then a sharp soprano spoke. "This is Lieutenant Avery at the water environment." A pause. "Kaymah says head down the z axis about fifty feet."

Her suit compass was synchronized to the Scattersky's. Alysha consulted it and sped down the open corridor.

"Northwest. About twenty feet."

She spun and headed that way. Her breathing had accelerated… she wondered if the heat was real or something she'd conjured.

"Down again, another forty feet. Kaymah says, 'What are you facing?'"

"Six cargo containers," Alysha reported, trying for briskness instead of fear. "Tilted up twenty degrees. Lying on the western plane. Behind them another six. And another six behind those."

Maurbery's voice cut through the channel. "Forrest, dammit, another five minutes and we won't be able to get you out of there!"

Avery's soprano: "The row behind the one you're looking at. That's the one. The Platies are sure of it. They're swooping around—"

"Forrest!"

Alysha dove for the base of the second row's axle. "I think I've found them, sir." The heat was no longer her imagination, but she ignored it to struggle with the controls that worked the mounts. She managed to start the unload routine and held her breath until the series of lights steadied and the machinery spun up. "Captain, they should be coming off. Hitch them."

"What about you?"

What indeed? Alysha stared up at the distant stars, felt anew the heat that had seemed so far away a few minutes ago. On an impulse, she leaped onto the last container and activated the magnetic pads on her softsuit, clinging to the container with open arms. Her speeding heart began to slow, and she had time to wonder at this unnatural calm before her container slid down the axle toward the dismount point and shot into space.

Alysha hung on, closing her eyes as her container cartwheeled away from the Alalbama. No one had ever researched the effects of a hitch on a suited individual, but it didn't seem important. When she was sure she wasn't going to vomit, she cracked her eyes apart and found the cargo ship. Its acceleration differed enough from hers that she could actually see it falling toward the giant. A shudder wracked her body.

"Forrest? Are you still out there?" The panic in Maurbery's voice jarred the entire situation into perspective and Alysha bit her teeth against another wave of nausea.

"Sir," she managed after a moment. "I'm here. On the last container."

"We're sending the shuttle out for you. I'm going to flay you alive, Commander."

"At least I'm alive to flay," Alysha managed wanly, and the sound of Maurbery's reluctant chuckle forced a small smile from her lips.

* * *

Two marks later in the Medplex, Alysha weakly propped herself up on her elbows as the captain entered. Maurbery stopped at the foot of her bunk, legs spread and arms folded over his chest. His dark brown ears were practically sealed to his skull, and fire lit his green eyes from within. Alysha met his gaze and waited for him to speak first, determined not to let his patent wrath sway her from observing proper military courtesy. She was faintly aware that the neat braids that had wound around her head had come undone and untidy wisps of black hair framed her face; she wished she'd had time to groom.

"Consulting the Platies and the Naysha for help saved your life," Maurbery said, and the statement was so far from what Alysha had been expecting to hear that she finally found herself off-guard.

"Sir?"

The Tam-illee didn't so much as twitch a nostril as he went on. "Saved your life, because from what I could see you would have searched that whole damn ship on your own until you fell into that monster. Against my specific orders."

That did not seem to invite a reply. She looked at the blanket in her hand until Maurbery wrenched her head around to meet his green eyes. She hadn't even noticed him drawing nearer — and now, confronted with his gaze she trembled, shocked at the implacable anger, the concern so obvious on his open face. Disarmed, Alysha stared at him.

"If you ever disobey orders like that again, Forrest, I will personally bust you down to ensign so hard there won't be any cheek left for you to fall on. Is that understood?"

The last three words hissed from his mouth, and she could only manage a weak, "Yes, sir."

She reeled when he let go, pulling the sheets closer. To have a superior officer touch her so flagrantly was so unusual that the warning echoed all the way into her bones. She watched with wide eyes as Maurbery strolled to the door, the appearance of calm restored, before turning back.

"You got them all out, by the way. All twelve hundred."

"All twelve... hundred?" she asked, stunned.

"Hawkins wasn't sure how many they took, but Lieutenant Kaymah reports that twelve hundred is it, give or take a few souls. There'll probably be a commendation in it for you." Maurbery grinned, eyes narrowed. "But for now, you will rest. Radiation poisoning is nothing to sniff off. And that is an order, Commander. I expect to be obeyed."

"Aye, sir," Alysha replied. And stared after him after he'd left.

A commendation? It hardly seemed real. But twelve hundred refugees, fleeing an Empire known for its capricious cruelty, now free to pursue their own lives...

Alysha laid down. She turned gingerly onto her side and slid a hand beneath the pillow, and smiled.

Charles Melville introduced his magical anthropomorphic world in a self-published comic book, The Champion of Katara *#1 (Crack O'Dawn Press, August-September 1987). It only lasted for one issue, but it introduced the animal peoples of Katara (felines), Dogonia (canids), Ra Kuna (raccoons), Bruinsland (bears), Bananaland (gorillas and other simians), Rodentia (mice), Scentas (skunks), and Lep'kufft (rabbits – wanderers without a homeland). Melville moved from Rochester, New York to Seattle in 1991, where he quickly got immersed in Seattle's Furry community. His comic-book world reappeared in several comics from Seattle publisher Edd Vick's MU Press, including the 184-page graphic novel* Felicia: Melari's Wish *(August 1994). In 2004 he began featuring Felicia in a series of five novellas published individually through Café Press, later collected together as the book* The Vixen Sorceress *(CreateSpace, December 2008).* Felicia and the Tailcutter's Curse *was the second of these; two others were finalists for an Ursa Major Award in their years of publication. Melville currently writes & draws both* The Champion of Katara *and* Felicia: Sorceress of Katara *as online full-page weekly comic strips.*

As sometimes happens in comic books and newspaper strips, a minor supporting character soon took over from the original main characters. Felicia cla di Burrows is a renegade vixen sorceress, expelled from the Magi Councils for refusing to renounce the forces of the Shadow. Felicia is less interested in Good or Evil than in gaining revenge against the rival cla di Howler (wolf) clan who killed her parents and drove her out of Dogonia, and she will not turn down any power that might help her gain that revenge. She operates as a lone "Magi for hire" from an isolated but comfortable tower in Katara. Although pledged from childhood for revenge, Felicia as an adult is often sidetracked by stronger concerns for her own comfort, and in helping out those less fortunate than herself.

Felicia and the Tailcutter's Curse

-or-

The Sorceress Takes A Vacation

Charles P. A. Melville

Prologue: "Cursed In Line"

There was no moon and they were grateful, for the night sky was clear and the stars burned too brightly as it was. The small band of felines slunk silently through the foliage and deep shadows outside of the tall city walls. Maryn glanced longingly back at the gates to Felina, knowing they were already shut and sealed with the mystic sigil of Aln. No one would pass through them again until sunrise. He stumbled on an exposed root and stepped on a twig. The sudden crack broke through the silence, and the others stopped, their breaths caught in their throats.

"Why don't you just wave a flag, Maryn?" hissed the closest shadow. It was Jenth, the town smith, a large and burly cougar. "I'm sure he doesn't know where we are yet! Perhaps you'd like to sing a little tune to call him right to us!"

"That's enough," admonished another whisper, coming up alongside them both. "This is dangerous enough without bickering." Strong fingers clamped around Maryn's arm and guided him through the dark. "This way, Maryn, and mind your step."

Maryn nodded nervously, even though he knew the other probably couldn't see him do so. "Are you sure he'll be here tonight, Kana?" he asked in a dry whisper. "He doesn't always come to us. Not every night."

Kana the Fearless chuckled grimly. "He'll come. He's due. And I can tell. Trust me, Maryn, he'll be here." They paused at the edge of a clearing barely lit by dim starlight, and the tall figure holding Maryn's arm pointed up towards a small knoll. "There! There's his perch. We can hide in the thickets until he shows."

"And he won't see us?" one of the others asked dubiously.

Kana surveyed the six friends who had followed him out of the city before the closing of the gates. "I've prepared for that, Astar. You shall see." He turned to Maryn. "Are you sure you still want to come, Maryn? I know this isn't easy for you. You can await us near the gate, since I am sure he will be too preoccupied to notice you."

"No," stammered Maryn. "I said I would come, and I'm coming!"

Kana grinned widely and gave Maryn's arm an encouraging squeeze. He led them all up the knoll. He knelt and searched for a moment under the bushes and stood up carrying something in both arms. "Take these," he instructed them. "I had these made especially for tonight."

"What are they?" Jenth asked suspiciously. He took one from the pile and snapped it open. It was a large blanket, and in its center was an embroidered sigil. The circle was woven of pure golden thread, and its simple features were that of two beady eyes and a wide, friendly smile. "Aln's seal!" gasped the cougar in surprise.

"Yes," said Kana. "With these pulled over us, we will be invisible to his eyes, and he will not see us. Now take these and cover yourselves. We will hide as we planned."

They all did as Kana instructed, each taking a blanket and slipping into the thickets. Silently they hid, laying down on the ground and concealing themselves with the blankets. And they waited. The stars high above wheeled slowly by as the night passed.

Maryn felt the approach before he heard the sound of beating wings. An overwhelming oppression suddenly filled the air and he feared that he would suffocate in it. Through the blanket he could hear the heavy thump of something large landing in the soft ground near him, and the loud, raspy breathing of some great beast. Maryn cowered for several moments, afraid to move, afraid to even breathe, and then, calling up the little courage he had been nurturing through these past days of preparation, he carefully lifted the corner of his blanket to peek up into the night sky.

Silhouetted against the starry sky was a terrible, ragged black shadow, tall and immense, towering at least as twice as tall as the tallest Kataran Maryn had ever known. It stalked in a crouch, and a long, serpentine tail snaked out behind it, wriggling almost of its own will. As though it suddenly sensed eyes watching it, the creature swiveled its head about in Maryn's direction. The darkness still hid it, but Maryn could see the head was vaguely canine in shape, with large tufted ears. Red eyes, like dull fire embers, stared at him. Maryn froze, feeling the stare drill through him and into his heart. But the moment passed and nothing further happened. The creature turned away and resumed stalking towards the walled city. The enchanted blankets had hidden him from the monster.

Maryn knew his task. He rose as silent as the morning mist and crept carefully behind the monster. So, too, did Kana and the others, each slowly emerging from their hiding places. The creature stopped suddenly and straightened, throwing its arms out wide in a gesture of placation. "Gentlebeings of Felina, O fair city..." it spoke in a voice as loud as thunder and dry as autumn. But it never spoke another word.

"Now!" cried Kana, and the seven companions threw aside their blankets. The creature knew them at once and turned to snarl at them. But Kana was swifter, and with his drawn sword made a single slice downwards on the beast's serpentine tail. The sword clove halfway into the tail before it was yanked away. A terrible scream of outraged pain echoed through the stillness. Red eyes flared as they turned to Kana, but two of the others also plunged their swords into the creature's tail. Another scream, and the creature limped away with a look of unaccustomed pain and horror upon its face.

Encouraged by the example of his fellows, Maryn took his turn and hacked at the bleeding tail with all his might. The impact of the sword striking the writhing mass reverberated up his arm like lightning, and he involuntarily let go of the sword as the tail whipped away from him. Kana leapt up, snatching a sword away from one of the closest of the other companions and with a mighty swing brought it down fully upon the first wound. The tail came away, hacked completely through at the very base. The creature screamed in agony and spread its ancient leathern wings, taking flight from its tormentors. The warriors all steeled themselves, watching the creature tensely, but the tailless shadow threw itself into the night sky away to the west, its screams of pain and fear ripping through the night.

The seven warriors stood and watched in mute disbelief. "We did it," one of them finally found the strength to whisper. "Bountiful Aln, we actually did it!"

Kana laughed loudly. "He's never had anyone defy him before! Never had anyone inflict injury to his person before! He'll remember this for a long time to come!" He laughed again and yelled a wild cheer. His companions all winced, unaccustomed to making loud noises at night; their own cheer was restrained. After a few minutes, Kana's exuberance was too much to resist, and they all joined him, cheering and congratulating one another. "Kana!" they cried. "Kana Wagajop!"

"Tailcutter?" Kana translated with amusement. "The fearless tailcutter, is it?" He laughed and playfully cuffed the nearest, sharing a few quick words with him. Kana turned and slapped Maryn on the back. "You showed greater heart than you thought possible, Maryn! You're as responsible for tonight as the rest of us. What are you doing?"

Maryn had dropped to his hands and knees and was searching through the grass. "My sword!" he replied with concern. "I dropped it after I struck him! I can't find it.!"

Kana the Fearless nodded. "We all dropped our swords, Maryn. Come, they're of no use to us now. We need to gather up twigs and branches! We need a fire!" He pointed at the bloody remains of the severed tail. "We must burn it. Cremate it and purify this spot, and not even the ashes should be left to remain!"

"Kana!" Jenth looked across the starlit field to their leader, and there was a note of renewed fear in the cougar's voice. "He's not dead." The others halted in their tracks and glanced at one another in abrupt realization. "He's not dead," Jenth repeated. "We've only wounded him. He'll be back."

But Kana broke into a raucous laugh. "Not tonight! He's fled home to lick his wound and marvel that mortal creatures could do such an injury to him, or dare to defy his will. He'll hide tonight, and he'll wonder." The fearless Kataran turned and gazed away to the western skies. "But you're right, Jenth. He will be back."

Maryn slept fitfully all through the next day, for the nightmares had him and would not let go. He dreamed of wielding a sword too large for his hands, of wielding it very awkwardly, and of piercing red eyes that always found him wherever he hid. He dreamed of the people cheering his brave act of slicing off the monster's tail, and then of those same folk accusing him of stirring up the creature's hatred and bringing them all directly to his attentions. And he dreamed of being carried bodily away through the night skies and of being dragged screaming into a ragged gash of a cavern opening, never to see the sun again.

He was jolted awake by a rough hand shaking his shoulder. His eyes popped open to see Jenth leaning over him. "Wake up!" the cougar told him in a quiet and low voice. "It's night! You've slept through the entire day!" The cougar straightened and looked fearfully out the window. "He's here," he continued in a faint whisper. "Can't you feel him?"

And Maryn could. The dreadful oppression of last night had returned, clutching at his heart like a claw. He hurriedly rose and dressed and followed the now quiet Jenth out into the city streets, and then up onto the ramparts of the wall. Kana was already there, staring stonily out into the night. Maryn edged to the side of the wall, drawn closer by an unspeakable compulsion, knowing what he would find but not wanting to see.

The creature has returned. It hung back at the very edge of the torchlight from the city, just barely illuminated. It was shrunken in appearance, and its body was wasted as though consumed from within. It was gaunt and bent, and malice was evident in its bony face. Thin, leathery wings curled behind it, unable to hide the rump that was marred by a large sore; a scarred stump was evident where the tail had been hacked away. It reached out a gnarled, taloned claw towards Kana and hissed balefully.

"Yes," said Kana, unconcerned. "I cut your tail off. Come again, and next time I will take your head."

Maryn and the others gathered around Kana caught their breaths at the declaration, and the creature's eyes grew wide with fury. It opened its maw to speak, and when it did so it carried none of the disguised sweetness of the night before.

"I will eat you. I will raze your city and devour you all. I will leave nothing, and I will defile your souls for all eternity!"

The Katarans recoiled from the unfettered venom of the creature's hatred. But Kana remained unimpressed and stood his ground. He laughed and sneered down at the creature. "Your power has waned, O Murk. You are not the powerful being you once were. And you have no power here anymore." The Murk appeared to wince and shrink in upon himself with each word. "Destroy us all? How shall you do that? Will you deceive your way in as you did in ancient Haven and Eeronwi? There are no dogs here, old shadow. Go away, before I cut your nose off next." Kana turned and walked away scornfully.

The Murk raised his claw again and pointed to the retreating back of the fearless Tailcutter. "You are damned! You shall know no peace, and your death shall not be pleasant! You shall go to it begging, begging for an end to your sufferings!" Kana ignored the Murk's ravings, but Maryn and the others fell away from the rampart side and dropped to their knees, cowering with their hands over their ears. "So shall it be!" the monster raged, "on through your children, and your children's children! And your children's children's children!"

Chapter 1 "The Best Of Times, The Cursed Of Times"

Felicia lounged alone, soaking contentedly in a hot bath, soap bubbles drifting lazily over her in a cozy blanket of suds. She lay limp in the warm water, arms hanging out of either side of the gilded porcelain tub, and her head resting on the rim at the end. Her eyes were rolled back, seeing nothing, and her mouth barely moved as she whispered in muted tones. On the floor near one outstretched hand was a small opened casket setting on a silver tray. A tiny trickle of fine dust glittered as it sifted through her open fingers and back into the casket.

Ghostly images drifted through the room, passing before the vixen's entranced eyes. A Siamese with large knowing eyes cast her gaze away from Felicia in grief and disappointment. A large burly wolf scowled balefully at her. A Kataran female with luxurious black fur and cold eyes studied her for a long moment with speculative interest. And then the dragon came. The dragon always came, and he always had a proposal, a promise, an exchange, or perhaps an offer. And he spoke to her, and called to her by name...

"Augh!" Felicia sat up with a start, splashing water all about the tub. She blinked and looked about her like a sleeper awakening from a long slumber. "Gur!" she muttered with a shiver as she stood and stepped from the tub. "These refreshenings are always more intense than I remember." Her hands shook as she gingerly lifted the casket and carefully sealed it shut.

"You know why that is," said a faint voice from behind her.

Felicia picked up a nearby towel and wrapped it around herself, barely acknowledging the arrival of the Archivist. "Of course I do," the vixen replied testily. "It's because my powers need occasional recharging, and the magikdust has... certain side effects." She glared for a moment at the prudish rabbit, silently daring her to challenge Felicia's evasion.

The Archivist frowned and shook her head sadly. Her pale white form fluttered as though disturbed by some breeze not present on the mortal plane. "You know that is not what I mean," she said in mild reproach. "You know full well what is wrong..."

"Yes," said Felicia abruptly. "You're right. I do know what's wrong." She sat on a chair and pouted. "I'm bored."

The ghost tilted her head inquisitively. "Bored?"

"Yes. I'm bored." The vixen stretched and yawned, then caught her towel before it fell away. "Bored, bored, bored, bored." She rose with an aristocratic languor and dried off her fur as she crossed over to her neatly folded clothing. "I simply haven't had a thing to do in weeks. All of my many projects are either currently caught up or in a state of progression to where I must wait for them to reach a stage that I may again involve myself with them. I have no research to do currently, nor do I have any clients. In fact, business has been slow of late; I haven't had a customer in quite some time. Not that I need to be concerned, since my personal coffers are plentiful at the moment." She sighed, and it was a long cry of dreary discontent. "I've read all my tomes many times over. And it's ever so peaceful in the surrounding towns and villages just now. Not even so much as a plague to make things interesting." She tossed the towel aside and dressed in silence.

"What will you do?" asked the Archivist curiously.

Felicia picked up a brush and stroked her fur thoughtfully for a few moments. She slowly smiled and a light shone in her green eyes. "I know exactly what I'll do!" she suddenly laughed in delight. "I'll go on holiday! Yes, that's what I'll do! I need a vacation!" With renewed animation she perked up and hurried into her study, still brushing at her fur. "I haven't been traveling in a while! I'll take a little trip for a few weeks, perhaps to the other side of Katara! Find some adventure or a romp! Hear some gossip from afar! Or a romance! Why, I haven't had a good romance since..." Her voice trailed off as she stepped up to her writing desk and picked up her diary. She winced at the thick coating of dust and cobwebs. "Oh, dear!"

"Where will you go?" asked the Archivist.

"Nowhere in particular. North seems like a good direction. Travel to a few inns and see what I find. I haven't yet made a circuit of inns without finding one or two good prospects!"

"For adventure?"

"Well, that too," Felicia smirked. She hurried away to her bedroom and threw open the wardrobe doors. "Let me see," she mused. "How shall I travel? Should I go in full regalia? Wear my best robes and jewelry? Or should I travel anonymously?" She nibbled at a clawtip for a moment as she scanned the contents of her wardrobe. "Hmm. Full regalia will turn heads and garner a lot of courtesy... but anonymity has its advantages as well. Sometimes you can pick up on the very most interesting bits of news when folks don't realize who you are." She pondered for a moment later, then nodded as she made her decision. "Anonymous it is! I'll travel incognito. But I'll pack away a robe or two just in case!"

So saying, the sorceress gestured and two voluminous magenta robes with plunging necklines rose and disengaged themselves from their hangers and floated across the room to deposit themselves into an open trunk. For the next few minutes Felicia pointed and called to several other articles of clothing or personal effects that she felt she would most likely need for her intended escapade, all while fetching and donning her good traveling cloak and boots.

"There!" she said at last, satisfied that she had collected everything she was going to need. She tapped the top of the trunk and it obediently locked itself secure and tight. "All done!" She slipped a pair of silk gloves over her black furred hands and smiled with eager delight. "The guardian spells are all in place, the proper notices are magically aligned for the specific attention of any visiting wizard who calls while I'm away, all of my personal effects and paraphernalia are mystically sealed, and I left a note for the milkman. All I need do is slip away to the stalls and fetch my horse..."

There was a sudden tolling of a huge bell, that rang loud and deep, resonating throughout the tower for several minutes before the echoes faded away.

"What was that?" asked Felicia in alarm and dismay.

"The doorbell," replied the Archivist solemnly.

"I know it's the doorbell!" snapped the vixen. "Who's calling now?"

"Hallo!" called out a voice from the main door downstairs. "Is the sorceress at home? Because I really got a problem and I need some one to be making with the magic to make it all better again!"

"It's a customer," observed the Archivist.

"Now?" Felicia huffed petulantly. "Now a customer wants to show up? When I'm all packed and ready to go on my vacation? Now someone wants me to work?" She glared indignantly at the window. "What nerve!"

"Hallo?" the voice outside persisted. "Listen, I'm not kidding! I hear you do miracle work, and I really need a miracle here!"

"That's it!" sighed the vixen dramatically, and she raised one hand imperiously. "I am so out of here!" And with a loud snap of her fingers she and her trunk vanished in a cloud of magenta smoke. The Archivist remained alone for a minute before she, too, faded away.

The voice below paused before continuing. "Hallo? I didn't come at a bad time, did I?" Another pause of quiet followed by low muttering that soon faded as the complainant eventually went away, unsatisfied.

Chapter 2 "Cursed In All Things"

"From Dogonia, you say?" The elderly noblewoman squinted her feline eyes in an effort to see the vixen sitting across from her more clearly. "Oh, are you from Canina, perhaps? I have a sister who lived there for a time. Her husband was an ambassador or some such nonsense. As though Katarans and Dogonians could ever maintain peaceful relations!" She sniffed and simpered before helping herself to another sip of her fine Kataran wine.

Felicia smiled indulgently. She sipped at her own wine and took in her surroundings. The inn was quiet tonight, with only a few travelers like herself dining in relative privacy, while a scant few local regulars were communing at the bar. Most were Kataran, of course, but there was at least one bruin and a handful of rabbits sitting by themselves. The rumble of conversation was a pleasantly low hum that hung just on the very precipice of audibility, punctuated from time to time by an occasional cheery laugh. Felicia's sharp fox ears could hear the happy greetings of the inevitable disciple of Jantorr the Deliverer who stood a post outside the inn's front door as they persistently solicited the tavern's arriving patrons and handing out flyers to any who would heed the call. The sorceress was content that the setting was complacent enough and that no danger threatened, either mortal or mystic. The aroma of meat sizzling in pans drifted in from the kitchen and hung in the air throughout the dining hall like a welcoming banner to all friendly passerby.

"Oh, I'm from the borderlands," she told the elderly feline. They had met and struck up a conversation and acquaintance soon after their separate arrivals at the inn earlier that evening, and had decided to dine together. That had been fine with Felicia, as it gave her the opportunity she had wanted to pick up on gossip. She raised her wine glass and took a moment to look at her reflection in the crystal to check that her disguise of a mature and matronly fox was still in place. She was still much too close to home to want to be recognized, and she wanted to maintain her anonymity for as long as it was possible. "I'm an immigrant, actually. My family emigrated here to Katara when I was a child."

"Good, good," said the old lady as she fished through her plate with her fork. "Makes a good deal of sense, really. Foxes don't really belong in Dogonia anyway, they're too catlike, do you know?" She reached out and caught the sleeve of a passing barmaid. "Dear, I think they forgot the fish on my fish platter. Do you see? Not even fishbones. Could you have them send me a nice fish? Thank you, dear."

"Wasn't there a fish on there when they brought it out?" Felicia asked when the barmaid had walked away off to the kitchen.

The old lady shushed her and set her purse down beside her on the bench, waving at a small stream of smoke wafting from it. "Now then, dear, where did you say you were going?"

"Nowhere special, more's the pity," sighed the vixen dramatically. "I just felt the need for a change. Life's become so routine lately."

"Oh, I know," the old feline sympathized. "One must get out and have a little fun now and then before one gets old." She also sighed dramatically. "Dear me, now that my tail is old and stiff it's all become dreary. I don't even dare sit in my rocker anymore. Because of the tail, you understand. That's why I'm going visiting to my cousin's in the west." The barmaid returned with a freshly steamed fish and set the platter before the old woman, who smiled pleasantly. "I know!" she said in sudden inspiration. "You must go to Felina!"

"Felina?" asked Felicia. "Why?"

"You must go to Lord Frisky's manor! He's going to have a big celebration in a week or so; I forget the date, I fear, but I know it's quite soon. It's his wedding anniversary, you see, and he's throwing a party for several friends and nobles. Why, it's just the thing you're looking for! There's even bound to be some young men there!"

Felicia smiled broadly. "I think you may have just the very idea. A celebration! Why, it does sound like fun! What is this Lord Frisky like?"

"Oh, very nice, very nice! A bit odd, you know, rather eccentric. But much loved by his tenants and people. A very fair cat by all accounts. Not much of a warrior, I hear, though I wouldn't really know about that. I've heard that he spends quite lavishly, especially when it comes to his parties!"

"Excuse me," Felicia overheard a voice speak up from the direction of the tavern bar. "I'm looking for this sorceress who does magic and might have been coming this way? She's a fox who's a real fox, if you know what I mean, and I'm having this problem I need a little help with?" The voice was drowned out by the low hum of background conversation, and Felicia ducked her head, hoping not to be noticed even with her disguise. She flicked an ear in annoyance at the thought of a persistent customer at a time when she didn't really want one. "And there are bound to be some young men? Yes, I think this is exactly what I'm looking for." Felicia couldn't resist a sly smile as she raised her glass to sip again at her wine.

The old lady giggled in girlish conspiracy before picking up her purse and slipping the newly steamed fish in with the previous one.

* * *

Felicia knew Felina well, though it had been many years since she had cause to journey through the old city. It was a trade city, and a major link between the nearest seaport, Linx, and the rest of Katara. It had prospered and grown, and fairly seethed with the energy of life as its populace bustled throughout the busy streets and markets. It had, for a time, been the seat of the Kataran throne before the monarchy moved across the mountains to erect the stately palace of Catalon. Now, even with the absence of the King and his retinue, it still managed an air of imperiality.

She caught a glimpse of it from the roadside as she rode around the side of a hill across the river from the main city gates. Little had changed since her last visit some years earlier. Buildings sprawled across three hills and a river, unrestrained by the old city walls that protected the ruling bureaucracy and the older and wealthier businesses. The sorceress still had some old business there to resolve, but then, she had unresolved business practically everywhere these days. But that wasn't a concern for today; she was on vacation. She turned away and urged her steed around the hill and away from Felina.

An hour later she rode into the estates of Lord Frisky and promptly up the paved road leading past the finely manicured lawn and meticulously trimmed hedges to the manor itself. A servant quickly came up and led her horse away to the stalls after she dismounted, and another directed her to the main entrance, where she announced herself to a doorman who promptly sent for the Steward.

The Steward was an old cat, bowed with age and bent of tail, and blessed with a face that resembled an irritated scrubbrush that had been teased to the point of intolerance. His whiskers had grown long and emerged from a shrub of facial fur that sprouted rebelliously under his nose, and both ears were scruffed and twitchy, and looked like animated barbs on a cactus.

"Good day, milady," the Steward said gruffly. "What's yer business with his lordship?"

Felicia smiled her absolute brightest and sweetest. "Good day, good steward! I was journeying through your lands and have come to pay my respects to Lord Frisky..."

"I'll tell 'im you called," the Steward muttered and reached out to close the door on the vixen.

Felicia frowned at the Steward's rudeness. "I have also been informed that he was throwing a celebration..."

The Steward paused with his hand still on the door. "Y 'got an invitation?" he asked suspiciously.

"Well, no..."

"Oh. A gatecrasher."

Felicia bristled. "I understood that it was an open affair..."

"It ain't."

"My sources say that it is," Felicia insisted firmly. "My sources are never wrong." She took a breath and reasserted a less aggressive tone. "Could there have been a misunderstanding perhaps?"

"Of course there was," huffed the Steward irritably. "Everytime he throws one of these dang-fool parties, there's a misunderstandin'! His Lordship sez, invite everyone, and I tell everybody, cut off the list after twenny-five folks. His Lordship's got this bloody stupid notion that he's rich or somethin',"

Felicia was puzzled. Apparently Lord Frisky's fortunes were a bit more exaggerated than she had been led to believe and this was evidently a sore point with the Steward. It might have been wiser for her to back away and continue on into Felina and spare herself a lot of further embarrassment. On the other hand, she had already come this far, and her horse was already being stabled, and she had been looking forward to this party for the past week. She played her high card. "Doesn't his Lordship have an open-door policy for Magi?" she innocently wondered aloud.

The Steward blinked. "Yer a Magi?" he asked doubtfully.

"Would you like me to turn... something... into a frog?" she offered with a smile. She waggled her fingers in demonstration.

The old cat frowned and rubbed the back of his neck. "Well... it is th' custom, I suppose." He looked at the vixen more sharply. "Ya swear yer a Magi, right?"

"Of course!"

"An' ya just happened to be droppin' by?"

"Yes."

He waved Felicia briskly into the manor hall, allowing the door to shut behind her brush of a tail. He then strode over to the elegant staircase and yelled, "Someone call for a wizard?"

"Sorceress," Felicia corrected him patiently, "And I told you, I was just passing by. No one sent for me."

"If yer a Magi," the Steward insisted gruffly, "then you ain't here by coincidence. Wizards and magicians and sorceresses don't do nothin' by chance, they don't show up by accident, and they don't crash parties without a reason." He stopped and eyed her with undisguised suspicion. "So why are ya here?"

He's a lot sharper than he appears, Felicia realized. "You're right, I do have a reason. I'm on vacation."

"Vacation?"

"Yes. And I'm trying to do so without drawing a lot of attention to myself. I heard there was a celebration here and that it was open and I thought I might be welcome here. However..." She drew in a breath and feigned a hurt countenance. "I can understand if I am not..."

"Did I say you wasn't?" the Steward demanded. "Yer here, ya might as well stay. B'sides, it's bad luck to turn a wizard away. You just wait a minute and I'll get some rooms ready for yer stay."

"Thank you," Felicia said, once more oozing with sweetness. "And where is his Lordship so I might pay my respects?"

"Ah, he'll be along. I 'spect he's up in th' gameroom."

"Oh! He has a gameroom here! How delightful! Does he have billiards? Darts? Chess or Parcheesi?"

"No, milady, those are all quite sensible games, so we ain't got none of those. His Lordship fancies himself quite a clever twit, so..." The Steward sighed and rolled his eyes. "He invents his own games."

"Jermond!"

"You're in luck," the Steward grumbled, indicating that he thought Felicia was anything but lucky at just that moment. "Here he comes now."

"Jermond! Ah, there you are!" A large fluffy feline of intolerably cheerful demeanor and ostentatious dress came bounding into the room. "But what is this? A visitor? Hello! Welcome to the Frisky Manor!"

"Thank you, milord," Felicia replied gracefully, performing a courtly curtsy.

"She's a Magi," the Steward muttered to the gregarious nobleman.

"Magi? Well, well." Frisky's face became quite serious. "I don't know about that. I don't know about that at all. You're not here to put a spell on me, are you?"

"Of course not, milord," Felicia assured him.

"And you're not after my treasury?"

"No."

"Oh, well then!" His face brightened again and he became extremely cheery. "That's all right then! Welcome! Jermond here will get you properly set away, and you'll join us all for dinner tonight, of course! I hope you'll excuse me, but I am so busy overseeing the preparations for our celebration tomorrow. And I need to finish my work in the game room. Oh, do you like to play games?" he asked eagerly.

"I've been known to play a few," Felicia replied with a barely restrained smirk.

"Splendid! Perhaps you'll join us later for a game of Yarnball!"

"Yarnball?"

"Yes! I invented the game myself! We stand in opposite corners of the room and bat a large ball of yarn at one another! You score points for inflicting Snags, Twirls and Snarls upon your opponents, and special bonus points for a Full Unravel!"

"His lordship's already done his share of Full Unravels," Jermond explained to Felicia, looking disapprovingly of his employer.

Lord Frisky beamed happily. "Yes, indeed!"

"Perhaps later, milord," Felicia deferred politely. "Perhaps after I've seen my rooms?"

"Ah! Right you are! My apologies! Later then! Anyway, I've already got a tournament lined up with Lord Puffy later this afternoon! We've got a little competition going." he confided to Felicia with a wide smile. "But I'll leave you to get settled in after your long ride – it was a long ride, wasn't it? Jermond will see that you're taken care of. Oh! I nearly forgot! Jermond! Please see to it that Lord Puffy is reminded of our match this afternoon, would you?"

"I'd be only too happy to waste m' time, milord," the old cat grumbled.

"There's a good fellow!" And the effervescent Lord Frisky vanished as cheerfully as he had arrived.

"He seems... nice," said Felicia politely.

Jermond the Steward waved a furious hand at the departed Lord Frisky. "Ahhh..." he growled. "Just another babbling idiot, like all nobility. Not as bad as some, though. It's th' curse, y' know. Come on, I'll show ya your rooms. Hope you don't mind the tower. If you do, tough; it's all we got left."

"The tower will be fine," Felicia reassured him as she followed him into the manor. "A curse you said. What curse?"

"What curse? You mean y' didn't know?" Jermond stared at Felicia as though he had just discovered another idiot and was wondering how much worse his day would become. "He's the last of the line. Inherited the family curse, he did. Lord Frisky is the last livin' descendent of Kana Wagajop!"

Felicia's pointed ears twitched in surprise. "Really? I am surprised! I had thought the line had died out many years ago."

Jermond snorted as they climbed a stairway. "Nah. Th' direct line died, but he's from one of th' branches. Th' last survivin' branch, as it happens. When he goes, the whole line is gone. All things considerin', that might be a good thing. Blitherin' idiots, th' whole branch."

The vixen studied the various tapestries and shield devices as they passed them on the climb upwards, lost in thought as she listened to the Steward. "Are you sure there's really a connection to Kana Wagajop? After so many years, that's an important historical connection, and quite prestigious in this region."

"If ya don't believe it, you can check it out for yourself. Wait a minute..." They paused before a door. "This is Lord Puffy's room." Jermond produced a notebook and a small metal box. He quickly scribbled a note and tore it from his book. He attached it to the wooden door with a metal tack from the small box. "I do this all th' time," he sighed. "I'm his Lordship's personal messenger service. Anyway," he continued as they resumed their walk, "he's got th' credentials. Y' look down in the main hall, hangin' over the mantelpiece is th' family heirloom, passed down from generation to generation."

"Which is?"

"Well, what do you think?" the Steward snapped. "It's th' sword! Kana Wagajop's sword, th' one he cut off the tail of th' Murk with!"

"Oh." The interest abruptly drained away from Felicia's voice. "I see." She shrugged to herself and followed the old cat silently as they wandered down the halls to her appointed rooms.

* * *

Once she was alone in her rooms and her trunk had been brought up, Felicia spent the next hour relaxing and unpacking. And she gave some thought to her options and priorities. Something was definitely awry here, but she was reluctant to say or do anything about it. It's none of my business, she decided. I'm on vacation and I'm not doing any magic while I'm here. She stepped to the window and opened it, allowing the late summer breeze to drift in.

The claim was false. She knew that. Kana Wagajop's line had long ago died out, as she had told Jermond, and it was unlikely that there any significant branches still existing, whatever claims Lord Frisky made. And the less said about the sword, the better. On the other hand, even though the lineage was phony, she hadn't detected any real deception from Lord Frisky, or from old Jermond; they obviously believed the family connection. Most likely the deception was begun some generations before and they were as much unknowing victims as anyone else.

Apart of the deception itself, Felicia didn't see what harm was being done. From what she had learned of Lord Frisky before arriving was that his reputation was solid and that he was well respected by his peers and subordinates. He was considered to be odd and eccentric, but generally harmless otherwise. No, this wasn't a matter to get concerned about, and she didn't intend to be. If Lord Frisky wanted to claim lineage to Kana Wagajop, then that was his concern and not hers. Let someone else deal with it. That wasn't why she was there.

Her attention was caught by the appearance below of the manor's gardener, a tall, lean cougar carrying a bucket of tools out to one of the lawn hedges. She pulled up a chair and sat down, careful not to take her eyes off of the handsome tawny feline as he set his instruments on the ground near the end of the hedge and set aside a large pair of shears. He removed his shirt to reveal a trim and muscular upper torso, and the vixen smiled broadly as she watched the gardener proceed to carefully trim the top of the hedge in the warm summer sun. This, Felicia said happily to herself as she propped her head upon her hand, is what I came out here for.

Chapter 3 "Appetizers And The Main Curse"

Felicia stole quietly down the hallway leading to the stairs. She'd decided it was time to familiarize herself with the guests and the household, and the best way was to become better acquainted with the servants. She intended to circumnavigate the Steward, who was too busy anyway and much too sharp for her to ask questions, even innocent ones, without making him more suspicious. Instead, she would try to speak with the kitchen help, if possible, or some of the outdoor servants, like the stablehands. And maybe the gardener, she smiled slyly to herself. It stood to reason that any significant information about what guests were attending and what they were really like and were there any unattached males among them would be fully known and documented by the servants by this time.

She paused at the sound of a loud voice coming from one of the adjoining apartments. A second voice shouted back a reply. A glance at a notice tacked to the door ("Dinner at Four PM in the Main Dining Hall" it read in Jermond's rough script) identified the occupants as a Lord cla di Snuffler and his wife. Dogonians, Felicia noted in surprise. As she listened, the intensity and the volume of the shouting increased and it became obvious that the Lord and Lady were having a row over something, although she still couldn't quite make out what was being said. She shrugged and walked on. It's none of my business, she reminded herself, and she left the furious shouting behind as she descended the stairs to the floor below.

Through carefully discreet questioning Felicia was able to learn that only a few guests had actually accepted Lord Frisky's invitation to attend his celebration, as many tended to believe very strongly in the reputation of the family's curse; those few who had actually accepted either didn't believe in it, or were very close to Lord Frisky and defied it, or simply weren't aware of it at all. She soon found out enough to satisfy the basic questions of who were attending and what rank of importance they held. And, to her disappointment, that there were no single males.

She strolled leisurely back to the manor house, taking an extra long shortcut all around the structure in order to pass by the hedges, where the gardener was still tending to his chores. She was delighted to notice that he hadn't yet replaced his shirt. "Good day, gardener," she greeted him courteously, smiling brightly as she approached.

The cougar looked up from his clipping as the vixen approached. "G'day, milady," he said courteously in a deep, pleasant voice. He watched her warily. "Can I help you?"

"I hope so," Felicia replied coyly, one hand idly stroking the tip of her long tail, which had curled around her side. "I've only recently arrived. I was wondering what you might tell me about the entertainments here..."

"Ah, there you are!" Felicia was brought up short by the appearance of the old Steward hurrying up behind her. "You got out of your room before I could leave a note for you," he accused her, waving one of his handwritten notes at her.

"I thought I would take a little tour of the grounds before dinner..." the vixen began, but the steward impatiently waved her off and took her arm, politely if gruffly, by the elbow.

"Yes, yes," he said irritably, half-pulling and half-dragging her back towards the manor. "But his nitwitship has decided to hold a little get together reception before dinner so all the guests could socialize and meet one another before dinner. Not that he bothered to note that little detail earlier so that we might have told everyone at an appropriate hour, oh no. You have just a half-hour if you want to change into something more appropriate..."

"A half-hour!" Felicia was horrified. That wasn't near enough time for her to bathe or even to choose what to wear for the evening.

"Take an hour if ya want," the old cat huffed as they hurried into the manor. "I'll tell everyone ya was worn out from the trip here and was takin' a nap. It's not like anyone else is gonna be breakin' into a sweat to be the first to show up, and not like anyone is goin' to notice if ya did."

Felicia sighed and hurried to keep up, sparing one quick regretful glance back at the gardener who watched back with a puzzled expression.

* * *

Felicia mumbled to herself as she rummaged through her trunk, searching for appropriate wear to the pre-dinner socializer. "Not that one, too busy... no, I'll want that for tomorrow's affair... no, a little too revealing for a first impression... no, too green!" She was barely cognizant of a faint and persistent knocking at her door. "Yes! Come in!" she called, not looking up. "Ah! This might do! A little on the conservative side, and just revealing enough...!" She held up the dress in consideration and fingered the high slit in the side of the skirt.

Turning to face the mirror, she noticed that the door hadn't opened. She walked over and opened it and looked out into the hallway. There was no one there. "Odd," she murmured. "I could have sworn I heard a knock..." She stepped back with a shrug and closed the door, and turned back to the mirror again.

"Hello!"

Felicia jumped, nearly dropping the dress, and raised a threatening finger. Red light sheathed the finger and throbbed dangerously. "Who are you?" She demanded with a snarl. Then she blinked and lowered her finger just a hair. Standing on top of her trunk was a mouse, barely a hand tall, dressed in hightop boots and a cloak, and topped with a very wide brimmed hat. He grinned cheerily and was carrying a bouquet of flowers that were taller than he was.

"I apologize for the intrusion," he chirped in a cheerful voice, "but I had wanted to pay my respects and welcome you to Frisky Manor, but, alas, this was my first opportunity to do so!" The mouse took a low bow and nearly fell over from the weight of the flowers, barely regaining his balance at the last moment. "I have the honor to be Sir Jack Sharpe of Bleucheese, ambassador from Rodentia. And these..." The mouse held out the flowers to Felicia. "...are for you, dear Lady!"

The vixen raised an eyebrow as she graciously accepted the bouquet. "Why, thank you! I'll see to it that these are placed in water." She half-turned and examined the door. Sure enough, there was a small mouse-door built into the base. Some manors and castles were built with special considerations for Rodentians, but she hadn't much dealings with them of late and had forgotten to check for such accesses.

"It is a pleasure, milady!" the mouse said with another sweeping bow. "Although their wild beauty pales before the grace of your own."

Oh, brother, thought Felicia as her whiskers tingled in warning. She cocked an ear at the mouse. "How kind of you," she demurred politely. She set the flowers into a vacant vase and turned back with her chosen dinner dress still in hand. "And now, if you'll forgive me, I do need to dress for the evening's socializer."

"Ah, yes! I beg your forgiveness! I'll leave you to your privacy! I'll have my own preparations to make as well!" The mouse leapt nimbly from the trunk to the floor, a feat that only a mouse could perform without breaking a leg. He paused before the mouse-sized door. "I pray I shall have the opportunity to speak again with you later?"

"It's possible," Felicia murmured with a polite smile.

"For the evening will be drab and bleak without the brightness of your presence to give it joy." He bowed deeply and swept out the door.

Felicia sighed and locked the small door with a gesture before undressing. She had been looking for a romantic encounter with a handsome stranger, but it was an unspoken requisite of hers that her suitors not only be at least over three feet tall, but preferably at least six feet in height. Still, he was polite and charming at least, and she didn't see much

difficulty in keeping him at bay. Despite the absurdity of a liaison between them, the vixen couldn't help smirk with smug satisfaction at the attention. It was a good beginning; now, if only there were a few more heads to be turned... But then she remembered there were no other unattached males among the guests and, with a sigh of regret, hastened to her bath.

* * *

After a hurried bath and a swift change of clothes into something more appropriate for the evening socializer, Felicia managed to appear fashionably late only scant moments after the others. She politely nodded as the Steward introduced her to everyone, and then proceeded to introduce the others to her. "Lord Cyril Plush, and his wife, the Lady Silky Plush." he announced as they paused before a stout Persian with wild and barely groomed white fur and his demure-but-pudgy female companion. There was a polite murmuring and bowing from each individual, and Jermond added as an aside while they walked on, "Plush owns lands on the other side of Felina and has his hands into most trading concerns around here, not to mention on most young beautiful women, especially those who are too fast to walk away when he lumbers up."

Felicia stifled a chuckle and made a mental note.

"Aha! There you all are!" Lord Frisky made his appearance, his cheerful countenance as every bit as dazzling as it had been during their brief encounter earlier. Arriving with him was a demure young lady with another couple in tow. "Dreadfully sorry we're so late, one and all, but old Puffy here and I –" he turned to indicate the other male who had entered behind him. "– had been caught up in a really smashing game of Yarnball! It was quite a near thing, too! The game was tied for quite a long time! Puffy is a fierce competitor! I like that! Made it a smashing game! But I was finally able to steal a march on him, and got him in a really good Snarl!" He threw out his arms triumphantly. "I won!" he announced.

Felicia broke the stony silence by applauding, which was swiftly taken up by Frisky's companions before finally spreading reluctantly to the other guests. "Congratulations, milord." Felicia said with an encouraging smile.

"Thank you! Thank you, all!" He beamed for a moment before turning to his steward. "Jermond! Have you introduced everybody yet?"

"Something so obvious would have never occurred to me, milord," said the old feline. He turned and continued for Felicia's benefit, introducing the lone Dogonian couple in the room, a grizzled Alsatian and his wife. "The Lord and Lady cla di Snuffler." The Alsatian rose and bowed stiffly, frowning sullenly as he did. The Lady acknowledged the introduction almost as cooly, but with more grace than her husband. "They are passing through Katara on an ambassadorial goodwill tour, courtesy of the Dogonian monarchy. As though goodwill between cats and dogs was any sort of a sane expectation..."

"What was that?" The Alsatian rose and reached for his sword, the fur bristling around his neck. "I've never been insulted by such a lowly servant!"

"This is nothing!" snapped the Steward. "Wait until you've had the dessert." When the Dogonian drew his sword and growled louder, the old cat refused to back down. "I'm not scared of you! I've fought your kind before: big, blustering, howling boobs..."

"Jermond!" intervened Frisky with a shocked expression. "That's enough! I want you to apologize to the big blustering boob right this moment!"

Without missing a beat or averting his glare from the ambassador, Jermond muttered, "I'm sorry you're such a big blustering boob." Snuffler hesitated a long beat before sheathing his sword and dropping back into his chair, barely mollified.

"Splendid, splendid!" said Frisky, totally oblivious to his servant's gruffness. "But here! I should be doing this! Let me continue, and you see how the dinner is coming along!"

"As you wish, milord," Jermond agreed, shuffling towards the kitchens. "Cook should have the appetizers ruined by about now. I'll just go see."

Lord cla di Snuffler bristled and growled under his breath. "The insolence of servants!"

"I pray you forgive my husband's manners, Lord Frisky," Lady cla di Snuffler apologized coolly, ignoring the burning glare her mate turned on her. "He has been out of sorts this evening, I'm afraid, since having mislaid some of his medals..."

"They were stolen!" The canine warrior slammed his fist onto the table, causing all of the silverware to bounce a foot into the air.

The Lady laid her hand upon his and dug her nails into his wrist. "Dear, I'm sure you've simply forgotten them..."

"What kind of sot do you think I am? Forget my medals?" Snuffler was indignant. "I nearly was killed earning those medals; do you think I would forget them? I packed them with the rest of my gear before we left Dogonia! Now they're gone! Someone has stolen them!"

"The way someone stole your favorite quilt last month?"

The Alsatian sulked. "That was different. The chambermaid took that to laundry. And I apologized to her family." He slammed his fist on the table again. Felicia snatched her fork before it flew to the floor. "I know I had those medals packed in my gear! Someone has taken them!"

"What's this?" asked Lord Frisky in surprise. "Gone? Your medals? Oh, dear! Well, I shouldn't worry; things are always disappearing around here. Why, I was missing a tea service one afternoon. An entire tea service! Just wasn't there. A week later, there it was. No, don't be concerned about your medals. They'll turn up again! They always do! All the same, I'll have the servants keep a watch for your medals. Never fear! We'll find them! Jermond! –oh, that's right, he's off to the kitchens. Well, I'll have him leave you a note once we find your medals."

Felicia frowned and inclined her head thoughtfully. Something was tickling her memory and she paused to reflect upon it. Unfortunately, she hadn't gotten far when her eyes were distracted by the appearance of the handsome cougar entering the room carrying a tray of rich pastries. She was puzzled at first, since she had assumed that he was the estate's gardener and not one of the kitchen help, but she then also recognized one or two of the stablehands and a plump feline she was certain was the laundry mistress. All were busy setting out trays of appetizers and hors d'oerves and pouring wine for all the guests. She watched for a moment, then let her eyes rove back to the cougar, now elegantly dressed in a smart butling suit, gracefully serving to each of the guests in turn, and soon found herself admiring the slow and idle curls of his long, ropelike tail.

"We're both so glad that you decided to attend our party, Lady Felicia," interjected a small voice next to her. The Lady who had entered alongside Lord Frisky had seated herself next to the sorceress. "We almost never see one of the Magi visit. I think Izzy despairs of their absence; he thinks they're afraid of the family curse."

It took Felicia a moment to connect the names properly. Izzy? Oh, yes! Izlane Frisky! Lord Frisky, of course. This must be his wife... what was her name? Lady Fluffy! "The curse of the Wagajop line was never a thing to be taken lightly," Felicia said, careful to keep rein on her doubts that the curse was still active after all these centuries, or that it would even affect someone not of that family line; whatever Frisky's deception, she didn't want to be the one to accidentally expose it. She took a swift moment to study the Lady who sat next to her. Lady Fluffy was shorter than her by half-a-head, had long and luxurious silky fur, and wide eyes of an aristocratic blue that brimmed with a childlike innocence. "Were you not concerned about the curse when you married into the family?"

"Oh, no!" replied Lady Fluffy in surprise. "Izzy has always been such a sweet and considerate soul, that I knew right from when I met him that the old curse must have long ago burnt away. I knew he could never be the cause of anything so harmful or vile! And he's such a cheerful and vital person! Do you know that he makes games?"

"So I've heard," Felicia said in amusement as she helped herself to a pastry from a tray carried by a passing chubby servant.

"They are the most delightful and entertaining things! He even lets me play sometimes, though he used to insist they were principally intended for men. I enjoy playing Yarnball. I don't quite understand the rules, but I like the feel of the yarn under my paws; it feels so... sensuous."

Jermond returned from the kitchen, leading another regiment of servants carrying trays to the long table in the adjoining rooms. "My Lords and Ladies," he announced as the servants continued past him with their burdens. "Dinner is served! If you will please follow to the dining hall and take yer chances."

"What did you say?" The Dogonian Ambassador's head snapped up as the Steward's words registered.

"I said, 'take yer chairs,'" the old feline replied without hesitation, meeting the Alsatian's glare evenly. The Dogonian frowned, but shrugged and followed the others into the dining hall, pausing long enough to allow the Ladies to precede him.

As Lord Frisky, his wife, and their guests were all seated, Jermond directed the other servants to laying out the steaming bowls they had carried from the kitchen. "Milords, the first course," the Steward announced. They all eagerly uncovered their bowls.

"What's this?" grumbled Lord Snuffler in suspicion and dismay.

"Oh!" cried Lady Plush in delight. "Warm milk! With nutmeg!"

Lord Snuffler was about to retort when he was preempted by a discreet elbow from his wife. "When in Katara..." she murmured warningly under her breath as she spooned her own milk. The Ambassador glowered at his bowl, but he accepted his wife's timely reminder. He took hold of the bowl between his two clublike hands and lifted it. Another elbow caught him before he could continue raising the bowl further. "Spoon, dear," Lady Snuffler tightly reminded him. Snuffler grimaced and lowered the bowl, taking quick note of how the cats and Felicia were all daintily slurping the milk from spoons. He sighed and reluctantly followed suit.

The servants returned just as the guests were finishing their milk, carrying in the next course. Felicia sniffed the air as a trace of aroma trailed in with the servants from the kitchen. "Chicken!" she said in delight. "Is that chicken I smell?" The second course was laid out before them. "The chef's special salad," Jermond announced. "The finest greens and vegetables from our own gardens." Oh, Felicia realized, the chicken must be the next course.

But the next course was an entree of noodles in a rich cream sauce. "What's that garnish?" Snuffler asked curiously. "I don't recognize it."

Jermond looked at the Ambassador as if he had asked something very, very stupid. "It's catnip," he said gruffly. "It's a common garnish here." The loud purrs of the Kataran diners rose in agreement.

"And the chicken is next?" asked Felicia hopefully.

Next was a serving of broiled fish in a butter sauce ("And now the chicken!"), followed by bowls of breads and a freshening of wine ("The chicken is the next course, right?") and a round of eggs and mushrooms, sautéed in a wine sauce ("There is chicken, isn't there?"). At the last, the servants carried in the main dish of broasted chicken. "Oh!" Felicia remarked in obvious delight. "Chicken! What a lovely and delightful surprise!" And she eagerly dug into her portion.

Desert and coffee passed more or less quietly in easy conversation, and the guests all passed back into the main hall. The remainder of the evening was quite pleasant, and Felicia found most of them to be charming folk to speak with, although Lord Snuffler tended to be loud and at times even arrogant. Lady Snuffler, who was obviously more sensitive to the need for discretion among their hosts, continued to keep his worst tendencies in check. Felicia found that she rather liked the Dogonian Lady, but had increasingly little patience for the Ambassador himself. She eventually tuned him out, felt a swell of pity for Lady Snuffler, and fell into conversation with the two Kataran Ladies for most of the evening. When the hour grew late and she felt herself heavy with wine and a good, full meal, she excused herself and returned to her rooms to prepare for bed. "Remember!" Lord Frisky called cheerfully after her. "Tomorrow eve is the big party! Lots of folks coming to celebrate! It'll be a day no one will ever forget!"

* * *

Felicia was awakened from a deep sleep late that night by a pounding on her door. She sat bolt upright in her bed. "What is it?" she called groggily. She heard someone call her name and beg for her to open the door; she wasn't yet registering words to the sounds, but she caught the note of urgency to them and she forced herself to turn and slip out of bed. "Just a minute," she called and she pulled on a robe. As a force of habit and vanity, she reached also for a brush she had set out on the bedstand. She was nonplussed when her hand found nothing, and for the moment she was distracted, searching the top of the stand for the brush. The pounding resumed at the door, recalling her attention. "All right, all right," she said sharply as she crossed the room to the door, hastily smoothing back her ruffled head fur. She unlocked and opened the door to find a harried Jermond on the other side.

"I'm sorry to disturb you, milady, but we need your assistance right away! It's horrible! Lord Snuffler has been smushed!"

Felicia woke fully. She secured the sash around her robe and followed the distraught steward down the hall. "I'll do what I can," she said reassuringly in her best professional manner. "Do you have a physician? You had best send for him as well –"

Jermond stopped suddenly and grabbed the vixen by the forearm. "I'm sorry, milady," he grated in an exasperated and distraught tone. "You bein' Magi, I took you for an intelligent woman. Lord Snuffler doesn't need a physician. I never said he was ill or that he had fallen down and bumped his knee. I said that he was smushed! Somone's smushed Lord Snuffler like he was a bug!"

Chapter 4 "Hel-loooo, Curse!"

Jermond hadn't exaggerated. There across the wall of one side of Lord Snuffler's room was Lord Snuffler himself. So she presumed. What there was, was a long bloody smear streaked across from one end of the wall to the other, reminiscent of a fly that had been swatted as it attempted to fly away. There was just enough remains of the body itself to be recognized – barely – as Lord Snuffler.

"Where's Lady Snuffler?" Felicia asked the Steward in a hushed voice as she stared at the grisly sight. "Have you notified Lord Frisky yet?"

"Th' Lady is down in the main hall, bein' comforted by Lady Fluffy," Jermond said in a shaken voice. "She was th' one who found th' body. What there is of it. Surprised ya didn't hear th' scream; woke me outta a sound sleep an' nearly give me a heart attack!" He edged back and dropped exhaustedly into a chair. "His Lordship's down there, too. They're tryin' to bring him around."

"Was he injured too?" Felicia asked in alarm.

"Nah. He ran in to see why th' Lady was screamin', seen the smush on th' wall, and fainted dead away. We got him revived out in th' hall, but he insisted on goin' back in t' properly identify th' body, and he fainted again. His lordship's got a low threshold for blood."

"What's the hour?"

"About... a couple of hours 'til dawn, I figure."

Felicia studied the wall again. "All right." She turned and walked away, out into the hallway. "I'll be off to bed, then."

"Bed?" Jermond jumped up and followed the vixen hurriedly. "What d'ya mean, yer off t'bed!?" he demanded.

"Well, what is it you expect me to do?" Felicia asked with some irritation. "He's dead. I can't revive him; that's not my line of magic."

"You can tell us what done it!"

"You have guards. You can also bring in the Royal Watch, if you need to. This is more their line, not mine. Besides, I'm on vacation."

"But there's somethin' unearthly goin' on here! What could smush a Dogonian... or anybody, for that matter, like they was just a bug?"

Felicia paused and sighed. "All right... I suppose I could put up some magical wards around the manor as a protection. But I am not an investigator."

There was a clamor from up the hall. They looked up to see an anxious Lord Frisky hurrying to them with a pair of guards hustling up behind him. "Have you seen it?" he asked Felicia. His face was drawn and pale.

"I've never seen anything so horrible! What could have done such a thing! Oh! How will I explain this to the Dogonian Royal Court? There'll be war! How will I tell this to the king! Our king, I mean! I could never explain it to their king! The Dogonian ambassador killed while in my safekeeping!"

"The sorceress was just about to examine the scene, milord," Jermond reassured the distraught noble as he gave the vixen a meaningful look. Felicia glared back through narrowed eyes before turning to Lord Frisky.

"I'll just have a quick look," she told him in a sweet voice. "It might not be all that serious..."

"Not that serious!" cried Lord Frisky. "Good Aln! He's a blot! We'd need spatulas to prepare the body for burial!"

"Relatively speaking," Felicia continued. "It might not be magic at all, or perhaps just some fluke of nature." She ignored the barely restrained snort from the Steward. "I'll just make a quick examination." She touched the noble's arm reassuringly before walking back into the room.

Alone, she folded her arms and stared at the gore-stained wall irritably. She did a quick scan with her mystic sight but could sense no trace of magic from the liquefied corpse; but she hadn't really expected to. It was obvious an act of some great feat of strength; a giant perhaps. It could have been done with a magically enhanced weapon, but that wouldn't have left a trace for her to detect. If she really wanted to, she could pull out her crystal and scrye into the recent past and pull out a vision or two that might lead her to the truth. But she didn't want to. She hadn't come out all this way to do anything but be fat and lazy for a week or two, and she certainly didn't intend to be pushed into doing Magi duty while she was on vacation. Besides, she hadn't liked Lord Snuffler.

She sighed to herself. On the other hand, it would be discourteous not to oblige her host, and the threat could be serious. She could at least put Lord Frisky's mind at ease. She continued to stare at the blot on the wall for a moment longer, then returned to the waiting party outside the room.

"Well?" asked Lord Frisky as he watched her anxiously.

Felicia stood and folded her hands before her. She glanced back at the room for a moment before returning her attention to Frisky. "I've made my examination."

"And?"

Felicia continued to lock eyes with Frisky, maintaining an expression of innocence and professionalism. "Sunspots."

* * *

"Sunspots!"

Lord Plush stared at Felicia as though she had suddenly sprouted an extra head.

"Sunspots are a natural occurrence that happen from time to time," Felicia explained patiently. "They appear and disappear on the face of the sun without warning and can cause unusual eruptions along the fields of magic."

They were all gathered down in the main hall following her brief examination of the smeared remains of the late Lord cla di Snuffler. Lord Frisky, still shaken, was slumped in a chair, while a weeping Lady Snuffler was comforted by the two Kataran Ladies. Lord Plush, obviously having been awoken from a deep sleep, was straining to fully understand the bizarre events of the night and was pacing erratically before the fireplace. "But these sunspots," he asked as he struggled to comprehend, "They can cause a body to go splat against a stone wall?"

"Oh, not usually," Felicia said carelessly. "But it's been known to happen. It's a very rare occurrence. But not unheard of. Mind you, my examination was a cursory one, but I've no doubt that a more thorough inspection will only confirm my conclusion." Especially if I make the inspection.

"This is terrible!" Lord Frisky moaned. "There will be war over this! I know it! And the King will have my head!"

"Oh, nothing of the sort," Felicia reassured him as she helped herself to some tea. "I'll certify the death myself. Deceased as a result of an extraordinary magic event. They'll accept the word of a Magi." I hope, she added to herself, not wanting to mention that her relations with the Dogonian monarchy tended to be strained at times.

"We'll have to cancel the party!" Frisky suddenly realized. "Can't have a party now under these circumstances! Good Gur, no! That would be absolutely ghoulish! We'll have to cancel! All those people to notify! Jermond!"

"I'll see to it that everyone is notified, Milord," the old Steward reassured Frisky.

"And the body... we'll have to – to prepare it for..."

"Yes, Milord. I'll see to it that's taken care of, too." He turned and shuffled out of the room. "We should have just enough towels to sop him up." He paused at the door long enough to fetch a tack from the wooden surface, crumpling the paper note he had left there at some earlier point during the day.

Felicia had fallen into a reverie, musing over the ruined night and pondering the cause of Snuffler's death. I may be making too light of this, she thought. Something bizarre certainly happened in there. Perhaps I should look further into this, if only for self-preservation. But there was no magic present, I could swear! No residue, no psychic impressions... She closed her eyes and meditated, sending out invisible feelers throughout the manor. Just a small search, a double-check to be sure...

A shiver suddenly ran down her spine as she 'touched' something icy and elusive. She recoiled at the impression of sliminess that slid away from her probe, and as she recovered from her initial surprise and pressed forward inquisitively, she was interrupted by the suddenly raised voice of Lord Frisky. The vixen growled under her breath as the contact vanished as swiftly as it had been made, all too quick for her to identify. Had it really been there, or had she just imagined it?

"We must have a proper and thorough investigation!" Lord Frisky was saying as she snapped out of her brief reverie. "We can leave nothing to chance! We must have as much information documented as possible to turn over to the Royal Watch!"

Jermond paused at the doorway as he snapped the lid on his box of tacks. "Investigation, Milord?" he asked suspiciously.

"Yes! The Royal Watch must be notified, after all, and we must do all we can to satisfy their inquiries! And I'm certain poor Lady Snuffler here would be satisfied with nothing less than our best efforts!" Felicia and Jermond both rolled their eyes skywards, but the Dogonian noblewoman ceased sobbing long enough to nod her head. "Very well! I'll put a guard on the door to Lord Snuffler's room, and no one is to enter but you, Jermond, and the good Sorceress here! We'll get Lady Snuffler accommodated in a different room for the night..."

"I think I should stay with her, dear," said Lady Fluffy as she held the stricken Alsatian in her arms.

"Yes, very well! Lady Felicia, I will leave the immediate investigation in your capable hands!"

"Mine?" asked Felicia, taken aback. "Whatever for?"

"Well, it's a very unusual death! That makes it the province of the Magi, does it not?"

It makes it the province of a Hero or a Champion, not a sorceress who's on vacation, she wanted to retort, but she held her tongue as a thought occurred to her. "I have full cooperation then? I may have full access to all and any I may need to interrogate?"

"Absolutely!"

"I shouldn't think you would have to look far," Lady Plush offered helpfully. "I mean, this is the Curse, isn't it?"

"Silky!" Lady Fluffy scolded her friend. Lord Frisky was stricken; he obviously hadn't considered it in all the confusion.

"Well, isn't it?" Lady Plush persisted.

"That," Felicia purred as she rose from her chair, "is a determination best left to be made by a professional." She was now rising to the task set before her. "If you'll forgive me, my Lords and Ladies, I will retire to bed for the remainder of the night, but I will begin my investigation immediately in the morning."

"Very good!" Lord Frisky agreed with great relief. "My household is at your disposal, Milady! Will you require anything?"

The vixen thought. "Some tea and a few cakes. Perhaps a bottle of wine."

"You shall have it!"

"Come, dear," Lady Fluffy encouraged Lady Snuffler as she helped the grieving widow to her feet. "We'll get you to another room, it'll be all right..." She spared a moments glare at Lady Plush, who made a whispered apology for her gaffe of a minute earlier, and the two felines guided the canine away from the hall.

Felicia retired back to her own rooms then, but as she made her way up the staircase and down the quiet corridor, she recalled the odd tinge of evil she had brushed earlier and attempted to locate it once more. To no avail, for whatever it was that she had sensed had since vanished. Perhaps I only imagined it, she thought, and she shrugged. No matter. Tragic as Snuffler's unexpected death was, it was bringing an unexpected opportunity to her, and she intended to make the best of it. She smiled slyly to herself in anticipation of an entertaining day.

Chapter 5 "Changing Curses In Midstream"

"All right then," said Felicia. She paused and carefully inscribed a note on the scrap of notepaper resting on her lap. She nibbled lightly on the tip of the feather end of her quill for a moment, and held a pose of thoughtful contemplation before lowering the quill to paper again, where she scribbled another note. It was late morning now and sunlight streamed in through the window behind her chair to light the wooden floor before her. She had changed into a dress of rich violets and resplendent gold trim, with a deep, plunging neckline and a strategically placed slit along the side of the skirt, which showed off just enough of her legs as she twisted into a comfortable lounging position in her chair. She smiled brightly as she looked up from her notes to her first interview. "Thank you for coming," she purred. "I regret the necessity, but this is an unpleasant business; I promise to be as gentle as possible, but I must be thorough, as I am sure you understand."

The puma fidgeted nervously as he stood waiting in front of the sorceress. "Yes, Ma'am," he replied, trying to keep his eyes locked on hers instead of either her legs or cleavage. It was a challenge he was having difficulty with, and the vixen wasn't making it easier for him by shifting her position every few minutes.

"As you've no doubt heard, there was an unusual death last night," Felicia said.

"Yes, ma'am. Everybody's heard about it by now."

"As it was a quite extraordinary death, it has fallen upon my shoulders," and she gave a winsome half-shrug that threatened to drop one side of her dress down over her shoulder, "to look into the possibility that magic may have been involved." There was a tiny flicker of worry in the gardener's eyes, but he continued to stand patiently waiting. "To this end, I need to speak to everyone here, from the nobility down to the lowest stable boy. This is nothing personal..." Yet, she thought. "I'm just required to be thorough."

"I understand," the puma mumbled, clasping his hands behind him.

"Good." Felicia rose and set her paper and quill aside. "You were at the dinner last evening? Oh!" she interjected, interrupting his reply. "Please remove your shirt, if you would."

"My shirt?" The feline was perplexed.

"Yes. It's to facilitate my investigation." She smiled disarmingly. "It allows me a better view... of your aura. So I can see if there's any sign of magic, or of mystic tampering with your spirit or mind."

"Oh." He slowly unbuttoned his shirt, fumbling nervously at the buttons. "Rather like a physician, is it?"

"Yes," Felicia agreed, still smiling. "Just like it." She paced idly around the puma as he uneasily undid the buttons on his shirt. "You were at the dinner?"

"Yes, ma'am. All of us servants were. There's only just a few of us, see, and we all have to do more than one job here on th' grounds."

"And where were you when the Ambassador was killed?"

"Uh... I was asleep, ma'am."

"Any witnesses?"

"No, ma'am. I was alone."

"Hard to believe," Felicia murmured. She maintained an admiring watch on the gardener as he stripped off his shirt. "Oh! And what is your name? For the record."

"Mason." He held the shirt bunched in one fist, and stood bare-chested for the sorceress' examination.

Felicia strolled slowly around Mason in a circle, her eyes roving lovingly over the firm pecs and muscular arms. The gardener obviously did a lot of hard work around the manor, for his overall body was trim and lean with very little fat showing. "Magnificent," Felicia breathed with admiration.

"Ma'am?"

"Your aura," the vixen said quickly. She stepped back against her nighttable for a better overall view. "Your... aura is... quite healthy."

The gardener's broad nose crinkled. "What's that smell?"

"Incense," Felicia replied. She reached out one hand towards the cat's brawny shoulder, and drew it back hastily. Not yet! Don't break the spell of the moment! "I had it imported from Scentas. It enhances... perceptions."

The puma seemed to accept that. "So... is my 'orra' okay?"

Felicia nodded as she absently reached for her grooming brush. "No problems at all there," she murmured. Her fingers tapped against the wooden surface of the table, and she fumbled for a moment trying to find the brush as she continued to gaze at the handsome, shirtless puma. But as the brush continued to elude her grasp, she frowned distractedly and glanced at the empty spot where her brush should have been, recalling suddenly that it had been missing the previous night as well.

The gardener watched the vixen's hand in its fruitless quest and he coughed nervously. "Am I goin' t' have to take off my pants too?"

"Oh," the vixen caught her breath and looked up at the gardener with bright eyes, the brush already forgotten. "Would you?"

There was a sharp knock at the door.

"Go away!" sang Felicia through clenched teeth as she smiled disarmingly at Mason.

The knocking continued.

"It might be important," Mason pointed out hesitantly.

Felicia continued to smile tightly. "I'll just be a minute," she told him sweetly, and pirouetted towards the door, which she flung open with a snarl. "I said I didn't want to be disturbed – " She broke off suddenly when she realized that she was speaking to an empty hallway. She craned her head to look up the hall, and then down the other direction, but saw no sign of anyone in either end.

"Ahem."

She looked down and discovered Sir Jack Sharpe of Bleucheese grinning up at her. "Ah, a good morning to you, fair lady!" He made a grand bow, tipping his broad hat to her with a smart flourish. The vixen blinked in disbelief. The mouse was standing on a long flat wheeled platform, just large enough to hold him, three lighted candles that were as tall as he was, and a small assortment of musical instruments which included a harpsichord, a mandolin, a silver flute, and a snare drum set. Before Felicia could open her mouth to speak, the mouse strummed the mandolin and began singing in a deep baritone (for a mouse) voice.

"Moonlight sets thy fur aglow
And sets thine eyes alight forevermore;
Thou'rt the beacon that guides my heart
Across the seas and to thy shore –"

"What are you doing?" Felicia demanded before the mouse could reach another verse.

"Why," Sir Jack replied with absolute reasonableness, "I'm serenading you!" The mouse seemed surprised that an explanation was needed. "I have been researching the most beautiful and passionate love songs ever written especially for this occasion..."

"Now is not a good time," Felicia said with a hasty glance back at the waiting puma behind her.

"Nonsense! I have plenty of time at the moment!" He sat down at the tiny harpsichord and played a few keys. "Allow me to woo you with a charming ballad of promised love between two young lovers... a traditional favorite..."

"Woo me!" The vixen was caught between amusement and outrage. She stared down at her diminutive suitor. "You don't think there might be a problem or two involved here? Like size differential, perhaps?"

"Oh, but no!" Sir Jack replied in surprise. He spread his hands in an expansive gesture, like the opening of a flower. "I prefer to think of you as... statuesque." He returned to playing lightly on the harpsichord. "Perhaps an aria from the opera of Jerbyl and Jasmine?"

"What, the legend of the mouse who was in love with a skunk!?" Felicia couldn't help laugh. "You do realize that story was a tragedy and both fared poorly in the end?"

Sir Jack laughed and waved off the protest. "Ah, but you've never heard the real story, of how they were reunited forever in a life of bliss! Love opens the doors of opportunity, my dear lady!" With that, the mouse threw himself into his keyboard playing, and singing again at the top of his voice. The vixen winced and scowled impatiently. Glancing up and down the corridor again to make certain no one was there to see her, she reached out and tapped the end of the tiny platform with her toe and pushed it gently down the hall, where gravity and the sloping floor combined to encourage the wheels to roll faster. Sir Jack had to stop and grab at the harpsichord to keep from falling off, as two of the candles did, arcing like tiny comets until they hit the floor. She heard the mouse cry out just before she closed the door, followed by the muted crash of cymbals.

The vixen turned back to the puma, who continued to stand with his hands on the clasp of his pant's waistband, and she smiled innocently at him. "Where were we?" she asked brightly.

There was another knock at the door, and her ears flattened back against her head. "Excuse me," she said with exaggerated sweetness, and she yanked the door open, prepared to send the mouse away on the crest of an enraged spell. But instead of the enraptured mouse, she found herself staring into the glum face of the Steward.

"I need t' speak with you, Sorceress," he grumbled as he pushed past the startled vixen. He paused when he caught sight of the half-dressed gardener standing in the center of the room. "What are you doing here?" he demanded of the embarrassed gardener.

"I'm interviewing him," Felicia answered testily as she followed close on the Steward's heels.

"For what? A pillow book!?" Jermond gestured to the puma with a scowl of disgust. "Get out of here. Go get to your duties!"

"Yes sir!" Mason muttered with barely disguised relief, and hastily slipped back into his shirt as he hurried out the door.

Jermond ignored the furious blaze of the vixen's eyes as he shut the door behind the departed Mason. "I want to know why you haven't been helpin' us find what killed th' Ambassador?" he demanded.

"I was interviewing the servants about it!" Felicia snapped.

"You interviewed Mason! One servant out of the whole household! Before that, y' spent th' whole blessed morning bathin' and primpin' like a schoolgirl! It's my impression that y' ain't takin' this matter very serious, and I want t' know why!"

Felicia's demeanor turned cold. "Do you realize," she asked dangerously, "who you are speaking to?"

"Yes! A freeloadin' Magi who's abusin' the hospitality of her host!" Jermond met Felicia scowl for scowl.

Felicia was taken aback by the Steward's accusation. "There isn't all that much to investigate," she temporized. "I already told you that it was sunspots, a fluke of nature that's all. I'm merely crossing the t's and dotting the i's by collecting information from the various household members. But there's nothing more to really be learned."

"Maybe you don't really realize how serious this is," Jermond insisted gruffly. "This is just another manifestation of the curse!"

"What curse?" Felicia asked carefully, watching the Steward closely for his reaction.

"The family curse!" he spat. "The curse of the Wagajop clan!"

"Oh, that." Felicia was unimpressed. She sat down on the edge of her bed. "All right, tell me why you think that's connected to last night's unfortunate death."

"Lord Frisky's been th' victim of th' curse alla his life!" Jermond insisted. "It's just manifested differently for him is all. Up to now." The old feline tapped the side of his head. "It's his mind, you see. He's crazy."

"Crazy?" Felicia tipped her head in a gesture of disbelief.

"All nobility are crazy t' begin with," Jermond continued. "They all got these notions of superiority an' such, an' put on airs an' attitudes. His Lordship's th' same , only diff'rent."

"Different? How?"

Jermond paced and rubbed furiously at his whiskers with an agitated hand as he considered his reply. "Well... y' know how nobles are always goin' on about talkin'bout their responsibilities t' their vassals an' servants and all th' common folk an' such? How they feel they got as much duty to their people as their people has got t' them?"

"The Noblese Oblige, do you mean?"

"Yes! That idiocy! It's crap, because none of them believe in it! Somethin' about bein' noble twists th' mind an' gives them, whattayacallit, delusions of grandeur. Instead of doin' their duties t' their people as they say their station demands, they's always out fightin' wars or curryin' favor or diddlin' each other, and the rest of us can go t' blazes."

"I see," Felicia said coolly. "And Lord Frisky...?"

"He's crazier than th' rest of the lot! He's th' only one who believes in the – what did you call it?"

"The Noblese Oblige."

"Yes!" Jermond paused to collect his thoughts, staring out the window for a moment. "I've been Steward here for twenty years now, since we came back from the border skirmishes, where we fought th' Dogonian's t'gether. In that time, I seen him respond to ev'ry kinda trouble hereabouts. When the river floods th' valley, he gets out an' directs th' rescues, an' sees to it that everyone's got food an' shelter 'til things return t' normal. When folks're havin' troubles, he mediates, or lends help... if tenant farms're doin' poorly, he lends 'em food an' money 'til they get past th' worst of it. An' never with any hidden strings, like interest rates, or 'I-done-you-a-favor-now-you-owe-me' kinda sneakery!"

Felicia was impressed in spite of herself. "You really do like him, don't you?" she said in wonder. "I was under the impression that you thought he was an idiot."

"He is an idiot!" fumed the grizzled feline. "He spends his free time throwin' dangfool parties or devisin' dangfool games that nobody'll ever play because they're so dangfool dumb!" He wheeled and jabbed a finger at the sorceress. "But he's our idiot! He's a fool, but he's a fool with a good heart. An' there's precious few of them in this rotten world." Jermond fidgeted and turned away, embarrassed at baring even so little of his true feelings. "He's a fool what doesn't have a real brain in his head. He'd have been ruined a long time ago, if it wasn't for me watchin' his interests."

"Oh!" Realization suddenly clicked in Felicia's head. "Of course! The rescues and the parties! You told me yourself when I first arrived: 'His Lordship's got this bloody stupid notion that he's rich', you said! His fortune is stretched to the limit, isn't it?"

"His Lordship can't carry a figure in his bloody skull. He doesn't know if he's got five fludels in his wallet or a million! I keep th' books, and I keep th' money flowin' for him, so he never knows th' difference."

Felicia remembered something else. "'Things disappear around here all the time', he told Lord Snuffler. And then they reappear again. You've been hocking valuables to keep the estate solvent!"

Jermond jerked his shoulders in a gruff shrug. "Had to. I try t' keep his worse tendencies under check, but sometimes his Lordship gets ahead'a me, and I have to come up with funds to cover th' expenses. Sometimes I hock th' tea service, or the silver; once I had to hock his best silver bridle and leather saddle, one of th' finest in these parts. But I always bought 'em back again when I could. There ain't nothin' that I've hocked that I wasn't able t' get back again." He sat heavily in a chair, relieved to finally be confiding some of his burden to someone. "Fortunately, his Lordship's got a few business interests here and there what do bring in some money – a few stocks in the Rakunian markets, an' sometimes the tenant farms pay some good money when th' harvest's good – or else he'd have been ruined a long time ago."

"Does this policy also extend to the belongings of guests?" Felicia asked. "Such as Lord Snuffler's medals?"

"I never touched those!" Jermond hissed. "Never! I never even knew the blowhard had any medals until he bitched about them bein' missin'! But I never touched or hocked anything that wasn't part of this manor! I wasn't about t' risk his Lordship's reputation that way! I knew he'd never miss any of his own stuff and that I could retrieve it before he did, but stealing a guest's belongin's was risky, and could ruin him once an' for all." Felicia nodded and accepted that. Jermond continued. "But that's th' other thing. His Lordship isn't really all that popular with th' other nobility 'round here. They think he's givin' them all a bad name. He's only got a few real friends, like Lord Plush. The rest would just as soon see him dead an' stop bein' such an example for them t' be expected t' live up to. Besides, they'd like t' get his lands."

"Ah," said Felicia. "Now I see the real dangers involved. Politics."

"Exactly, Milady." Jermond was pleased that Felicia was finally on the same page as he was. "They'd like nothin' better than t' use th' curse against his Lordship and take everythin' away from him. And apart of that bein' a vile and cruel thing t' do to th' poor fool who's only sin is that he's too bloody nice t' everybody, it would be a cruel thing for everyone else who lives and works on these lands. If Lord Frisky is ruined and his lands are taken, who will look after their interests?"

Felicia rose and paced thoughtfully. "I see," she said. "The death of the Dogonian Ambassador under mysterious circumstances could be the straw to break the camel's back. The threat of war could be enough for his foes to gain favor and petition the King to take Lord Frisky's lands and remove his titles. I wonder..." She tapped her chin as she considered further. "Could that be behind all this? A deliberate murder to implicate Lord Frisky? There's certainly motive... but who and how?"

"Murder?" Jermond was puzzled. "You don't think it was th' curse what done it?"

"Hardly," Felicia murmured. She shot a quick look at the old steward. He obviously believed in the curse, so he was therefore unaware that Frisky was unrelated to Kana Wagajop. "Tell me... you said you both returned from the border wars? You were referring to Lord Frisky? You served under him?"

"Just a footsoldier, another grunt under the direction of the nobles and knights on horseback. I'd been a career man, such as it was a career, fightin' my whole life for a little piece of mine. But I lost that when the Dogs took back a few miles of the land. Little strip of property on a creek, with an old shack. Weren't much, but it were mine. Gone now, I imagine, burnt or torn down for some Dog family to build their own.

"Almost lost my life, too. Took a sword in the side. Didn't kill me right off, but left me rather badly. That's how his Lordship found me. Brought me back t' safety, back t' the Kataran camps. Weren't easy either, what with him faintin' every few steps. Longest night I ever spent, me too weak t' stand and losing blood, an' him gettin' up an' draggin' me a few feet under cover of th' dark. Then he'd see me bleedin' and he'd faint away like a big sissy. His Lordship's got no sensibility for blood, y' see. But he never stopped draggin' me back. All night long, he'd drag, faint, and get back up again an' start all over, until we finally got back t' camp. I was more dead than alive, but I'd have been all dead if it weren't for him.

"When th' fightin' was done an' he heard I had no home t' go back to, he come t' me an' said, 'Why don't you come and work for me?' An' then he fainted dead away when he saw the blood on my bandages. That's when I knew for damn sure he was a fool, wantin' a body to work for him what he had t' drag through the night all the while he was faintin'. But I had nothin' better, so I came. Came t' this big, fancy manor, with its fine history and its fine treasures and its fine heirlooms. Me, closest I ever got t' havin' an heirloom is this old box of tacks m' dad gived me 'fore I went to war. But his Lordship brung me here an' showed me th' sword, th' very one I heard of in the old stories when I was a boy, th' very sword what was used to cut off th' tail of the Murk." Jermond roused himself and stood. "Anyways, you can see how you needs to be doin' more serious at gettin' to th' bottom of this matter."

"I don't know," Felicia said reluctantly. "I understand your concern, but this isn't what I came here for. I'm not on duty; I'm on vacation. Besides, I'm not sure what you expect for me to do. I grant it's a serious matter, but I don't see where a Magi is needed more than a simple investigator or a—"

She was interrupted by a loud and terrified scream. As the last echoes died away, she and Jermond were already racing down the hall, and down the stairs, until they came to one of the other guest rooms. Lady Fluffy was just outside the doorway, cowering against a wall and covering her eyes with her hands, weeping and screaming. Other servants arrived within moments of Felicia and Jermond, and the Steward directed them to the stricken Lady. Felicia stepped cautiously through the door, sparing only a swift glance at the note addressed to Lord and Lady Plush tacked to the door, and paused at the horrible sight within. The room was splashed with blood, and there was gore everywhere. The remains of a body had been torn and scattered like a child's doll.

Jermond came up behind the sorceress. "Who is it?" he asked in a trembling voice.

"If I'm not mistaken," Felicia said somberly, "it used to be Lady Plush." She jumped as a hand clutched tightly at her forearm, and she turned to find Lady Fluffy at her side. The feline's face was pale and her eyes wide with terror. "I don't think," she said in a small and shaken voice, "that it's sunspots!"

Chapter 6 "A Curse With No Name"

"I was so angry at her," Lady Fluffy said with a barely checked sob. "For having mentioned the curse, you remember? We had a row once we were alone and we each retired to our own rooms. I... I was coming back to apologize to her..."

"You were alone in your room?" Felicia asked. They had gathered again in the main hall following the grim discovery of Lady Plush's ravaged body. Lord Frisky was consoling a stricken Lord Plush as best he could. Jermond hovered at the doorway, speaking to servants as they drifted by the hallway, giving them instructions in gathering together the remains of the body and tidying the room following the sorceress' examination.

"Well, not my room; I mean, I took Lady Snuffler to her room and stayed there with her." Lady Snuffler solemnly nodded in acknowledgement.

"Someone else then," said Felicia. "Or some thing. Something powerful. Strong enough to rip a body apart or flatten them with a single blow. But what could roam so freely about the manor and do such harm without being seen? It sounds like a monster, but what monster leaves no track save for its attack?"

"Could it be invisible?" asked Lord Puffy timidly.

Felicia could only shrug. "Anything is possible. But something so powerful could scarcely be dainty or discreet in its movements. I would have expected more damage of a casual nature: broken door latches, overturned furniture..."

"This cannot go on," Lord Frisky said solemnly. Lady Fluffy and Jermond both looked to him in alarm. "This cannot be ignored. It must, after all, be the family curse coming to life once more."

"I hardly think..." Felicia began, but Lord Frisky continued on.

"I cannot avoid the responsibility of this matter, Lady Felicia; it is much too serious. We must find a means to end it, or, failing that, I must forfeit my lands and title and go into exile and hope to take the curse away with me."

"Izzy!" cried Lady Fluffy in shock.

"Milord, surely that's not necessary!" Jermond protested.

"I agree," said Felicia. "That is far too drastic a measure to take, especially when we don't yet know the true cause of these horrible deaths."

"But what else can it be?" Lord Frisky asked in exasperation. "There is no one here with motive to kill both Lord Snuffler and Lady Plush, and no one with power enough to do it in such monstrous fashion. No, it must be the curse, and although I take no blame, I nevertheless must take the responsibility."

The Steward looked helplessly to the sorceress. "Your Lordship, perhaps the sorceress might be able to... remove the curse?"

"Eh?" Lord Frisky brightened. "Good Aln! Neutralize the curse? I hadn't thought of that!" He turned hopefully to Felicia. "Can you do that?"

Felicia frowned impatiently. "It won't do any good! There is no —"

"It would be the sword, wouldn't it?" Lord Frisky said with unusual insight. "The sword was used to cut off the Murk's tail; wouldn't the curse be connected with such an object?"

"Well, yes," agreed Felicia with reluctance, "But you don't understand —"

"Why would anyone even keep such an article in their household?" Lord Plush asked angrily.

"As a trophy," said Lady Snuffler quietly. "That's not hard to understand. The Murk caused so much harm in the elder days. We Dogs understand that well. He humiliated our people, and we bore the shame of Haven's fall for many centuries afterward. No, I understand fully why such a trophy would be proudly displayed. There is no blame in that, Lord Fluffy, and in spite of all, I do not hold either you nor your family ill will for my husband's death. I believe it is indeed the curse, and that it is another evil mischief laid at the paws of the Murk!" The Dogonian spat as she spoke the name of the dreaded Lord of Shadow.

Lord Fluffy turned and gravely bowed to the Lady. "Thank you, Lady Snuffler. All the same, I cannot ignore my responsibility. I cannot have anyone else suffer as a result of this curse."

"All well and fine," Felicia interjected, "But the point is—"

"It shouldn't hurt t' have a looksee," insisted Jermond.

The vixen sighed in resignation. "Fine!" She dropped wearily into a large, high-backed chair. "Fetch me the sword!"

Jermond crossed over to the mantelpiece and climbed a stepladder to retrieve the sword from its resting place. He brought it gingerly to the waiting vixen, who took it in both hands, and held it out before her, weighing it carefully in her open palms.

"It's a fine sword," Felicia observed. "It has a good weight. A fine balance." She turned it carefully over. "Excellent craftsmanship. Appears to be well tempered steel. It should be a most formidable weapon." She turned it about and held it with the handle upwards. "It's a fine sword," she repeated. She handed it over to Lord Frisky, who nearly recoiled at its offering, but took it very gingerly from the vixen's grasp. "But," Felicia concluded, "It is not the sword of Kana Wagajop."

There was a stunned silence. Most of the room's occupants stood with their jaws dropped open. Lord Frisky nearly fell backwards onto the floor, still holding the sword, but recovered his equilibrium after a faltering step back. Jermond was equally shell-shocked and stared at the sorceress as though she had turned into a dragon. Felicia looked back at the old Steward sternly. "Close and secure the door," she told him firmly.

"Not Kana Wagajop's sword!" Lord Frisky gasped.

"You cannot be serious!" protested Jermond as he closed the door to the room, ensuring privacy from the rest of the household.

"Do you mean," Lord Frisky persisted, "that the sword is a forgery? That someone has switched a phony for the real one!?"

"But that's not possible, milord!" Jermond insisted as he hurried up to examine the sword. "I swear this is the same sword that has been hanging in this room ever since I first came here! I've dusted it enough to know it by sight! This is the sword of Kana Wagajop!"

"It is the same sword that has hung in this room for many years, I have no doubt," said Felicia. "But it is not Kana Wagajop's sword. What I mean to tell you, Lord Frisky, is that Kana Wagajop's sword doesn't exist."

There was another stunned silence, broken only by a croaking whisper from Lord Frisky. "Doesn't exist?"

"Kana Wagajop and his band of followers surprised and attacked the Murk outside the gates of Felina that night many centuries ago, and together they all cut off the demon's tail. But their swords never survived that act. The blood of the Murk was venomous and destroyed all that it touched. The land where it spilled was barren for many years, and required a spell of cleansing to purify it again. The swords used by Kana and his followers were destroyed. There was nothing for them to bring back, let alone hand down through the generations." Felicia looked sadly at the Kataran noble. "I'm sorry. I've known all along it was a fake, but saw no reason before now to say so."

Lord Frisky stared numbly at the sword in his hand. "I don't understand," he mumbled weakly. "Why would this have been handed down through my family for so long? And what of the curse? Why should it be connected to this sword?"

Felicia sighed. "There is no curse connected to this sword. It is just a sword. It is a fine weapon, but nothing extraordinary in any other way."

"But the curse!" Lord Frisky persisted.

"Has no bearing on you!" the vixen snapped irritably. She paused, and caught a breath before continuing. "I'm sorry to inform you, Lord Frisky, but there is no family curse where you are concerned. You are not of Kana Wagajop's lineage. The Wagajop line died out many years ago. The last descendant left no heirs."

Jermond broke the renewed stunned silence with an indignant snort. "That's not possible!"

"I speak from absolute knowledge!" the sorceress returned evenly. "Do you think the Magi wouldn't have kept track of the lineage of such a famous personage with such an infamous curse? We've long known of the fate of the Wagajop line. And I tell you with all certainty that you are not his descendant."

"It's all been a lie?" Lady Snuffler looked at Lord Frisky with renewed suspicion, but Felicia hastily raised a hand.

"Not a lie, though certainly a deception. But not on the part of Lord Frisky, for he was no more aware of it than any of you. I suspect that one of his ancestors somehow saw the opportunity and took advantage of stepping into the role of a descendant of the Wagajop clan, telling no one the truth. And the deception was kept even from later family members."

"But that can't be right," Lord Frisky protested. "I have family records! Accounts! Memoirs and memorabilia! Artifacts and heirlooms that can all be traced back through the Wagajop line!"

"Like the sword?" Lord Plush asked coldly.

"We're overlooking something," Lord Puffy intervened. "What of the curse? If it is not the Wagajop Curse that is causing the killing... then what is?"

The nobility all turned to look expectantly at the sorceress. Felicia frowned and stood. "An excellent question. And one that I cannot answer just yet. All we've managed to determine is what it is not." She paused and touched the crestfallen Lord Frisky on the forearm. "I'm sorry, milord. I would have not spoken if there had been another choice."

"No, no," Frisky muttered as he drew himself up. "It's better this way. The truth must come out, after all, if it is indeed the truth. I – I just find it difficult to assimilate. All these years, and I find out that I'm not who I think I am...!"

"Rubbish!" Jermond growled fiercely. "You're just who you've always been, milord, name or no name!"

"That's right, Frisky!" Lord Puffy reassured his friend with a slap on his back. "Name isn't always everything! It's how you carry it! And you've always carried your name well. Even if it isn't your name after all!" There was a low murmur of agreement, and Lady Fluffy shot a quick withering glare at Felicia before stepping up to put an encouraging arm around her husband.

"All the same," warned Felicia, "I think this should be kept discreetly among ourselves for the time being. This matter is far from being resolved, and the matter of the curse, whether real or not, is most certainly at the heart of these incidents."

"What do you propose to do?" asked Lord Plush.

Felicia stared at the empty slot over the mantelpiece where the sword had hung. "I'm not sure," she admitted with a sigh. "I'm not sure.

Chapter 7 "Profiles In Curses"

"No, it's not in here either!" Felicia sat back from her trunk and dropped the pile of clothing she had lifted from it back into the opening. She frowned as she contemplated the open trunk, and then made an abrupt gesture of annoyance. "I remember now! I left my crystal ball at home. I didn't want to bring it. I didn't think I would need it while on vacation. Bother!"

The vixen stood and ran a hand through her head fur. She had returned to the privacy of her rooms to think, feeling both irritable and frustrated by the constant interruptions to her attempts to have a troublefree vacation. She also felt irrationally guilty over the revelations she had been forced to make concerning Lord Frisky's heritage, and now felt responsible for helping him to some sort of resolution. And if she ever wanted to get that scrumptious cougar alone, she was just going to have to get rid of all of the distractions once and for all. It had occurred to her to just get the sordid business over with once and for all by using her crystal ball to scrye for some solid clues to the source of the deaths, now that she was more firmly convinced of their seriousness. But, as she now discovered, she didn't even have that option.

"Bother!" she muttered again. "Just one thing after another!" She crossed over to her nightstand to fetch her brush and stopped up short when she saw the empty space. "And where has that brush gotten to?" she snapped furiously. She pulled the stand away from the wall to search the floor behind it, but was then interrupted by a hesitant knock at the door. "Come in!"

One of the kitchen servants entered, pushing a cart before him. "Beggin' your pardon, ma'am," he said as he wheeled the cart into an empty space near the window. "His Lordship felt you might wish a bite t' eat while you was meditatin' alone."

"Yes, thank you!" said Felicia. She rose from her fruitless search of the floor behind the nightstand and brushed the dust from her robe. "That was kind of him. Please convey my gratitude to Lord Frisky." The servant bowed and slipped quietly out, latching the door behind him. Felicia glared again at the nightstand and dismissed it from her mind as she returned to the more immediate problem. "What is at the heart of these killings?" she mused aloud to herself. "How are they being done? It must be magic... but what is the means? If there was another Magi, black or white, I would sense it. The same is true if there were a talisman or an artifact. The curse seems most likely... but there's no connection; there's no family line to follow, no cursed item." She halted in her steps. "Damn! I had sensed something last night! I had nearly forgotten! But it was so brief, and I hadn't sensed it since. But then again, I really hadn't been trying!"

The sorceress crossed to the window and drew the curtains close to shut out the daylight, enclosing the room in a deep afternoon gloom. She sat on the edge of her bed and fell into a light trance and allowed herself to feel with her inner senses, once more sending feelers throughout the manor. At first there was nothing. Little by little, she began to sense the emotions of various household members, like tiny beacons of light floating on a dark pool of water. There were ripples of fear and worry resonating throughout. And then she found something odd: little pinpricks of malevolence. Tiny and almost imperceptible, they were like tiny sparks against a background of sunlight; she might never have noticed them if she hadn't been specifically looking for them. But what were they? She couldn't seem to narrow them down, and the magic, black and vile as it was, was weak and almost insignificant; it was like trying to focus on a single firefly from a distance of a mile away.

Felicia was rudely roused from her trance by a muffled sneeze. The vixen started involuntarily and her sharp ears swiveled towards the sound. She rose and cautiously edged towards the luncheon cart. There was a small pitcher of fruit juice and two covered dishes. She cautiously lifted one and found an assortment of cheese and meat. She then lifted the other lid.

"Hello!"

The sorceress nearly dropped the lid with a cry. Lying across the platter in his most seductive manner, was Sir Jack of Bleucheese, totally naked with only a leaf of lettuce to protect his modesty. Felicia stared at the mouse in open-mouthed surprise. "What are you doing?" she demanded when she found her breath again.

"I overheard the cook say you might be in the mood for a snack," the Rodentian said with a suggestive smirk. He propped his head up on his hand, and toyed with the protective lettuce. "I thought that perhaps you were more in the mood for some company. Let us compromise! Let us indulge in the feast of love together!" Sir Jack smiled his most dazzling smile at the vixen.

Felicia just stared, her ears slowly dropping to either side of her head. She lifted the platter and turned to the window, sweeping the curtains aside and pushing the window open with a single gesture. Then, without further ceremony, she turned the platter over, dumping mouse and lettuce over the edge of the sill. The mouse's startled cry diminished as he dropped, until it was punctuated by the splash from the garden pool below. As she pulled the windows shut again, she heard his faint voice drift from below, "Is that a 'maybe', then?"

"Gur!" swore the vixen. "I can't think around here! There are too many distractions! I need information!" She strode across the room to the wardrobe, and stood before it, raising both arms. Light sparked and arced across the gap between her hands and the wardrobe, and she murmured a spell under her breath. The wardrobe was suffused with an intense light that just as quickly faded. Felicia reached out and opened it, and then stepped into the wardrobe, and carefully closed the door behind her.

The sorceress took three steps to the back of the wardrobe, where she found the latch to another door. She opened that and stepped through into the light of her own study, in her own tower on the other side of Katara. She glanced behind her to note the closet door she had just stepped through. "Good," she muttered. "Now to do some real research." Closing her eyes, she took hold of the closet door and stepped back into the closet again. But when she opened her eyes, she was neither in the closet nor in the wardrobe, but inside of a vast library. Rows and rows of shelves, each filled to capacity with books and tomes.

Like all Magi, Felicia had the ability to walk through the 'between-worlds', as they were known, small realms beyond the experience of mortals. Some were little more than amorphous limbos, but others were inhabited and reflected the aspects of their inhabitants' interests or lives. Some were metaphorical, others were quite literal. This realm, the library, Felicia knew quite well; it belonged to the Archivist, the ghost who haunted her tower.

The sorceress wandered down the aisles for a moment, casually glancing at the titles. Each book represented the life of some individual, past or present, or of some major event. Some even recorded events years into the future, but Felicia knew these were seldom reliable, since they related probable futures and nothing of certainty. She didn't generally like browsing through the library – well, this library, she noted – as there was always the danger of learning too much too soon, but at times she found it invaluable for specific research. Like now. She stopped in the center of one long aisle. "I know you're here!" she said to the open air. "I need some information!"

"I know," answered a soft voice behind her. Felicia turned to find the Archivist there, standing placidly as though she had been there all along, waiting for the sorceress' arrival.

"I need to review the history of ancient Katara," the vixen told the rabbit as they walked together down the aisles past the seemingly infinite rows of volumes stacked neatly on the shelves. "In particular, I need the account of Kana Wagajop's encounter with the Murk."

"I thought that you had discounted the influence of the curse," the ghost said mildly.

Felicia hid her annoyance at the Archivist's apparent omniscience of the events at Frisky Manor; she had long since become used to the rabbit's awareness of things beyond her confinement at the tower, even if it continued to irk the sorceress. "I can't afford to discount anything. It doesn't seem likely that the curse could be at the root of the problem, but I need to be absolutely certain of it."

The Archivist halted at the end of an aisle and withdrew a thick volume. She handed it to Felicia, who carried it to a reading desk and opened the book. "All right, let's just see… 'Bravely did the hero band smite the evil Lord of Night, and together did they strike off his tail. The Murk did scream and hop about liketh a stuck toad and wailed loudly like a little girl…' Hmm." The vixen scanned the page swiftly, running her finger down the text. "Ah! Just as I remembered! Their swords were lost, dissolved away in the blood of the Murk, useless following the success of their heroic deed, for so corrupt and vile was the Murk's blood was as corrupt and vile as he and naught could survive its touch.' That confirms the matter of the sword." She looked up from the book. "Is there a cross-reference to this? I need a record of Kana Wagajop's family line."

The Archivist nodded and reached into another shelf and produced another text. Felicia took it and opened it to the last pages. She read it silently for a few minutes before closing it with a sigh. "No, this confirms the rest of what I already knew, that Kana Wagajop's last descendant died childless many, many years ago. So the curse can't be to blame."

"Couldn't it?"

"Not without a focus." Felicia propped an elbow upon the book and dropped her chin into the palm of her hand as she frowned and reflected upon the matter. "The curse was specific. The Murk had cursed Kana's bloodline, down through his children, his children's children, ad infinitum. But with the line having been extinguished, the curse cannot continue. Now, if the sword were intact, it's possible the curse might have lived on through that, having been in contact with the Murk's body and having been doused with his blood, it would have resonated with his evil and been linked to the curse in that manner. But the sword is destroyed, so there's a dead end."

"Is it?" The Archivist stood patiently by, neither encouraged nor discouraged by the sorceress' findings. Felicia spared the ghost an annoyed glance before looking away into the flickering of the desk's solitary candle.

"But the nature of the deaths at the manor," the vixen mused, "sound like the results of a curse. Could it be the work of a different curse altogether? Or a magic attack that's unrelated, but taking advantage of the notoriety of the curse in order to throw us off the track and hide the true reasons for the attack? But why couldn't I detect any magic at work? No, strike that! I did detect magic, but weak and dispersed; something evil, but faint and unfocused. Surely that couldn't have been the source. Could it?"

"There is a way for you to solve the mystery," the Archivist said quietly. She walked over to the nearest shelf and withdrew another book, and brought it to the desk. "Here is the history of Frisky Manor, complete to the present moment. You only need to read through the last few pages to learn the truth of the matter."

Felicia scowled. "Take that away!" she growled. "I won't look at that! That's cheating!"

The rabbit raised an eyebrow. "You're cheating now," she said, pointing to the books in front of the sorceress.

"Well, I'm not cheating anymore!" Felicia snapped, slamming the book shut. She glowered at the ghost for a long minute. "This isn't the same thing. I am doing research, which is not the same thing! I won't take the easy way and look through any books that give away the present or future! That is unethical! It's dangerous!" Felicia shrugged. "And it isn't much fun. Besides, I'm a Magi! I should be able to figure this out on my own without resorting to arcane cheat sheets!"

"And yet you're consulting books that contain information that could not be found in any other library," the rabbit reminded her. "And you were ready to use your crystal ball."

"The crystal would have only revealed stray images and psychic clues for me to follow up on! And these books only show me the past; they are a part of a very unique reference library. I won't cheat by using magic!"

"'What good is magic if you can't use it?'"

"That's a lovely quote," Felicia said wearily. "What brilliant soul said that?"

The Archivist produced a wine-colored volume from the small stack she had been carrying under her arm. "The sorceress, Felicia cla di Burrows, to her mother and mentor, on the day she left home following a bitter dispute."

Felicia's head snapped up, her eyes ablaze with a red light. "I told you to never show me that book," she growled in a low voice. "Take it away! Get out!" She reopened the book of Kana Wagajop's family history with an angry motion that allowed the cover to slam loudly against the desk surface. The Archivist sadly bowed her head and withdrew into the shadows. Felicia stared unseeing at the open pages, seething inwardly as she struggled to contain her anger. Her breathing quieted and the words slowly focused before her. She looked numbly at the family line for a minute, noting the long procession from scion to scion.

The vulpine head suddenly snapped up. "Could it be?" she wondered. "Would he have done that?" She flipped the pages backwards and scanned through the lists again. "Wait!" she called. "Come back!" The rabbit rematerialized beside her. "Family lists! I need more family trees! Lord Frisky's, especially! I need to backtrack his tree! Perhaps he's connected to the Wagajop line after all, in some connection that might have been formally overlooked! And bring me the family trees of the other guests and inhabitants of the manor! I don't want to overlook anybody!"

The rabbit withdrew and reappeared again, carrying an armful of books. She deposited them before the waiting vixen, who eagerly pulled a volume out and pored over its contents. "No, it's as I thought originally. He has no blood connection to the Wagajop's. But his family has had the manor and lands and titles going back four hundred years... Hmm." She pulled another book out of the stack and opened it. "While I'm at it, bring me the family histories of the others who had stood with Kana Wagajop outside the gates of Felina. His friends, the other heroes – oh, I can't even remember their names! But I might as well be thorough!" As the Archivist went in search of the requested material, Felicia scanned through the book in her hand and stopped at a passage. "Ah! Here's something of interest!

Yes, that would explain things! In part, at least. Never underestimate the spitefulness of the Murk!" She looked up and gazed thoughtfully into the candle flame. "A catalyst, perhaps... yes... but it still needs a key! What could be the key to the magic?"

She continued to pore over the books before her, finding nothing further of value, and pausing only when the Archivist returned with a new selection of titles. Felicia eagerly took them from the ghost and read through them quickly, tossing each finished volume into a pile of discards. It was only after she had read a few pages of the very last book that she abruptly paused and sat up fully alert. "Now, this never got into the old stories!" she murmured in excitement. "'Maryn went back to the hill the morning following the last visit of the Murk, and he found the place where they had attacked the Lord of Shadow. The grass had died and the nearest trees were withering, and the ground was bare and rocky. He found the remains of their swords, for such he had sought in hopes of retrieving his own. But they were spoiled by the blood of the Murk, which corrupted all it touched, and there was naught but a pile of slag. He instead took the slag back into Felina with him...!'" The vixen flipped the pages of the book, scanning the recorded events of Maryn's life over the next few days. "Ah! Maryn was a smith of minor abilities, who also ran a general store in Felina! He melted down the slag and reused it, not wanting it to go to waste! He never told Kana nor the others, because he never saw the need; he didn't think it was important!"

"What did he recast it as?" asked the Archivist, curious in spite of herself. "A new sword?"

Felicia smirked, pleased at having found something that the seemingly-omniscient rabbit didn't know. "No! He recast it as..." She flipped more pages, and came to a halt, frowning again. "Cloak hangers." The Archivist raised an eyebrow in surprise. Felicia continued to scan, running her finger under the lines on the printed page. "Um... there wasn't all that much metal in the slag, certainly not enough for any large items, and it wasn't strong enough for him to make a sword. Not his expertise anyway. He instead turned the metal into items of utility, such as hangers and hairpins and safety pins and tacks..." She stopped and glanced up. "Oh, dear."

"What is it?"

"I think..." Felicia suddenly lunged for the pile of discarded books. "Where is that book? Not that one... Ah!" She yanked one of the volumes from the center of the pile, nearly spilling those on top onto the floor, and spread it open. She jabbed her finger into the center of a page and ran it back and up, tracing the intricate family tree back to its origins. And stopped when she came to a name she recognized. "It never occurred to me that there would be another descendant," she remarked in triumph. She looked up at the Archivist and grinned broadly. "I know how it was done. I know the magic and I know what triggers it. I even know who." She paused and reflected. "No – I don't know who; not fully. There's still one, no, two more pieces to the puzzle I haven't yet uncovered. But I know who to start with. The rest will all fall into place now!"

With that, the sorceress leapt up from her chair and hurried across the span of the library, hurrying away down the aisles to the door she had originally entered through. "Who was it?" called the Archivist after her. "What connection does the Tailcutter's Curse have in all this?" The vixen's laughter trailed behind her.

"I can't stop now! I've a vacation to hurry back to! You can read how it turns out in my book!"

The Archivist could only watch as Felicia passed through the exit, leaving her alone once more in her library. With a small sigh of resignation, she retired to her own reading desk and opened the book with the wine-colored cover, turning the pages until coming to Felicia's return to Frisky Manor.

Chapter 8 "A Curse Of A Different Color"

Upon her return to the manor, Felicia went in search of Jermond. When he was not to be found at any of his duties, she went straight to his room. She didn't bother to knock, but eased the door open quietly. The window was shuttered and dark, except for the glow of a single, small candle on a short wooden table. Jermond was kneeling before it, his back to the sorceress and his head bowed low. Felicia could hear him muttering low, and caught a snatch or two of an old and familiar prayer. The steward paused, sensing the vixen's silent presence, and raised his head, half-turning to look over his shoulder at her. His grizzled face was troubled.

"I didn't know," he told her, not rising from his place before the candle. "I figgered it out a little while ago. But I swear I didn't know before that. I had 'em since I was a lad. My old Dad give 'em t' me, said they was th' only heritage our poor family had, though he never rightfully knew why or where they'd come from. Never thought they was anything important, 'cept that they was mine." He turned back to the candle again, and gripped his knees with trembling hands. Felicia said nothing, but remained standing quietly near the door. "When you said the sword was a fake, it got me thinkin'. Th' only other thing I could think of around here that was old enough t' carry a curse was mine. I collected them all, t' make sure I had 'em all, an' I brought 'em back here t' see for myself, th' only way I knew how." He waved a hand towards a trunk in the corner of the room. "See f'r yerself."

Felicia crossed over to the trunk and found the small metal box sitting atop of it. She took it and opened it, revealing the small, dull metal tacks that Jermond used for leaving messages around the manor. The vixen turned away from the light so that her shadow covered it completely. Even without her trained mystic senses, she could see the faint, sickly green glow from the tacks, like small smoldering coals. "Yes," she agreed. "These are the source. They've been corrupted with evil."

"I never knew," the steward said again. "I never really looked at 'em before. They was only tacks, for Aln's sake, heirloom or not. Never needed t' look at 'em in th' dark before, an' never noticed them glowin' when they was used."

"Well," Felicia said quietly. "The glow is faint. Unless one was really looking for it, it might not be noticed." She reached under her skirt and pulled forth a small silver dagger. She used the edge of the blade to scrape the side of the metal case, scratching away the dull color to reveal a brighter sheen beneath. "See this!" she told Jermond, holding the box out so that he might see the scratching. "Silver! The box is really silver, painted to look like common iron. That kept the magic in check while they were contained."

Jermond swore under his breath. "You mean t' say that all these years I been carryin' around a silver box? I could have hocked that t' pay bills a dozen times over!" He shook his head and lowered it in shame. "Instead, I failed in my duties and brought harm t' my master. But I swear that I never knew!"

"I believe you," Felicia reassured him, laying a sympathetic hand upon the steward's shoulder. "What you have here, believe it or not, is the true remains of the sword of Kana Wagajop." Jermond looked up, his eyes wide with surprise. Felicia nodded and continued. "As well as the other swords used by his companions. You see, it was as I said: the swords were all destroyed that night, as a result of having been corrupted by the blood of the Murk. They had been dissolved into a worthless pile of slag. But one of the companions went back a few days later and collected the slag, and took it back into Felina, where he melted it down and recast it into ordinary items, never realizing that it had been tainted by the Murk."

"How did they come t' my family, then?"

"Well, Jermond, it seems that it isn't Lord Frisky who has a famous ancestor, but rather that it's you. You see, I did some checking. You happen to be a direct descendant of Kana's companion, Maryn."

"Maryn? Maryn the Hesitant?" Jermond stared at Felicia in dumbfound amazement.

"Hesitant indeed!" scoffed the vixen. "True, he was not the most courageous of the band, and he lagged behind; he wasn't a warrior like the others, after all. But when the time came, he went, and like the others he plunged his sword into the Murk. Hesitant he might have been, but he proved his courage that night with the others." Jermond seemed to take some comfort in that, so Felicia went on. "Maryn's only mistake was in retrieving the slag. He was a smith at heart and couldn't bear to see the metal go to waste. It never occurred to him that it would be harmful in any way." She hefted the small box in her hand. "But there's no blame to you either, Jermond. There was no way for you to know these were cursed."

"Does that matter," Jermond said bitterly. "Two people are dead, one of 'em an ambassador. My master'll take th' blame, even if he learns th' truth, an' he'll lose everythin' here. It still makes it my fault."

"No." Felicia carefully placed the box in her purse for safekeeping. "The tacks themselves couldn't have done the harm caused here."

"What d' ya mean?"

"I mean that the evil influence of the Murk is weak and diffused throughout the tacks. A single tack of itself could not inflict such damage as we've seen. The magic, in fact, is dormant until evoked. It needs a catalyst. In fact, the Tailcutter's Curse itself wouldn't apply without a blood descendant of Kana Wagajop. Come! We must find Lord Frisky! We need to set his mind at ease, and a killer to apprehend."

"Just a minute," Jermond protested as they hurried out into the hallway. "I thought you said his Lordship wasn't related t' Kana Wagajop?"

"He's not," Felicia replied. "The bloodline died out generations ago..." She paused as a thought suddenly struck her. "Oh, Gur!" She came to a complete stop and slapped herself in the forehead. "I am such an idiot! That's what she was trying to tell me! That's why she mentioned Mother!"

"How's that?" The steward was puzzled.

"I keep forgetting that she's a ghost! It was a riddle, and I didn't see it!"

"I'm sorry, milady, but I've completely lost th' thread of yer meanin'," the old feline said with some impatience. "If I were to bang my head against th' wall here, would it make any more sense t' me?"

"The Archivist!" Felicia explained. "She's a ghost! You see, ghosts have their haunts, and they have their specialties, and the Archivist's specialty is knowledge! But being a ghost, she can't impart it directly; she can only guide me to it! Even so, she needed for me to know something about Lord Frisky, but she wasn't able to come right out and tell me! So she tried to clue me in by indirect means, by reminding me of my mother!"

"Oh, yes?" Jermond was anything but educated by this information. "Well, that's so much clearer," he grumbled.

"It's such an obvious answer; why didn't I see it before? I've no time to go back and recheck the histories. You must have family records here, surely?"

"Of course we do, in th' library..."

"Good! Fetch them! It has no real bearing on the curse, but it may very well resolve any issues of legitimacy." Another thought came to her, and she patted her purse cautiously. "The tacks. You said you had collected them all?"

"Soon as I figgered them out."

"You're sure they're all here? Think carefully! It's important."

Jermond frowned and furrowed his brow. His whiskers splayed and quivered while he thought. "I – think so. I use so many of 'em that I lose track of where I put them sometimes. I usually collect 'em when I pass 'em, once th' notes've done their business. I can't always remember where I use 'em. But I think I got 'em all."

But there was a faint note of uncertainty that didn't escape the vixen's attention. There was, she realized, still a potential of danger present. "Fetch the family history," she told Jermond. "I'll find Lord Frisky."

Felicia hastened down the stone corridors to the main hall, her cloak rustling behind her. *Next time I vacation in Bananaland,* she told herself. *Sultry, tropical nights on an isolated island. Exotic food and private beaches. Lots of sailors.* She hurried down a flight of stairs. *Next time I do an extensive historical research on the region I plan to vacation in, in order to avoid all of this nuisance.*

Luck was with her, for both Lord Frisky and Lady Fluffy were sitting together in the main hall. "Good!" said Felicia breathlessly as she entered. "I've found you both! Listen! I've unraveled the mystery –"

There was a sudden and sharp scream of rage from outside the window, causing them all to jump. The window exploded inwards, showering shards of glass everywhere, and a massive shadow hurtled in through the rain of fragments and landed with a heavy thump on the floor. Lady Fluffy screamed and ran to her husband, who drew her behind him while he turned and called for his guards. Felicia stared at the intruder in surprise, and then cried out in disappointment, "Oh, no! It had to be you, didn't it?"

The shadow snarled and lumbered towards her, swiping the air with a massive paw, barely missing the sorceress as she stepped hastily backwards. The vixen brought both of her hands upwards in a defensive gesture and hot, white light erupted from her fingertips, arcing across the space between her and the monstrous intruder and striking it firmly in its chest. The creature staggered backwards, surprised by the unexpected resistance, and roared in anger. The brilliance of the light illuminated his features and both Lord and Lady gasped in recognition. Enlarged to monstrous proportions and distorted into an evil caricature of his former self, it was nevertheless recognizable as the gardener, Mason!

With another scream of rage, the creature lunged again at Felicia and swung a massive fist at her. She nimbly leapt aside, and the fist instead struck a table and pulverized it into kindling. The sorceress again raised her hands and uttered an incantation. Blue light enveloped the transformed gardener, and his motions slowed until he moved with great difficulty. He was caught in the spell, like a fly in amber, and his enlarged muscles flexed and bulged as he strained against his constraint.

"I can't hold him long," Felicia gritted as she maintained the spell. "He's been ensorcelled by a magic greater than mine. Quickly! Look about for a tack!"

"A tack?" Frisky asked in bafflement.

"Look in the door!" Felicia snapped. "See if one of Jermond's tacks is still holding a note... or is imbedded in the wood!"

"I don't think you can hurt it with a tack..." Frisky protested, and a low, gurgling roar, drawn out by Felicia's spell, burbled out of the monster.

"The tacks are what carry the curse!" Felicia explained curtly as she strained to keep Mason contained. She could feel tiny cracks erupting around the perimeter of her spell as Mason continued to force his way free. "Hurry! I can't keep him at bay forever!"

"There's no tack in the door!" Lady Fluffy cried from the doorway.

Felicia cursed. "Look about! There must be one in this room!"

Lord Frisky directed the arriving guards to search the room for any sign of a tack, and he joined them in a search of the walls and tables while Felicia held off the ensorcelled Mason. "Here!" cried one of the guards as he fell to his hands and knees. He groped under the furniture in a far corner of the room and reemerged with a single tack. "It must have fallen to the floor and gotten lost!"

"Bring it here," said Felicia. The pure blue light holding Mason was being slowly corrupted by a sickly, pale green that threaded through the aura like a network of veins. "I have Jermond's box in my purse. Take it, and quickly place the tack in with the others, and reseal the box. That will break the spell!" A pulse of green light pierced one side of the blue aura. "Hurry!"

The guard hurried up with the tack, and Lord Frisky took it from him and did as Felicia instructed. As soon as the box was open and all of the tacks were exposed, Mason flexed with a powerful surge and the blue aura popped like a child's balloon. The monster roared with indignant fury and lunged at the sorceress who had fallen over backwards when her spell was disabled. Lord Frisky fumbled with the tacks, dropped the lost tack in with its brothers and clumsily replaced the lid.

Mason fell heavily onto the floor next to Felicia, flat on his stomach. The spell broken, he shriveled and contorted until his body took on its normal form once more. The gardener shakily raised his head and looked about him with a befuddled expression. "What happened?" he asked in a small voice. He was immediately surrounded by the guards who raised him roughly to his feet.

"Easy, lads! Easy!" said Lord Frisky as he helped Felicia to her feet. He handed her the box of tacks which she replaced in her purse. "No need to be rough! It's obvious he wasn't to blame for his condition! He's not responsible for what he's done!"

"Like hell!" seethed Felicia. She stared at the bewildered cougar through narrowed eyes, and then bent to retrieve an object from where Mason had fallen to the floor. She turned the object over in her hand and passed it over to Lord Frisky. "This slipped from his pocket when he fell." Lord Frisky frowned severely, all friendly demeanor fading from his countenance as he examined the Dogonian Medal of Courage.

Chapter 9 "Cutting The Curse Strings"

"Well, I'm all in a topsy, I don't mind saying," Lord Frisky said. "I'm not related to Kana Wagajop, but the Tailcutter's Curse was still the cause of the murders? And you say that Jermond is descended from one of Kana's companions!?"

It was evening now, and the main hall had been cleaned and straightened, and except for the absence of the table that Mason had destroyed, all seemed as if nothing unusual had occurred earlier. Felicia sat in a comfortable, high-backed chair and sipped at a cup of tea while Lord Frisky paced nervously in a circle, trying to fathom the day's events. Lady Fluffy sat nearby, and Jermond waited by a writing desk on which he had set a huge book. "Yes," said Felicia. "That's about it, in a nutshell."

"Well, I suppose I understand that just fine, except for all the bits I still don't understand." Frisky paused in his pacing. "For example, I understand that the tacks were made from the swords, which were all cursed. But why didn't they ever affect us before? Jermond here has been using them for years!"

"But until recently you were missing two very important things to trigger the curse. By themselves, the tacks were minor; the magic was diffused over the quantity of tiny items, and most of them were kept in check by the silver box they were kept in." Felicia held out her cup, and Jermond stepped forward to refill it from a silver teapot. "What is the most important event in your life this past year, milord?"

"Well, nothing really," Lord Frisky replied thoughtfully as he scratched his head. "Except for getting married..."

"Exactly!"

Lady Fluffy cocked her head in puzzlement. "Why would our marriage make a difference where the curse is concerned?"

Felicia smiled widely. "Because it was of great importance to the curse. Lord Frisky is not a blood relation to Kana Wagajop. But you are."

The Lady's eyes widened in surprise. "But I am not! I assure you I am not!"

"Oh," said Felicia, wagging a finger in gentle admonishment. "I can assure you that you are! After a fashion." She leaned forward in her chair. "You see, the standard for ascendancy is through the male's side of the family tree. The son inherits, and passes titles and land and name on to his sons, and so forth. But the daughter rarely inherits, but becomes part of the family she marries into. That's tradition. But the Murk doesn't care about legalities. His curse was on the blood of the family, and that follows down through son and daughter. The bloodline died out when the last male died childless, and the Magi took no further notice. But the distaff side had long since been forgotten, and the mingling of other bloodlines has diluted the original curse so that it never manifested." She sat back again and stirred her tea. "I can trace your line back through your mother and grandmother's ancestry back to the Wagajop line."

"But," Lord Frisky protested, "that's not a legitimate bloodline!"

Felicia shrugged. "You can argue it with the Murk if you like. Like I said, he wasn't concerned with tradition. Only mischief. The curse was linked to family blood, and he didn't much care which way it spilled."

"You say the curse was diluted on my side of the family," Lady Fluffy said. "Why then should our marriage make a difference?"

"Well, only in that it brought you into contact with Jermond's tacks, which were infected by the Murk's magic. The two together had an affinity. Even so, they were still weak and needed more to become active. Tell me, Lord Frisky," Felicia said, turning to face him. "Have you ever known Lady Fluffy to lose her temper."

Frisky was surprised. "Why, no! She has the sweetest and most gentle demeanor I've ever known in a person!"

"I'll vouch for that," Jermond agreed. "She never gets the little bit irritable. Not even with me."

"You see?" Frisky said proudly. "A paragon of patience!"

"And yet, I saw her show signs of temperament at least three times these past few days."

"What? Never!"

"I saw her glare at Lord Snuffler for his accusations during the dinner. And again at Lady Plush for having mentioned the curse following the death of Lord Snuffler. And a third time at me after I had told you that you were not related to Kana Wagajop."

"It's true," Lady Fluffy admitted, dropping her eyes in shame. "I was upset with Lady Plush for having mentioned the curse at such an indelicate moment... and I was horrified that you dared suggested that Izzy's titles were false. And that awful Lord Snuffler!"

"And each preceded their deaths, or in my case, an attempted murder."

"But surely you're not saying that Fluffy is to blame!"

"Oh, no!" Felicia said hurriedly. "Not at all! I've no doubt that she's every bit the gentle person you believe her to be, milord! There was never any intent to do harm in her at all. But even so, she is still a mortal like the rest of us, and given to piques. Her flashes of anger were on your behalf, in

response to what she felt were attacks on your name and reputation. And it was those piques that evoked the latent curse."

"Really?" Lord Frisky was intrigued. "How?"

"Through the tacks. As I said, there was an affinity between the family curse and the afflicted metal. Even so, the power was so diluted that it might never have manifested if it weren't for Mason."

"Yes, what was his part in all this?"

"A necessary pawn for the curse to channel itself through. Mason was a recent addition to the staff, I presume?"

"Yes, milady," said Jermond. "Only a few months with us."

"I thought so! Well, you might have noticed, milord, that objects around the manor tend to disappear at times and then reappear elsewhere at a later point?"

Jermond fidgeted nervously, but Frisky nodded. "Yes! All the time!"

"Well," Felicia said breezily, "that's just normal housekeeping for a house as large as this. Things get moved, stored, inventoried, etcetera, etcetera, all the time. Easy to become misplaced and forgotten and then later replaced when relocated."

"Of course," Lord Frisky said reasonably, though a bit puzzled by this line of conversation. Jermond breathed a quiet sigh of relief.

"Well, Mason observed this as well, and saw an opportunity for some small theft, thinking that if he kept it small it might never be noticed. And for a long time, it worked. And then he overstepped himself when your guests began arriving." She gestured to a waiting guard who brought in a small sack. The guard opened the sack and spilled the contents onto a small table. Felicia reached out and took a small silver brush from the pile. "This is mine," she said. "The other items you might recognize."

"My pins!" cried Lady Fluffy. "Why, I thought I had lost those!"

"And the rest of Lord Snuffler's medals," observed Lord Frisky. "And that's a clasp belonging to Lord Puffy! I recognize it! Good Aln! Mason was a thief!"

"Yes, he was," Felicia said with a sad sigh. "And I'd thought I was making him nervous; he was only afraid that I'd found him out. With so many rich targets to choose from, his greed couldn't be swayed by common sense, and so he stole small items from each of us as well. But unlike the household items, these were more readily missed."

"But how does this connect with the curse?"

"The curse needed a pawn to manifest through. It needed an evil individual, or at least a corrupted or corruptible soul. Mason was the one most closely suitable to its purpose. He was never aware of what he had done; in that regard, he was a helpless and unwitting puppet. His only true crime was the thievery." Felicia rose and placed the silver brush in her purse. "So there you have it. The curse revealed and dealt with! The curse lives, diluted and otherwise inert, in the Lady Fluffy's bloodline, acting in accord with the cursed tacks of Jermond, and manifested through the personage of a corrupt thief. Mason will be incarcerated, I will dispose of the tacks, and without either to influence, the curse will be forever silent, and continue to become more and more diluted down through the generations."

"Excellent! But," Lord Frisky added sadly, "too late to save me from ruin, I'm afraid."

"Ah!," said Felicia with a bright smile, "I have a surprise for you there as well!" And she briskly brought Lord and Lady to the open book that Jermond had brought at her instruction, and she turned the pages until she reached a certain entry. "There! Do you see?"

Lord Frisky read through the entry and the last ounce of worry fell away from his face as his whiskers quivered with excitement. "Great Gur! That had never occurred to me! How perfectly simple!"

"Why," Lady Fluffy exclaimed in amazement, "it just explains everything!"

"Indeed it does," Felicia said triumphantly. "And so the last threads of any charge of illegitimacy falls away from the grasp of your enemies."

* * *

By late afternoon of the next day Felicia was lounging by a fountain in the estate's garden, enjoying the afternoon sun with Lord and Lady Frisky. The Royal Investigators had been sent for and Mason was being held in a cell in the dungeon until their arrival. Felicia had locked the accursed thumbtacks in her trunk where they would be secure, their magic stifled by their silver case, until she could hand deliver them to the Magi Council. Frisky had regained most of his cheer, but now let out a disappointed sigh.

"Ah, me! It's a shame about the party. I had such grand hopes for it."

"Never mind, dear," Fluffy reassured him. "There's always next year. At least now we know there will be a next year."

"Well, that's true!" Frisky brightened even more at the thought. "And this gives me time to pursue a new idea for a game that I had!"

"A new game, dear?"

"Yes! A variation of Yarnball for the common fellow to play! Seems they don't much like Yarnball; not rigorous enough for them, you know. So I thought, something with a club! And a net! And instead of a ball, a little birdie!"

"Oh, not a birdie, Izzy!" Fluffy was horrified.

"Not a real birdie, good Gur, no! But a mockery, something that looks like a birdie! And they can whack it across the net with all of their might! Whack it against their opponents! Whack the living bejeebers out of it against the ground! That ought to be rigorous enough for them, what do you think?"

"It might do," agreed Fluffy. "What will you call it?"

Frisky preened proudly. "I'll call it... Birdieball!" He turned to Felicia. "What do you think, Sorceress?"

Felicia looked up distractedly from her ice tea. "Ah! Yes, I think that would be splendid."

"Dear me," Frisky said, leaning towards the vixen with concern. "Is everything all right? You look positively funkyish, if you understand me."

"Oh, I'm all right," Felicia said with a small sigh. "But I was reflecting that in the middle of this happy ending that everybody has got what they wanted or needed... except me!" She thought of the handsome cougar in detention, and almost regretted his imprisonment. If he hadn't tried to rob her as well she might still have half an inkling to sneak him out to safety across the country, but while she was forgiving of many things, there were many more that she was not forgiving of. "A fine way to spend a vacation! And to find that so many things were not as they appeared to be. Well, I should expect that, I suppose, but it's a nuisance all the same. That reminds me," she said with an abrupt sharpness. "I had almost forgotten! There is still a plot thread dangling and there is something I must ask Jermond. Where is he?"

"Here, Milady!" panted the old steward as he came into the garden from the direction of the manor. A stranger followed at his anger. "Forgive me for not responding immediately to your peevishness, but there was a knock at the door." He turned to indicate the stranger. "Says he's here to see you."

Felicia frowned and stared at the stranger, a road-weary sheepdog who was large and very broad of shoulder and whose face was lost in a sea of long white fur, and who fidgeted restlessly from one foot to the other. "Yes? Do I know you?"

"Are you the sorceress?" There was a desperate edge to the sheepdog's voice. "You do the magic and the spells and make with the curses going away and stop with the doing of nasty things?"

Felicia hesitated and eyed the stranger with suspicion. "Yes..."

"Oh, thank Aln! I've been following your trail for a week up and down the road and over the river and at the inns with the expensive menus just trying to catch up to you on the fast horse! I got a curse like you wouldn't believe and I need it made to go away, please! Sure, the signs said 'don't touch the diamond or something bad'll happen', but you think they could have been more specific!" He spread his arms in a plaintive gesture. "Just look at me!"

Felicia took a step back to view the sheepdog with a critical eye. Apart from his obvious distress, he appeared perfectly fine and fit. "What, exactly, is the problem?"

The sheepdog hung his head in shame and said in a small voice, "I'm a raccoon."

Felicia sighed deeply and shook her head sadly. "Rakunes..." she muttered under her breath. She gestured and led the way back to the manor. The raccoon-turned-sheepdog followed anxiously behind her.

"Now, this will be without the pain and the hurting, right...?"

Epilogue

Sir Jack of Bleucheese entered the darkness of the small, mouse-sized room he kept in the manor. With a weary sigh, he made his way through the dark to where he knew his candle was kept on a small, barren table. He struck a light and carefully put the flame to the wick, casting a pale yellow light over the small and nondescript room. The mouse pulled the wide brimmed hat from his head and held it for a moment, staring at it sadly before hanging it atop of a tall pole next to the door.

"You lied to me," said a soft voice from behind him.

The mouse jumped in surprise. He grabbed the candleholder and raised it to better disperse the shadows in the opposite side of the room. "Who's there?" he demanded.

"You told me you were a knight and a guest. The truth is that you are neither."

Sir Jack raised the candle higher, approaching the source of the voice. The shadows fled at the approach of the light, revealing first the silhouette of a figure with sharp pointed ears and muzzle. He nearly dropped the candle in surprise. "Lady Felicia?"

The vixen sat in an overstuffed chair with her cloak wrapped about her like a magenta cocoon. "It finally occurred to me that I hadn't seen you at any of the dinners or social events since I arrived, nor did Lord Frisky or anyone else mention your presence in the manor. When I asked Jermond what had become of Sir Jack of Bleucheese, the Ambassador from Rodentia, he thought I was mad, and then couldn't stop laughing."

"How did you –" The mouse swallowed nervously. "You're so small!"

Felicia shrugged, allowing a bare shoulder to emerge from beneath the cloak. "Not a difficult spell for a Magi. How else can we deal with mice in their homeland?" She sat forward in the chair. "It would seem, 'Sir Jack', that you are an impostor. What do you say to that?"

Jack hung his head. "It's true," he sighed. "I'm no knight. My name is Jack. No 'Sir' to it at all."

"I know," Felicia said quietly. "Jermond told me. You are an employee of Lord Frisky. You are, in fact, an accountant. You help Jermond keep the books and even helped him with the rather tricky business of keeping the estate solvent. You helped him, in fact, to find buyers for the items he had to sell to obtain funds to cover Lord Frisky's excesses, and to later buy those items back again."

"Yes, ma'am," Jack admitted. "I have a pretty good head for money and numbers, and I know most of the business dealings in Felina. I've been in

Jermond's confidence for years now, and we've done our best to keep his lordship from going too far over the edge with his spending."

"So I was told," the vixen smiled.

"For all the good it will do us," the mouse added sadly. "I've heard the truth about Lord Frisky's past, how he isn't really a descendant of Kana Wagajop. Once word gets to his enemies, it won't be long until they bring pressure on him, financial and social, to ruin him. They'll convince the king that he has no legitimacy to his title and his lands. He'll be dispossessed and stripped of honors."

"No," said Felicia. "That won't happen." Jack looked across at her, a frown of doubt tugging at the corners of his mouth. Felicia gestured with a hand, allowing the cloak to slide down her bare arm. "You see, Lord Frisky really is the heir to the Wagajop lands and title. His claim is perfectly legitimate."

"But... I thought it was proven that he wasn't related? That the Wagajop line died out years ago!"

"It did," the vixen confirmed. "But I was reminded by an acquaintance of mine of something rather obvious that I had overlooked. It's a little-known fact that my parents were killed when I was a child."

Jack tipped his head and twitched his whiskers. "I'm sorry, milady, but I don't understand the connection."

"When I was orphaned, I was taken in by a Kataran woman, who adopted me and raised me as her own."

The mouse didn't immediately respond, but continued to puzzle over the revelation. A minute passed before his expression brightened with surprise. "Oh! I see! You're saying that Lord Frisky is also adopted!"

Felicia laughed. "Almost! Not him, but certainly his ancestor. The last of the Wagajops had been childless, but they took in an orphaned waif and adopted him as their own; he became their heir, and the lands and titles were passed down ever since. Lord Frisky is the legitimate heir to Frisky Manor and all that comes with it. As I said, it was obvious, but I hadn't thought of it right off. But it was right there in the family history, all duly recorded and witnessed. I had Jermond bring me the books so that we could verify it. Furthermore, we discovered that the estate is smaller than it should be; seems that one or two of his neighbors have encroached on his lands and annexed it as their own over the generations. Looks like they may be too busy scrambling to fight to keep it to be too overly concerned with whispering poison into the king's ear."

"I see!" Jack was rubbing his muzzle thoughtfully, his whiskers twitching with excitement. "I'm going to have my work cut out for me, aren't I? There will be assays to make, damages and fines to assess... dear me! Jermond and I will have to get on this right away!"

"It can wait," said the vixen. She rose from the chair, still clutching the cloak about her. "We still have unfinished business," she said sternly. Jack's face fell in apprehension. "You still haven't explained your behavior and your deception to me yet."

Jack bowed his head in shame. He set the candle back on the table. "I'm sorry," he said in a small voice. "I meant no harm. But I –" He faltered and struggled for words. "I just wanted to meet you."

Felicia raised an eyebrow.

"And – and I knew that a fine lady like yourself wouldn't be interested in an ordinary mouse like myself... just an accountant. You'd want to be impressed by somebody bold and flamboyant."

"So you lied to me."

"Yes."

"To impress me."

Jack swallowed and nodded. "Yes."

"That's rather dangerous to do with a sorceress." the vixen told him severely.

"I know – but..." The mouse steeled himself and straightened his back. "Better to have tried and failed than to not have made the attempt!" Felicia said nothing but continued to stare at him, her green eyes glowing in the candlelight. "What's more," Jack added while the spark of courage was still present, "given half a chance, I'd do it again!"

"Would you?"

"Yes! If I must go down in flames, then let it be the flames of passion!" With a sudden cry of alarm, the mouse covered his mouth with both hands. "Oh, my! Did I really say that!?" His eyes widened in horror and humiliation, but the vixen threw her head back and laughed heartily. Jack cringed for a moment, but Felicia reached out and placed a hand upon his shoulder.

"Ah, well, Sir Jack! You've succeeded!" she laughed more softly. "I am impressed." She slipped into the arms of the surprised mouse and kissed him. "Now," she whispered to him as she allowed her cloak to fall to the floor. "Would you like to see some magic?"

With that, she reached out and snuffed out the candle flame between her fingers.

This story originally appeared in Tales of the Tai-Pan Universe #39, *July 2005.* Tales of the Tai-Pan Universe *is both a fanzine and the group of (mostly) Seattle Furry fans who produce that fanzine, the Tai-Pan Literary & Arts Project, a registered not-for-profit corporation. The project dates back to March 1988, when seven Seattle Furry fans had dinner at a Denny's during the Norwescon X s-f convention. They decided to publish a shared-world Furry space-opera fanzine, set in the 36th century against an interstellar background, with a group of writers and artists featuring the same Furry characters, in stories edited to be mutually consistent. The first issue of what was then titled* The Tai-Pan, *named after the merchant cargo spaceship that was the original focus of the stories, appeared in March 1991. The fanzine has averaged two issues a year since then, currently up to #50, edited at monthly social/editorial dinner meetings among the Project's editorial staff, which has been headed by Gene Breshears since 1994. The slow pace is largely due to making sure that each new story is consistent in the increasingly-detailed 36th-century saga of the Furry crews of the Tai-Pan and the other gradually-added spaceships with which she intersects – the Quantum Lady (a luxurious cruise ship), the Iktomé (a pirate vessel masquerading as a heavy freighter), and the Ramanujan (a scientific research ship) – plus the planets of the Gold Road region of the galaxy in which they all roam.*

Kristin Fontaine is the current Recording Secretary and Associate Editor of the Tai-Pan Project, as well as a frequent author of its stories since #4. "In His Own Country" is a direct sequel to the two-part "Dancing on My Grave" by Gene Breshears in #24 & #26, which dealt with an unsuccessful but bloody pirate attack on the Tai-Pan aided by the sabotage of one of her own crew. The protagonist is Aubrey Took, the Tai-Pan's young skunk assistant security officer, who is suddenly thrust from what had been a nominal and fairly solitary position into the aftermath of a life-threatening situation. He has been forced to kill for the first time, and he suddenly is promoted after the death of the security chief. He now has the safety of all his crewmates resting on his ability to do his job well. This is the story that makes Aubrey really feel like one of the Tai-Pan's crew.

In His Own Country

story by Kristin Fontaine
illustrations by C.D. Woodbury

35.84.10

Rasputin entered engineering, pleased to see that the frantic working pace of an hour ago had settled down to a calm, by-the-numbers routine. Blood still stained the walls where the pirates had died at the hands of Mac and his crew but the bodies had been removed and the floor was now dry.

MacQuarrie, J.T., Ajax, Citron, and Sky were spread throughout the massive space. Rasputin couldn't see Citron or Sky but he could hear both otters' rapid-fire patter from behind one of the start-up reactors.

"Cap'n on deck," J.T. bellowed, her voice carrying to every part of the echoing room.

"Come to check on me progress?" MacQuarrie asked, handing a report back to Ajax. The red panda took it and headed quickly back to where Citron and Sky were working.

"Yes. I heard a change in the engines as I was walking down here," Rasputin said.

"I'll make an engineer of you yet." The gorilla was pleased. "We're nearly up to full power."

"That's good news." Rasputin looked at his own computer and frowned. "Aki's given me a preliminary report on our casualties. Barbara Frise and Shirogiin Kuroi are dead. Bob and Arther are struggling—Aki and Isis are still working on them. Walter's been drafted to look after Kelson and Gaitz. If either Bob or Arther survive surgery they must have access to a full-scale hospital as soon as possible."

MacQuarrie pulled in on himself, water standing in the corners of his eyes. J.T. looked away from his distress. "The engines don't seem to have been damaged by mishandling," J.T. said after a long pause. "But the log shows that they tried to restart several times after the pirates took control—apparently spontaneously."

"The problem now, Cap'n," MacQuarrie said, "is that we're going much faster than I'd like this deep in system. Getting to Serengeti quickly won't be a problem. Stopping in time might be. We may be forced to veer wide. That would add five to seven days to our ETA."

"Bob and Arther don't have time to waste," Rasputin said, tightly.

"I hear that. Rufus and Spike are running the fuel numbers now."

"I'm appointing Eli temporary first mate until Aki certifies Gaitz for duty."

"What about Kiakiru?" J.T. asked, puzzled.

"We're down two pilots as it is. Kia won't have time to supervise another shift, and with Gaitz in sickbay, we're down two shift commanders. Work with Kiakiru, Faust, and Eli, and give me the fastest possible arrival timeline."

"How is Aubrey holding up?" J.T. asked, looking at Mac.

"Better than I expected," Rasputin said. "He's searching Frise's quarters now. I've assigned Karaya to help him set up a monitoring post in crew country. Aubrey will be setting up his investigation from there."

"Stan volunteered to come down and help us out," Mac said. "Knowing what load Aubrey is carrying, I'd rather second Stan to him."

"That's a good thought. I certainly can't pull anyone else away from their departments. Communications is the only group that has a full crew and Tina's going to be dumping the computer log analysis on them."

"We've worked short before," Mac said. "You just tell Aki to fix my people. I'll handle engineering."

* * *

Aubrey's search of Barbie's quarters yielded very little. Her clothes had been left in place, but jewelry, personal comp, and small items of high monetary or sentimental value were missing. Aubrey made a note to search for a suitcase or bag containing her effects. She hadn't had it with her by the time she and the leader of the pirates took the bridge.

The small skunk sighed. The Tai-Pan wasn't equipped for a full-scale crime scene evaluation. Now that he was certain there were no time bombs waiting in the cabin, he would have to seal the room and read up on the proper procedures.

He wasn't sure what to do next. The prisoners were contained in one of the empty passenger cabins. He wondered if Shirogiin would handle the interrogations?

He stopped short, reminded afresh that his mentor was dead. He was on his own.

"I don't know enough," Aubrey said to the empty room. No answers came. Aubrey battled his own inertia, left Barbie's cabin, and locked it down.

Karaya was coming down the hall with a small cargo sled. "The captain asked me to help you set up a monitoring post near the prisoners."

The sled had a desk and a chair perched on it. After a few minutes the hare and skunk were able to find a niche in the corridor that would allow someone sitting at the desk to see both the monitor and the door to the makeshift brig.

"Why are all the prisoners in the same room?" Karaya asked.

"It was the best we could come up with quickly," Aubery said, defensively. The skunk switched the datastream from his handheld to the monitoring station. "I have been recording their conversations since we locked them in. If they have tried to get their stories straight we will have a full A/V record of it."

"It would have been better if you'd separated them from the beginning," Karaya said pedantically.

"I know procedure." Aubrey's exhaustion was the only thing keeping him from shouting. "And so far all I've heard is the two ferrets arguing over whether the ship is haunted or not. The bear hasn't said anything at all."

Karaya smoothed back one long ear and changed the subject. "I'm off-shift now," she said. "I could keep watch while you get some rest." She watched him think over her offer. "I cleared it with Jasmine and the captain. He's the one who sent me down here."

"Right." Aubrey blew out a deep breath. "I do need a break, but first I need to go find Stan. Call me when you need to be relieved."

* * *

He found Stan in the cargo hold, clearing a path to a refrigerated container.

"What are you doing?" Aubrey asked.

"Eli says that TPFM 268731 is empty this trip. I'm going to hook it up to the power grid and make a temporary morgue," Stan said, pointing out the container.

"What did we last haul in there?" Aubrey asked.

Stan checked his wristcomp. "Barrels of fish, sealed." He scrolled down the holo-display. "Says here the customer took delivery of the entire shipment with no loss of cargo." He read further, "My notes say that I cleaned it out before we left port."

"It should be as good a place as any then," Aubrey commented. "Where are the bodies?"

"On a cargo sled behind those containers over there," Stan said. "I couldn't work when I could see them."

Aubrey frowned. If Shirogiin had been alive Aubrey could have overseen this task while Shirogiin searched Barbie's quarters.

Stan caught Aubrey's expression. "I did have one of the bots record everything before I moved the bodies."

"I should have looked at everything myself," Aubrey said, feeling the quicksand of the investigation rising.

"There wasn't time," Stan said shortly.

Aubrey nodded, not really in agreement, but more to keep himself from saying something he would regret. Stan was trying to help.

* * *

Rasputin keyed open the door to the bridge. Chester and Satin started in their seats at the sound. Seeing he was no threat, they settled back to work.

"Eli." Rasputin gestured to the command chair. "I'm here to relieve you."

The raccoon jumped out of the chair to make room for the captain. "Thank goodness."

"It's normal to say, 'I stand relieved,'" Rasputin said mildly.

"I just hope Gaitz gets his voice back soon," Eli said fervently.

"So do we all." Rasputin settled in his chair. "Any word from Aki?"

"Not yet," Eli called over his shoulder as he exited the bridge.

Rasputin turned to his navigator. "Satin, what's our status?"

"We'll be dumping velocity in ten minutes, sir," Satin said as she watched numbers flow across the navigation board. "Once I have the numbers from this dump, I'll know if we'll need to swing wide or not."

"Does Aki know the plan?" Rasputin asked.

"Yes, sir. She asked Chester to give her a countdown from the five-minute mark."

"Very well, carry on." Rasputin turned his attention to his own station. He listened as his crew prepped their boards for the stutter warp that would determine if they could dock at Fossey Station on the first pass. Getting it right would give Bob and Arther a better chance of survival.

Satin counted it down and Rael hit the mark. Rasputin felt a slight shift sideways as the stutter warp kicked in. He waited for Satin to work through the new numbers that were coming off her board.

"That's done it, sir!" she said. "We're well within normal speed and I have a clear course to Fossey."

"Lock it in, Satin, best speed. Chester, confirm that Fossey knows we're coming in damaged and carrying prisoners. Get us as high on the priority docking list as you can."

"Yes, sir," Chester said, all business.

A message appeared on Rasputin's board. Aki wanted to talk to him. He keyed on his headset and watched as Aki's face appeared on the monitor. The knot in his gut tightened at the sight of her tear-streaked muzzle.

"Yes, Aki?" Rasputin said. At the mention of the doctor's name the bridge crew fell silent. They weren't trying to listen in but were unable to carry on with normal business. If Aki was on the line, she wasn't in the operating room.

"I regret..." Aki choked up, then took a deep breath. "I regret to inform you that Arther Debroge died as of 1802 ship time. The damage to his brain proved too extensive to repair."

"And Bob?"

"Bob is critical but stable. The operation to repair the damage to his neck and skull is a conditional success. I'll know more in a few days."

"Thank you, Aki," Rasputin said softly.

"I'm going off duty," the exhausted ermine said. "Isis and Walter will monitor the patients."

"You're relieved," Rasputin said, simultaniously sending an order to Chester's board, putting Aki on do-not-disturb status.

"Yes, sir." Aki signed off.

Rasputin looked up at the bridge crew. They had heard his side of the conversation with Aki and he could tell by the droop in their ears and tails that they had guessed the news. Best to make it official. "Aki just reported that Bob has survived his surgery and is in recovery." Rasputin felt tears welling in his own eyes. "Arther is dead."

* * *

Aubrey put his head down on the cool surface of the desk in his quarters. He couldn't bring himself to work in the small office he and Kuroi had shared, and the monitoring station was too public to allow him to concentrate.

Karaya was covering for him once again. He just needed a few minutes to collect his thoughts and begin drafting a timeline of the events since the Tai-Pan had jumped into Serengeti. Before he could do that he would need to take his head out of his hands and start the document. He closed his eyes instead.

Shirogiin was dead.

Arther was dead.

Barbie was dead, killed by his own hand.

That was even harder to wrap his thoughts around. Acerbic and sometimes annoying, Barbie had been crew, one of the people he was supposed to protect. Now no one would mourn her, at least not publicly. People were already Not Talking About her, finding ways to construct sentences so that her name wasn't used, or using only her last name. As if the person "Frise" was somehow different than "Barbie."

Maybe she was.

Aubrey opened his eyes and lifted his head from the desk. Regardless of the name, he was required to investigate her life and document her death.

* * *

Aubrey checked his monitor. It was nearly time to relieve Karaya.

He closed down the timeline he had begun and checked his in-box. There was a note from Aki inquiring as to who should preform the autopsies: the Tai-Pan's medical staff or the Serengeti security force. Aubrey started to compose a note to Shirogiin and was brought up short as his fingers refused to type the dead Kilinji's name.

He re-routed the query to Rasputin, snapped his terminal shut, and went to relieve Karaya.

A wave of anger swept over him as he neared the monitoring station. Anger at all the pirates had taken from him, at what Barbie had done to his ship, and to his crew. His fur stood on end. He could feel heat radiating from his ears. He wanted to run screaming down to the hold and throw the bodies of the dead pirates out the nearest airlock— followed closely by the living pirates in his custody.

He paused in the empty corridor. Karaya was just one turn away, waiting for him to come and relieve her. Aubrey took a deep breath and settled his fur.

Shirogiin guide me. I'm the responsible one now.

Karaya looked him over as he rounded the last bend. "You don't look very rested," she said doubtfully.

Aubrey waved her off. "Anything to report?"

"I bet you didn't eat any of the food Stan brought you either," Karaya said, continuing her own train of thought. Aubrey thought guiltily of the now-cold tray of food sitting on the floor of his quarters. He hadn't even taken the lid off when Stan brought it to him.

Much to Aubrey's frustration, Karaya correctly interpreted what had not been said. "I knew I should've told Stan to stand over you and make you eat," she said.

"Anything to report?" he repeated, teeth clenched in a not-quite-growl.

Karaya froze for a moment and then reached for a control on the monitor. "The two ferrets have done nothing but sleep, eat, and argue." She stroked her long, trailing ears, pushing one back to drape over her shoulder.

"What do they argue about?" Aubrey asked.

"I could hear one trying to blame everything that had gone wrong on a 'ship's ghost.'" She shrugged. "They were yelling at each other, and at one point I thought I'd have to find someone to help me break it up. The whole time that was going on, the bear sat in the corner murmuring to himself. I turned up the gain on the mic, to hear what he was saying. He was praying." Karaya frowned. "I hope his higher power wasn't listening. He finally got fed up with the bickering brothers and shouted them down. It's been quiet in there since. I really think we should separate them."

"Yes, yes, I know," said Aubrey, testily. "As soon as I figure out a way to secure them separately we'll do it."

"Don't put it off too long," Karaya said as she got up from the chair. "Things are getting tense in there."

* * *

Rasputin read the query from security that came up on his board on the bridge. "Dae, is Eli still awake?"

"Aye, sir. He's active in the system," the husky replied.

Rasputin pulled Eli up on his board. The raccoon came into focus wearing a nightshirt. "Eli, I need someone to research Serengeti police procedures. Aubrey needs to know who should do the autopsies."

Eli yawned. "I was just about to follow your order and get some sleep. How urgent is it?"

"With the time lag between here and Fossey Station, we should get someone on it as quickly as possible."

"So we need a researcher who is actually awake." Eli yawned again.

Rasputin mulled over the possibilities. He glanced at the medical update from Isis, and put Eli on hold. He read over the orders: No heavy lifting or straining. Complete rest of vocal cords. Otherwise, he was to be released to light duty upon Rasputin's request.

"Eli, it looks like Gaitz could handle the job."

Eli perked up. "He's cleared for duty?"

"Light duty, no talking."

"That's some good news to sleep on."

"Aye," Rasputin said softly, as he cut the connection.

* * *

Aubrey walked down the corridor to sick bay trying to think of what he could say to Gaitz that wouldn't make the first mate feel worse. Aubrey didn't want to provoke the Rhianian into responding and further hurting his voice but, the skunk couldn't help thinking how terribly alone he must be feeling in his mourning of Barbie.

He rapped on the door frame to let Isis know he was there, and to give the snoozing bird a chance to come to full alertness.

"Why are you still on duty?" Aubrey asked curiously.

"We drew straws and Aki lost," Isis said, curtly. "I could ask you the same thing."

"I'm here to meet with Gaitz," Aubrey said, sidestepping the issue of sleep. Isis turned her head to focus one eye, then the other, on the skunk. Whatever she was thinking, she kept it to herself.

"Rasputin alerted me that you have a job for him," Isis confirmed.

Aubrey quickly outlined the job requirements and Isis nodded.

"That is just the thing. Gaitz needs something to focus on. Aki doesn't want him alone and idle any more than can be helped—at least not for a while." Isis led the way to her patient.

Gaitz was sitting on the bed, fully dressed and reading from his viewer. He looked up as he heard the rustle of Isis's feathers and his lips turned up in a ghost of a smile when he saw Aubrey. He opened his mouth. Isis snapped her foot-long beak at him and he closed it again.

"Aubrey's come with captain's orders to put you to work," Isis said. "It's work you can do here so I can continue to monitor your progress."

Aubrey felt a curious reluctance to say anything. It was as if Gaitz's prescribed silence was his as well.

He ported Aki's query over to Gaitz's viewer. The system flag indicating new data started flashing. They must have just passed a navigation buoy. He keyed open the flag. Sure enough, there was the response from the report they'd sent in twenty-three hours ago, reporting the pirate attack and prisoners and requesting instructions from local law enforcement.

"Your job just got simpler," he said aloud.

Gaitz clenched his jaw to keep himself from responding.

Aubrey took a quick look at the file. "I think I spoke too soon. It looks like they sent us their entire law library."

"You may set up your work there," Isis said, sweeping her wing toward a table in a corner of the lab. "Remember, no talking! Not even to yourself."

Gaitz nodded curtly to Isis, made himself comfortable at the table, and set to work on the data bonanza.

* * *

"Cap'n," Rael Fellis said as the shift changed on the bridge. "Can I have a quick chat with you?"

"Faust, remain at your station. Tina, you have the con," Rasputin said briskly.

"Aye, sir," Te Teko said as the shift change continued around her. The panda steered Rael out into the corridor and Te Teko shut the door to the bridge behind them.

"Yes, Rael?"

"I've a concern with the duty roster."

"There's not much I can do about it," Rasputin said. "I'm afraid the double shifts are with us for the duration."

"It's not my schedule I'm worried about— Kia, Faust, and I have a good thing going," the big lion said, stuffing his hands in his pockets. "It's Aubrey, he's running himself ragged keeping tabs on prisoners and rounding up evidence. And I heard Cory getting on his case for not eating. You know that boy doesn't have a spare gram on him."

"I'm aware of the problem," Rasputin said. "Stan and Karaya have been helping with guard duty. I can't spare anyone else."

"I still think he needs someone to ride herd on him," Rael said stubbornly. "He's way out of his league. I'd volunteer myself if we weren't missing two pilots already."

"Thank you for your concern, Mr. Fellis," Rasputin said. "I will take it under advisement."

"It's not that I don't think he's doing a good job," the lion said. "But he's just a kid—and he's wearing himself out trying to do it all."

"You have made your point," Rasputin said, exasperated. "Return to your duty station and relieve Faust."

"Aye, sir," the lion said. The door to the bridge opened and Rael slipped inside to take his place in the pilot's seat.

* * *

Aubrey heard the take-hold klaxon and T'Narah's voice counting down to stutterwarp. His vision flickered for a moment and then everything returned to normal. He checked the terminal at the monitoring station.

The navigation report confirmed that the most recent velocity dump was part of the flight plan. The next one was scheduled in six hours. The Tai-Pan was on course for Fossey Station.

Aubrey glared at the prisoners on the monitor. The bear was sitting in the corner and the ferrets were asleep. He still hadn't thought of a good way to separate them—at least they hadn't killed each other, yet.

The skunk shifted in his chair and keyed open the medical status report from Aki. Gaitz had been released to full duty, Kelson was on light duty, and Bob's condition was unchanged, holding at critical but stable.

Aubrey worked his way through automated security log reports and recordings made by the bots. He noticed that Stan had put an alert in the system to check on Shirogiin and Arther's cabins when time permitted. Aubrey followed the thought through. Shirogiin, at least, would enjoy one last chance to provide a service to the ship.

He keyed in a request for Stan to join him. The hyena showed up a few minutes later.

"I've had an idea for how we can separate the prisoners," Aubrey said to the puzzled-looking hyena. "Would you mind if I cleaned out Arther and Shirogiin's cabins?"

Stan understood immediately. "We could use them for cells. That would be fine with me. Will you be all right? It can be spooky, going though a dead person's things."

"I'll be fine," Aubrey said firmly.

"Before you start you'd better check with the captain," Stan said as he ported over his procedures for closing out a cabin. "You can get some storage crates from locker D-19. I have a stash there."

Aubrey glanced at the files that Stan dropped on his handcomp. "I'll check with him next. How long can you cover the desk?"

"Will six hours do you?"

"Thanks, Stan," Aubrey said, and went to meet with Rasputin.

* * *

"Are you sure you want to help with this?" Aubrey asked Gaitz. The first mate had volunteered to help once Aubrey had cleared the suggestion with Rasputin.

"I'm sure," the Rhianian said, only a slight roughness to his voice. "It is one of my duties as first mate."

Aubrey made no mention of Barbie's sealed cabin. He and Gaitz stopped by the storage locker that Stan had mentioned and stacked some of the storage crates on a small cargo sled.

Neither of them said much as they walked the sled to crew country.

"I'll take Shirogiin's room," Aubrey suggested, handing Gaitz the keycard to Arther's quarters.

Gaitz nodded, took the card and a crate from the sled.

Aubrey walked down the hall and keyed open Shirogiin's quarters. Shirogiin had been one of the most private individuals on the ship. He had mentioned to Aubrey, once, how important it was for him to have a space apart from the rest of the crew.

Shirogiin's scent had not yet dissipated. Its fine, slight musk caused Aubrey to look over his shoulder. Aubrey felt like a trespasser on his mentor's sacred ground. His heart beat faster.

He took a deep breath, as Kuroi had taught him. Kuroi's scent intensified and for a moment Aubrey could feel his mentor's presence.

He tried to focus on the here and now. Kuroi's cabin was clean and bare, with a single wall hanging written in Kilinji. Kuroi's collection of antique weapons was stored in the built-ins along one wall of the cabin. Shirogiin would never come back, never pull the bookmark from the book he had been reading, never return the cup on his nightstand to the galley.

Aubrey exhaled gently, reluctant to disturb the air. A tear threaded its way down the side of his muzzle. He could taste the faint salt tang as he went to get a packing crate from the sled.

He found Gaitz at the sled, staring into space with tears darkening his face fur. The Rhianian made no sound in his grief. The skunk reached out and gently took the empty crate from the first mate. Gaitz seemed not to notice.

Aubrey steered Gaitz to take a seat on the sled. He sat next to the first mate and put one arm around him.

Gaitz hugged Aubrey tightly to him. The small skunk was forcibly reminded of how much strength lay in Gaitz's wiry arms. Gaitz had carried him not too long ago.

Gaitz's body shook with unvoiced sobs.

Aubrey was overwhelmed. This shouldn't be happening. Gaitz was... older... stronger.

Gaitz began making odd little gasping sounds. Aubrey pulled away enough to look the Rhianian in the face and ensure that he was breathing properly.

The spasm passed. Gaitz's breathing quieted and his grip on Aubrey relaxed. Aubrey shifted away but did not get up from the sled.

"I'm sorry, Aubrey." Gaitz put his head in his claw-tipped hands. "I thought I could handle this."

"You're not ready," Aubrey said quietly. "It's all right."

"I should be able to do this," Gaitz said fiercely. "I did it for Chance and all the other friends I lost at New Queensland. Why break down now?"

Aubrey thought he knew the answer but kept his thoughts behind his teeth. *New Queensland wasn't your fault.* "Give yourself time," was all he said.

"I don't think I can go back in there," Gaitz said.

"Don't worry about it. I'll do both rooms."

"You're sure?" Gaitz asked, rapidly resuming his adult role.

"I'm sure. Besides, the captain needs you on-shift. Get some sleep and you'll feel better."

Gaitz stood, steadied himself, and walked away.

Aubrey picked up the crate and returned to Shirogiin's room.

Aubrey loaded the last crate of Arther's belongings onto the cargo sled next to Shirogiin's possessions. Neither spacer had left much behind. Aubrey checked his comp and found that Eli had responded to his question on where to secure the crates until the Tai-Pan could dock at Fossey Station. Aubrey switched his comp over to remote mode and guided the sled down to one of the smaller storage closets just off the main cargo hold.

It took longer than he thought to transfer the crates to the locker and secure them. He was on his way back to the makeshift brig when his comp beeped.

Karaya's voice came out of the tiny speaker. "Aubrey, I need you back at the desk. Where are you?"

"I'm on my way," Aubrey said, picking up his pace. "What's the trouble?" Sudden visions of the bear tearing the ferrets limb from limb filled his mind. She had warned him that there was trouble brewing.

"I'm covering for Stan but I'm going to be late for my bridge shift," the hare said sharply.

"I'm on my way—I'll let Jasmine know you're on your way to her." Aubrey sprinted down the hall, caught the lift up two levels, and arrived at the security desk only slightly winded. He waved Karaya out of the chair and on to her duties on the bridge. He quickly checked the video feed and the security log and found, to his relief, that the prisoners were ignoring each other for once. There was no blood on the walls, no hard-to-answer questions about accidents to prisoners in his care—just three very bored-looking pirates.

Aubrey flicked the security log closed more forcefully than necessary. "Stupid kid," he muttered to himself. He had gotten himself all worked up over nothing.

He thumped his head onto the desk. He wanted to hit something. He wanted to cry. He'd done what he had to. Couldn't he just stop now?

* * *

"Okay, folks." Rasputin got the attention of his senior staff. "Let's keep this short so we can get back to work or sleep. I want your suggestions on a replacement for Shirogiin Kuroi. We need someone in that position as soon as possible. We'll be docking at Serengeti in twenty-seven hours."

"I thought Aubrey was doing Shirogiin's job," Eli said.

"He's been doing his best to cover both positions," Rasputin said. "But nothing formal has been decided."

"Not that I am anxious to lose any of my staff," Jasmine said, "but Karaya has some security training. She's been working extra shifts to help

Aubrey out. She may have more formal training than Aubrey in this sort of work."

"Thank you, Jasmine," Rasputin said. "Any other suggestions?"

"Depends," MacQuarrie chimed in from further down the table. "Are ye talking about a temporary or permanent deal?"

"Temporary, at this time," Rasputin said. "After this disaster, I want to take my time hiring the next person."

"Me an' J.T. have been talking. She'd be willing to take over if it's just temporary—six months at the outside."

"Mac, I can't take one of your engineers!" Rasputin said.

"It sounds like you're wanting to give young Aubrey some backup. We can manage without J.T. for a bit and she's got the chops to do the job. She served with the Military Police during her enlistment. She's helped Shirogiin out before when we were short-handed. She won't take guff from anyone." The gorilla turned to Jasmine. "And as much as I like Karaya, I've a feeling she's a bit better at inciting trouble than stopping it."

Rasputin waited a bit to see if anyone else had a comment. He noticed that Gaitz was shifting uncomfortably in his chair. Rasputin leaned back and waited.

"Before we write Aubrey off," Gaitz said, his voice quiet and hoarse, "I'd like to remind everyone that he stopped four heavily armed pirates with only the help of Jonesy. He saved my life. I think he can do the job. I'd trust him to protect both the ship and our lives."

Rasputin saw Tina nodding and Kiakiru flexing his flukes and made a note of their reactions. "He's been under tremendous strain this last week. Mac, I'm going to take you up on your offer. Have J.T. set up a time to meet with me and we'll discuss terms."

"Aye, Cap'n," the gorilla said.

Rasputin looked around as the meeting broke up. His staff were all moving slowly. He had expected a more spirited debate—with at least one joke about Chester or Frith as possible candidates. The staff shortage was taking its toll on all of them. The sooner they got into port, and got some downtime, the better. He knew the real help would be getting the dead bodies out of the hold and the live pirates off the ship.

Rasputin gathered his own comp and headed down the hall to his quarters. Maybe this time he would take the sleeping draught Aki had prescribed. Gods knew he needed it.

* * *

Aubrey heard footsteps in the corridor and sat up before Karaya came around the corner.

"You're early," he said to the hare.

"Not by much—I figured you could use a break." Karaya's long ears hung down her back, giving away very little about her emotions.

"I really appreciate the extra shifts you've been pulling," Aubrey said, all business.

"Everyone's pulling extra duty—how could I not help out?" Karaya sounded sad. "Besides, I was trained for this. I just should have figured out what was going on with Barbie sooner."

"You couldn't have stopped her," Aubrey said quietly.

"Yes, I could have!" Karaya hit the desk with her small fist. "I'm supposed to see the things no one else does. I just didn't want to intrude. And I thought that it was something petty, like Frise being jealous of Satin," Karaya said bitterly.

"She was jealous of Satin?" Aubrey was surprised.

"Desperately so," Karaya said. "Remember, she hired on while Satin was off at that hospital on Dunstan. While Satin was gone, Barbie had Kelson hopping. Frankly, I think that's part of the reason Barbie seduced Gaitz. There were other ways for her to access the system, but not in a way that would hurt Gaitz, and by extension, Satin."

Aubrey's attention was caught by part of what Karaya said. "Could you write up the alternate methods she could have used to get the information?"

"Sure, no problem," Karaya said. She waved a hand at the monitor. "I'll do it while I keep an eye on the bickering boys."

"It's gotten a lot quieter since we separated them." Aubrey rubbed his eyes. "I'll be in the security office for a few hours—I'm still trying to assemble all the recordings of the incident that I can. Not all of the cameras were working during the power outage. I promised Mac I'd send him a list of the cameras that failed so he could add them to the list of things to check."

"Just remember to get some sleep." Karaya sat down behind the desk. "Stan will be relieving me so you should have a full eight hours before you need to be back here."

* * *

Aubrey worked in the security office, sorting the recordings. Vid after vid of empty hallways, bots catching glimpses of each other in their cameras, then an occasional brutal flash of pirate violence. The most extensive coverage of the damage done by and to the pirates was from the cameras in engineering, the main cargo hold, and the bridge.

Aubrey had already reviewed the engineering footage. He had put off the cargo hold and bridge as long as he could by watching hour after hour of quiet corridors and normal crew interaction. He had only found two sequences showing Frise's betrayal of the ship. She'd disabled or avoided most of the cameras but there were a few in engineering that she must not have known about. That, or she had not cared that her murderous actions toward Bob, Arther, and Shirogiin had been recorded.

He had felt sick on the bridge, just after shooting her. He had managed to hide his nausea by focusing on Gaitz and Kelson, both of whom Frise had injured.

Now, cold anger soured his stomach as he watched her gun down Arther and Bob and drag their bodies into hiding. When Shirogiin entered engineering there was no one to warn him. Aubrey caught himself before calling out to the recording, as if he could stop it from happening, bring them back by replaying the recording and stopping just short of Barbie's trechery. *If only I had been faster. If I had seen the signs. Karaya is not the only one who should have noticed.* Tears blurred his vision. Gaitz and Barbie had seemed so happy together.

He cued the last recording. The pirates were dead or incapacitated by the time this recording was made—all but one. He would face what he had done and try to learn from it as Shirogiin had taught him to.

The door chimed, startling Aubrey into twitching off the viewer with a guilty start as the captain entered the small space.

"Sorry to disturb you, Aubrey. I need to speak with you," Rasputin said, settling into the larger of the two office chairs that crowded round the desk.

"It's no trouble, sir." Aubrey folded his hands in his lap. "How can I be of assistance?"

"What were you working on?" Rasputin asked, ignoring the skunk's question.

"Trying to see if I could have done better, sir," Aubrey said. "Shirogiin—" his voice broke on the name. "Shirogiin recommended a performance review as soon as possible after a security breach. No one else has had time so I thought I would do for myself."

"You've had a bit too much of doing for yourself in the past week, son," Rasputin said. "I wish I could have gotten to this sooner, but with the shortage of bridge crew and with trying to get the ship slowed down and on course to Fossey, I've been busy."

"I've got everything under control," Aubrey said, anxiously.

"At the cost of your sleep and meal periods," Rasputin said. "You've done a fine job handling things so far. I'm noting that in your personnel record." He paused long enough to let the skunk take in his words. "However, I need security to be rock-solid at Serengeti and that means more than one person doing the work."

"Stan and Karaya have been helping me," Aubrey protested.

"I know," Rasputin said, softly. "However, the crew is still very shaken up. It's going to be months before we all stop jumping at every clang or bump this ship makes. It's normal, but it means that I need to do all I can to make the crew feel protected. To that end, I've asked J.T. to step in as temporary head of security until we can find a replacement for Kuroi."

Aubrey felt a strange mixture of relief and disappointment. He knew he needed the help but he was suddenly reluctant to give up control of the investigation. He saw by the set of Rasputin's black-furred ears that the decision was made.

"Yes, sir," he said, bowing to the captain's authority.

* * *

Aubrey hustled down the hallway to Kuroi's... he stopped the thought. It was J.T.'s office now and he was going to be late if he didn't hurry. Aubrey swallowed hard.

"Morning... ahh...," he trailed off wondering what to call her now that J.T. was his section chief. Ma'am was a death-wish, Sir was a military pretense, and just J.T. seemed disrespectful.

"Morning, Aubrey," J.T. rumbled. If she noticed the skunk's confusion she gave no sign of it. "Come with me, I want to go over a few things on our way to the meeting with the rest of the senior staff?"

"Should I really be attending the meeting?" Aubrey asked, diverted to this new worry. "Juniors don't, usually."

J.T. waved a white paw dismissively. "We have a job to do and I'm not going to let you wiggle out of the boring parts. Besides, I don't want the rest of the senior staff to get used to me as Chief of Security. I'm doing this job as a favor to the captain. We've got to sort out how Frise sold us out to the pirates and keep security running smoothly all at the same time—that's more than enough work for us."

Aubrey shrank in on himself, missing Shirogiin more at that moment than he had in days.

J.T. narrowed her eyes and glanced down at Aubrey as they made their way down the hall to the briefing room. "I'm not Kuroi," she said, in a deep, quiet rumble. "I want you to work with me on this."

Aubrey nodded his assent. He couldn't trust his voice. They walked through the door to the briefing room.

"Glad you could join us," Captain Rasputin said from his chair at the head of the table. All the senior staff, save Gaitz, were settling in. The Rhianian was on the bridge, keeping the Tai-Pan true to her course.

J.T. took a seat at the table. Aubrey set a chair against a wall, trying to be unobtrusive.

"I invited Aubrey to attend this meeting," J.T. said in advance of any questions. "He and I will be working closely together to figure out what went wrong and how we can prevent such attacks in the future."

"We know what went wrong," Jasmine said, puzzled. "Barbie betrayed us to those pirates."

"But we want to know how she did it," Te Teko said. "She got an awful lot done without any of us noticing."

"Exactly," J.T. said. "Barbie managed to hide the charges for our weapons, infiltrate the computer system, initiate a full engine shutdown, and hide an entire pirate ship from view. That's a helluva lot to pull off."

"Do you think she had help?" Jasmine asked, in a very small voice.

"On the Tai-Pan?" J.T. asked. "Nothing in the records points to it so far, but that is one of the reasons we need to do a thorough investigation. Officers of the Serengeti Port Authority have asked for depositions from the entire surviving crew to allow them to prosecute the three bastards in custody."

"I had intended that we would lay over for a few extra days at Serengeti," Rasputin said. "Bob needs some specialized help. Correct Aki?"

"He and I have appointments at a neuro-clinic," Aki said crisply. "We will be out the door as soon as the ship docks."

Silence spread around the table. MacQuarrie swallowed hard. "Losing Arther, having Bob out, and loanin' J.T. to security is putting quite a strain on my other lads. Walter has been a godsend. I'd hire him away from you, Tina, if that wouldn't leave you short. Sky is working hard but he's takin' a bit too much of a load on his stubby shoulders."

"I'll come in and help out on my off shift," J.T. said.

"No, lassie. You've an important job to do and I agree with the cap'n, you're the one to do it. Find out all you can—we'll work on getting the ship back together. You and Aubrey—you make it safe for her to fly."

"Aye, Mac, we'll do our best," J.T. said softly.

Rasputin checked his watch "We'll be docking in fourteen hours. How is the crew holding up? Is there anyone in the rotation that we should be concerned about?"

"It-t is hard on every <kt> one," Kiakiru said. "Our family mourns."

"I've seen a general increase in requests for sleep aids," Aki said briskly. "However, nothing that is out of line given the stress we are all under."

"It was a big help to get Gaitz back in the rotation," Eli commented. "I'm relieved to be out of the hot seat."

"I am a bit worried about Tyr," Jasmine said.

"Oh?" Tina looked up from her notes.

"Maybe we can talk after this meeting," Jasmine suggested.

"I'll want to know if something is affecting his performance," Rasputin said.

"Yes, sir," Jasmine said.

"You bet," Tina chimed in.

"Have you set a time for services for Arther and Shirogiin?" MacQuarrie asked.

"No," Rasputin said, rubbing his face. "I'm afraid it will have to wait until we are docked. I'd like everyone who wants to attend to be able to."

"It would be disturbing, to have a memorial for them and know that their bodies were still down in the hold," Jasmine said.

"Yes, <kt> we must-t wait for the right t-time to say farewell," Kiakiru said, moving his head from side to side.

"You mentioned that port-side security would be taking depositions— will they also be taking the bodies?" Tina asked.

"Yes," Rasputin said. "Gaitz's research confirmed our hunch that they would want to process the bodies and evidence in their own labs."

J.T. leaned in. "I've reviewed Aubrey's work so far and I'd say it's a pretty fair match to the procedures they sent us. Though we might get some guff for moving the bodies so quickly."

"If you do, refer them to me," Rasputin responded. "The bodies were cleared by my order."

"Aye, sir," J.T. said.

"I'd also like you to take over the negotiations for prisoner transfer," Rasputin continued.

Aubrey and J.T. both made a note of this request.

"Eli, what's our cargo status?" Rasputin asked.

Eli shuffled his pile of flimsies. "Neko and I have been working on contacting all of our clients. We may have some difficulty getting one of them to take delivery."

"Why?" Jasmine said sharply.

"They are trying to claim that the cargo may not be intact. It seems that our encounter has become public and captured the attention of the news-net, at least long enough to make a splash. Neko's checking on our options if they drop the shipment. I've been looking at the markets and we might have a hard time unloading this to a third party for a profit."

"Just what we need," Tina groaned.

"I don't think we'll ultimately lose money this trip—though it depends on what kind of cargo we can get outbound and how long it will take for our insurance to come through. We still have the cargo that the pirates were after and our other buyers have confirmed that they plan to take delivery. Things are just going to be a bit more—complicated at this stop."

"Is that everything?" Rasputin asked the table at large. A chorus of nods met his question. "Very well, dismissed."

Aubrey closed his comp and shoved it into a side pocket. His comfortable sarongs languished in his closet, exiled by too many duty shifts and a lack of pockets.

The rest of the staff got up, gathered piles of flimsies, and headed off to meet with their juniors or to get some sleep. Sleep was sounding good to Aubrey for the first time since the attack.

J.T. stood up and stretched. "Did ya get all that?" she asked, waving her white-furred paw at the now-empty table.

"I had the computer transcribe it," Aubrey said. "I've also got notes on the security-related items."

"Good." She nodded in approval. "Let's get back to that hole of an office and divvy up the work. I wish we could stay here to hash things out but Shirogiin was right about one thing, security needs to be private—or at least discreet." J.T. shrugged to herself and let the little skunk lead the way to the security office.

Walter Gasdan was waiting for them outside the door.

"Can I help you?" Aubrey asked, reaching to key open the door.

The human looked at Aubrey and then up at J.T. "Yeah, I wanna talk to you 'bout somethin."

"Um, we're kind of busy," Aubrey said.

"Damn, boy. Everyone on this ship is busy!" Walter burst out. "Saving your presence, ma'am," he said to J.T. with the odd courtesy he had shown the polar bear ever since he figured out she was female.

"Five minutes," J.T. said, holding up a paw as big as the human's head.

"Not out here in the hall," Walter said.

"Fine, in the office then," J.T. said, sharply.

Aubrey fumbled with the controls and got the door open without dropping the pile of documents he carried.

The office had one desk shared between two chairs, two terminals back-to-back, and just enough space to get from one side of the desk to the other.

"No wonder you can't do your job right, crammed in this little sardine can," Walter muttered as Aubrey gestured for the human to take one of the seats. J.T. settled in the other one. Aubrey parked himself against the back wall.

Walter rubbed a hand across his pale face. "Darn it, that wasn't how I wanted to start things." Aubrey noticed that the man's face had more lines in it than usual and there were dark circles under his eyes. Human faces showed strain more easily than their furred kindred. Aubrey wondered if Walter had ever figured out how to see the signs of stress and age in his furred crewmates. Probably. The man had been in space for many years now, and not just on human-crewed ships.

"What do you have to tell us?" J.T. asked, the tone of her voice telling Aubrey that she was going to stop being patient any moment now.

"Listen, I only signed on to this tin-can a month ago and already she's being hit by pirates. I didn't really know any of our folks who got killed but even I can see that there was some sort of massive security failure. Now that's what killed my nephew all those years ago and I want to make sure that I'm not the next of the Gasdans to die in a crossfire."

"That's what you needed to tell us?" J.T. said, in disbelief.

"Yeah," the human said. "That, and I don't know who to trust. If Barbie was a pirate, who's next? She's been on the Tai-Pan, almost forever, and she went whacko and sold us out to a bunch of scum. What if she had a partner on the ship?"

"That's why we're conducting an investigation," J.T. said coldly. "We'll figure out how Barbie got around our security."

"All of the senior staff are working with us on this," Aubrey added.

"But can you trust 'em, kid?" Walter stood and looked the skunk in the eye. "This was an inside job, everyone's talking about it—and comparing it to the smuggling that got my nephew killed on New Queensland. Then there was that pair of bobcats that went crazy and cut Chester up, and I heard rumors that some engineer tried to blow up the captain once..." Walter trailed off. "I know I'm not bein' very clear, but what I am is worried. That darn doctor of yours prescribed sleeping pills and I'm too scared to take 'em. I'm afraid that I'll sleep through the next attack. Just like..."

"Just like you did this most recent one?" J.T. snapped, rolling her cigar from one side of her mouth to the other.

Walter's shoulders slumped. "I feel like a damn fool coming to you with this. Distracting you from your work."

J.T. narrowed her eyes. "We can make the ship more secure, but Aubrey and I can't make you feel safe. This is something you really should talk to Aki about."

"We will find out if anyone else was involved," Aubrey said, with more firmness than he felt.

"Thank ye for yer time," Walter said, as he opened the door and, head down, walked out.

"Those other failures," J.T. asked, "did Shirogiin ever do anything about them?"

"I don't know how he handled things before I became his second," Aubrey replied. "But he had me write up reports on the incidents as a training exercise."

"What happened to the reports?"

"He gave me suggestions for other areas I could research to make them more complete. I made some changes and turned them in," Aubrey said.

"You wouldn't have a copy?" J.T. asked.

"I'll have to look," Aubrey said, unreasonably anxious.

"You do that," J.T. said. "I'm particularly interested in any of the copies with Shirogiin's comments on them. I think we need to look at everything we can find about the history of the Tai-Pan's security. Neither of us has been here from the beginning and it might be useful to look at what has gone wrong before."

"Aye, ma'am," Aubrey said.

"Don't you start," J.T. said with a mock growl.

"What should I call you then?" Aubrey asked.

"Just J.T. is fine, son," she said.

"What about when we are off-ship?"

"Good thought. I'll check with Rasputin and see if he would mind me using my old military rank." She grinned at Aubrey showing two-inch incisors. "Do you think 'Sergeant' would be official enough for you?"

"Yes, ma—I mean, sure, J.T." Aubrey said.

* * *

"Welcome aboard, Inspector Trilbae," J.T. said as she and Aubrey met the Serengeti security officer at the Tai-Pan's airlock.

"Good to meet you in person, Sergeant Thalarctos, Mr. Took." Trilbae nodded to each of them in turn. She was a petite schipperke with stiff black fur and bright, observant eyes. "Your crew has been the talk of the station ever since we got your first transmission."

"Has there been any progress in scheduling the prisoner transfer?" J.T. asked, following up on the concern that was uppermost in her mind.

"My boss is working on it," Trilbae said with a shrug. "We can't put them in with the general prison population if we want them to survive more than a day. Until we can get a secure facility set up they will have to stay here."

"You've had a week to figure this out," J.T. growled.

Trilbae raised a hand in protest. "We're doing the best we can. My boss knows that you're on a schedule and she's working on it. Now I would like to see the prisoners before we continue."

"This way, Inspector," Aubrey said, leading the schipperke into crew country.

"Somehow I thought you'd have them locked in the cargo hold or something," Trilbae said.

"There's too much trouble they could get into in the hold," J.T. said.

"They're safer in the cabins anyway," Aubrey said. "None of the containers we're carrying are rated for sentient occupation. This way we can control their air, water, computer access, everything."

"Have you kept them separated since their capture?"

"No," J.T. said bluntly. "We were short of space and time."

"We separated them once we had breathing space," Aubrey put in. "I have recordings of the entire time they were together."

Trilbae looked them over. "I'll have to make a note in my log." Her lips thinned in aggravation.

Stan was watching the desk when they arrived.

"Any change?" J.T. asked.

"Nope," Stan said and waved them over. He spun the displays so they could see the prisoners. "They had their lunch thirty minutes ago. The bear is still not eating much."

"They look healthy enough," Trilbae commented.

"Do you want to speak to them?" Stan asked.

"Not right now. I'd rather wait until we've moved them off your ship," Trilbae said. "To start with, I'll review the records on the pirate attack and your personnel's response to it." She grimaced. "I have only the five days you are in port to complete my investigation and I would like to get started right away."

"We can set you up in the security office. Neither of us is really using it right now," J.T. said.

"Great, I'll check in with my boss and let her know how to reach me."

* * *

Aubrey returned to the security office after escorting the inspector off the ship. It had turned into a very long workday. The schipperke left the Tai-Pan with a comp full of recordings to review and had given Aubrey a long list of what needed to be accomplished in the remaining four days.

J.T. was sitting in the larger of the two chairs, attention focused on the screen on her side of the desk. The polar bear looked up as Aubrey entered.

"Did you get the inspector's note about the evidence team coming in day after tomorrow?" the skunk asked.

"Aye," J.T. said absently, eyes returning to the screen briefly before focusing sharply on the skunk. "I want you to handle as much of that detail as possible. I'm going to take a walk around our perimeter on station and see if I can't talk to someone higher up about getting those damned pirates off our ship."

Aubrey moved to settle in on his side of the desk. J.T. waved him over to take a look at the document she had up on her screen. It was the report he had written for Shirogiin on the Elijah North incident.

"You've really been thinking about this," J.T. said.

Aubrey's tail fluffed in anxiety. "They weren't meant to be official," he said. "Shirogiin had me do them as an exercise."

J.T. snorted. "They're very methodical—I like that in a report." She went back to reading.

Aubrey stood awkwardly for a moment. J.T. glanced his direction and indicated that he could take his seat. He pulled his chair up to the other side of the desk and spread out his flimsies. Propping his comp book up in front of him, he made notes on the day's work while J.T. continued to read.

He reached for a stylus and knocked his pile of flimsies to the floor. Nose dry with embarrassment, he bent down to pick them up. J.T. appeared not to notice.

"Based on your examination of previous security breaches what do you think will show up as the main cause of the security failure this time?" J.T. asked abruptly.

Aubrey thought for a moment. "There have been two types of security breaches. In one, a person sets out to harm one or more of the currently serving crew. That was the case in both the Elijah North and Harvard Chahoi situations. They both had some sort of problem with an individual crew member and were predisposed to act out violently when their expectations were not met. Aki, Captain Rasputin, and the rest of the section heads have all changed the hiring procedures to help screen out this type of individual. Also, their problems surfaced within a year of being hired.

"The other type of security breach has been much more serious and has caused long-term complications for the ship and crew. Geoffrey and Chance both occupied positions of trust and authority on the ship and both of them abused that trust. There was no indication of a problem until things went wrong. In Chance's case he had extra motivation to be careful that his activities were not discovered as it would put his sister at risk."

Aubrey took a sip of water. J.T. gestured for the skunk to continue. "From the evidence I have seen so far, Barbara Frise acted as a normal crew member for over four years. She did not show any of the signs of the mental instability that Chahoi or North did, and she served competently. There was no reason to suspect she worked for anyone besides the Tai-Pan.

"The same held true for Chance. He was a trusted member of the crew until his death at New Queensland Station. It was not until after Satin's abduction that the captain had cause to look more deeply into Chance's activities while he was first mate of the Tai-Pan. By the time Chance died he had served with the ship for over seven years and had given the captain no reason to suspect that anything out of the ordinary was going on.

"The Tai-Pan has a pattern of showing unwavering trust in its crew once they have demonstrated that they will be staying with the ship for the long haul. I think," he paused and swallowed hard, "that such trust should not be extended indefinitely. As much as I want the Tai-Pan to be a family, I want the crew to be safe. Audits of all crew activities need to be made on a regular basis, and questionable actions need to be brought to light before someone else gets killed."

"Or before you are forced to kill anyone else?" J.T. asked in a soft rumble.

Aubrey lowered his head.

"It's nothing to be ashamed of," J.T. said.

Aubrey was not sure if she meant the shooting or his urge to keep it from happening again.

* * *

Aubrey watched as Inspector Trilbae supervised two teams of technicians. The first team was checking Aubrey's evidence against an inventory he had provided. The second team was working its way though the makeshift morgue in the refrigerated cargo container.

This area of the cargo hold had been off-limits for the past two days while Fossey Spaceport shuttled up enough techs to process the scene. Eli had three different customers whose cargo was trapped behind the police line. Since the Tai-Pan had gotten in ahead of schedule the delay wasn't yet problematic. Though, as Eli had said, "Once the cargo is in, it doesn't matter how early you are, the customer still wants it yesterday."

Aubrey answered questions as best he could when the evidence techs ran into something they didn't understand. Otherwise he stood off to the side and watched as the mortuary techs unsealed the cargo container and began processing the bodies.

"You don't have to stay here for this," Inspector Trilbae said.

"Thanks," Aubrey said. "I would rather know what is going on."

"We can record everything for you," the schipperke said.

"I'll stay."

She shrugged. "We'll be a few hours with this many bodies."

The doors to the container opened and Aubrey could see Shirogiin's horn and Arther's hand underneath the coverings that Stan had laid over each of them. Stan had run out of body bags with the third pirate. The other bodies had been laid down over a tarp. There was a patch of empty floor between the pirates and the Tai-Pan crew. The tech crew directed hovering lights and cameras to illuminate and record the container's contents. Freezing cold air spread through the cargo bay from the container, making the techs' breath show white in the air.

"Can we get the chiller turned off?" a tech yelled across the bay.

"I thought Dr. Humboldt shut it down already," Trilbae said to Aubrey.

"He did. He also said that this container will keep producing cold air for up to forty minutes after shutdown."

Trilbae crossed the hold to pass the information to her lead tech. Aubrey watched the schipperke as she gestured to an area of the hold that he had marked off. It was just a bare patch of floor now. Aki had insisted that the blood here, in engineering, and on the bridge be cleaned up. He had wanted to leave it as evidence, but Aki had pointed out that safety regulations prohibited it. She had gone into more detail than Aubrey needed in explaining just why those areas of the ship needed to be decontaminated but had helped him take samples before cleaning up the gore.

Shirogiin and Arther and the pirates in the body bags were examined, videoed, scanned, and loaded onto gurneys. Aubrey bit his lip and looked at his feet as the bodies were guided off to the station's morgue. He tried not to think about what would happen to them during the autopsy. He had read Gaitz's report on Serengeti investigation autopsy procedures with the mistaken idea that he might need the information later. Aki had warned him that even she got queasy contemplating an autopsy on a crew member. He should have listened. He sat down against the wall, put his head on his knees, and took several calming breaths. He was just levering himself to stand, when Trilbae and one of her techs crossed to where he was holding up the wall.

"We're going to have to let the container warm up a bit before we can finish up, sir," the tech was saying.

Trilbae held up a hand, forestalling further details. "How long?"

"An hour or so," the tech said.

"Carry on," Trilbae said. The tech returned to the roped-off area.

Aubrey's comm beeped. He turned away from the schipperke to take the call.

"Aubrey," Jasmine said, "the inspector's prisoner transfer team is at the lock asking permission to board. The captain has given the okay but wants you and J.T. to supervise the removal."

"Got it, Jasmine," Aubrey said. "Have J.T. meet us at the lock."

"J.T. is outside on patrol," Jasmine replied. "She's heading back in now."

Trilbae paused to give orders to the lead tech before she and Aubrey made their way to the airlock. J.T. cycled in just as they arrived.

"G'damn gawkers," the polar bear cursed as she exited the lock. "There's at least two dozen people out there watching our lock for no good reason." Aubrey could see the police cordon around the Tai-Pan's berth on the airlock's monitor. Two bobbing cameras floated above the heads of the crowd behind the police line. "Your team is coming through behind me," J.T. said with a curt nod to Trilbae.

"I thought any interest in us would have faded by now," Aubrey said. "Aren't we old news?"

"Unfortunately not," Trilbae said, strain evident in her voice. "You should see the gauntlet I ran at my office this morning. The local newscasters can't get enough of the story."

"I've had damn well enough," J.T. said. "What's the plan for transferring the prisoners?"

"We've got a team for each prisoner," Trilbae said. "We'll pull them out one at a time, search them, and send the team on its way."

"We pulled all their weapons and tools off them when we locked them up," Aubrey said.

"Regardless, we have procedures we must follow," Trilbae said as her troopers stepped through the inner lock, and the sergeant in charge came to attention.

"Reporting for prisoner transfer duty, sir." He was a schipperke, like Trilbae. Two zebras, a Mishikhan wolverine, a honey badger, and a hare smaller than Aubrey rounded out the pack. The hare caught Aubrey looking down at her and grinned.

"At ease," Trilbae said. She opened one hand, indicating the polar bear and the skunk. "This is Sergeant Thalarctos and Mr. Took. They are the Tai-Pan's security contingent."

"Follow me," J.T. said, setting off down the corridor. "This is the route you'll use when moving the prisoners."

Trilbae and her group followed while Aubrey brought up the rear. Deep in crew country they found the three cabins serving as the brig for the prisoners. Stan was on duty, watching the monitors.

"They've come to take our prisoners off to a proper storage facility," J.T. was saying.

"I'm certainly tired of watching them. Eat, sleep, that's all they do," the hyena grumbled. "I sent in some books with one of their meals. The bear ignored them and the ferrets each independently asked for technical specs on our engines."

"You didn't give those to them, did you?" Trilbae asked.

"No, but I did ask 'em what they wanted them for. Seems they'd wrangled over why our engines wouldn't stay shut down at first. They each wanted the docs to prove the other one wrong."

"Techs," one of the zebra guards muttered, disgustedly.

Trilbae looked over the situation for a moment. "Let's bring the big one out first while we've got the whole team here."

"He's been sitting in the corner of his room for the past week and a half," Stan commented.

"He could be waiting for his chance," the sergeant said briskly.

"He's wearing my clothes," J.T. said.

"Do you want them back?" Trilbae asked.

"Gods, no," J.T. said, holding her paws up as if to avert the thought. "I just thought you'd want to know for your records. He wasn't wearing much underneath his armor, that's all."

The schipperke made a note on her comp. "Okay, are we ready?" she asked her sergeant. The troopers took up a formation around the door. Stan keyed the door open from the board at the monitoring station. At Trilbae's command the hare and the zebra quietly entered the room. The bear's hands were secured behind his back and he was quickly searched. His small red eyes gleamed dully in the corridor lamps but he gave no resistance to his escort.

J.T. walked the prisoner and the two troopers escorting him to the airlock and watched on the monitor as they cycled through and loaded him into the transport. She was soon joined by Aubrey and Stan as each of them took a turn escorting a prisoner and detail to the airlock. Trilbae brought up the rear.

"I have to go with the transport and register the prisoners," she said. "I'd like to leave the tech crews to finish their work in the cargo bay. I should be back before they finish up for the day."

"That would be fine," J.T. said.

Aubrey nodded in agreement. "I'll go back down there now."

Trilbae cycled through the lock to the dock.

"Thanks for your assistance, Stan," J.T. said.

"Both you and Karaya have been a big help," Aubrey added.

"You're welcome. It is a relief to hand them over to someone who knows what they're doing," Stan said. "I should get back to crew quarters. I promised Tina that I would let her know when the rooms were open again. She and MacQuarrie want to check them over before I clean up." The hyena paused and read a note on his comp. "Aubrey, do you know when the cargo hold will be ready for cleanup? I need to put that on the schedule. I have to finish cleaning the hold before we can take on any new cargo."

"When I know, you'll know," Aubrey said, mildly. "The techs weren't sure. I'll check with them when I get back down there."

* * *

Aubrey sat in the bowl-bed in his dim quarters. It was the end of another very long day. A second shift of technicians had come back with the inspector. They had worked into the ship's night and Aubrey had stayed to watch and learn—all the while hoping never to have to do this again.

Three crew dead, one by his own hand. Never mind that Frise had been holding a gun on Gaitz with the rest of the bridge crew hostage to her intentions. She was crew, and the biggest threat to the family he'd constructed for himself. That she had intended to kill Gaitz he had no doubt. In the moment he'd drawn her attention to himself he could see her plans in the movement of her body. She would shoot Satin first, and because she still held onto a hard core of sanity, Gaitz would be next.

He'd known all this in his gut, but it had taken Karaya's insight to show it to him. Barbie had wanted Gaitz to suffer but Satin, sitting pale-nosed and holding an unconscious Kelson in her lap, was just as much a target of Barbie's fury. Aubrey wondered if Barbie had known any of this in the moment that he killed her.

Shirogiin himself had seen the danger. Aubrey could hear his dead-level voice. "Remember, the most dangerous people are the ones you know. The most grievous threats come from within."

Shirogiin had lived apart from the crew, convinced that good security came from objectivity, from not getting too close to the people he was both responsible for and wary of. Packing Kuroi's belongings had been an exercise in loneliness and isolation.

Aubrey could feel the heavy weight of his mentor's teachings pressing him down into the bed. The small skunk shrank under the weight, curling up into a ball, his black-and-white striped tail curling to meet his paws.

The captain should be notified that the ship was clear. There were reports to finish, memorial services to plan, crew to interview, and three hundred twenty-seven other urgent things to attend to, all before the ship could pull out of Fossey Station, and leave the burden of her dead behind for Serengeti officials like Trilbae to deal with.

Barbie was destined for anonymous disposal after the necessary evidence had been collected. Arther and Shirogiin would be remembered publicly by the crew. Aubrey knew from hard experience that time would ease the pain of their loss. Barbie, privately mourned, publicly reviled, was a different story. Her body and effects were to be left in the custody of the Serengeti police. News of her death would spread in slow, uneven ripples out from Serengeti as ships and infopedoes carried the news from port to port in the loose network of stars making up known space.

Aubrey knew that Gaitz, of all the crew, would mourn the woman Barbie and castigate himself for letting the pirate, Frise, take advantage of him. There was more pain on the way. Once Aubrey and J.T. finished their report, Gaitz likely would read it and relive choices he could not unmake. Aubrey would spare his friend, the closest thing he had to a father, if he could, but Gaitz was also the first mate and would not spare himself if it meant shirking responsibilities to ship and crew.

Aubrey felt his muscles tighten, anxiety washing over him. He wanted to cut himself off from the world and never leave the quiet of his cabin again. Minutes passed; his hammering heart slowed, his breathing deepened.

Cutting himself off hadn't saved Shirogiin.

Aubrey's eyes popped open at the thought. Shirogiin had lived a life apart from the messy relationships of a crew that lived, worked, and played together. Three to five days a month were spent port-side, the rest of the time they relied on each other for entertainment, support, employment, conversation—and, occasionally, love.

I don't want to lose that.

But until he could figure out how, there were still the three hundred twenty-seven things that needed to be done, and none of them would happen while he was holed up, feeling sorry for himself.

* * *

Aubrey and Inspector Trilbae worked in companionable silence in the security office. Trilbae was cross-checking her document and evidence inventory against Aubrey's log as the last step in her investigation.

Aubrey worked on some paperwork Eli needed so a shipment could be released. The health inspectors had been in that morning, confirming that the hold was safe to haul cargo. Aubrey appended the health certificate to the form and sent it on its way.

Trilbae made a note in her files, looked up at Aubrey, and smiled before going back to work.

Aubrey reviewed Stan's note confirming that Arther and Shirogiin's personal effects were packed and awaiting Eli's appraisal for sale. Barbie's possessions had already been taken away by Trilbae's evidence team. Copies of the dead crew members' files had been archived; the information could be forwarded at the request of their families.

"I've finished the inventory," Trilbae announced after an hour had passed.

"Do you have everything?" Aubrey asked.

"Everything except Dr. Nagykanizsai's medical assessment."

"Aki should be in. We could walk down there and pick up a copy," Aubrey suggested.

"I could use a chance to stretch my legs," Trilbae confessed. She stood and packed up her files. "I'll be ready to go once I have the assessment and if I remember correctly the infirmary is on the way to the main lock."

"It didn't take you long to learn your way around our ship," Aubrey said, showing the schipperke out into the hall.

"Hazard of the profession." She shrugged. "Have you thought about what you are going to do after this investigation wraps up?"

"Not really," Aubrey said, walking alongside her. "I expect that the crew and procedures will begin to return to normal once we leave port. Hanging around and having to deal with the aftermath of… well, everything has been hard."

"I understand," Trilbae said. "I was more wondering what will happen to you, specifically."

"I don't know," Aubrey said, trying to keep the anxiety out of his voice. "The captain has said that he will keep me on when we leave. I just don't know in what capacity."

"Have you thought about finding another job?" Trilbae asked.

"You mean leave the Tai-Pan?"

"Yes, stay on Serengeti. There are good security jobs to be found at Fossey Spaceport." Trilbae pushed on, oblivious to the mulish look on

Aubrey's face. "You have real-life security expertise, something not all of my co-workers can say."

Aubrey looked away, blinking furiously. "Inspector Trilbae," he said hoarsely, "I appreciate your confidence in me but if there is any way I can stay aboard the Tai-Pan, I will. They are my family in a way you wouldn't understand."

"Because I'm a 'dirtsucker,'" Trilbae responded, the admiration in her voice souring.

Aubrey looked at her in puzzlement. "I don't understand."

"Spacers are always making excuses, saying we don't understand, that 'dirtsuckers' can't understand." Her ears were flat in remembered anger.

Aubrey stopped and looked at her. She stopped to keep from outpacing him.

"That's not the reason," he said quietly. "It's—I owe them more than I can ever repay."

Trilbae closed her mouth on a reply as the door to sick bay opened.

Aki was just setting her empty coffee mug down. "Can I help you?" the ermine asked.

"Dr. Nagykanizsai," Trilbae began.

"Call me Aki. I only use my surname on court documents." Aki smiled tightly, determined to be polite. "Isis and I need to finish our inventory before we ship out. Given how nervous the crew's likely to feel, I don't want to be caught short of any supplies."

"We just need a copy of your casualty report and damage estimate," Aubrey said. He could hear the rustle of Isis's feathers and the tick of her claws on the metal floor in the back room.

"Didn't I send that to you already?" Aki asked.

"That's the problem. It's on my list of received docs but I can't find the actual report. I want to be sure I have everything before you ship out."

Aki was quickly back behind her desk, typing at her terminal. "Here it is," she said, more to herself than anyone in the room. Trilbae canted her ears forward in anticipation. With a few quick keystrokes Aki transferred the data to Trilbae's comp.

"That file documents the physical injuries to the crew and the cost of treatment. In Mr. Fulton's case, many of the costs are estimates, as he has a long rehabilitation ahead of him. First Mate Gaitz, Mr. Fulton, and Kelson have agreed to my release of this medical information."

"Thank you Dr... Aki," Trilbae said.

Isis rustled out of the back and handed Aki a clipboard to review.

"When will you rip the entrails out of the ones you have in custody?" Isis asked casually. "I would very much like to see that."

"I don't know what will happen to the three you captured," Trilbae said. "We'll have a trial and hopefully they'll tell us what they know about the crew they were working for. There's still a pirate ship out in the beyond. If we don't catch them, one of our neighbors might. My office's main concern is keeping the prisoners alive long enough to get at that information. Whoever this pirate is, he has connections. Connections we'd like to sever."

"On my world we disembowel murderers and leave them to rot in the sun," Isis said, wistfully. She fluffed her feathers out and settled them sleekly once more.

"After seeing what they did to your ship, I can see why," Trilbae said.

Aubrey and Trilbae left the lab together.

The schipperke looked at the skunk. "I meant what I said, earlier. You are good at this work. Given time and experience, you will only get better."

* * *

Aubrey looked at his messages. He and J.T. were crowded in the security office working on the first draft of their report to the captain. "Karaya sent in her report."

"What report?" J.T. asked.

"She and I were talking, back before Rasputin asked you to step in, and she suggested that there were simpler ways to get around our security than sleeping with the first mate. I asked her to write them up for me."

"That reminds me," J.T. said. "The captain stopped by earlier. He's interviewing someone for the security position and he wants you to sit in on part of the interview if the first half goes well."

"When?" Aubrey asked.

"Cap'n said he'd page you when he was done giving the guy the tour." J.T. chewed on her cigar. "In the meantime, give me the short version of Karaya's report."

Aubrey suppressed his desire to ask more about J.T.'s conversation with Rasputin. Instead he scanned down Karaya's report. "Tweaking the ship's sensors to hide the pirate ship could have been done with the codes that Barbie had as navigator. The tricky part was ensuring that the bad data wasn't caught until it was too late. Having Gaitz's codes simplified this part of the plan, but was not necessary for it to succeed." Aubrey paused. "Karaya goes on to detail six methods of feeding the blinding data to the sensors without leaving a flag in the system."

J.T.'s forehead fur rippled in consternation.

"She goes on to assure us that none of these weaknesses can be exploited by someone not physically present on the Tai-Pan." Aubrey paused and appeared to be counting. "The second section of the report deals with methods of disabling the weapons lockers. Karaya has four different approaches, listed in order of risk of discovery."

"What do you think of Karaya's analysis?" J.T. asked.

"I'd have to read it more closely, but she makes a good point that Frise's motivations were not strictly profit-based."

"We knew that as soon as we read her personal log," J.T. said.

Aubrey nodded in agreement. "I felt like she was serving on a different ship than we were. I had always thought that she was trying to be tough and sarcastic to hide her feelings."

"She was," J.T. said. "We just didn't know that what she was hiding was even worse." J.T. made a note on a flimsy. "Send me a copy of Karaya's report. I'm minded to include the whole thing as an appendix to our report but it sounds like there are a few things we might want to forward on to Tina."

"Will do," Aubrey said. "In the meantime, how detailed should the event chronology be? I'm down to five-minute increments during the boarding but there's a lot of detail to include."

"Have you tracked down how Barbie was able to dispose of the weapons charges without having Gaitz show up twice in the system?"

"It was mostly a question of timing, and since she was intimate with him, she could pretty much depend on being able to use his card at a time when he was not logged in, on duty elsewhere. The charges themselves were stashed in three caches on the ship. If she'd known more about explosives she could have rigged some very messy bombs. As it is, our engineers accounted for all of the missing battery packs and ammunition. They also found a bag of her personal belongings—it looks like the contents match with what she took from her room, so no surprises there."

"That's a relief," J.T. said.

"That was the last issue to be resolved," Aubrey said. "Now it's just a matter of finishing this report."

"Bureaucratic rule, boy," J.T. said, using her cigar as a pointer. "It always takes longer to write the report than to do the investigation. It's a good thing you wrote all those reports for Shirogiin. We can crib some of what we need from those, especially your recommendations. If Shirogiin had passed on some of your ideas, Frise's job would have been a lot harder."

* * *

"Thank you for coming, Aubrey," Rasputin said as he welcomed the skunk to his office. A strange zebra was seated in one of the chairs opposite the panda's desk. Rasputin's tea set was out on his desk with an extra cup next to the teapot.

"What can I do for you, Captain?" Aubrey stood in front of the desk. Rasputin, seated, was nearly as tall as he was.

"May I introduce Mr. Yadto. He is interviewing for the senior security position." Rasputin turned to the zebra. "Mr. Yadto this is Mr. Aubrey Took. He has been with us for over eighteen months. He trained under our previous security chief and is coordinating the current investigation with the local authorities."

Mr. Yadto looked at the skunk carefully. "You are young for such work. Have you always wanted to be in security?"

Rasputin poured Aubrey a cup of red tea and indicated that the skunk should sit in the remaining chair. "I never really thought about it when I was growing up," Aubrey said honestly. "I was born in space and figured that I would wind up working for a ship in some capacity."

"So you feel no particular passion for this job, over any crew position?" Mr. Yadto asked.

"I didn't say that," Aubrey said, stung. He wondered why Rasputin was allowing this line of questioning. "The Tai-Pan is my home. I would

do any job required of me. Making her secure, knowing that I am helping to keep the crew safe, is important to me. I can do that by helping Stan in the hydroponics bays or working with J.T. on security. Whatever helps the ship helps me."

"So it is not the job but the crew that is important to you? That is a good attitude for a security person." Mr. Yadto turned to Rasputin. "Your Sergeant Thalarctos does not want the job of supervising this youngster?"

"She's helping out because of her previous military security experience." Rasputin took a sip of tea. "Sergeant Thalarctos has made it clear she wants to go back to engineering. It doesn't have anything to do with Aubrey."

"And you, Mr. Took. I take it you have not applied for the position?" Mr. Yadto asked.

"No, sir."

"May I ask why?" the zebra continued.

Aubrey looked at Rasputin. A cascade of questions filled his head at the zebra's question. Would Rasputin consider me? Could I do the job? Do I want to? The panda's face was unreadable. "I guess I haven't given it much thought."

"Mr. Took, you have answered all of my questions. Thank you for taking time to visit with me." He turned to Rasputin. "What will you do if the person you wish to hire does not feel they could work well with Mr. Took?"

"I think it would depend on the candidate, Mr. Yadto. Regardless, Mr. Took would not be leaving the ship. I can always find room for good people. You, for example, come highly recommended by Ms. Zuvela."

"Thank you," said Mr. Yadto, after finishing his last sip of tea.

"Now that you have had the tour, what do you think of the Tai-Pan?"

"It pains me to say this, but your ship is terribly misaligned," Mr. Yadto said in a deep, patient voice.

"What do you mean?" Rasputin asked, leaning forward in his chair.

"Surely you realize that having the security office in a dead-end corridor creates a pool where energy collects and stagnates?"

Rasputin wrinkled his muzzle in confusion. "I'm afraid I don't understand. We just checked the conduits throughout the ship and repaired any that were damaged."

"It is not physical energy of which I speak. I am surprised that you prosper as well as you do. Though I sense that a protective hand is held over this ship and crew." He gazed into the distance and then shook his head. "No, even that is not enough. I'm afraid I could not serve on this ship unless major modifications were made to correct the energy flow."

"I am sorry to have wasted your time, Mr. Yadto," Rasputin said, rising to his feet to show the visitor out. He gestured and Aubrey kept his seat.

"Oh, it was not a waste. I am pleased to meet someone Ms. Zuvela speaks so highly of. Never fear, Captain. With patience you will find the one whose energy matches that of your ship, and when you do, you will both know."

* * *

Aubrey woke from his first sound sleep since the Tai-Pan had jumped into Serengeti. His alarm chirped quietly. He crossed to it and turned it off. He had a good twenty minutes before he was due to open the security office for the day. A shower or breakfast? What would it be this morning? His stomach rumbled, deciding the issue. He threw on a clean pair of cargo pants and a shirt and made his way to the galley.

He could feel the tension in the air as he walked in. Cory was issuing terse commands to Gasdan and Spike. The latter's brown fur was covered in white flour, though the galley was nearly spotless.

Cory caught sight of him. "Aubrey, has J.T. found whoever did this?"

"Everything was quiet when I went to bed last night, Cory. I was just stopping in to get some breakfast on my way to the office."

Aubrey saw Spike making don't-get-her-started motions from behind the wolf's back. Rather than the explosion Spike apparently feared, Cory took a deep breath and let it out again in resignation.

"I'll let J.T. update you, then," she said. Spike puffed his cheeks out in relief. Cory turned to her helpers. "Thanks guys, I can get to work now," Cory said, her voice one of forced cheer floating on boiling anger.

"No problem, Cory," Spike said quickly.

"Anything to help," Walter said as they both edged their way out of the galley and broke for the hall.

Aubrey filled his coffee mug then followed Spike and Walter's example, leaving Cory alone in her domain.

As he keyed open the door to the office, questions about Cory's mysterious behavior were blown out of his mind by J.T.'s ferocious roar.

"What do you think has changed in the last twenty months that gives you permission to leave the galley in such a state!"

It took Aubrey a moment to realize that her anger was directed at a cowering honey badger and not at himself. Even so, his hands shook, sloshing the coffee around in the, thankfully, lidded container.

"I'm just... Jeg vet ikke... anxious, I guess," Tyr stammered.

"In Standard, please," J.T. said, sharply.

"I was craving banana-nut bread and didn't want to disturb Cory." Tyr rushed to get the words out.

J.T. checked her comp. Aubrey could see that she was pulling up Tyr's personnel file.

"This is your second and final warning," J.T. said, voice quieter but somehow more menacing as she added a note to the file. "If there is a next time we will activate the lock on the galley and you will not get the passkey. Do I have to tell you how unhappy the rest of the crew will be if we have to lock the galley and give them one more access key to remember?"

Tyr shook his head.

"I'm also requesting that you make an appointment with Aki," J.T. said. "See if she can help you get these cravings under control, understand?"

Tyr nodded miserably, embarrassment reddening the tips of his ears and making his nose sweat. Aubrey stood aside as the honey badger slunk past him into the hall. The door shut behind him.

J.T. sighed and sank back into the too-small chair that was Shirogiin's legacy. "Sorry you had to walk in on that," she said, swiveling her chair around to face Aubrey and tracking him as he moved around the room to sit at his side of the desk.

"I figured something was going on when I got to the galley."

"Did Cory find anyone to help her clean up the mess Tyr left?" J.T. asked.

"Spike and Walter were both finishing up when I got there—as a crime scene it's a bust."

J.T. smiled slightly. "Good. You should have seen it when Cory called me at oh-dark-thirty this morning. Tyr and his nut-bread really did a number on the galley. Hopefully Aki will be able to sort out what's behind that 'cause I'll be number one in the cranky line if we have to lock the galley."

Aubrey scanned the overnight reports on his terminal. "Other than that it looks like it was a quiet night," he said.

"Yep, but don't let it fool ya." J.T. tossed a chewed-down stub of cigar in the trash and pulled a fresh one from her pocket. "Everyone's gonna be jumpy this time out. Don't be surprised if we're called out a lot more than normal the next few weeks."

"I thought everyone was starting to settle down now that the investigation was over and we know that Frise was the only crew behind the attack."

"Their brains are calming down," J.T. said. "The rest of 'em will be jumping out of their skins at the least little noise—especially once we're inbound again. You'll want ta keep an eye on the ex-military types in particular– some of us have been around a few too many explosions and are likely to over-react."

Aubrey's ears flicked back in alarm. "You're leaving security?"

"Not until the captain hires a new chief of security, and even then he'll likely have me hang around until we're sure the new guy knows the ropes."

"The captain had a few folks apply for the security job while we were in port," Aubrey said.

"There'll be more like that once we jump," J.T. said glumly. "I don't know how long it's going to take to find someone to replace Shirogiin."

"Have you thought about taking the position permanently?" Aubrey asked.

"No!" J.T. said, explosively. "Especially not after this morning. I don't mind helping out in a pinch, but I like engines a lot better than people. And good security, regardless of what Shirogiin might have told you, is all about people. People are a damn sight more complicated than a jump drive."

Aubrey suppressed a smile.

"And I hope you'll squash any rumors supportin' that crazy notion," J.T. continued.

"I promise," he said. He paused for a moment, considering his words. "What would you think if I applied for the position?" He tried to sound more confident than his rapidly sinking gut would let him.

The polar bear sat back in her chair and looked him over appraisingly.

Aubrey waited anxiously for her to speak.

"I think you could do the job," she said very seriously. "More importantly, I think you care about the job and about this crew in a way that would be hard to match with anyone hired from outside."

Aubrey breathed in.

"Do you really want it?" J.T. asked. "I know I couldn't stand it. Dealing with Tyr this morning reminded me how much I miss Mac's crew."

"I do want the job. I want to make the Tai-Pan safe again. These past few weeks have been hard but if I'm going to do this work, I want it to be for people I care about. It just took me a while to realize it."

"You had a lot to deal with," J.T. said. "And I don't think Rasputin would have taken you seriously if you had spoken up before the blood was dry."

"Do you think he will now?" Aubrey asked.

"That I do," J.T. said, a big grin revealing her scrimshawed incisors. "Not only that, but I know where you can get a sterling recommendation."

The phrase "took by storm" seems too mild to describe the Furry community's reaction to Kyell Gold when he showed up in 2005. His first appearance was with the novel Volle, the first of his "Tales of Argaea", published by Sofawolf Press in January 2005. It debuted at that January's Further Confusion convention, where it was greeted with gasps of, "My God! This has explicit sex scenes! Scenes of homoerotic sex!" "Yes, but ... look at how well-written it is. This is real literature, not just gay pornography!" Despite (or because of) all its controversy, Volle won the Ursa Major Award as the Best Anthropomorphic Novel of 2005.

Since then, Gold has won seven more Ursa Major Awards for his novels and short fiction. His persona as a red fox is mega-popular on LiveJournal, and he has become a familiar guest at Furry conventions around the world, often as the guest of honor. His story "Race to the Moon" (New Fables #3, Summer 2009) was a finalist for the Washington Science Fiction Association's Small Press Award in 2010 (earning more controversy because of news reports that "Kyell Gold has finally been nominated for a real award!", implying that Furry literature and the UMA are "not real"). His latest book is Green Fairy, which premiered at the Furry Weekend Atlanta convention in March, and is already widely expected to win next year's Ursa Major Award in the Best Novel category.

"Jacks to Open" is typical of Gold's take on alternate-world fiction. It is superficially our world, set in a gambling-mecca Las Vegas with a Suncoast, a Caesar's and a Luxor; with references to L.A. and New Orleans, to movies like Oceans Eleven and The Sting, and to historical philosophers Nietzsche, Hegel, Locke, Descartes, and Rousseau. At the same time it is definitely a Furry world, designed for inhabitants with a much sharper sense of smell than humans have, where the people need less clothing because they have fur, where there is some species segregation based upon their separate senses and instincts. "Jacks to Open" takes place largely in a casino that does not allow smoking, and as a result the canids who are particularly sensitive to the stink of burning tobacco tend to frequent it. Other Gold stories have been set in cities with neighborhoods where the nocturnal species live together, and where the homes of otters have waterways connecting the rooms.

Jacks to Open

Kyell Gold

When you think of Las Vegas, you think of the flash, the glitter, the sparkle, the neon, the light. But there's another Las Vegas, too, if you go behind the Strip, behind the standalone casinos scattered through the town at Suncoast, Boulder Station, Palace Station, and down a shopping arcade called Easy Street. You might notice that the parking garage is always full from the basement to the roof, even though its eight levels seem extravagant for the two blocks of small stores below. But if you turn right at the end of Easy Street onto Siegel Avenue, you'll see a series of small clubs in large buildings, and these are the casinos that do not need to advertise their presence.

They are the old breed of casino, a place for gamblers to wander from blackjack to craps, where you still pull the handle on the one-armed bandits, where the dealers deal from their paws and not from a shoe, keeping up a line of patter all the while. There are no celebrity chefs, no hotel rooms, no gift shops, only a bar, the slapping of cards, the ringing of slots, and, in some casinos, the thick haze of smoke overhead.

There was no haze of smoke in the Persian, even by the bar where Sean was sitting. As far as he could see and smell, the patrons of the Persian were entirely canid: wolves, coyotes, foxes, dingos, and dholes. No other red wolves, but that was okay. He was used to being mistaken for a coyote, and used to being the only red wolf in the room.

It was illegal, of course, to restrict entry based on species, and the Persian did no such thing. But it was one of the few casinos in town that did restrict smoking in deference to the sensitive noses of their canine patrons. Because the casino depended more on word of muzzle than advertising, its canid regulars tended to tell their friends, and a haze of canine scent was as off-putting for some other species as smoke was to canids. There are no shortage of casinos in Las Vegas, and if one doesn't exactly suit, then it's easy enough to go elsewhere and leave the Persian to the canids.

Even apart from the lack of smoke, the Persian was the perfect place for Sean. His nondescript tan shirt, collar unbuttoned, and pair of ordinary brown slacks served to mute rather than highlight the red accents in his fur. On any evening, he spoke rarely; in the Persian, there was no shortage of things to listen to and watch, a constant barking over the jingling of paying slots. Tonight, Sean's attention was focused on one particular thing.

The fat wolf sitting next to him was a perfect companion, because he appeared to have some kind of affliction that made it hard for him to stop talking. The guy was like a caricature of a 1950s businessman, wearing a blue suit with a yellow striped tie and a white shirt with gold cufflinks, chomping on a cigar—unlit, of course, just for the taste of it. He wore three rings and had a pocketwatch with a gold chain. But his tie was stained and the cufflinks tarnished, and at this distance, Sean could smell that the wolf was using some cheap cologne that stung his nose.

Sean knew his type and knew why he was here rather than over on the Strip where he belonged. He was here because he thought the Persian was a nice exclusive place, and he was the sort who wanted to be in exclusive places, even ones where he didn't belong. And when he started to realize that he didn't belong here, well, sometimes he called someone like Sean. And Sean's job was to make him feel better.

"Anyway," the wolf said as he drained his gin and tonic, "the table's over there. I'll see you there in a bit."

Sean took another sip from his half-filled club soda. He didn't gamble well while drunk. "When there's an opening."

The wolf nodded, pushed his bulk off the chair, and set off for the table. Sean watched him go with some distaste. His tail flopped back and forth over the seat of his pants like a rag, and one of his shirttails had come untucked as he sat at the bar. Really, you'd think someone with all that money would take better care of himself.

Sean sipped his drink and sighed. Still he had to play nice, impress the guy. He wasn't worried about his skill at the cards. He was more worried that he would say something about the smell. But he was very good at lying to people. He had to be.

The wolf shouldered his way onto the blackjack table they'd been watching. Sean leaned against the bar and studied the dealer yet again.

The casino's ancient Persia theme was mostly executed in the names of the drinks at the bar and the pictures on the slot machines. None of the employees wore particularly Persian costumes, and the blackjack dealers were no exception. The dealer Sean was watching was a slender silver fox, his fur jet black with creamy white under the muzzle and down the chest. Sean only knew he was wearing a plain black vest because he also wore a name tag and a shiny pin on one shoulder, and although the vest was invisible against his fur, he wouldn't have fastened the pin in his fur.

It wasn't out of the question that he would be shirtless, though, because he was a flirty little thing, smiling at each of the players at his table and curling his tail up so the white tip was just visible over the edge of the table. His paws moved around the cards like hummingbirds, a blur of motion and then stillness as he waited for the players to make their decisions.

At the Persian, each of the dealers was a personality. Next to the black fox, a coyote in a parti-colored shirt tossed her deck from paw to paw and let the cards flutter theatrically to the table. At the table closest to Sean, a vixen bounced on her heels, highlighting the twin attractions that most of the males at her table were ogling. He could hear the patter of the coyote one more table down, telling jokes as he dealt the cards. Each of the dealers was well known, with regulars who just played to be at the table and would-be regulars who just wanted to be seen at the table.

Sean took out the worn deck of cards he carried in his pocket and shuffled them. The feel of the smooth card backs soothed his paws. He shuffled them a couple more times than was strictly necessary, watching the simple double circle pattern on the back. When he felt relaxed, he dealt out his standard layout on the bar: three cards. He got the Jack of Clubs, Three of Hearts, and Ace of Clubs. Then he looked again and saw that the Three of Hearts was actually the Three of Clubs.

The wolf frowned. He hadn't drunk enough to be seeing things. It wasn't unheard of to get flickers of uncertainty in the cards like that, especially in a casino where there was so much luck and magic swirling around, but his readings were so simple that he rarely saw the phenomenon. He scooped the cards up in his paw before someone could come over and ask what he was doing. The Jack of Clubs meant a reliable friend, but he would hardly count the fat wolf as reliable, and he was more of a King signifier, anyway. The other cards were clearer: the Three meant money or help coming from a partner, and the Ace signified new endeavors. He often saw that combination at the beginning of a job that was going to turn out well. Of course the Three of Hearts meant caution, being careful what you say. He rubbed his whiskers and thought over that combination, and the flicker he'd seen.

It wouldn't do him much good to deal out another spread. Unless you asked a completely different question, the cards tended to muddle things in their attempt to clarify, focusing in on details and projecting other possibilities. The first reading would have to be sufficient for him to get a sense of what was going on.

He hadn't quite finished his soda when a dhole at the silver fox's table finally got fed up. Sean left a tip for the bartender and sauntered over to the table, giving the fox a big smile as he sat down and pretending not to know the fat wolf three seats to his left.

"Well, hello, Slim," the fox said. "Welcome to the table." His lapel pin was a Club, and his name tag read "Jack."

Sean indicated it with his muzzle, and grinned. "Thanks, Jack." Of course his name was Jack. What else could it be? He pushed three hundred over the table, two fifties and a bunch of twenties, and then took one more crumpled twenty from his pocket and added it to the stack. "Hope this is enough to let me play for a while."

Jack scooped it up and riffled the stack of bills casually. "Three twenty," he said, dropping it into his till and sliding a stack of chips back over to Sean. "Good luck, Slim."

Sean experienced an odd and powerful urge to breach casino protocol and touch the fox's fingers before he withdrew them from the chips, but he held back until the chips sat alone on the table, and only then did he pull them all back. He made a show of looking at the minimum for the table—twenty-five dollars—and then slid out a single $25 chip in front of him.

"Everybody in? Cheer up, Angel, your luck is about to turn. I feel it." The fox shuffled the cards in his paws, and almost effortlessly dealt. Sean's cards seemed to appear in front of him: Three of Clubs followed by the Eight of Diamonds. An interesting combination, he thought, reading them automatically. The Three of Clubs again: a wealthy partner, but in conjunction with the Eight, it meant that the money would arrive through practicing an art or skill, jointly between both partners.

Of more practical import, of course, was the fact that he'd been dealt an eleven. He glanced at the fat wolf and saw an Eight of Spades and the Ace of Hearts. Nineteen—not bad. The other players had less promising hands: two that added to seven, and the busty female wolf just to his left had drawn a Nine and Six for fifteen. He saw her frown and saw Jack's apologetic smile in response; apparently she was "Angel."

The dealer had the King of Diamonds showing. That would have been a good significator for the fat wolf, Sean thought. Rich, influential person. Influential in this case, because it promised a good hand for the dealer, especially given the lack of face cards on the table. Dealer's twenty was a hard hand to beat.

Apparently reading the odds the same way he had, the fat wolf used the flexibility of his Ace to hit again, and got a Six for fifteen. He scowled, hit again and busted. The next two players both hit and ended with seventeen and twenty, and Angel looked much happier with her twenty than she had with fifteen.

Sean slid another chip out beside his first. "Double down," he said.

Jack grinned at him. "Good to listen to the cards," he said as he flipped the Jack of Clubs to Sean's hand. "Well, look at that. Twenty-one, and with my namesake at that."

Sean leaned back, one paw just resting on the edge of the table. "That Eight wouldn't lie to me," he said, almost to himself.

Jack paused in the act of turning to the coyote seated to Sean's right, then completed the motion, but as he dealt out a Five and then an Eight to the coyote, leaving him with twenty, Sean noticed that his eyes flicked over once or twice to meet Sean's own. With the coyote's deal done, the fox returned his full attention to his own hand.

"Oh, my," Jack said, "I've got a twenty-one and a couple twenties on the table. And dealer has…" He turned over the Queen of Clubs. "Twenty. So sorry, ladies and gents, a bad round for the table. I promise the next one will make up for it." He raked in everyone's chips, sent two of them to Sean, and followed them with a look that made Sean's ears flick back in surprise. It wasn't one of the casually flirty looks he obviously had in his extensive repertoire. It was a look of honest curiosity, and even though it lasted only a second, Sean sat up straighter and perked his ears.

"So, Slim," Jack said as he dealt the cards, not looking at Sean now, "haven't seen you around before, I don't think."

"I don't gamble much." He took his winnings and left a single chip out as ante again.

"You know the cards, though." That remark was delivered with the same tone as the look: curious, not flirty, though he threw in an empty smile.

"I play lots of Gin Rummy with my mother," Sean said. He reminded himself that he especially should not be flirting now, not with the fat wolf sitting right down at the other end of the table glowering at him.

It was hard not to, though, especially when Jack stopped in front of him, vest hanging open to reveal his smooth chest and tight, flat stomach. Sean kept having to shake the image of his paws sliding behind that vest to hold the fox against him, and it didn't help that he couldn't remember the last time he'd been on an honest-to-goodness date with someone he'd chosen to spend the night with. It also didn't help that Jack seemed to pause longer in front of his seat than any of the others.

"Is your name really Jack?" Sean said during one pause while a new player took Angel's place. The female wolf had finally cashed in her last few chips, taking Jack's apology that the "cards just weren't falling tonight" with a smile and a bounce of her chest. Sean had no doubt that she'd find someone to make her and her painted-on dress feel better.

"Sure as the skies are blue," the fox said.

Sean chuckled. "It's nighttime out now," he pointed out, just to keep the conversation going.

Jack riffled the edge of the deck with his thumb and grinned back. "Nothing but blue skies do I see," he said.

The red wolf, whose eyes were blue, smiled. "Irving Berlin," he murmured as Jack dealt the cards out.

"Him and ol' Blue Eyes," Jack said, pointing to the ceiling, where Sean could now hear the strains of "Strangers In The Night," and he wondered if Jack had waited to point out the music until that song came on, or if the casino just played a lot of songs that encouraged people to hook up.

"Not a bad choice," Sean murmured, and then caught a glare from the fat wolf, who had to be down four hundred already, and looked at his cards.

He lost that hand, but won the next two, and was actually up a hundred fifty after half an hour. He usually bet conservatively enough not to lose, but the cards were falling well for him tonight. Along with Jack's flirting, it gave him a sense of well-being that was not unlike being buzzed.

The wolf finally stood and walked away, and that was Sean's signal to do the same. He had been hoping the wolf would stay because he was enjoying himself so much, but on the next hand he was dealt the Four of Hearts, a change or journey card, and he tapped it when Jack came back around. "I'm being called away," he said casually, as if the card had nothing to do with it.

Jack looked at the card and smiled. "Sorry to lose you, though my bosses won't be," he said, nodding at Sean's pile of chips. "Hope it's not for a couple more hands, though. I hate to see those blue skies go."

Sean couldn't see the fat wolf any more, but he could make excuses for remaining at the table. He pushed ten chips out and grinned. "Deal me in, tall, dark, and handsome."

The eyebrow the fox raised was black with silver edging. He smiled and dealt out the next hand, and though he made a point to flirt with the other players and not with Sean, the Jack of Clubs he dealt Sean said more than any words could. The Jack of Clubs, in addition to signifying a dark-furred youth, also signified a reliable friend, and Jack had as much as announced in that first hand that it was his card. The next card Sean got was the Seven of Diamonds, which meant a surprise or a reward from consistent effort. Again Jack delivered the card without a word, after telling the dhole to Sean's left how his eighteen was a good hand. He went on to deal an eleven to the coyote to Sean's right, who eyed Sean's stake and then prepared to double down.

Seventeen, Sean thought as Jack went back to the beginning of the table. He should stay on seventeen, but that card combination was tempting him. A surprise or a reward from a reliable friend. Was Jack telling him to hit? He tapped his fingers on the table. That was the feeling he was getting, and if he had learned nothing else in his line of work, it was to trust his feelings.

"You'll stand on seventeen?" Jack had come quickly around to him, but was hesitating.

"Hit," Sean said.

The coyote next to him said, "Hang on!" to Jack, and then laid a paw on Sean's arm. "Son," he said, "you got seventeen. You always stay on seventeen."

"I know," Sean said. "I just have a feeling." The coyote tilted his muzzle and put his ears to the side, so Sean made something up. "That girl who took the wolf's place, she's a red fox, and whenever a new red fox joins the table, if I get a red card, I have to hit on it."

The coyote grinned, and slapped a paw on the table. "Here I took you for a tenderfoot. You go on ahead and hit. Don't let me mess with your mojo."

Sean was watching Jack's muzzle, while everyone else was watching the cards, and he could swear that Jack's grin started before he even flipped the card over. "Four of Diamonds," Jack said. "Looks like your finances are definitely improving."

That was the meaning of the Four. Sean tapped his fingers on the cards, not even bothering to hide his grin as the coyote next to him whooped. Jack knew the cards, and it sure felt like he was dealing out whatever cards he wanted. Sean would never be able to follow those nimble paws with just his eyes, though he kept imagining them on his tail, his rear, his thighs. He collected his winnings and cleared his head of those thoughts, but even though he watched the next deal closely, he couldn't follow the movement of the black fingers. If he was cheating, Jack was good.

He was good anyway, of course, and that was the problem. The next hand the red wolf got was the Seven of Hearts and the Seven of Diamonds, and that had to be intentional. Apart they were good cards, the Heart somewhat less than the Diamond, but together they meant love and pleasure.

Jack grinned down at him. "Quite a pair," he said. "Want to split those up?"

Sean gave him a wide, answering smile. "No, I'd like to keep these together. Don't think I need anything else."

The coyote scratched his ears. "Son, I can't argue with your winnin's, but you got some mighty peculiar superstitions there."

"Whatever keeps him happy," Jack said, and Sean noticed the tip of the fox's tail twitching back and forth.

"Winnin's what keeps me happy," the coyote said. "And another one o'them sevens would just about do the trick right now."

Jack skipped a card towards the coyote's thirteen, and the three of them watched as the Seven of Clubs came to rest. "Usually I don't take orders," Jack said. "But for the gentleman, this once..."

The coyote shook his head at Sean. "You'd have hit twenty-one, son. Maybe you should re-think."

"Oh, I don't know," Sean said, his eyes on Jack. "I have a winning feeling."

Jack winked, unmistakably, but just as the coyote was saying something like, "Hey," Jack revealed the dealer's eighteen, and the coyote's objection vanished as Jack swept Sean's chips over to his.

"And I think that'll do it for me," Sean said. He pushed four of his chips forward and smiled at Jack. "For you," he said.

"Sorry, sir," Jack said, and pushed the chips back. "I don't take tips at the table."

Sean's ears stayed up through an effort of will. Of course they were allowed to accept tips at the table; he knew that. But if Jack didn't want his money, there was nothing he could do about it. He took the chips back and then tilted his muzzle to one side. "Is there anywhere you can accept tips?"

The fox's tail jumped, but Jack didn't react otherwise. "It's very kind of you to ask," he said. "But you seem so familiar with the cards that I can't help but think you already know the answer." He gave Sean a wink, and started the deal again.

As Sean got up from the table, confused, the coyote turned and laid a paw on his arm. "Y'aint the first to try to get into Black Jack's pants, and you won't be the last," he said in a low voice. "But shoot, you got closer than anyone I seen in a while. I thought for a minute you two was old friends."

"No," Sean said. "Just met." He smiled and nodded. "Good luck."

At the newer casinos, it was all done with electronic tickets, but at the Persian, they still had chips and cashiers. Sean leaned on the cashier's window ledge looking at Jack as she counted out his money. He felt obscurely disappointed, not in Jack, but in the cards. Had Jack been manipulating them to get Sean to stay longer? Had the whole flirting just been an act? Sean was pretty good at reading people, and he'd thought there was some genuine attraction there, but maybe he'd been fooling himself. Jack was a professional just like he was.

The cashier had to say "Hey" twice to get his attention.

He turned. The plain wolf behind the grille was holding up a white chip. "This isn't one of ours."

Sean blinked, and saw writing on the chip that said, "Full House Café." An image of Jack's paws sliding his tip back to him flashed through his head. "Oh, sorry," he said, and took the chip back. A gold-embossed '1' was all that was on the other side. "Don't know how that got in there."

She slid his money over to him, and he pocketed it and walked quickly to the sports book area. The fat wolf was there at the bar, pretending to watch some game. His tail was twitching; it was definitely not wagging. One paw was tapping the bar, and Sean could feel the intensity of the wolf's attention in how studiously he was not looking around.

The red wolf slid a rumpled ten into the video poker machine next to his client. "Took long enough," the wolf growled under his breath.

"Just doing my job," Sean said.

"Looked like you were enjoying yourself a little too much," the wolf replied, and then shut up as the bartender came over to take Sean's order. When he'd delivered the club soda, the wolf started up again. "I'm not paying you to flirt."

Sean sipped his drink and tapped the video poker buttons almost at random. "You're paying me to do a job," he said, "not for the privilege of telling me how to do it."

The wolf didn't respond to this, just kept tapping his paw on the bar. "Look at that," he said to the screen. "Goddamn Holy Cross can't buy a bucket." The bartender moved away again, and the wolf lowered his voice. "So, did you spot anything?"

You're terrible at being sneaky, Sean wanted to tell him. Instead, he said, "No. If he's cheating you, he's good enough that I can't spot him and he's even fooling the casino cameras."

The wolf made a growling noise, a frustrated snarl that drew some looks. He gestured at the screen again. "They're terrible!" he said loudly, and the other patrons turned back to their own business. "So what next?"

Sean could feel the weight of the white chip in the pocket of his shirt. "I might be able to get a little closer," he said. "All that flirting wasn't for nothing, you know."

"How's that going to help? He doesn't cheat unless he's at the table."

"No, but he might keep something elsewhere that would help us."

"Like what?"

"If I knew that, I wouldn't have to go look."

The wolf took a drink of his beer and was silent. Finally, he said, "I'm not paying for you to go screw the guy who's screwing me."

Sean restrained his initial reaction. "You want me to keep investigating or not?"

Another long drink, and the beer was gone. "Tomorrow, same time. I'll expect a full report."

"I have your number. I'll call you if anything develops before then."

The wolf pushed himself gracelessly off the chair and left without a word. Sean shook his head and played the video poker machine until his money was gone, then headed out to the dark Las Vegas night. His work day was just beginning.

The Full House Café, like any other place in Vegas where someone might stop for more than twenty seconds, featured automated gambling machines. Sean was amused to see that in addition to the table-top video poker, the café had a video slot in the corner on which a cartoony rendition of an old yak in white robes with a long beard was dancing on a pile of gold coins. Above the old yak was written the name of the game: "Philosopher's Stone," and beneath that, in smaller letters, "turn wisdom into gold!!"

At the counter where he ordered his coffee, black, he saw a pile of white chips similar to the one in his shirt pocket, and realized that they were a clever type of business card. "Take one," the rabbit behind the counter said when she saw Sean looking. "They're lucky."

"Got one." He patted his shirt pocket.

"All right, then. Good luck," she said, which seemed to have replaced "good-bye" as a parting expression in some parts of Vegas.

The "Philosopher's Stone" machine featured Nietzsche, Hegel, Locke, Descartes, and Rousseau, as well as various symbols, and if you got four in a row of one of the philosophers, you got to debate him for extra credits. The game looked too silly for Sean to pass up.

Being a slot machine, of course, it was long on promise and short on delivery, but he finally lined up four Nietzsches. The machine display sprang to life with a picture of the old wolf and three phrases that were apparently attributed to him. Sean chose "Error has made man of animals," and got 40 credits and moved on to another set of three phrases. The actual "debate" was somewhat of a letdown, but he made most of his starting ten dollars back.

"I like a fellow who can take on Neitzsche," said a voice behind him.

He turned to see Jack, still wearing his vest with the club pin but without the name badge, his scent lost amidst the strong coffee smell of the shop. Sean grinned, feeling his tail wag. "You did show up."

"Of course," Jack said. "The cards said I would."

"I have a feeling they had a little help," Sean said as they cashed out and returned to the table. The initial feeling of delight was fading and now he was a little wary. The flirting at the table was nice, but here they were in a different element, on equal footing. Jack sipped some sort of latté while Sean lapped at his now-lukewarm coffee.

Ignoring his comment about the cards, Jack asked immediately whether Sean was a tourist, and Sean admitted he wasn't, that he just didn't get to Siegel much. Jack conversed as smoothly as he dealt, and Sean found it impossible to work any more questions about his dealing into the conversation. He did find out that the fox had been born and raised in Las Vegas and had been dealing blackjack for various casinos since he was seventeen. He blamed his career on his name. "What else is a black fox named Jack going to do in Vegas?" he said.

Jack's laugh, sincere and light, put Sean at ease. By the time his coffee was gone, so was his nervousness. He was comfortable telling the fox about his childhood in New Orleans, mimicking the Cajun accent of his youth, and telling him that he lived over near downtown, though he didn't mention where.

"Well," Jack said. "I live a block away, you seem like a nice guy, and I'm tired of this coffee shop. Want to come over?"

Sean grinned. "You always move this fast?"

"I don't have time to move slow." The fox got up from the table and inclined his head. "Coming?"

The red wolf hesitated. His only worry was that Jack was onto him and that this was some kind of trap, but his whiskers weren't tingling. "Hang on a second," he said, and reached into his pocket for the cards. "Just want to check with my friends."

Jack grinned at him and watched him deal out a three-card layout. For a moment, Sean studied them, then swept them back to the deck and stood. "All right," he said. "Let's go."

"You put a lot of faith in them," Jack said as they walked out into the night. To the south, Sean could see the glow of the Strip and the single beam of the Luxor shooting up to the sky. "Wish I had friends that are that reliable."

"This was my mother's deck," Sean said. "She gave 'em to me when I left home."

The fox gave him a sidewise look. "So you asked your mother if you could come back to my place?"

Sean laughed. "Not my mother. Just a family friend."

"What would you have done if they'd said no?"

The red wolf examined Jack. He saw no reason to dissemble. "I'd have politely—and regretfully—declined."

Jack shook his head. "You're an odd one, all right."

He'd said it almost affectionately, so Sean wasn't offended. "Isn't everyone in this town?"

The fox grinned as they stopped at an apartment building. "Touché." He tapped a code to open the gate and held it for Sean, who had been studying the resident list trying to figure out which one was Jack. "I'm not on there," Jack said, grinning. "Like to keep a low profile."

"Okay," Sean said, embarrassed at having been caught. He walked into the lobby.

The building was plain, but clean and relatively new. Tile floors and wood paneling made Sean think it had been built as part of the boom of the late 90s, when a lot of people searching for a cheap alternative to L.A. had driven up demand for homes in the Vegas area. Jack stepped past him to the stairs and led him down a second floor hall that smelled of carpet cleaner, to an apartment with "206" on the door, and inside.

The fox slid out of his vest easily, but it was the coming-home action of shedding a coat, not an invitation to Sean. He walked across the small living room they'd entered to a cabinet, and opened it. "Something stronger than coffee?" he asked, looking back.

Sean was looking at his slender chest with its white throat ruff and the thick black fur down his shoulders and back. "Only if it's tall and black," he said with a grin.

"All right then." Jack grinned. "I keep that in here." He beckoned Sean into the next room.

There was nothing in the living room to help Sean's investigation, and he wasn't sure what he was looking for anyway. A book on "how to cheat at card dealing?" A membership card to the International Federation of Underhanded Blackjack Dealers? He had a phone bug in his pocket; illegal, but usable in his case because they weren't looking to bring criminal charges anyway. What he really hoped was that exposing the cards to this place would give him a good read on how his case was going to turn out. For that, he'd have to stick around here for a while.

The final swish of the fox's black tail as he disappeared into the other room suggested a pleasant way to pass that time. Sean unbuttoned the top button of his shirt and walked into the bedroom after Jack.

The fox caught him by surprise, paws around his waist and warm breath in his ear, murmuring, "Now, let's see what kind of hand we've been dealt." He brushed his muzzle within an inch of Sean's, giving Sean time and chance to inhale his scent in return.

Sean made a practice of learning people's scents from a distance, but preferred to smell someone up close. Jack's strong vulpine scent masked a myriad of details, which shifted through his nose like the nuances in a fine wine. He wouldn't have been able to put a name to many of them, but he compared them to other people he knew: here the same excitement as his friend Michael, here the same touch of passion as an ex-lover or two, here the same caution he knew in himself.

He always savored that moment of introduction, especially in this context where he expected the encounter to progress to something more intimate quickly. This getting to know his partner, being let into their private space, was special to him on a personal level, but also excited the part of him that liked finding out about people, liked getting more information about them. He kept his eyes open, too, and looked around the small bedroom.

Jack kept a pair of dressers, a vanity, a bed, and a bookcase that was full of not only books, but also DVDs, CDs, and various trinkets. The DVDs included "Ocean's Eleven," obligatory viewing for any Vegas resident, as well as "Rounders," "The Sting," "The Cincinnati Kid," and "The Hustler," and those were just the ones that leapt out at Sean before the fox's paws slid inside his shirt and around his midriff. Funny; he hadn't even felt his shirt's buttons being undone.

The touch made him shiver. Jack's paws were as sure as they were quick, claws tracing just close enough to his skin to be felt without exerting any pressure. He placed his paws on the fox's slender form in return, brushing down the sleek black fur to come to rest on his hips. They rubbed their long muzzles together, teasing each other's whiskers while their paws pulled their bodies close. Sean realized that somehow, all of his shirt's buttons had been undone, and the shirt itself was hanging off his shoulders. He pulled back a little bit and looked into a grin as Jack's paws moved up his chest and over his shoulders, slowly forcing the shirt off.

He had to take his paws off the fox to let it fall, and that brought a brief flash of self-consciousness, because Jack was thin and sleek, and Sean, though he worked out, did not do so regularly enough to get rid of a little extra weight around his waist. But Jack didn't look anything but pleased at what he saw, and his paws wandered happily down the ivory fur on the red wolf's chest and stomach. Sean put his paws back on Jack's hips and slid his fingers under the waistband of the fox's pants, exploring the thick black fur and slender hips, and then worked around to feel the base of the long, fluffy, black tail.

Jack pulled the wolf against him with surprising force, and Sean found that, mysteriously, his pants had been unfastened as well. They slid down his hips, guided by a confident pair of paws that let them hang around his knees before moving back up the outside of his legs to cup his rump. His tail started to wag of its own accord, and then he put more energy into it as he felt Jack's tail match his enthusiasm.

It had definitely been a while, he thought. There was no reason he shouldn't be undoing Jack's pants the same way the fox had undone his, except that the fastening was pressed up against his boxers, pressing, in fact, right into his warm arousal, and not only did he not want to relieve that pressure, he didn't want to change Jack's paws, which felt so good on his rear, under his wagging tail. Sean was sure that if he were more used to this type of encounter, he would know how and when to get Jack's pants open, too. As it was, all he could do was slide his paws further inside the still-fastened pants.

He thought at first that he'd accidentally slid inside the fox's underpants as well, and congratulated himself on his luck in moving forward, but as he explored the slender hips and ventured around to the fox's tight rear, he realized that Jack wasn't actually wearing underwear. He felt a little embarrassed at his white cotton boxers, until Jack's paws slipped inside them, brushing under his tail and driving any embarrassment out of Sean's mind. He whimpered softly, answered by a low "mmmm" from Jack. "Feels like someone's ready to move to the bed," the fox murmured.

"Yeah," Sean said, and took the opportunity to reach around the front and fumble with Jack's pants until he got them open.

"Right behind you, Slim," Jack said.

The red wolf rubbed his muzzle against the fox's and licked up the edge of one of Jack's long, triangular ears, following it as it flicked around. Jack squirmed, the first sign that his arousal was overwhelming his composure, and Sean pressed the advantage, licking further into the ear as Jack buried his slender muzzle into the red wolf's shoulder ruff.

"Bed. Right," Sean whispered into the fox's ear. He turned Jack around, keeping his muzzle in the fox's ear and pressing his hips up against the big fluffy tail. The lithe black form pressed back, tight and hard. "Lead the way," Sean murmured.

Once on the bed, the remainder of their clothes didn't last long. Sean was used to first dates that ended short of bed, and even the ones that made it that far usually left some intimacy for later. But Jack didn't pause, and it was Sean who did when Jack rummaged in the bedside drawer and flipped a condom to the wolf, as easily as dealing a card. "You sure?" Sean asked, but he was sure enough of the answer that his claw had already popped the wrapper open before Jack's grinning nod.

The fox was warm and tight, slender and alive with energy below him. Some guys just lay there and let the top do all the work, but Sean felt Jack was an equal partner in their lovemaking. They moved together, spoke and answered each other with short yips and moans, and shuddered in concert.

Sean lowered his muzzle as his body tightened, gripping the fox's ruff in his teeth and inhaling, filling his nose with the sweet vulpine scent. He pulled up, panting hard through his nose and moaning into the black fur as his hips drove the smaller canid into the bed. Dimly, he was aware of the fox squirming below him, and he knew that Jack's arousal had crested as well.

"Uhhh," he moaned, letting go of the ruff, and Jack echoed his moan with a contented exhalation. Sean nuzzled the tall black ear again, making the fox squirm and turn his head away from the tickling whiskers. "Definitely...a winning hand..." Sean panted.

The fox wriggled back until Sean giggled and squirmed himself, and Jack said, "No argument here...I think you take the pot."

Sean slowly extricated his paw from below the fox and said, "Let's share it."

"Mmm. Deal." Jack relaxed. "What's your tie time?"

"Ten minutes, usually."

"Not bad. You like to talk or just cuddle?"

"Whatever. I'm easy."

"Oh, I wouldn't say that." Jack brought one of his slender paws to Sean's and held it against his chest. "You weren't difficult, but you weren't easy, either. I had to drop a bunch of hints."

"The cards?" Sean kept his demeanor casual, but turned on his detective mind.

"Words, and the chip," Jack said. "I always let the cards guide me, not the other way round."

"Oh."

"Disappointed?" Jack curled his tail around under Sean's, laying across the red wolf's rump. "You thought I was picking those cards?"

Sean thought for a moment before answering, and then decided, to hell with it, and told the truth. "I thought it would be extraordinary if you hadn't. But the cards know. It's just been a long time since..."

Jack turned his head and fixed Sean with one eye. "Since?"

The red wolf wriggled and grinned. "Since I met someone so in tune."

"Don't get the wrong idea here," Jack said. "I'm not looking for an attachment."

"Me neither," said Sean, and after a moment's silence, he said what he thought they were both thinking. "But what if the cards..."

Jack shrugged, but Sean could see the corners of his grin. "I didn't say I wasn't open to one."

* * *

The water pressure in Jack's shower wasn't great, but Sean didn't mind. It almost took him longer to choose which scented soap to use than to get his fur clean. He had scanned the bathroom for anything that might be a clue, as if to convince himself that he really was here for work and not just following his libido. Really, he was relieved to have nothing to report to the fat wolf, though he told himself sternly that if Jack had admitted to cheating, he would have done his duty to his employer. His groin tingled in mild reproach as he soaped it, recalling the tight warmth of the fox and the way he'd abandoned himself to it, but it had been expected of him, he reasoned. Jack would've been suspicious if he hadn't gone to bed with him.

That didn't sound very convincing, but it was the best he could do. He got out of the shower and dried as much of his fur as he could with the large towel he found folded neatly on the toilet seat. For a moment, he debated whether to wrap it around himself before walking back out, but he'd feel silly if Jack were still naked, as he suspected the black fox would be.

He was right. Jack swung his legs off the bed as Sean walked out of the bathroom. "You clean up nice."

"Your turn." Sean watched the fox swing his rump and tail back and forth as he walked into the bathroom; a moment later the water began running.

The red wolf stretched and pulled on his boxers and pants, and then thought, might as well do a little detective work. He walked around the bedroom, looking sharply at the neatly arranged bookshelves and making note of the titles. A few science fiction novels, a few spiritual books, a little of everything, in fact. Just the sort of book collection he would have if he didn't want anyone to be able to learn anything from it. No books on the cards, though he wasn't surprised; he didn't keep his in plain view either. They were full of his notations and he wouldn't want anyone seeing some of the titles anyway.

In the living room, the same things he'd noticed before. Nothing new presented itself, but something nagged at him. He looked around at the coffee table, the low black sofa, the television, and couldn't see what it was. The kitchen, though full of interesting smells, was similarly unhelpful. He returned to the living room and, cocking an ear to the shower to make sure it was still running, lifted the fox's vest carefully from the coat rack. He slipped his fingers into the pockets and found the business card holder that held the casino ID and, behind it, a driver's license.

Jack Filcher. Not an auspicious name. But the IDs were all in order. He memorized the driver's license number and replaced the small card holder, and that's when he realized what was nagging at him.

He took his wallet out of his back pocket and opened it. Bringing it to his nose, he caught the very faint scent of fox.

Jack had been in his wallet while he was in the shower. He closed it again and then laughed silently. Turnabout was fair play, after all. His detective license was in there, but at this point it didn't really matter whether Jack knew he was a detective. Replacing his wallet, he went into the other pocket and took out his cards.

He sat on the couch as he shuffled, inhaling the scent of the apartment and focusing on his question: was Jack cheating the fat wolf? The noise of the shower stopped suddenly, and Sean found his mind occupied with images of the sleek black naked fox, wondering what he would look like all wet, the water running through his fur in trails. He shook his head and laid down the third card, and stared. All three were the Jack of Clubs.

He rubbed his eyes and looked again, and now only the first was the Jack of Clubs; the other two were blank.

Slowly, Sean picked up one of the blank cards and turned it over. The back was the same deck he had known since he was a cub, the double circles soothing in their regularity. He turned the card back over and saw a Three of Hearts. When he set it down on the table again, the design vanished.

The third card, when he picked it up, revealed four clubs, and he shivered. The Three of Hearts was a warning: careful what you say. He'd seen it at the beginning of the job, too. The Four of Clubs was worse: lies and betrayal. Alone, it would have meant bad things for Jack. Together with the previously negative card, though, it seemed to be intimating that Jack would be betrayed if he weren't careful. Or if Sean weren't careful. He picked up all three cards and shuffled them back into the deck, paws moving automatically while his mind worked.

Jack ruffled through clothes in the other room. Sean slid the cards back into his pocket. Whether Jack was causing the odd effect or just happened to be drawn to it, he could investigate later, on his own time. He had only encountered this effect once before, the day he'd left New Orleans. In any event, the unreliability of the cards was hardly enough for him to follow up. If Jack were cheating, he wasn't doing it by any detectable means that would satisfy the fat wolf.

"Want something to drink before you go?" The fox came out into the living room wearing a silk robe with an Oriental pattern.

Sean got up and shook his head. "No, thanks. I should get back home." He walked over to Jack and extended a paw. "Thanks for a nice night."

The fox grinned an open grin, tongue hanging slightly out. He stepped into Sean and slid his arms around him. "Anyone who just stuck the pot gets a hug before he goes."

"Mmm. Okay." Sean couldn't detect any hint that Jack was annoyed at the information he'd found in Sean's wallet. He hugged back and let himself enjoy the feel of the fox's slender body against him.

* * *

"There's no evidence that he's cheating you purposefully," he told the fat wolf the next evening. They'd met at the bar in the Persian again, and Sean had braced himself for the wolf's anger with a scotch and a written copy of the contract he'd signed.

"That's fine," the wolf said. He was on his second beer. "Glad to hear it. Here's your money."

He slid an envelope across the bar to Sean, apparently not caring whether anyone saw it. Sean picked it up and stared at him. "So that's it?"

"Yeah. If he ain't doing it intentionally, then..." The fat wolf shrugged. "I'll play some other table." He appeared to turn his attention to whatever game was on the TV for real this night, but Sean looked closer, at the twitching of the tip of his tail and the curl of a smile at the corners of his muzzle. He felt a shiver then, all down his own tail, and without even looking at the check he grabbed it and shoved it into his jacket.

"Nice doing business with you," he said, and slid off the stool, the scotch overwhelmed by the bad taste in his muzzle.

He searched the casino floor, but Jack was nowhere in sight. Not working, or just on break? The cards in his pocket were tingling. His fur stood on end. The sense of urgency made his ears and tail twitch. He had to do a layout, or did he? He knew something was wrong, involving the fat wolf and Jack. He should find out what it was before asking the cards for direction.

The big-bosomed vixen at the next blackjack table told him Jack had called in sick that night. She looked oddly at him when he asked if Jack had called himself. "Who else would have called?" she said, and that he didn't know.

The Full House Café was another dead end. No black foxes stood by the Philosopher's Stone machines. He hurried out, down the street, to Jack's apartment building, even though he hadn't watched Jack enter the code, and he had no way of getting in.

Luck, decidedly, was on his side. The gate was ajar. He checked up and down the street and then slipped inside.

There, the insistent tingling of his cards grew stronger, raising his fur. He padded quickly to Jack's apartment and listened at the door. No sound came from inside. He bent to sniff the door handle, and caught Jack's scent, strong, and wolf, not him. Standing again, he considered the door. Knock, or just barge in? He lowered a paw to the door handle, and felt a brush against his tail. The tingling of the cards vanished.

Sean turned and clapped a paw to his pocket. As soon as he turned, he saw Jack in the hallway, holding his deck of cards gingerly and looking grim.

"I wouldn't go in," he said softly. "Your friends are mighty annoyed they haven't been able to catch me."

"They're not my friends," Sean hissed.

Jack arched an eyebrow. "They know a lot of things only you know." He inclined his head toward the apartment door.

"I didn't tell them. They must have followed me."

"Very convenient. Plausible, even. I congratulate you." His fingers riffled through the deck. "Good detective work."

"Jack..."

"I think these will be adequate payment for the inconvenience of moving again," the fox said, to himself. "I haven't seen a deck as sensitive as these in a long time."

"They were my mother's," Sean said.

Jack's paws stopped and squared the deck. He looked up at Sean. "Fair trade, then."

"Listen, I didn't mean to...I came back to warn you!"

"Did you now?"

"I believe you're not really cheating him, but he thinks you are!"

Their ears caught the noise at the same time. Jack reacted quicker than Sean would have thought possible, flipping over the banister of the staircase in a moment.

Sean, left alone in the hallway, held up a paw to his ear, a well-conditioned reaction to surprise.

The door opened, allowing a large grey wolf muzzle to poke out into the hall. The nose twitched, smelling the air. "Hang on a second," Sean said to nobody, and turned his attention to the wolf. "Sorry. My girlfriend was supposed to be home but she's still playing the slots over at Caesar's. With my money." Without waiting for a reaction, he turned his attention back to the imaginary earpiece. "I know I gave it to you, honey, but it is my money. Yes, it is. Look, I'm coming over there. Don't move." He waved to the wolf and looked up from his imaginary conversation. "Sorry if I bothered you. You know how it is."

The wolf narrowed his eyes. "You seen a black fox?"

"What, ever?"

"In the building. Why you here in the building?"

"Buddy of mine lives up on four." Sean pointed up the stairs. "I was hoping to have a few beers with him, but now I gotta go to Caesar's before all my goddamn beer money is gone. That okay with you?"

The wolf studied him for a moment. Faintly, from below, Sean heard the flick of cards, and thought he felt a sympathetic twitch to his fur. He itched to run down there, but he waited, and finally the wolf just grumbled and stepped back into the room. He saw, for a moment, the door to Jack's bedroom, and another part of him twitched. As soon as the door was closed, he spun and ran down the stairs to the next landing.

"Jack?" he whispered.

No response. The stair was empty.

He hurried downstairs, skipping steps. Beyond the empty lobby, the gate stood closed. He was about to run outside when he spotted a card stuck into the row of mailboxes: the Jack of Clubs.

On the back, he saw when he took it down, was his double circle pattern. The mailbox swung open easily. He reached inside, and pulled out his deck of cards.

The tingling was gone from them, the crisis apparently passed. He sighed and sat with his back to the wall of the lobby, and then set the Jack of Clubs down on the floor. Slowly, he dealt out the top two cards, keeping his mind blank. Jack had been the last to shuffle this deck, and his imprint would remain on it for a little while. Sean was as sure of that as he was that Jack had not had to search the deck to find his significator. It would have risen to his fingers, drawn by the pull of the black fox.

He dealt the Five of Spades and the Seven of Diamonds, and his muzzle curved into a grin. A change of opinion, victory achieved at cost; and the reward from consistent effort, a card he seemed to see a lot. He looked at the tableau one more time and then scooped the cards up.

So Sean's little performance had changed Jack's mind, at least enough to leave Sean his cards. And he knew they had power, so he knew that he did, too. Sean was interested in Jack for that, but he was also intrigued by the fox. What did he do with all that power? Just deal tables? As he walked out of the building, even though it was night, he whistled a tune to himself, singing the lyrics in his head.

I was blue, just as blue as I could be
Ev'ry day was a cloudy day for me
Then good luck came a-knocking at my door
Skies were gray but they're not gray anymore.

It appeared that he had himself a case.

If Gold's "real world" settings are designed for inhabitants who still have species' instincts and individual physical traits, what about a Furry world with anthropomorphic-animal costumed superheroes? "Don't Blink" was originally published in Heat *#4 (Sofawolf Press, July), later revised and integrated into Gold's collection* In the Doghouse of Justice *(Sofawolf Press, August 2011). It features Jake Kellin, a.k.a. the teleporting Blink Coyote of the League of Crimefighting Canids, a team of eleven masked and (mostly) superpowered canids (wolves, foxes, a dingo, and a fennec) in a general anthropomorphic world. Their costumes are lined with Neutra-Scent to keep their real identities a secret from the sharp noses of the citizenry. Blink, new to the League, is anxious to get "his own" super-villain, as each of the other heroes seems to have a particular foe. But all the super-villains are "taken" by one or another of the other heroes. All…?*

Don't Blink

Kyell Gold

Jake knew that training was necessary to become a top-flight superhero, so he endured it patiently. When Marcia took his training into her own paws, however, he usually attended those sessions with enthusiasm. So it felt odd, on this late spring night, to be hesitating in the doorway of her bedroom as she slipped out of her jacket and blouse.

"Well?" she said. Her long ears twitched, satellite dishes rotating to focus on him.

The coyote unbuttoned one button on his shirt, reached for the next. "Sorry, I just…"

"No, no." She placed a finger on the third button as the coyote was about to unbutton it. "Undress your way."

She stepped back from him, lowered her skirt to the floor and then tossed it into the hamper in the corner. Her short, fluffy tail rested against the vanity as she leaned back, folded her arms under her bra, and watched him.

He eyed the cleavage her pose created, and grinned. "You got it." He concentrated, extending his arms forward for dramatic effect. He hesitated only for a moment—toward her or away?—and then figured out how he could use the mirror behind her. He closed his eyes and pictured himself in front of her, and when he flexed his power, he contracted the 'field' as much as he could.

In the mirror, over her shoulder, he watched his clothes hang in the air where he'd been one second ago and then fall to the floor. That never got old.

Her paws reached out for his sides, fingers sinking into his tawny pelt, her thumbs rubbing at the border where the tawny dissolved into ivory. He returned his attention to her, fitting his paws neatly around the curve of her dark brown shoulders.

"You've gotten really good at that." She reached down between his legs, finding plenty with which to pull him forward. "C'mere, now."

"Come in handy if I ever need to strip for a supervillain," he said. "Maybe like some evil woman I need to distract." He moved his large paws down to her small rear, shoving his fingers under her pink panties and pulling her hips against his.

Their muzzles met. Her long ears folded over to touch the tips of his. He pushed her panties further down and broke the kiss, licking up her pink nose and the gentle slope of her muzzle.

"Jake," she said in mild reproach, turning her head to the side.

His ears flicked back. She didn't let him go, though, so he didn't stop pushing her panties down, crouching to finish the job. She stepped out of them and shook her head. "You canids with your tongues. Come on, onto the bed."

He licked at her, but she stepped away from him, unhooked her bra and dropped it in the hamper. He watched her bare white rear sashay to the bed and plop down on it, bouncing with the springs. Her lithe form turned around, showing off the curves as she sat back and beckoned him with a finger. He wagged his tail and jumped up to the bed in a moment, burying his muzzle in her stomach fur.

She squealed and batted at his head, leaning back on her elbows. "Jake!"

"What?" He grinned up, but she didn't really seem to want to be tickled. So he got serious, trying not to get distracted, trying to remember what kind of foreplay she'd told him she liked. Marcia wasn't the first girl he'd slept with, but she was the first he'd taken instruction from.

She stopped complaining, then, and got into it herself, her gentle fingers getting him as excited as she smelled. At her touch he moaned and pushed her down onto the bed, washing his tongue across her body.

She shuddered, slipping her paws around to his rear to pull him down against her. He gasped in excitement and worked his hips, feeling her moan building in her chest before he heard it. He wrapped his arms around her body, pressed close, feeling her warmth slowly engulf him. "Don't forget to concentrate," she whispered.

"I know." For a moment he held there, making her wait, annoyed that she'd broken the mood, and then he pressed in slowly, all the way. She squirmed as he held her, bucking up against him, pulling his muzzle from her chest up to her mouth so her tongue could slide between his lips in a hot, wild kiss.

They kissed, while his hips bucked, and that lasted a grand total of two minutes by her bedside clock until he heard her high squeals and felt her body shake as the familiar surge of imminent release built in him—

—and suddenly he was in his own bedroom on all fours, moaning and shaking the rickety frame of his double bed, and the warmth of the rabbit was gone. He panted, unable to stop himself from consummating the act with empty air, and then sighed at the musky smell of his passion and sweat, his ears flat. "Shit," he said to the empty room.

He blinked back to her bedroom, ears flat. She was getting under the covers, and if she saw him appear, she gave no sign.

"I'm sorry," he said.

Marcia shook her head. "You weren't concentrating." She lay back on the pillows and looked at the ceiling.

"I tried," he said. "But if you weren't so damn hot..."

Now she looked at him. "Don't try that, Jake, it's not going to work. A real superhero has to think fast and keep his power completely under his control. You had to have felt the power building up, and you should have been able to stop it. Do we have to look at the monitor record again to look at how long you had?"

He glanced at the machine in the corner, and tucked his tail between his legs. "No."

She sighed. "You know this is all for your career, right, Jake?" He nodded. "Well, look. There are worse things than having to practice that some more."

When he looked up, she was smiling. "I just feel like I screwed up this whole night. I really have been practicing."

"By yourself?" She arched an eyebrow.

"Well...yeah." He looked away and flicked his ears.

"That's cute. Do you think of me?"

"Oh yeah!"

"Nice to know you think of me at least then." She turned onto her side.

Jake started to collect his clothes. "Sorry," he mumbled. He pulled the briefs on, then stood there awkwardly.

"You can stay if you want to." She sounded tired.

"I was going to do my rounds."

"All right." She turned out the light. Just before he blinked to the rooftop, he heard her say, "Be safe."

* * *

Marcia's condo building was not tall, but there were few tall buildings between it and downtown Dunstown, so it gave him a nice view of the suburbs and the gaslamp district, and the cracks in between where dirty things happened. He lay on the edge, eyes closed, listening to the city below. The wind ruffled the dark streak of fur down his back and tugged his tail back and forth, slowly carrying away the glow and warmth of sex.

No noise reached his ears this night, and after ten minutes, he was feeling a little chilly even through his fur. He took one last look around this area and blinked back to his apartment, on the other side of town.

Back in his bedroom, Jake dropped his clothes and put on his costume, a tight black jumpsuit with a yellow eye logo in the center. He'd wanted it smaller and over the left breast, but Marcia had overruled him. "It has to be big. We want people to remember it so the brand takes hold. You won't be doing much hand-to-hand fighting or sneaking around. Pop in, pop out. We'll put a kevlar sheet behind this so if people aim at it, you can survive being shot. That's what I'm most worried about. Someone taking a shot at you that you don't see."

So Jake had kevlar on the front and back, a hood he could pull over his head to avoid exposing his identity if he needed to, and black gloves that had a well-textured grip, because early on he had a tendency to blink into someplace off balance and put his hands out to break his fall. He was much better now, but he still kept the gloves because he didn't know what he would be appearing next to.

BLINK COYOTE

His portable police scanner fit into the pocket on his right hip. He seated the earbud that was connected to it in his right ear before blinking to the roof of his building, his safe spot numero uno. From there he could see and hear several blocks into the Swamp, his low-rent, low-class neighborhood where he'd started breaking up small crimes when he first got his powers. As his confidence had grown, so had his beat, but he always began and ended in the Swamp.

It was quiet tonight, so he blinked over to spot numero dos, in the financial district, Dunstown's euphemistic name for the three buildings that housed the city's largest bank and four financial services companies. There he heard some activity, and turned up the volume until he caught the code: 211-S. Robbery in progress, silent alarm. 221 Redwood, cross street 3rd—that was only six blocks away, a small office complex. Someone after the computers, no doubt. That happened a few times a month. He blinked to the closest roof he could see, and then the next, until he was looking down at the intersection.

Jake knew that the four-story plain brown building with schoolhouse-regular windows was older than he was, but the collection of antennas on the roof and the black wire at each window showed him that the inside had been brought up to modern standards. He tapped his paw impatiently, itching to blink inside and find out what was going on. He hated having to wait for the police.

They pulled up ten minutes later, lights and sirens off. Two officers got out, and Jake sighed when he saw the six-foot-tall frame and huge rack of antlers. The presence of Officer Rosen meant he'd most likely be wasting his time, but he had to try. He put his hood up and blinked down to the street, in full view of both the large elk and his new partner, a young fox.

The fox clapped a paw to his gun in alarm, but Rosen barely twitched. "Blinky," he said. "Wondered when we'd see you."

"Just offering my services, Officer," Jake said, keeping his ears up and smiling, not reacting to the elk's condescension.

"We don't need the League butting in," Rosen said. "We've got this under control." He looked over his shoulder. "Collins, you have the building entry code?"

"I'm not here representing the League," Jake said. "When I am, I have to wear this red and blue armband, and I can only do that anyway if there are supervillains involved or if there are research laboratory thefts—"

Rosen cut him off with a wave as the fox tapped a code into the security panel. "I'm not interested in your accessorizing tips. We've got this under control. Isn't there a liquor store somewhere you should be staking out?"

"Sergeant," the fox said, "It would be helpful if he could pop in and..."

OFFICER ROSEN

"Collins, just get that door open." Rosen didn't even turn, just kept Jake fixed with his eyes as though he could prevent him from blinking away. Jake glanced over at the fox, and saw a logo that looked like a circuit design and the word Intagrated on the wall at the far end of the lobby.

The fox's ears went down. "Yes, sir."

Jake shrugged, trying not to betray his disappointment. "Just call on the radio if you need me."

"Don't hold your—"

He was on the roof before the elk finished speaking. Keeping his hood up, he sat next to the ledge at the edge of the roof and rested his elbow on it, looking over as the two policemen entered the building. If there was gunfire, or if they called, he could get inside pretty quickly.

A breeze wafted past his nose, carrying a familiar avian scent. She was quiet and his hood muffled surrounding sounds, so he hadn't heard her, but she was good about approaching him from downwind. "Hi, Moxy," he said in a low voice.

"Rosen run you off again?" A tall, stately raven settled herself a few feet in front of him, leaning her arm on the ledge in a mirror image of his

202

pose. Her beak clacked lightly as she talked. Like most avians, she wore no clothes, as all but the lightest garments made it difficult to fly. She had fingers on the ends of her wings and clawed talons at the ends of her skinny black legs, but when she had her arms spread out, she looked like a person in a bird suit.

"Yeah." Jake looked over at her bright black eyes. "I thought things would get better once I got in the League, but it's just gotten worse."

The raven clacked her beak and grinned at him. "They were threatened by a superhero horning in on their turf, and you thought that joining with a bunch of other superheroes would make that better?"

Jake shrugged. "I just thought, y'know, they'd see that I'm legit, that I'm not just some cocky kid out there who doesn't know what I'm doing."

"Cops have long memories. Why d'you think the cop beat at the paper turns over every year?"

"I thought it was cause most reporters are lightweights and once they see their first murder, they ask to be transferred to the society pages."

"Ha ha." She clacked at him again. "For your information, that was a promotion. I'm still on good terms with some of the cops."

"But not all of them."

"Do you want to trade or not?"

He grinned. "What'cha got?"

"Some info the cops aren't talking about on their scanner."

That perked his ears up. "Really? Why not?"

"Why do you think?" She fluffed her wings. "They don't want you and the League hearing about it and getting involved."

Jake couldn't stop his tail from wagging. "A supervillain? Here in Dunstown?"

"Maybe. But no, just a couple thefts from research labs specializing in supernormals."

"Which labs?"

"Tell me about your girlfriend," she countered.

He jumped. "How did you know..." Then he stopped, because her beak was open in a laugh. "Dammit, Moxy..."

"So you do have a girlfriend. That's sweet. How long you been going out? Does she know your secret identity?"

"One question," he said. "Since you already got a bit of info. She's gonna kill me anyway."

"Does she know your secret identity?"

He nodded. "Yeah." He hadn't really been able to hide it, when he'd blinked out during sex on their fourth date.

"So you trust her. Wedding bells in the future?"

"Which labs?" He was determined to hold her to one question. Moxy often dug up good information for him, and if he didn't parcel out the things she wanted to know about him, he wouldn't get far with her. She'd already asked about his family and once about the League in the four months since she'd first met him on a rooftop in the gaslamp district.

"Ling Scientific and the Mount Cedar government facility. The cops are really worried about the Mount Cedar one because it had state of the art locks. They think it might be a new gadgethead."

"Cripes, not another one. You know the League has a list of about a hundred of them?"

"I've heard." She cocked her head as he took out his handheld phone and started jotting notes. "You're just going to send that unsecured?"

"Oh, Crypto does all kinds of security on it," he said, tapping a quick message.

"Yeah, but if I pick that up, or knock you out and take it, I could just read it from there."

He grinned and tossed it to her. "Go for it."

It clattered to the roof as she swiped and missed, unprepared. She picked it up and stared at him, then down at the handheld. Her black eyes blinked, and she looked back up. "It won't turn on."

"Thumbprint reader on the side, keyed to me. I have to be holding it for it to be on."

"What if I sever your thumb?"

He shuddered. "Come on, Moxy."

She tossed the device back to him. "Hey, you have to think like a supervillain."

"Well, it has to stay warm. And I think it checks for a pulse too." He applied his thumb to the pad and watched the screen light up.

"Okay," she said. "So I just have to tie your paw to it and keep you in restraints."

He grinned. "You seen a restraint that could hold me?"

"If I'm a gadgethead, that's the first thing I try to build. Mount Cedar had a lab devoted to power negation."

"What?"

"You think the government likes the idea of you guys running around?"

"The League has a government contract…"

"Wake up, Blink," she said, now sounding cross. "The government defaults on contracts every day. You expect them to rely on the innate honor of anyone else? They expect in others what they would expect from themselves. They just want a way to control you guys in case…in case they need to."

"But why here? Why not in Port City, or Crystal City?"

"In the big two's backyards? Nah. Dunstown was a good, medium-sized town without a superhero, until a couple years ago." She laughed again, a breathy ah-ah-ah sound. "The radiation burst you got your powers from was a malfunction in a machine headed for Mount Cedar, right? Hella ironic, eh?"

"I guess. I don't really go for irony."

"To each his own." She grinned. "This'll make for a good couple articles. 'Ms. Blink,' I think we'll call her. Probably a coyote, right? No, wait, cubs would be a big liability for you. So probably not a coyote." She tapped the ledge. "Probably not a canid. Oh well. I'll make up a few likely candidates and profile them. Should get me through the month. Hey, look. Your cops missed the guy."

Sure enough, Rosen and Collins were coming out of the entrance of the building alone. They got in the car, and Jake turned up his scanner in time to hear Rosen's gruff voice saying, "…no suspects found at the scene. Security company rep arrived and reset the alarm."

He turned the scanner down. "Did you see a truck from the security company pull up?"

"Yeah." Moxy pointed down to where the police car was driving away. "It's around the corner from here. There goes the guy." A bear in a dark uniform was tapping a code at the security panel and then walked off and out of view.

MOXY

Jake watched him go, and looked back up at the building. No lights flickered behind any of the windows, no flashlight appeared now that the police and security were gone. Still…

"Don't go in," Moxy said, watching him.

Jake didn't take his eyes from the windows. "It just doesn't feel right."

"Alarms go off sometimes," she said. "But look, you go in there now and the best thing that can happen is you don't find anything, nobody sees you, and you come back here to this spot. So let's just pretend you've already done that, and move on?"

"What about truth and justice?" he said, trying to keep the bitterness out of his voice.

"What about 'em?" She rustled her feathers. "Sorry, kiddo. You get caught snooping around in there, you're breaking the law. You catch a thief after the cops have already been here, you're making things worse. Just move on. Keep an ear to the scanner, and don't worry. You're a good kid and you'll get a break eventually."

Jake sighed and forced himself to look away from the building, working his paws against the frustration building up inside him. A few mistakes he'd made in the past couple years as an overzealous kid, and suddenly the cops wouldn't let him help with anything. And the League gave him nothing but petty assignments and food duty. "I sure hope so," he said sourly.

"I'll see to it," Moxy said, standing and stretching her wings. "After all, someone's got to be your Lois Lane, right?"

"You're first in line." He waved as she leaped from the roof, spreading her wings and soaring down over the street.

Sometimes he wished he could fly, more for the experience than anything else. He liked being able to hop from place to place in no time, though; he wouldn't trade gifts with Moxy. Besides, any avian or bat could fly around. Only he, so far as he knew, could teleport.

* * *

He watched the papers for the next few days, but saw no mention of a break-in at Intagrated. Moxy'd been right, as he was finding she often was. She'd reported on the police for a year with the Dunstown Herald, and before that she was covering the wires, so she knew her stuff.

Jake caught a car thief two nights later, blinking onto the hood of the car long enough to startle the driver and get a look at the interior, and then he'd blinked into the passenger seat and grabbed the horse's gun, blinked with it to the back seat, and held it on the suddenly terrified driver until he slammed on the brake and stopped the car. The police had grudgingly given him credit for that one, but of course nobody at the League meeting had noticed it except for Red Lightning.

"Nice work on that car thief," the whip-thin fox said, sauntering over to Jake during a break.

"Oh, you noticed?" Jake played with the League pen, doodling on the memo pad.

Red squeezed his shoulder. "I was the youngest once, too. Just be patient, 'kay?"

Jake glanced up at the narrow russet muzzle, encouraged by the smile. "You were? When?"

"'Til you joined."

Jake barked a laugh. "Really? How old are you?"

"I graduated from Whitford two years ago."

"You're kidding. You've only been a superhero for two years?"

The fox leaned against the table, looking down at Jake. "Now, who says I wasn't doing a bit on the side in college? I just went pro after graduation."

"But I read your bio! You collared the Dastardly Dingos, and brought down F.R.I.G.H.T. almost single-pawed, and—"

The fox waved him silent. "Ah, you know, the Dastardly Dingos weren't that dastardly. It was just the alliteration they liked."

"I thought I'd never get into the League. There's no criminal genius masterminds or organizations in Dunstown. I won't even get to investigate the Mount Cedar thing."

Red put a paw on his shoulder again and grinned down. "You'll get there. Just wait 'til the other guys get to know you a little better. The barbecue will be good. Bringin' anyone?" Red grinned. "I saw that article."

"Oh, that." Jake shook his head. "The papers, you know. They make up shit..." He flicked his ears. "Nah, not bringing anyone."

Red nodded, and rubbed his chin with a paw. "You'll meet my wife there. Those things are always kind of awkward, though. Tell ya what. Why don't you come by the house for Sunday brunch? We can sit down and just talk."

"Sure!" Jake wagged his tail. "Love to!"

"I do love my Sarah's biscuits an' gravy, and I bet dollars to donuts you will too."

"Doesn't show." Jake grinned, pointedly eyeing the fox's waistline.

Red laughed. He leaned closer. "I'm not 'llowed to talk about it around Vicious Vixen, but I just can't keep weight on. Anything I eat vanishes quicker'n a chicken leg at my mom's Sunday dinner."

"I'm kinda the same," Jake said.

"You could just blink off the extra weight, couldn't you?" Red cocked his head.

"Eww." Jake shook off the vision of a pile of fat lying on the ground. "I dunno, never tried."

"Crypto reckons you could. He's pretty excited about seein' the range of your powers."

"Really?" Jake looked across the table at the scruffy fox, lost in his laptop computer. "He hasn't given me anything to do. I wonder if he ever will."

Red rubbed his chin again. "Hold on just a tick." He patted the coyote on the shoulder and then navigated through the chairs and heroes to Crypto's side. The smaller fox jumped when Red tapped his shoulder, then perked his ears, looked over at Jake as Red talked, and finally nodded. Red looked up and gave Jake a thumbs-up.

"I swapped with you," he said a moment later, strolling back to Jake's side. "P.K.'s investigating the Mount Cedar research item you brought in, and Crypto'd assigned me as backup, but I convinced him to switch with you. I'll do that cleanup over in Millenport for ya."

"P.K.?"

"Psycho Coyote. Sorry, Power Coyote."

Jake stifled a giggle, looking over at the tall coyote engaged in conversation with Vicious Vixen, three pens twirling lazily in the air above his paws. "Psycho?"

CRYPTO FOX

"Psycho-Kinetic. But also, yeah, that." Red grinned. "Wait 'til the barbecue. Watch him try to pick out a fork. The tines all have to be exactly the same length. He's an okay guy, though. Just be flexible with your schedule."

Jake found out what he meant after the meeting, when P.K. came over to work out the schedule. The floating pens in front of the jarring red on black patterned uniform distracted Jake, so he had a little trouble following the conversation.

"I'm sorry, we can't meet there at noon?"

The pens twirled more quickly. Jake had to look away. "I have to eat lunch at 12:45 p.m.," P.K. said. "And I have to eat dinner at seven. So we'll have to leave the labs at five."

"I could just blink you home."

One of the pens nearly fell. "Oh, no no no. I can't do that. No, my private jet will be fine. We just need to be done by five so I can get home."

Jake caught the eye of Red Lightning, who was grinning at him over MultiWolf's shoulder. "Okay. If we meet at three, will that work?"

The pens froze in the air for a moment. P.K.'s eyes seemed to unfocus. "Three is bad," he said. "It has a bad resonance on that day." He focused on Jake again, as the pens started moving. "Three-thirty?"

"Two-thirty would give us more time." Jake watched the pens' reaction to that. They kept twirling calmly.

"All right." P.K. nodded. "Two-thirty. Two-thirty. Two-thirty. Meet out in front of the labs? I'll have Jumal call someone there to set up an appointment. The idea is to pick up reference points for us to come back that night and investigate further if need be."

"Got it." Jake grinned.

P.K. peered behind him. "I hope you don't wag your tail that much all the time," he said. "It's quite distracting."

"Sorry." Jake stilled it, but when P.K. turned away, he gave Red a thumbs-up and a huge grin.

* * *

His first real assignment had Jake excited enough that when he blinked into Marcia's place that night and saw her holding the Herald society page, he had completely forgotten about Moxy's article. "Guess what?" he said, bouncing from foot to foot. "I've got an assignment, a real one, with P.K. next week! I can't tell you what it is 'til it's over, official League business, but it's—what?"

Marcia held up the paper, open to a page 2 article titled "Local Hero Has Romantic Side." Beneath one of the stock photos of him, Moxy had drawn a generically canid silhouette with a large chest and a white question mark inside it. "Oh," Jake said. "That."

"Let's see," Marcia said. "I could be Genevieve Hightower, the kangaroo heiress to the Hightower fortune—classy, her internet sex video must be losing steam—or I could be Janice Margolies, high-powered criminal attorney—met her once or twice, she needs that long neck for looking down on people, plus she has no fashion sense—or I could be Adrienne Bazure, that slut of a lioness over at Macy's—and why do they have you linked to all these exotic women anyway? Oh, and listen to this: 'Rumors linking Blink Coyote to the Herald's own Moxy Nightwing are almost certainly untrue.' Almost certainly." She snorted. "Considering she just made them up, I'm sure they are. Aren't they?"

It took Jake a second to realize she was talking to him. "Oh. Oh, yes, of course! I mean, I couldn't tell her anything about you, but she tricked me into telling her that I have a girlfriend."

"I know." Marcia sighed. "It's just frustrating, doing all this work and being such a part of your career and not being able to take any credit for it. You know, yesterday all the girls at work were talking about that carjacking."

"They were?" Jake's ears perked up. "What did they say?"

"Oh, the usual." Marcia splayed her long ears and clasped her paws under her chin. "'He's so brave, I bet he's really handsome under that hood, and so mysterious!'"

"Was that that cute, um, what's her name, Crystal?" Marcia's eyes narrowed, and Jake flattened his ears, dropping the look of interest. "Sorry, sorry. So, uh, where are we going tonight?"

"Bertolucci's. My treat."

Jake wagged his tail as Marcia dropped the newspaper. "Is this my birthday dinner?"

"No, no." She smiled. "You get your birthday dinner next week on your birthday. I've got something special planned. No, this is just a dinner. Then I thought maybe we'd come back here and work on your concentration."

"Oh, if we have to." His tail wagged even faster.

She grinned. "Like I have to ask. Come on, hero. I'll drive."

That was their standing joke; Jake had a car, for appearances, but it barely ran. He preferred to walk or blink anywhere he went. He could get to places he could see, or get back to places he'd been, and having grown up in Dunstown meant he could get almost anywhere in the city within five minutes at most.

They were walking down to the car when his handheld went off. He flicked it on and skimmed the messages while Marcia sighed audibly. "Oh, for…" He tapped a message back. "Hang on. I can't believe these guys have never heard of Justin Timberwolf…I can't believe they don't know who sings 'Howl of My Heart.' Crypto really needs to go home and not be at the office all night. Okay, there." He flipped the device off and grinned at her. "Dinner?"

They had just gotten their drinks when the handheld buzzed again. Marcia glared at it. "What now?"

Jake's claw moved over the screen, writing in quick shorthand as he talked absently. "Another check up. They're worried about Dr. Malevola escaping from his cell, and they want me to pop in at random intervals."

"Can't they wait until after dinner?"

"Crypto says that might constitute a predictable pattern." He looked up, putting the device down on the table. "I'll be right back. Sorry."

"Jake, listen, don't—"

He didn't hear the end of her sentence. When he blinked back, she was sipping her beer. The lines of annoyance above her eyes smoothed out as she saw him. That was one thing Jake was learning to appreciate about his ability: the chance to see people candidly in the moment before they registered his presence. He made a note to be nicer to Marcia for the rest of the night.

"Dr. Malevola all safe and sound?"

"Yeah, he was, uh, well, kinda embarrassed to see me." Jake grinned. "I think someone's been sneaking him dirty magazines."

The rabbit shook her head. "You shouldn't do that, darling. The waiter could've come over."

Jake shrugged. "No biggie. I'd sign an autograph or two and we'd get the meal comped." He slid the handheld into the pocket of the yellow dress shirt he wore.

The rabbit arched an eyebrow. "That's never happened."

Jake looked off towards the bar. "I got a free salad once after I stopped a guy from robbing the Sizzler."

"But you did that in costume."

"Marcia, I'm fine, really." The handheld in his pocket buzzed again, and he took it out and started tapping on it.

The rabbit looked over the table. "Another follow-up?"

"Nah, P.K.'s asking me if I can take care of the potato salad for the barbecue this weekend. He was supposed to, but I'm the new kid, so they're dumping all the stuff they don't want to do on me. Red Lightning already asked if I could get the chips for him. I'm like, how long will it take you to run to the store? A minute?" He grinned and waved his paw.

"Oh." Marcia leaned back in the booth. "I didn't know we were going to a barbecue this weekend."

Jake's ears went back. He looked up at her and then back at the handheld. "Oh, I, uh, didn't think you'd want to go…"

Marcia folded her arms across her dark blue jacket. "What made you think that? All the times I asked if I could meet some of the other League members? The strings I pulled to get you an interview to get into the League in the first place? The huge poster of WonderWolf I used to have in my college dorm?"

"I never saw your college dorm."

"First the publicist position, now this."

"It's just a boring function. I don't know if anyone else is bringing their, uh, SOs…"

"Of course they are," she snapped back at him, and then softened her voice, giving him a smile. "But most of them aren't single. You just have to be more assertive."

"I just feel like I have a long way to go," Jake said after a moment. "I've only been doing this for two years. They've all got these great stories they swap. And my name…"

"What's wrong with your name?" Marcia narrowed her eyes.

"Blink Coyote? It sounds like I have some kind of neurological condition."

"We picked that name out together." Marcia's tone was growing frostier.

"You picked it. Anyway, I don't even have a nemesis yet."

"Oh, not this again." Marcia rolled her eyes. "Forgive my prosaic spirit, but I'm glad you don't have one of those."

"But I should! I'm the only big hero in Dunstown. The only one in the League, anyway. WonderWolf has at least three." Jake tapped the table. "I wonder if he'd give me one, if I asked."

The waiter returned then with their pizza. Jake took one of the pepperoni and sausage slices and ripped a huge bite out of it, while Marcia nibbled on the green pepper and onion side.

"You've got a lot to be proud of," she said after a bit. "I mean, crime in Dunstown is down thirty percent since you started working the streets."

"I know," he said, "but it's all purse-snatchers and liquor store holdups. Nothing really big. You hear that Night Wolf captured three terrorists and half a pound of weapons-grade plutonium last week?"

Marcia blinked. "No."

"I guess Stormy was going to release the news tomorrow. Yeah, he just got back from Kurdistan and he was in D.C. with the CIA all day yesterday and today."

"Stormy? Is that Coyote Rain?"

Jake finished his slice of pizza. "Nah, Stormy's the...uh..." He grabbed another slice and chewed on it, his ears back..

Marcia put down her pizza. "Oh. So that's his name."

"Her name."

"Cute. Sounds like she really fits in. Is she a wolf? Coyote?"

He chewed on the pizza, searching for an answer that wouldn't prolong the conversation. "Um. Wolf, I think."

"You think?"

"I only met her the one time, WonderWolf was introducing her and it was real quick, but yeah, she's a wolf."

"Of course she is. The League of Crimefighting Canids couldn't hire a rabbit publicist. Did you see the press release I did last week got picked up by two of the major networks?"

Jake started to shake his head, then caught himself. "Oh, yeah!"

"If I'm not fighting crime, I don't have to be a canid, right?"

"Yeah, but everyone else is."

"That's discrimination."

Jake sighed. "I did try to tell them…but I'm just a kid, you know, and I'm new..."

The rabbit picked up her pizza. "It's all right. I'm probably not qualified. It would have been nice to have been asked, is all." She paused, then visibly put it aside and chirped cheerfully, "I'm glad to hear things are going well there."

Jake took another slice of pizza and munched it slowly. Her dismissal of their disagreements made him vaguely uneasy, each one feeling like a cloud in their sky, a storm postponed until later.

They walked along the tree-lined streets back to her condo, a second-floor unit in an upscale complex just a few blocks from the Dunstown gaslamp district. The conversation along the way back was bland and neutral, friends of theirs going on trips, people in Marcia's office getting promoted, government initiatives. Nothing to add to the storm; nothing to dispel it.

Jake felt the tension, or at least thought he did. Best to cut his losses tonight and start fresh tomorrow, or even wait 'til his birthday, he thought. They'd reached her building, and she was waiting expectantly, so he said, "I'm kind of tired."

She tugged on his jacket. "You need to keep practicing."

He sighed. "Mmm. I really am kind of tired…"

She nuzzled up at the base of his ears and then a bit inside. His ears flicked. He was getting excited, and he could smell that she was too. She angled her hip into his groin and sighed against him. "Why don't you stay the night and tuck me in?"

He gave in, of course; he was young and male. What else could he do? At least he would do his best to enjoy it. And while this time he managed to hold on until his climax, he still blinked out in mid-convulsion, returning contritely to Marcia's remonstrations. At home in his own bed, Jake thought he would rest for just a little while before making his rounds, but when he yawned and cracked his eyes open, the sun greeted him through the bedroom window.

Guilt over missing his rounds drove him to check the Internet and the paper for any crimes he might have prevented, and finding none helped only a little. He worked assiduously the next few nights, meeting Moxy once but getting no new information from her.

Marcia was unaccountably busy the entire weekend, leaving him messages with instructions to come to her place on Tuesday night at 6 pm. Making his birthday present, he presumed, with some relief, as it freed him from having to explain that he was going to meet Red Lightning for Sunday brunch without her.

Red's wife was a charming vixen, a little older than Red, and she told him they'd been married out of high school, since before the lab accident that had given Red his powers. He told Jake about that over beers (Red drank only one, saying "I'm a lightweight" with a grin), and Jake told him the story of discovering his power, the radiation burst from the machine he was unloading from a truck at his summer job. Jake envied the rapport he seemed to have with his wife, how they each knew each other's stories and kept taking small moments to look at each other or touch each other. They were so likable, however, and laughed so genuinely at his stories, that he couldn't let envy grow into anything else.

Their real names were Mike and Sarah, and as they were shaking hands, Mike said, "Well, now you've been here, I guess you can get back anytime, eh?"

"Just to the front porch." Jake grinned. "I never blink in uninvited."

Sarah smiled hesitantly. "Could I…see?"

Mike grinned at Jake. He pointed to a tree in the front yard. "Race you to the tree and back?"

"Oh, I don't know," Jake said. "I don't usually…"

"Come on. Don't worry about beating me."

"No, it's just…" They were both looking at him. "Okay."

"Give us a start, hon," Mike said.

Sarah held up her black paw. "Ready…steady…go!"

Jake appeared next to the tree and touched it just as a red blur slapped a black paw to the bark. He got his bearings and reappeared inside next to Sarah, a fraction of a second after Mike had skidded to a halt.

"I think Mike won," Sarah said. "But you did a very nice job."

"Of course you would say that." Jake grinned as he said it.

"Home court advantage!" Mike crowed, raising both paws in the air.

"Now let's try it with the door closed," Jake said, and they all laughed. "All right, I gotta get going. Thanks again for the great brunch, Sarah."

"Lovely to meet you," Sarah said, extending her paw.

"Likewise," he said, taking it gently. "You're a lucky guy, Mike."

"Oh, I dunno," he said. "I heard you're dating Jenny Hightower." He winked as Jake's ears flicked back in a blush.

"Stop it, Mike," Sarah said.

"Yeah, don't worry, you won't see me on the Internet anytime soon." Jake grinned. "So long, guys."

He blinked back to his apartment and spent the rest of the day doing mundane tasks: laundry, some housecleaning, grocery shopping. His mom called just before sunset to wish him a happy birthday in advance, and after an hour talking to both parents, the city was growing dark and he could go out on his rounds.

On Tuesday, he was woken up at quarter past seven by a phone call from his sister in Europe wishing him a happy birthday. He talked to her while he rubbed the sleep from his eyes, went in to work, and found himself growing more and more excited as the clock inched towards six.

At 5:57 pm, unable to wait any longer, he blinked to Marcia's apartment. "Birthday boy's here!" he announced, dropping to the living room carpet.

Soft music played from the bedroom. Otherwise, the apartment was silent. Jake straightened his shirt with a grin. "Oh, some concentration lessons? Well, I'm all for that." He pushed open the door to the bedroom.

Marcia sat on the bed. It took him a moment to see that her arms were tied behind her back and her mouth bound securely with tape. Her eyes widened when she saw him, and she motioned him back with her head, straining to talk through the tape.

He heard a small noise to his right and felt a prick in his side. In an instant, he was back in his bedroom, landing unsteadily on the bed and falling to the floor. Dizzy, he got up and braced himself. He'd been shot with…something. And Marcia was caught.

The yellow eye logo stared at him from the open closet. Had to get his suit on and go back and rescue her, he thought. He fumbled for a moment with the buttons on his shirt, wondering why his fingers seemed thicker. "Hell," he said, and blinked out of his clothes, appearing naked in front of the closet and already reaching for the outfit. He got both legs in it and then his arms, fastening the snaps up the side and pulling the hood over his ears. The room was spinning slowly. He pulled the gloves on. Had to save Marcia. Had to…

He blinked to her bedroom, intending to pop in, assess the situation, and pop out, like he'd done with the car thief. But he materialized a good two feet above the edge of her bed, landed awkwardly, and fell to the floor after getting only a glimpse of a white-robed figure striding toward him. Hands circled his neck as he struggled to keep his balance in the room, which was now not only spinning, but crazily tilted. He tried unsuccessfully to blink out twice before blackness rose up and swallowed him.

* * *

Awareness came back to him in a reddish haze on the inside of his eyelids. His mouth felt gummy and tasted horrible. He ran his tongue around his dry lips and tried to open his eyes, but they felt gummy as well. He couldn't bring his paws up; they were bound behind him somehow. His ankle hurt, too. The room he was in smelled sterile and antiseptic, but there was a person in it with him. Male, some kind of scientist or doctor, he thought. He could smell laboratory chemicals and the person's scent under it, a light musk, like raccoon, but different.

He forced his eyes open, letting in a bright white light that made him close them immediately. After several blinks, tears dripping down his muzzle, he was able to see the blurry outlines of what was in the room with him.

Directly in front of him was some kind of lab bench, with two metal stools in front of it and a shiny metal contraption, probably a faucet. He could see a yellowish rectangular object to his right, approximately filing-cabinet-shaped, and beside it a long flat thing that looked as though another filing cabinet had exploded on top of it, showering papers and folders everywhere.

His vision cleared somewhat as he looked over to his left, and saw the figure in white.

It stood just a bit shorter than him, and not only was its lab coat white, but most of the fur he could see was white. Only a grayish patch between the two small pinkish ears marred the otherwise ivory fur. Behind him, a thick and furless pink tail curled up from the ground, and Jake could see his feet, covered in shoes. The dark brown eyes behind a pair of round glasses held his when he met them, and the long pointed muzzle below them curved into a smile, showing a mouth full of small, pointed teeth. A possum. Jake had never met a possum before.

First time for everything, he thought, trying to clear his head. He'd find out what the story was, blink out of his bonds and subdue this guy, and then go rescue Marcia.

"Welcome to my laboratory, Blink Coyote. Or may I call you Jake?" The possum had a deceptively pleasant voice, with a bit of a quaver to it. Jake cursed inwardly. His secret identity was out, less than two years into his career! It had taken WonderWolf thirteen to be found out.

"Jake, then," the possum went on. "I'm sure you're wondering what you're doing here. I've been working on some projects involving you and your fellow supernormals, and I reached a point in my work where it became necessary to prove a hypothesis before I could proceed any further. I required the presence of an actual supernormal in order to conduct a series of controlled tests, with myself as the control subject, to follow proper scientific method…" He blinked, looked around, and cleared his throat. "That is to say, I have been indulging in some extra research of my own, that my employer is not aware of. For my own benefit. With your power at my disposal, I will build a weapon that will make governments tremble!"

Jake ignored the odd discontinuity of this exposition. "Who are you?" he croaked, and then immediately thought of a thousand better things to say. Why not, 'you have the advantage of me, sir'? Or 'you seem to know me, but I'm afraid I'm not familiar with you'? Or even the classic, 'you're mad!'? But no, he had to come up with the most trite line ever, and deliver it badly on top of that.

"You will be the first to know me as Doctor…" He hesitated. "Doctor Defiance."

Jake frowned. "What are you defying?"

The possum blinked at him. "Um, authority. Governments! You know."

"It's not a very good name. I suggest you keep trying." That was better.

"Listen…you're not in a position to discuss this!" Doctor Defiance was clearly as uncomfortable with his name as Jake was with his, if not more. "We'll have plenty of time to compare names."

"Where's Marcia?" Jake demanded.

"Oh, she's down the hall. After she saw me, I had to bring her along. She'll be extra insurance to make sure you behave."

Fleetingly, Jake wondered how the possum had gotten them both to this lab. Must have henchmen, of course, so there'll be someone guarding Marcia. I'll be ready for them. He flexed his fists. "This has all been very interesting, but I think it's time for me to go." He closed his eyes and blinked…

...and opened them again to see the possum's sneer. "Go on, then," Doctor Defiance said.

Jake felt a sinking feeling in his chest that passed a rising panic on the way down, a feeling he remembered last from looking up two years ago and seeing the red glow even through the wood of the crate as he balanced it on his shoulder. He tried again, and again went nowhere.

"Not so easy, is it?" The possum clapped his paws. "It looks like my first hypothesis is proven correct! The collar works!"

"Collar?" Jake could feel it now, constricting the fur around his neck. If he swiveled his ears downward, he could hear a very faint, high-pitched electronic whine.

"Yes, my hypothesis about the mechanism of your powers was accurate. Once I had figured that out, it was child's play to create a blocker."

This was not heading in a direction Jake was happy with. "How did you…"

The possum waved a paw. "Oh, it's a simple matter of working out the displacement factor and the transference energy. After that, there's enough supernormal research to narrow it down. But perhaps I'm being too modest. It did take me six months, after all." He hid a small laugh behind his paw.

Jake felt his tail droop. Six months? This guy had come up with a way to negate his powers in six months? His career was over anyway. It didn't really matter if some idiot with a stupid name was going to keep him captive to do experiments on. If it wasn't this jerk, it'd be some other one.

No! He was a member of the League of Crimefighting Canids, after all!

Even if, he now realized, he had completely neglected to call the League and notify them of a dangerous situation. So none of them knew where he was, to come to his rescue, or even that he was in trouble. They might not figure it out until late in the week, when he didn't show up for the League meeting.

He still had his wits, though. Maybe he could trick the possum into taking the collar off. If he pretended to be choking, or something. Not right away, but…later, when his guard was down. His tail drooped further. Lame dialogue, lame escape plans. What kind of superhero was he?

"Let's start with a blood sample. I've been dying for that. Fortunately, you won't have to. Ha ha ha."

The laughter sounded forced, but Jake couldn't see how that would help him. He studied the possum for any sign of weakness, but without powers and with his hands and feet bound, he wasn't sure what he could do.

The possum tapped his muzzle with one claw, staring up and down Jake's uniform. "Now, how does this thing come off?" he wondered, and Jake kept quiet.

For all his supposed intelligence, it took Doctor Defiance a full minute to find the snaps down the right side of the chest of Jake's outfit. His delicate pink fingers pulled apart the first one, then another and another. He exposed Jake's shoulder and upper chest, and seemed to be staring for several moments to decide where to stick the syringe he held in his left paw.

The possum cleared his throat. "Okay. Now, this might hurt a bit." His dark eyes drifted up from Jake's chest to meet the coyote's eyes, and he blinked. "Not that I care!" He pulled loose several more snaps from the uniform and pushed the sleeve down Jake's arm, exposing his elbow and his stomach down to the top of his hip. Once again, the possum paused and stared.

"You go commando, huh?" he said finally.

Jake was very aware of the cool lab air on his privates. He said, "I was kind of in a hurry when I put the uniform on tonight."

"Right, of course." Doctor Defiance put one of his delicate pink paws on Jake's chest. "You work out?"

"Not really." This looked like maybe a sign of weakness. Or something. Jake wasn't quite sure what was going on.

"You should. It's important to stay healthy."

"That's your job, now," Jake said bitterly.

The possum looked genuinely startled. "What?"

"To keep me healthy. As your prisoner?"

"Oh. Of course! Yes, I'll do all that." His paw was curling in Jake's chest fur, his muzzle close to the coyote's. Jake searched his eyes for any sign of trickery, but saw only reflected curiosity.

Then Doctor Defiance leaned in and kissed him on the mouth.

It lasted only for a couple seconds. The possum stepped back, holding a paw to his muzzle as if horrified. The syringe clattered to the floor.

Jake blinked, trying to figure out what was going on. "How long have you been a villain?" he said. "Because I think you need some more practice." Hey, he thought. That was pretty good.

"Oh my God," the possum moaned, "this isn't going well at all."

Damn, Jake thought. Maybe he's got a secret crush on me. Maybe that's the weakness I can use. I can take another kiss if it'll set me free. Actually, even if it won't… "Maybe you should've asked me first," he said.

"Asked you?" The possum straightened. "Doctor Destiny does not ask!"

"Doctor what?"

"Defiance." The possum's shoulders sagged. "What did I say?"

"Destiny." Jake couldn't help but grin. If this guy didn't have him prisoner, he'd be kind of cute, actually.

"Well, uh, would you mind if I kissed you again?"

Jake knew he was going to say 'no,' but what surprised him when he did say it was the swelling in his sheath. And when the possum stepped timidly up and touched his lips again, Jake felt himself reacting, very fast. As fast as if it had been Marcia kissing him. Good job, body, he told himself unconvincingly. Way to, uh, pretend that I'm aroused…interested…and then he stopped telling himself anything, because his long tongue was being rubbed by a shorter, thicker one and his uniform's snaps were coming undone one by one under a set of gentle fingers.

"Mmm," Doctor Defiance said, pulling back from the kiss. He looked down Jake's body. "God, you're gorgeous."

Jake swallowed. "Look, I don't, uh, I'm not, I mean…" He stammered, aware of how little his words meant against the proof his own body was unwillingly supplying.

Smiling nervously, the possum stepped back and shrugged off his lab coat, then pulled off his shirt and slid his pants down.

Jake stared. "Oh, my God. Are you okay?"

Doctor Defiance glanced down at himself. "Yeah, all possums are like this. You never saw one before?" Jake shook his head. "I got teased a lot in gym class."

"I bet."

The possum hesitated for a moment, then leaned up to kiss him again, and he found himself kissing back, and both of them nearly got the tips of their tongues bitten off a moment later when a shrill female voice echoed through the room.

"What the hell is going on?"

Jake snapped his head around as the possum flinched, then dove for his lab coat. Marcia walked towards the possum, a gun held loosely in her right paw. "Charles?" Her tone carried that sharp warning that Jake knew meant trouble. Usually it was enough to send him blinking home.

"How did you get free?" Jake asked, trying to distract her, but she held up a stubby paw to him.

"Charles, maybe you didn't understand your role in all of this. You were supposed to be Doctor Defiance, budding supervillain. You have captured Blink Coyote and are beginning to perform experiments on him." She eyed the lab coat he was hastily buttoning shut. "Of a medical nature."

"Marcia…" Jake started, and this time succeeded in distracting her.

"And you!" She whirled, pointing the gun at him. "I set up this whole scenario, and it was not cheap, let me tell you, all to give you a nemesis and an adventure for your birthday, and I walk in to rescue you and find you kissing your nemesis?"

"Rescue me?" Jake said, just as the possum said, "Nemesis?"

"And," she said, pointedly looking down to the open flaps of his suit, "you're into it. Does your little feathered friend know about that secret romantic side?"

While Jake sputtered to reply, she turned on the possum again. "What were you thinking?"

"That you don't know how lucky you are. My God! He's gorgeous! Look at that body!"

They both turned to look at Jake, who squirmed under the scrutiny. "Hey, uh…"

Marcia ignored him. "If I'd known you cruised that side of the street, I never would have hired you."

"I, uh, don't really go out of my way to keep it secret," Doctor Defiance—Charles—said. "I mean, did you see the poster of WonderWolf on the wall of my office?"

"What does that prove?" Marcia waved the gun dismissively. "I've got that same poster. So does everyone."

WONDER WOLF

Jake didn't want to draw attention to himself again, but he was talking before he knew it. "The one of him looking over his shoulder from behind, where he's naked?"

"He's not naked," Marcia said pointedly, looking again at Jake's crotch, which appeared to be enjoying the attention and begging for more. "He's got a speedo on."

"It's a butt shot," Charles said. "The speedo doesn't cover anything."

"That's what I say!" Jake said.

"Great butt," Charles said, and inclined his head as though he were trying to see Jake's. "Yours is too."

"All right," Marcia snapped, "enough. Come on, Jake." She reached up to his neck and unbuckled the collar. "Go on home. I'll be there soon. Though I don't really feel like celebrating any more."

She'd left his uniform unbuttoned. The possum noticed, and reached out quickly to pull the flap up. "Hey!" the rabbit said as he pressed one of the snaps together, restoring some modesty to the bound coyote. "Paws off!"

He looked at the gun and then looked at her over his glasses. "It's not loaded."

"I don't care! Get away from him!" Her voice echoed shrilly through the lab.

The possum raised his paws and stepped back. "Okay, okay."

"And you're wrong," she snapped. "I know exactly how lucky I am. Come on, Jake. Let's go."

He was almost afraid to try blinking, because the feeling when it hadn't worked had been so terrifying. He looked at the space just behind Marcia and just like that, he was out of the restraints and standing behind her. Before she could register his presence, he grabbed the collar out of her paw.

It was a black leather strap with small electronics embedded all around it. One light was on, burning green. Jake held it to his ear so he could hear the hum of the electronics, though it was hard to hear over Marcia's insisting that he give it back.

He dropped his paw to his side. "So," he said, "let me get this straight, because I know I'm not as smart as you. For my birthday, you paid some guy to create a device that takes away my power and then kidnap me?"

Marcia had dropped the gun to the floor, and now folded her arms. "I was doing it for us," she said. "I thought it could help with your…problem."

Jake couldn't find any words to make light of that. He could only look down at the strap lying across his paw, and back up to the rabbit's brown and white face, now bearing a more placating expression. The change felt wrong, felt too fast to be sincere, and then he realized with a shock what he should have seen all along. She wasn't just good at pushing away her hurt and guilt all those times they argued. She wasn't hurt at all, because she didn't care what he thought about her. She just wanted to keep him close and control him.

"It was supposed to be an adventure," she said. "Remember, sweetie? You wanted a nemesis, more excitement…"

"Go home," he said, interrupting her.

Her blue eyes narrowed. "I'm not leaving without you."

He closed his paw over the collar. "I said, go home, Marcia."

"Come with me."

Not only did he not want to go with her, he wasn't sure he wanted to see her again. The moment he let himself think that, he felt a huge wash of relief. To be able to live without being scrutinized, without being corrected, without being hemmed in, without having all his failings analyzed… "No. I don't think I want to see you again."

"You listen to me, Jake Kellin. You are not going to throw away everything we've worked for. All right, this evening didn't go quite the way I'd planned it, but that's no reason to…to…" He could see her trying to work up tears, but the build up was so obvious that when she squeezed one out of the corner of one eye, he was unmoved. "Please, Jake. I love you."

Jake shook his head. "No, you don't."

She wiped the tear away, and there were no more. Her eyes flashed now. "Fine. I won't beg any more. I'll be home, and if you're not there by midnight, then we are over." When the coyote didn't respond, she held out her paw. "Give me the collar."

"Oh ho ho," Jake said. "Not a chance."

"I paid for it!"

"You should take better care of your things," he said.

She lunged for it, and he tried to blink back without success. Damn thing, he thought as she grabbed the collar. He wrested it back from her without much trouble and pushed her back a foot. She glared at him.

"You do not want me as an enemy," she said.

"I don't want you at all," he said, which was a bit of a lie, but not much.

She glared for another few seconds, then turned on her heel and marched out of the room, slamming the door shut behind her.

Jake let the reverberation from the slamming door die down before he exhaled and looked at the possum.

Charles stammered. "I…I was just doing what she paid me…"

Jake smiled. "It's okay. I know." He held up the collar. "Mind if I break this?"

The possum hesitated, then shook his head. "She paid for it. It's not mine."

Jake walked over to the metal stools and dropped the collar to the floor, where he stood and stared down at it. "What's the point, though? You really built this in six months?" The possum nodded. "No offense, but I assume you're not the most brilliant scientist in the world. So there's got to be someone else who could do this if they wanted to. So what's the point?"

Charles cleared his throat. "Well, actually, I was sort of exaggerating. You know, I was trying to be in character. I did it in six months because your, uh, friend kept monitoring devices in her apartment and fed me months of data on your ability. Anyone without access to that much data would have a much harder time replicating my results. So, uh, if you destroy that, then probably I'm the only one who could build another one. And you can have my notebooks if you want."

"Thanks." Jake brought the stool down on the collar over and over, until the delicate electronics were shattered. He picked up the leather strap and held it to his neck, then blinked across the room without any problem. "That's that," he said, and looked at the collar. "It's a nice leather," he said. "Maybe I'll wear it just to remind me."

"Of what?" The possum looked confused.

"Who to trust."

"Oh." Charles looked down and fidgeted. Jake waited until he looked up again, and saw the surprise come into his eyes. "You're still here."

"What's your name?"

"Charles," the possum said. "Goldstein. Dr. Charles Goldstein."

"So you really are a doctor."

"Oh, yes. Ph.D., electrical engineering. This isn't really my lab. Marcia, uh, thought it was more 'evil villain' than my office." He adjusted his glasses.

"Well, you know my secret identity now." Jake sighed.

Charles blinked. "Oh, I swore I wouldn't reveal it. I mean, I swear I won't…you don't have to worry about that."

Jake smiled. "You know the weird thing? I trust you."

"Thanks." Charles looked away again.

Jake studied him. The possum's tail was curled around his legs, and he was fidgeting from side to side. He tried to work out how he felt, himself. Even though his body was still warm from their kiss, it seemed like a long time ago. It would be easy to push it away and forget about it.

If he wanted to.

"So," Jake said after a moment, "since you're done working for Marcia, I guess you might have some time on your paws?"

"I do have a job at Mount Cedar," Charles said, then hurriedly added, "but yes, yes, I should. Um, why?"

"You'd be a pretty good gadgethead," Jake said. "I'd sure rather have you working with me than against me."

Now Charles let his muzzle slip into a small grin. "Is that a job offer?"

"I can't pay you," Jake said. "Marcia had all the money."

"Oh, I'd do it for free," Charles said.

Jake smiled. "I was kind of thinking of making you part of the team, eventually."

"Like, your partner?" Charles squeaked, and then clapped a paw to his muzzle. "I mean, um, sidekick."

Jake laughed softly at the possum's stricken expression. "Let's say sidekick to start. But you know…I can't believe this, but…I'd be willing to talk about terms, say, over dinner?"

Charles gaped at him. "After…"

"You couldn't tell I was enjoying it? Hell, it surprised me, too. I want to take it slow, but I'm interested enough to give it a shot. Even if it meant I would be the only guy in the League with a boyfriend."

"You wouldn't be the only gay one." Charles grinned when he saw Jake's eyes widen. "You didn't know about WonderWolf?"

"Really?"

"Well, he can't keep a steady boyfriend, but why do you think he does all those butt posters? It's advertising."

Jake giggled, and then his stomach rumbled. "How about that dinner? You might want to put some clothes on, though." He started to button up his uniform, then stopped. "And I should get out of this uniform."

Charles picked up his clothes. "I'll be here and dressed in five minutes."

"I'll be back." Jake paused. "You know, I'd much rather have a friend than a nemesis as a birthday present."

Charles glanced at the door. "I think you might have gotten both."

Jake's ears perked up. "Hey, yeah! You know, she was a lousy girlfriend, but I bet she'd be a great villain."

"Hopefully not too good."

"With you on my side, I'm not worried." Jake grinned, and impulsively blinked to right in front of Charles and kissed him on the nose. He answered the wide smile on the possum's face with one of his own, flicked his ears jauntily, and blinked.

227

Six

I cannot think of anything to say about "Six" that would not be a spoiler, except that it is a stand-alone story, not connected to any series. Just read it. You will not be disappointed!

Dr. (of chemistry, Dartmouth '91) Samuel C. Conway is one of the best-known, most-familiar, and influential leaders in Furry fandom. As "Uncle Kage", from his persona as Kagemushi Goro (Goro, the Shadow Bug), a giant anthropomorphic cockroach, he is a popular figure in a white lab smock at numerous Furry conventions on three continents, usually as a guest-of-honor or program participant. He has been the Chairman of Anthrocon since 1999, two years after it was founded as the Albany Anthrocon. Conway was responsible for its incorporation as Anthrocon, Inc. and its relocations to Valley Forge (1999-2000), Philadelphia (2001-2005), and currently Pittsburgh (2006-present). He can largely take credit for its growth from 845 members in 1999 to 4,400 in 2011. Aside from his omnipresence in his white lab smock, he is the popular stand-up raconteur of "Uncle Kage's Story Hour" and the frequent lead auctioneer for the conventions' for-charity auctions. Conway has been inducted into the Furry Writers' Guild and the Furry Hall of Fame. He says that "Six" is "based on a true story" from his period as a Red Cross volunteer.

In addition to his Furry activities, Conway leads an active professional career. He is currently employed by West Pharmaceutical Services of Lionville, Pennsylvania, near Philadelphia. He has written numerous scientific papers, and has two patents, one in organic chemistry and one regarding recyclable packaging material.

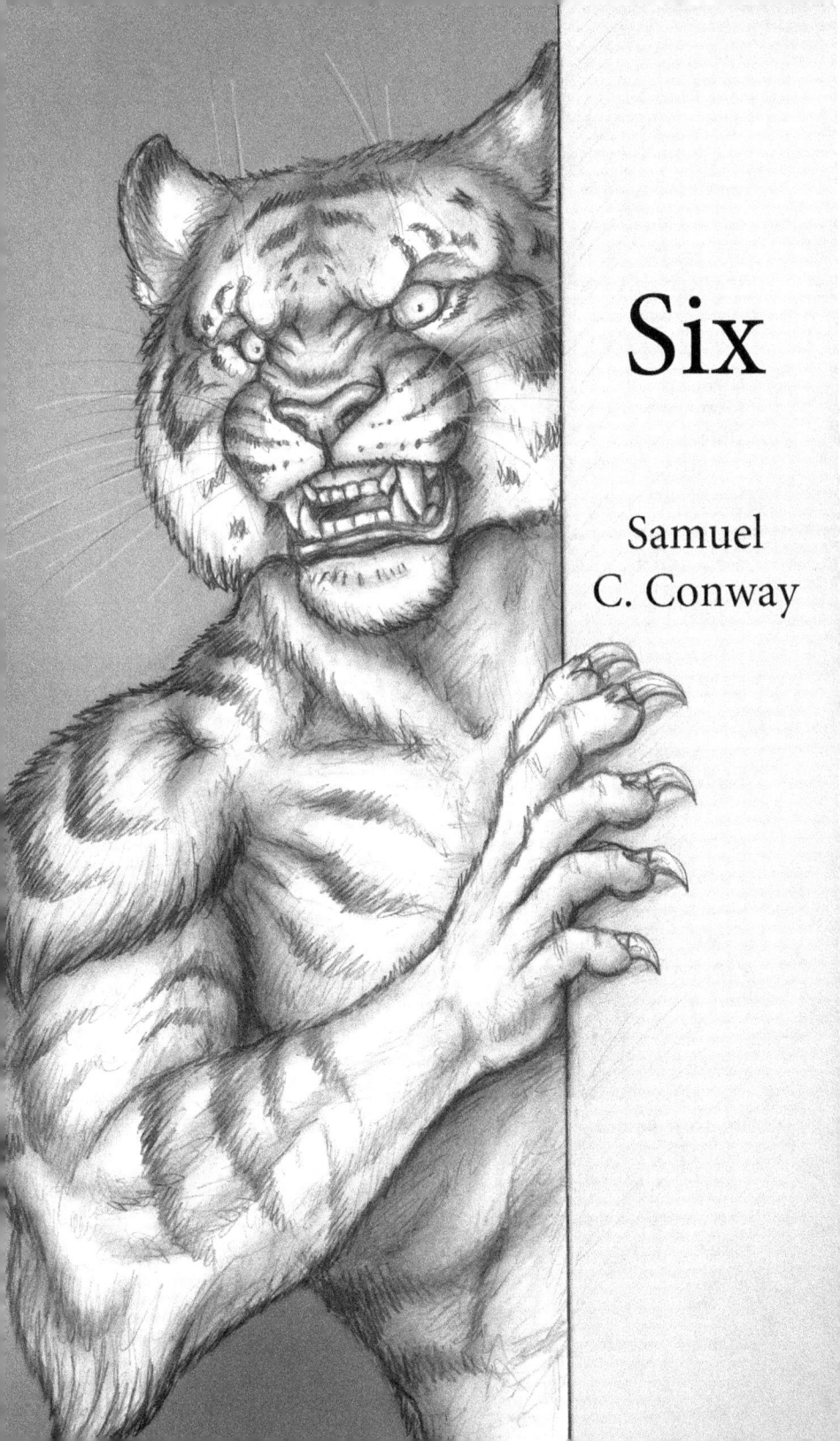

Six

Samuel
C. Conway

I am all at once a scientist, a humanitarian and a lover of animals. Those traits often combine to produce some truly memorable experiences. Such events as those of a winter night not too long ago become almost an inevitability when you throw into the mix a cat named Elvis.

Volunteering for the Red Cross, specifically in disaster recovery service, satisfies the humanitarian part of me. There is no joy that can rival that gained from helping out a fellow human being in an hour of great need. There is also no greater discomfort than standing up to your waist in sewage-swirled floodwater, but the humanitarian side never really minded that much. In the end, I suppose I'm a martyr. It helps to explain why I found myself choking on the smoke of a burning building in a section of Philadelphia we called The Badlands.

It was a row home, of course. Most of Philadelphia is made of row homes. They are a sad remnant of the city's industrial past, and like the skeletal factory buildings that are crumbling on every block, many of them are abandoned. Up in The Badlands it is not uncommon for only one single house to be occupied on an entire block of leaning, gutted structures. That was the sort of area that I was called to that night. Four empty homes were burning, which might not have been such a crisis if the fifth did not contain an old lady in a wheelchair. When I arrived I could see a fireman rushing inside as smoke billowed out of the doorway around him. From outside I could hear him arguing with her. "No, you can't stay!," the fireman's voice barked. "You gotta get out of here or you're gonna burn up! Come on!"

I squinted through the smoke but could see nothing. It was like trying to look through a chalkboard, or would have been if I had been able to keep my eyes open for more than a second. Smoke from a house fire wreaks havoc on the eyes, even when it looks thin and harmless. It's one of the reasons people are often found dead just inches away from a convenient exit. Struggling to see, I called out, "This is the Red Cross. Do you need help in there?"

"Yeah!" the fireman shouted back. "Reach in and grab the front of this wheelchair."

I groped forward through the pall, and finding a metal bar, grabbed it and pulled. A wheelchair slid ponderously out of the smoke and into view. Crammed into its seat was what was undoubtedly the most morbidly obese woman I had ever seen. She was so immense that the wheels on her chair were warped from the weight they had to carry. The humanitarian side of me began to falter slightly, worrying, along with the other sides, about the fact that volunteers do not get Workman's Compensation.

There were six steps leading down from her front door. Small wonder that the poor thing was a shut-in. Fortunately, one of my teammates, Mark, came running from across the street, and between the three of us we were able to wrestle her and her chair down the stairs and onto the sidewalk. As we stopped to rest, a little black and white shape darted out of the smoke, down the sidewalk, and straight into the basement window of the next vacant house in line. The poor lady immediately started to sob. "My kitty!" she wailed. "Someone get my kitty!"

Mark gave me a pained look, and gently patted her hand, "He's safe, Ma'am," he said soothingly. "He went right into that basement there." We both cringed as she began to cry harder. Mark tried again. "He's not in any danger. We'll get him later. He'll be all right down there, really..."

Inconsolable, the woman become hysterical. "He won't be all right! He's never been outside before! He'll get lost! Oh, I can't lose him! He's all I have!"

My heart broke. As I said, I do love animals, and I happen to have a particular affinity for cats. My concern for the cat and pity for the poor lady overwhelmed my common sense, and I committed the First Mortal Sin of disaster service. "Don't worry, Ma'am," I said firmly, "I'll get your kitty for you. I promise."

Mark looked at me as if I'd lost my mind, and dragged me a few yards away while the paramedics worked on the victim. "You nut case!" he whispered harshly. "How could you say that to her?"

"Why not?" I said stubbornly. "I'm going to go get her cat."

"Like hell you are. You can't go in there."

"Sure I can. It's our job to provide comfort, right? She's not going to get any comfort without her cat."

Mark shook his head. "Fine," he muttered. "I don't know you." He turned and stalked away. We had been through similar disagreements before, although the fact that Mark was always right about them never did deter me from doing stupid things.

I thought it would be a simple matter to retrieve the cat, but when I stepped through the open doorway of the house I could see that the floor was too badly rotted to support my weight. Undaunted, I slipped back out and crouched down by the broken window into which the cat had disappeared.

The basement was piled high with garbage and pieces of the floor that had collapsed decades ago. I could hear the cat yowling unhappily in the darkness, and as I played my flashlight beam across a mountain of old rags I caught sight of two green eyes glowing eerily back at me. "Well," I said with a mournful sigh, "it's why they give us helmets." I sat down, then fed my legs through the narrow window and slithered my way inside. The floor felt solid enough under my feet when they landed. "Here, kitty

kitty," I whispered. "Here, puss puss." I stumbled over some old tires that had been thrown down there and cursed under my breath. "Come on, you stupid cat!"

Mark's voice suddenly floated in through the window. "His name is Elvis."

"What?"

"I said his name is Elvis." I could almost hear the smirk in his voice. "Try calling him."

"Cats don't come when you call them."

"Maybe not. But I just wanna hear you say it."

I wanted to make a snappy retort, but instead I just grunted as I tripped over something else that lay unseen in the darkness. Whatever it was, it was probably horrible. Mark laughed. "Serves you right. Give me a call if you need rescuing."

I swore again as I heard him moving away from the window. He was right, of course. Never make a promise to a disaster victim, especially one you can't keep. I'd opened my mouth though, and thus I had committed myself. Shuffling my feet to keep from falling, I inched my way over to the rag-pile and shined the light on it. The beam again caught two luminous orbs peering out from the depths of the pile. "There you are. Come on out now. The fat lady's waiting."

There was a pitiful mewl off to my left. Swinging the light around, I caught a flash of black and white fur. There, prancing nervously atop an overturned oil tank, was Elvis. His ears were tucked back and his tail was puffed out thicker than my wrist. His eyes, I could not help noticing, were glowing orange in the light. "What the hell?"

Suddenly I felt very, very cold.

Very slowly I turned the flashlight back to where those green orbs were still peering balefully back at me. I stood motionless and just stared as my brain registered what lay before me. I was certain that the smoke had damaged my eyes somehow, or maybe the fire had burned up something the crack dealers had left behind in one of the vacant houses. The only thing that I knew was that what lay before me could not possibly be real.

Half-hidden in the rag pile was a monster. At first I would have called it a tiger, since that is what its head and face most closely resembled. But the arm that was visible was distinctly human, although it was covered with dark orange fur, complete with black tiger stripes. There were other stripes, too, which I realized were dark trails of blood. For a moment I feared that the thing had recently killed something and that no doubt I was going to be next, but then I realized that the blood had come from the creature itself. Its eyes, now that I could see them more clearly, were dull and drooping. Its mouth was open, its breath ragged and wheezing.

"Yo, Sam!"

I almost jumped out of my boots. Mark's flashlight beam played through the window. "Did you get that damned cat yet?"

"No, I—I found... Mark, there's..."

His voice grew concerned. "What?"

The words caught in my throat. The creature's eyes had closed. It was too weak even to keep them open any longer.

I am still not certain why I didn't tell Mark. Maybe I was afraid that the thing was all in my head, and Mark would think I was a lunatic. More than likely, though, my fear was that the creature was real, and somehow I could not bear to face the implications of such a staggering discovery.

"Sam?" Mark's voice was agitated. He was starting to climb down through the window.

"I got him," I blurted out, still staring at the silent hulk before me. "I mean, I had him. He's pretty scared. Give me some light over there to the left."

Mark's flashlight beam found the cat. "Well, grab him and throw him out here. We're taking the old lady to her sister's."

It took a tremendous force of will to drag myself away from the creature. I kept looking back, as though I thought it might vanish if I took my attention off of it for too long.

Elvis seemed more than happy to see me when I reached him, his first time outside having proven not at all to his liking. He purred and clung tightly to my sleeve when I picked him up. I picked my way to the window with him and handed him out to Mark, who tucked the cat safely inside his vest and then held a hand down to help me up.

I paused one more time and swung the beam back toward the pile.

From where I stood I could see only rags. Had there really been anything else there?

"What is it?" Mark said.

I chewed my lip, convinced that I should tell Mark that there was something down in the basement, something that I could not believe and that he had to see for himself, but what came out was, "Nothing. Just creepy down here. Give me a hand."

For me, the rest of the evening was a blur. A valiant effort by the firemen saved the old lady's house, although it would take several days of airing out before she and Elvis could return. Mark kept asking me if I was all right, and I told him that I'd gotten too much smoke that evening and that I was going to go home and rest. Instead, I drove around the quiet streets of the neighborhoods just south of the Badlands and tried to make sense of what I thought I had seen.

There was one undeniable fact: what I had seen in the basement of that rotting home was simply impossible. No such creature could exist. The combination of the smoke, the stress, and yes, probably something illicit floating in the air had surely made my mind play tricks. I reminded myself how the tiger-like face had vanished once I stepped back from the pile. In fact, I hadn't seen it all that clearly to begin with. Some of the old rags were probably orange and striped with motor oil or something.

The whole situation was laughable. Imagine, a grown man, a scientific professional at that, getting so frightened by an imaginary monster in the basement. I laughed as I told myself over and over how silly and childish I was being, all the way back to the Badlands in the small hours of the morning.

The neighborhood, naturally, was utterly dark when I arrived. The woman in the wheelchair had been its only permanent resident, if you did not count the dealers who occasionally used the empty houses as places of business. Even those were few and far between in that part of the city. It was as though even they could not bear to stay for long in the endless, decaying rows. Even so, one or two might have decided to pay a visit once the firemen had left, perhaps to see what might be stirred up out of the ashes. I was furious with myself for taking my life into my hands that way, for purposefully marching into something out of a post-apocalyptic nightmare just because of a stupid hallucination.

But I had to be sure.

The air that wafted up from the empty window frame reeked of smoke and mildew. If anything was down there, it was unlikely that it could breathe that noxious mixture. It was a miracle that Elvis and I had not asphyxiated during our brief stay. I played the flashlight beam inside and squinted through the lingering haze of smoke at the pile of rags.

There was nothing there to see. It was just old, dirty, decomposing cloth. That was why I was cursing so viciously as I slithered back down through the window and felt my way across the debris toward the pile. I knew that the only way I could relax would be to convince myself once and for all that the monster was entirely in my mind, so I leaned down and placed a hand upon the first patch of orange I saw.

I felt warmth, and fur. Then something slammed hard into my chest with the force of an onrushing truck. For a second I had an odd sensation of weightlessness, and then my back crashed painfully into a post. The wood gave way with a dull crack and clattered to the floor behind me. The flashlight flew out of my hand and whirled to the floor. In the wildly spinning beam I could see a hulking figure rising from the pile. Green eyes flashed above terrifying fangs. The scream that tore out of my mouth was loud and shrill, the kind a mouse makes as a hungry cat seizes it in its claws.

The beast raised its arms and made itself look immense, and then almost at once the ferocious glow of its eyes faded. It shuddered, then lurched backward, landing with a muffled sound amongst the rags.

The basement was silent, except for the sound of my own tortured breathing. My eyes were burning from the smoke and tears were flowing down my cheeks, but I could not close them, nor could I take them away from the hulking shape in front of me. I realized only later that I had wet my pants.

It took quite a long time for me to gather enough courage to reach for the flashlight. I was terrified that if I so much as twitched the beast would come to life once more. At last I had the light in my hand and began painfully inching toward the window, which seemed to be a mile and a half away. My back ached terribly, but fortunately the rotted old post had broken before any of my bones had. I did not have time to reflect on my injuries, though, for fear that I would sustain quite a few more if I did not get myself out of there fast.

It seemed to take forever before I reached the window. I held the flashlight out ahead of me, hoping that I might be able to fend the monster off for the precious few seconds it would take me to scramble up and out. In my mind's eye I could see myself clawing my way out, only to be seized by the ankle by a huge striped hand and dragged helplessly back down inside. The image unnerved me to the point of panic, but I knew that to bolt now would surely bring the monster lurching after me. I moved a single inch and then stopped, then another inch, then waited again. The window was behind my head now. If I could only get enough leverage to worm my shoulders through...

A low, rumbling groan rose from the rag pile and I froze. It was a surprisingly feeble sound, filled with unimaginable pain. The monster turned its face toward me, its eyes once again glowing green in the light. The ferocious teeth were hidden now. Its eyes fluttered and then sagged shut. Trails of moisture gleamed along either side of the creature's muzzle. No doubt it was suffering just as much as I was from the acrid, tenacious smoke that hung in the air.

But it still looked as though the monster was crying.

It groaned again, a pitiful sound, and turned its face away. There was no other movement save for the slow rise and fall of its chest as it struggled to breathe. It was a precious opportunity for me to make my getaway, and like an idiot, I did not take it. I was scared beyond belief, but there was something in that agonized groan that managed to hold me back despite my fear.

Once I climbed into a burning car to pull a trapped passenger out, and simple-minded people called me a hero for it. In reality, it was just a manifestation of a desire to help those in trouble that runs so deep in me that it often overwhelms my common sense. That is the only way to explain it. It was the same thing that made me crawl into filth-choked basement to retrieve a cat named Elvis that kept me from scrambling through that window and never looking back. The thing that lay before me was suffering, perhaps even dying, and somehow the thought of leaving it behind was worse than what it might do to me if I stayed.

"What are you?" I heard myself saying.

The green eyes opened halfway and the creature bared its teeth ferociously, but for only a second. It shuddered and groaned, then went limp, as though the effort had taken the last of its strength. Its breathing grew more shallow.

Before I knew what I was doing I had crept forward, holding the flashlight before me like a weapon. The monster had buried itself halfway in the rags, probably in an effort to hide while it nursed its wounds. It did not react as I approached. With a quivering hand I snatched the rags away, ready to dart away if the thing made even the slightest move. It did not open its eyes, however, and I snatched away more of the rags, and before long I had uncovered it completely. Without taking my eyes from its face I stretched forth a wary hand and touched the creature's arm.

It had not been a hallucination. I could feel the fur warm under my fingers, the flesh beneath trembling slightly. Emboldened by the lack of response, I began to explore the remarkable form. It was indeed shaped like a man, although with a tiger's head and fur. A long, thin tail lay motionless beside it. Its hands, to my surprise, bore six fingers each, and if not for the odd digit and the furry covering they could have been the hands of any man.

I had not imagined the blood, either. It matted the fur around a dozen or more deep gashes in the creature's hide. The worst injury was a trio of holes in its left thigh. Bullet holes, obviously. Two were neat and round—entry wounds—while one was jagged and ugly. That meant that one of the slugs was still inside. "Oh, man," I whispered. "You really caught some hell, didn't you?"

The creature still did not awaken. I stepped back and swiped at my stinging eyes as I tried to think of what to do. I thought to call the police, but then what? They would be just as likely to kill the thing as soon as they saw it. Even if they did not, what would they do with it? It would probably wind up on a dissecting table in some government laboratory somewhere. I certainly could not leave it where it was, which left me very little choice. I did not relish the idea of taking what was possibly a dangerous wild animal to my home, but at the time I could see no other way to help it. If I did not do something soon it would almost surely die.

And if it did, I would never know what it was.

That clinched it for me. Scientific curiosity always tips the balance, and usually at the cost of common sense, which I never used much anyway.

I used some of the rags to bind the creature's wounds. That was difficult since my hands could not stop shaking. Any minute, I feared, the thing could wake up again and tear me apart. At the rear of the basement I found a boarded-up door that led to the outside. It made for a welcome exit, since it would have been impossible to hoist the creature through the window, and the plywood, once I wrenched it free, made an excellent ramp.

In the trunk of my car I used to keep an old sleeping bag, which came very much in handy that evening. There was a tense moment when the creature stirred as I was trying to roll it onto the bag. I jumped so high I nearly hit my head on the rafters above. The green eyes opened briefly and the creature grunted. It struggled briefly as though trying to rise, and then once again it groaned and fell unconscious. I approached it cautiously, and then hurriedly zipped the sleeping bag shut around it. If it woke up again, the sleeping bag might at least contain it for as long as it would take me to run away.

It took all the strength I could muster to drag the heavy body toward the door and up the makeshift ramp. A wise old Greek once stated that he could move the world with a lever and fulcrum upon which to place it. I owe him one for that.

I drove home with great care, since the last thing I needed was to be pulled over by the police with such a passenger slumped across my back seat. With every bump I glanced nervously over my shoulder, in constant fear that the beast might awaken and be unhappy with me for having stolen him from his hiding place. I have dealt with wild animals before and know that the old line about them knowing when you are trying to help them is a load of crap. They know you are trying to help them. The trouble is that they do not want your help. I had no reason to think that this tiger, or whatever it was, would be any different once he came to.

Thank God I live in a one-story house. With what was left of my strength I dragged the limp form into the bedroom. It was a miracle that he was still breathing after such treatment. Panting, I turned on the light and carefully unzipped the sleeping bag to get a better look at what was inside. Seeing him for the first time in full light took my breath away. Whatever had created him, be it Nature or Science or Whatever, it knew exactly what it was doing. The creature was magnificent, a perfect blend of tiger and man in a single body, a masterpiece.

And dying, I thought bitterly.

I hardly knew where to start. I could not guess how much blood he had lost; he was definitely dehydrated and probably in shock. My manhandling him couldn't have been much help. Again I thought about calling for assistance, maybe from a veterinarian, but again I dismissed the idea. It was unthinkable that the creature's existence could be kept secret if I involved other people, and I knew that once word got out, the creature would face a life of imprisonment, if he was even permitted to live. I had to help him, and I was on my own.

"You're not going to die," I whispered to him. "Not after I went through so much work to get you here."

I left him in my room and hurriedly scribbled a list of the things I would need: baby formula and medical supplies from the late-night supermarket, some syringes and needles that I could swipe from the lab at work on my way back. This time I drove as fast as I could, and within an hour I was ready to begin work on my patient.

Years ago, I worked summers at a local nature center where I learned a few tricks for nursing injured animals back to life. Those had been mostly birds, though, with the occasional raccoon or squirrel. This thing, though, was well beyond anything I had ever experienced. I had no idea where he had come from, or even if he was even a natural being. The sixth finger was a troubling reminder of that. All the way home I worried that I would wind up killing him through simple ignorance of his physiology.

The creature was still lying motionless when I returned. I had brought some tablets from the lab that were used to tranquilize pigs, but I was hesitant to use them on something in such a weakened condition, so I worked quickly to take advantage of his unconsciousness. After removing the dressings I'd fashioned from the filthy rags, I carefully cleaned each wound and bandaged it. The leg wounds I saved for last. I could only imagine how he had managed to get shot. Perhaps someone had chased him as he escaped from a secret laboratory somewhere. Maybe he had encountered some of the drug dealers who lurked in such old buildings as he had been hiding in. That would explain the gashes all over his body as well. It sent a shudder through me to think of why there might have been no witnesses to report such an encounter.

The creature's peculiar hand suddenly clenched as I probed for the bullet in his leg. I caught my breath and sweat started to trickle down my brow, but there was no further movement from the patient. My probing had reopened the wound, which was now bleeding copiously. Fighting to control the trembling in my hands I gripped the bullet with a pair of tweezers and tugged it from the hole. The hand went limp, but the creature gave no other indication of having regained consciousness. "I guess that hurt a lot, Six," I said half to myself. "I'm sorry. Just stay asleep until I'm done, OK? I don't think I want to be torn apart just yet."

I reflected on the odd name that I had given him as I flushed the bullet wounds with disinfectant. It seemed as fitting as any.

The sky was starting to lighten outside the window as I sewed the angry wound shut. I spoke in a quiet monotone as I worked—not that he could understand me, but it helped to keep my own nerves steady. "All right, last but not least," I mumbled as I injected some sterile saline under the skin beneath his arm. The thin white fur there swelled up in a big balloon, and just as quickly began to subside as his parched flesh eagerly absorbed the fluid. At least he would not die of dehydration.

There was nothing more that I could do. "It's up to you now," I said softly. "Let's hope you're still alive in the morning." I stood back and stared at him for several long minutes and then closed the curtains, turned off the light, and left him in peace. Stretching out on the living room sofa, I fell almost instantly into an exhausted sleep.

It almost noon before I woke again. My back was stiff and sore from where Six had slammed me against the post. I could not see it, but I imagined I had quite a bruise. It was persistent evidence that the events of the night before had not been more than some bizarre dream. As quietly as I could I tiptoed to the bedroom door. There was no sound from inside. I placed my hand hesitantly on the doorknob and turned it. The click it made sounded terribly loud and made me wince. Cautiously I cracked the door open and peeked inside.

Neither the sleeping bag nor the patient was where I had left them. Curious, I opened the door further and leaned my head in. A low growl sent a shiver of fright through me, and I hurriedly slammed the door shut again. "Holy shit," I gasped out loud. "He's alive!" My elation quickly turned to alarm as question of the day became, Now what? It hit me all at once that I had not fully thought the matter through. The remarkable creature had survived. Now it was awake, and in my bedroom.

Even more slowly this time I opened the door and once again peered inside. Six had climbed onto the bed and was huddled upon it beneath the sleeping bag. All I could see was his angry tiger-face, his eyes glaring back at me warily.

I bit my lip. "Hello." I really did not know what else to say. "I see you're awake."

Six growled in reply and retreated further beneath the sleeping bag.

"Can you understand me?"

He only glared, which disappointed me. It seemed unthinkable that a creature who looked so much like a man could have only an animal's intellect. I wanted more than anything to communicate with him, to find out where he had come from. Maybe he was still getting over the shock, I told myself. Maybe he was just too frightened and confused at the moment.

Or maybe he's a wild animal that will rip you to shreds the first chance he gets?

I tried not to think too much of the latter possibility as I closed the door again. Intelligent or not, my guest was no doubt going to be hungry. Still concerned that he might not be strong enough for solid food, I poured baby formula into a large bowl and carried it back to the bedroom, opening the door just far enough and just long enough to slip the offering inside.

There was no sound from within the room. Frowning, I leaned forward and pressed my ear to the door. There was no way to get the formula into him if Six did not recognize it on his own as food. I did not want to offer him solid food, since in his weakened condition it could very well kill him. Several more silent minutes passed, and then finally I heard the creaking

of the bedsprings. The floorboards depressed under my feet. I held my breath, ear pressed tightly to the door, and smiled as I heard the sound of lapping from the other side. "Good boy," I said silently.

It struck me that I was going to be stuck with this odd houseguest for possibly a considerable time, and hence I was going to need a few more supplies. For more than an hour I wandered from store to store until I managed to find one whose manager was willing to drag a child's wading pool out of storage and sell it to me. The rest of the items I needed were much easier to obtain, and I was able to return home before sunset.

Six hid under his blanket and glowered at me as I cracked opened the bedroom door and reached inside with one of my new purchases, an electric stun gun. It at least gave me the illusion of being on an even footing with a creature whose fangs were as big as my thumb. "Hi there," I said soothingly. "I'm not going to hurt you." Without taking my eyes off of him I groped for the empty bowl and held it up. "See? I brought you this. Nummy! I'll bring you some more later." As I spoke I eased the door open further. It was hard to keep a grip on the stun gun with the amount of sweat my palm was generating. Six watched intently as I edged into the room, dragging along the big plastic pool. "This is for you." I eased it down onto the floor and backed into the hallway. The next to come in was the first of five fifty-pound bags of kitty litter. That notion had been borne of desperation. It was extremely unlikely that my patient would be toilet trained, and perhaps just as unlikely that he would know how to use a litterbox, but I could not think of what else to do. The other alternative was too distasteful. I just prayed that Six would get the idea.

I was soaked with sweat by the time the last bag was emptied into the pool, though only a small part of that was from the exertion. Six made no movements other than an occasional blink. I finished by splashing a little ammonia onto the litter in hopes that it would give him a hint, then left him with another bowl of formula before backing out of the room and closing the door.

The next morning I called in sick to work, using my most convincing fever-voice, then I went to check on Six. He looked as though he had not moved at all, still huddled under his sleeping bag on the bed. The sand in the makeshift litterbox was disturbed, though, much to my delight, and there were other signs that Six had explored the room while I slept.

"Hello again," I whispered as I slipped into the room. "Remember me?" He did not stir as I crouched down on the floor and tried to look as non-threatening as possible. "I'm not here to hurt you. I want to help." I paused, and then shuffled a little closer, keeping my thumb on the stun gun's trigger. "Can you speak?" There was silence. "No, I guess you can't. Can you understand me, though? Can you give me some sign?"

He did not even blink. His icy stare was unnerving. The stun gun gave me courage, though, and I inched a little closer. "I'm your friend," I said soothingly. "I won't hurt you. Do you understand? You're wounded. I'll help you get better."

There was no reaction. Slowly I crept up to the bed. "It would help if you trusted me. I don't want to have to dope you up. It's dangerous. I know how much you're scared." With an exaggeratedly slow movement I lifted a gauze pad from my belt pouch and touched it to my chest. "See this? Your bandages need to be changed. I didn't nurse you this far to have you die of infection." Closer. "It won't hurt. I promise." As gingerly as I could I reached for the edge of the sleeping bag and gripped it between two fingers.

Six erupted with a furious snarl. I saw a black-and-orange wall of muscle rocketing off the bed toward me and fell back, throwing my arm up to defend myself. Claws flashed through the air. I felt a tug at my arm and a sting, and in panic I thrust the stun gun forward and squeezed the trigger as hard as I could.

Nothing happened.

My belly turned into a block of ice. I sat immobile, the stun gun wavering before me as my thumb squeezed itself white on the trigger. Not even a tiny spark crackled between the electrodes. Damned cheap import. It had left me defenseless in the face of an enraged tiger. I wet my pants again.

Six retreated back onto the bed, his teeth bared threateningly and his eyes ablaze. His hand was upraised, each finger sprouting a claw that looked the size of a steak knife. For a long time neither of us moved, until finally Six relaxed and began to lick at the back of his hand. He kept his eyes on me the whole time and growled under his breath. It was an even longer time before I dared to move myself, and I slunk as hastily as I could from the room and yanked the door shut behind me. Only then did I notice that my left shirt sleeve was gone entirely. On my forearm were six pale-red lines, from which here and there tiny droplets of blood oozed. I could hear the quiet rasp of the tiger grooming himself on the other side of the door.

The message had been delivered with crystal clarity. He could have taken my arm off; he just did not want to. I figured it was the closest I was going to get to gratitude from him. "Fine," I said shakily. "We'll do it your way."

Six got a treat that afternoon with his bowl of formula. I left a small chunk of steak on a plate next to the bowl, and heard him greedily devouring it before he lapped up the rest of his meal. A satisfied smile came to my face moments later as the bedsprings creaked and Six began to groan. The tablet that I had hidden in the meat had done its job. It still worried me that I had to tranquilize him, but it was better than losing body parts.

He was sprawled on his side when I ventured back into the room. Much to my relief he was still breathing. A little spot of drool darkened the sheet under his muzzle. I took a moment to gather my courage, and then crept closer. "Hey," I said. "Hey, you." Six groaned in reply, his eyes blinking, unfocused. I had brought a yardstick with me, which I used to poke him in the shoulder. He only groaned again, and did not move. It was a pitiful sight. "Sorry I had to do that to you," I said as I knelt on the floor beside the bed. With trepidation I reached for his muzzle and held his jaws open, and with my other hand pulled his tongue out to keep him from choking. He growled indignantly, and then closed his eyes.

At least I could get a look at his bandages, which were in sorry shape. Blood had seeped through the gauze that covered some of his larger wounds. A few of the smaller bandages were gone altogether, probably licked away. I was worried that he might have swallowed them, but after a quick search I found that they had fallen between the bed and the wall.

When I was finished changing his bandages I sat on the edge of the bed and laid a hand on his chest. It was warm and powerful, and twitched just slightly at my touch. The fact that I could not do this without tranquilizing him depressed me. It was a sad reminder that the creature that lay upon my bed was not human. Whatever his origin, whatever secrets he held, it was all out of my reach. I had wanted so much for him to be an intelligent creature, a wondrous being that I could talk to and learn from. Maybe that was why I had been so eager to take him home, despite the danger. As

surely as he was unique, though, inside he was nothing more than a dumb animal.

I sighed, and for a while I sat and petted him. The fur was soft, like velvet, and the muscles underneath were hard and well-toned. I explored him for a while, moving down his arm to his hand with its curious extra finger, and then I brushed my fingers along his big round ears. So much like a man, yet at the same time so much like a tiger. How could such a creature have come to be? Was he a construct? An alien? Something from the future? Or had he simply been there all along, unseen?

I stayed for a long time with my hand simply resting on his chest. Some of my disappointment with his savage nature faded with the feel of his fur against my skin. Though a brute, he was still no less a wonder. Gazing down at him filled me with pity. He had suffered so much and was very likely alone in the world, and despite his obvious strength he surely had to struggle every day against hunger and fear. It was not fair that such a magnificent creature had to lead what I imagined to be a miserable existence. Overcome for a moment, I leaned down and touched my nose to his, and whispered, "I won't let anything happen to you."

His eyes snapped open, and again I felt my innards turn to ice. I stood up quickly and backed away as his tongue drew back into his mouth and he began to growl. Marvel that he was, it was no excuse for me to forget that the pill I had slipped him had only a limited duration. Thankfully he was still groggy and could not focus his eyes. It was a sure bet that he would not be happy if I was still there when his senses returned, so keeping a wary eye on him I gathered up my medical supplies and retreated from the room.

Later that evening I heard Six moving about, exploring his surroundings, and decided that he was strong enough for solid food. That led to another quandary. There was no way to know exactly how close to a tiger Six was, and it worried me that he might require an ungodly amount of raw meat each day, which I could never afford. It seemed almost insulting to offer him cat food. I reasoned that as he did not seem to be starved when I found him, obviously he did not require that much meat, since he could never have found that much on his own in his environment. Then I thought of how strangely few drug dealers and homeless people could be found in the Badlands, and quickly put that thought out of my mind. Cat food it would be.

After another trip to the supermarket, with a detour to the hardware store where I had bought the stun gun to give the clerk a piece of my mind, I returned with four huge, heavy bags filled with canned cat food and several cheap cuts of meat. Six eyed me warily as I slunk into the room with a bowl of water and a tray of the smelly mush. "Sorry," I whispered to him. "It's all I can afford." I closed the door, and listened with satisfaction to the sounds he made while he devoured his meal.

The next morning I thought it would be best if I did not take the day off of work as I had planned to. There was little need for me to hover over my patient, and Six would probably appreciate being left alone for a while. It was hard to concentrate in the lab, though. Distracted, I kept spilling things, and broke three beakers before it was even lunchtime. My coworkers were concerned, of course, but I just waved my hand and said that I was exhausted after my bout of "fever." My mind, of course, was preoccupied with Six and the hundreds of questions surrounding him. More than anything, I could not keep my thoughts away from the soft warmth of his fur.

As soon as I returned from work it was time for Six to take his medicine again. His glare seemed somehow darker as I reached through the door to deliver his offering of meat. "What's wrong?" I said, worried that he had somehow made a connection between the meat and the terrible hangover that I imagined he suffered after the drug wore off. I waited impatiently outside the door, growing ever more concerned that he was wise to my trick, and was relieved when I heard him gulping down the treat. There was some scratching in the litter-pool, and then a creak of the bedsprings, and then silence. I waited several minutes and then slipped inside.

Six lay on his belly this time, eyes half open and glazed, staring at the wall. I had to roll his ponderous body over to reach his bandages. His head flopped to the side and his tongue fell from his mouth of its own accord. It was a relief to be spared the unsettling job of reaching between his teeth.

Many of his wounds bore healthy scabs, much to my satisfaction, although the bullet holes in his leg were still worrying. I changed his dressings, then raked through his litter-pool, which thank God he had learned to use without any urging. I pulled it closer to the bed so that he would not have to risk tearing his stitches to reach it, and then sat once again beside him and stroked his fur. I knew that I should not linger, not wanting to repeat the previous day's indiscretion, but I could not resist burying my hand in his pelt. It was as soft as I remember it and just as warm, and this time I fancied I could feel a subtle vibration under my fingers. I wanted to think it was a response to my touch, or maybe in his drugged stupor Six was simply dreaming pleasant feline dreams. Whatever the reason, I found it soothing, almost hypnotic. I realized that through that touch I had found a tenuous means, perhaps the only way, to commune with this wonderful creature. The feeling of his strength beneath my hand gave me a fleeting glimpse into his world. It was a fellowship in which I could easily lose myself, and I hoped that somehow, deep in his savage thoughts, Six felt it, too.

The week settled into a routine. Six got a hearty breakfast of cat food in the morning before I left for work, then afterward, a tasty chunk of meat with its hidden tablet allowed me time to tend his wounds, and moreover to sit beside him. His injuries were healing at an impressive rate, giving me a greater understanding of how he had managed to survive in what must have been a very hostile world. As the days passed it was probably no longer necessary for me to treat him on a daily basis, but I could not bear to give up the peaceful communion. I knew that it was wrong to keep drugging him as I did for such a selfish need, but it had become almost an addiction for me. Every night as he lay safely in a daze I would sit by his side, my hands caressing his fur, marveling at his fierce beauty and pondering his impenetrable secrets. Each night I would leave behind an untainted piece of meat and some fresh tuna, little gifts for him that I thought might help to assuage my growing sense of guilt.

At the end of the second week I finally admitted to myself that Six no longer needed my treatment. I had taken the stitches from his leg and his other wounds were healing well. There would be no more tablets hidden in his evening meal. Now I was faced with the dilemma of what I was going to do with him. It seemed cruel to keep him in my room like a prisoner, but it seemed equally cruel to just release him where I had found him. I agonized over the question all evening long, and went to bed with a dreadful headache.

I awoke later from my uneasy sleep with a deep sense of dread. It was a sensation I had not felt since I was a little boy when I would awaken positive that I was not alone in my room. I was sweating and shivering, and was actually hesitant to reach for my glasses on the coffee table. My rational mind scoffed, reminding me that I was a scientist and that it was shameful to tremble in the dark like some frightened child.

My groping fingers encountered fur.

The room abruptly grew much colder.

I could not move a muscle. I do not even think my heart was beating. My mind reeled as the reality of the looming danger sunk in. Don't move, I told myself. Stay perfectly still, or you're as good as dead.

There was a sudden pressure on my chest. A hand, huge and warm and furry, was holding me down. I had seen a cat once pin a mouse the same way before ripping it to pieces. My breath escaped in a hoarse whimper, which caught in my throat as I felt the prick of claws against my skin. Don't move.

An hour went by, or perhaps just a minute. There was no sound in the room save for the thunder of the blood in my ears. The hand on my chest did not budge, not even a twitch, until the pressure abruptly lifted away. I panted but remained motionless, straining in the darkness for the slightest sound.

There was none. Time passed, and I managed to gather enough courage to fumble for my glasses. Peering into the darkness I could make out the familiar shapes of my furniture, but nothing threatening, no looming monstrosity waiting in the shadows, not even when I turned the light on. With shaking legs I stumbled to the bedroom and threw open the door.

The window stood open. Chilly air blew in through it and rustled the curtains. The bed stood empty. Even the sleeping bag was gone.

I shut the door slowly and felt tears burning behind my eyes. "You're welcome," I said in a choked whisper.

I told myself that it was for the better. After all, what was I supposed to have done with him? Six had survived for a long time on his own, and now that he had his health back, he no longer needed me to look after him. It was supposed to be a consoling thought, but it did not work. He was more than just another wounded animal that I had nursed back to health. He was a living mystery, one that I sorrowfully knew that I would never solve. I did not appreciate the true depth of that mystery, however, until the next evening, when I discovered that of the dozen cans of cat food that I had left in the kitchen, not one could be found. Later, as I set about the sad task of cleaning the bedroom, I was astonished to find hidden behind the bed a neat little collection of white tablets. There were fifteen of them, one for each night of Six's stay, their surfaces pockmarked and rough from the moisture in the meat in which they had been hidden.

I sat down on the bed and cried for a very long time.

To this day I carry the stun gun with me. It still does not work, of course. I keep it as a memento. My coworkers find it odd but I don't care. Let them think what they will. They already think I'm crazy for insisting on driving once every week to a lonely, desolate neighborhood to leave a can of cat food in the doorway of an empty house.

Sometimes, the only element of fantasy that a Furry story needs is that the characters live in an anthropomorphic animal world. Tobias, a lemur; Dylan, a black panther; and Marty, a fox, are three young males who live together (in one sense or another of the phrase) in a modern city. They have a relationship. Relationships drift around over the years. Hey, it happens. Are Tobias and Dylan through with each other? How does Marty come into it? "Drifting" depicts their slowly evolving relationship with sensitivity.

Drifting

Kyell Gold

It had been four long years since Tobias had looked forward to a bedtime. He and Dylan had shared a bed for eight, and the first four had been delightful, everything he could've hoped for. Well, okay. The first three had been delightful—two and a half, technically, if you counted the ski trip as the last really delightful time. It had been good for a year or so after that, or at least for eight months, but it had taken almost six months for Tobias to say something about it, which he remembered because it was right after they'd come back from their fourth and last ski trip, standing in the living room with the ski gear still resting against the couch and his tentative words hanging unanswered in the air. Dylan had just mumbled something and gone into the bathroom, leaving Tobias with nothing to do but unpack and remember the cold of the weekend.

So now, because Dylan always stayed up late on the computer, Tobias retired early to their empty bed, made sure his alarm was set, and pressed his face into the pillow, trying not to think about the giant empty space in the bed. It was better than lying next to the inert black panther, thinking about touching him and playing the loop over and over in his mind: his paw reaching out, the shiver of muscle at his touch—because Dylan still slept naked—and then the panther relaxing again, trying to pretend Tobias hadn't touched him. Maybe this time it'd be different, sang a tiny, irrepressible voice in his head, but it had been so long since that voice had been right about anything that it, too, felt like a stuck tape loop, as perky as Tobias's assistant at the office and with as little sense.

Tobias now slept in boxers, his long ringed tail flat between his legs. He usually managed to fall asleep before Dylan came to bed, and his alarm never woke up the panther. Or if it did, Dylan never actually got up while Tobias slid himself out of bed, threw on sweats, and went to the gym.

Gymnasiums in Tobias's home country were very public affairs, some with showers literally open to the changing room. He'd been puzzled when he saw the walled-off areas here, wondering why people who were working so hard to get in shape would be shy about their naked bodies, but now it was specifically because the Steel Body Fitness gym had private shower stalls that Tobias had started going back there. Dylan had a membership too, one of those things they were going to do together, but as far as Tobias knew, Dylan hadn't been to a gym—or done any sort of exercise—in quite a while.

He wasn't particularly fond of exercise either, but he didn't want to show up at work at seven in the morning, and spending two hours in a coffee shop would only take care of part of his morning needs. And yet, he couldn't just show up at the gym and shower, so he'd reluctantly started a limited workout routine, half an hour on the treadmills. And then, looking around at the pine marten huffing away at twice Tobias's speed, at the red wolf straining at the bicep curl, he'd felt ashamed of his indolence and had started setting goals for himself: faster speed, more time. He'd paid for three training sessions, and had been assigned Marty, a lean fox who'd started him on a progressive exercise regimen. Tobias still suspected he wasn't working as hard as he could, but he felt better, and when he cut back his lattes to one a day from three at Marty's suggestion, he'd started to lose weight.

Not that Dylan would ever notice, he thought, his paws thumping in time on the speeding treadmill, tail kept carefully up out of the way (once you've stepped on your tail during a run, you always remember to keep it up). Actually, for all Tobias knew, Dylan could've gained twenty pounds. Or lost it. The panther favored loose shirts and baggy jeans, so it was impossible to tell. And he seemed to be eating the same as he always had, to judge from what he got when they went out to dinner (which they still did three or four times a week).

But Tobias had had to buy some new pants. He'd dragged Dylan shopping, and Dylan had helped him pick out the new wardrobe without once commenting on why he needed it. "These'd look good on you," he'd said, as if he were picking out a color of house paint. Which, in its own way, had a nice comforting domesticity to it, and Tobias wouldn't have minded it at all if it'd been accompanied by a wink, or even just by the knowledge that that night, or the next, or maybe the next, Dylan might be watching him take those pants off with lustful eyes. Tobias would've settled for affectionate eyes, even.

There was no use dwelling on it. It was what it was. Tobias had moved to Riviera knowing only Dylan, and when things were going well, he hadn't bothered to make friends of his own. When things went bad, he'd made a few attempts to connect with co-workers, or friends of Dylan he got along well with, but inevitably he found himself wanting to complain about his relationship, and he didn't like himself when he was complaining. Besides, it felt disloyal to Dylan, as if he were giving up. So he remained cordial with his co-workers, saw Dylan's friends with Dylan, and ignored the few times people approached him at the gym.

And when he had finished his workout, his body pleasantly warm and sweaty, he stripped down in the changing room and took his shampoo into the private shower stall. There, finally, he let himself long for the Dylan he'd fallen in love with, his own black paw becoming the panther's in his mind as he gave himself his release, alone.

Then it was time for a long, thorough scrub, long enough that he would be presentable when he walked out. Long enough for him to reflect on how pathetic he was, jerking off at the local gym because he didn't want his boyfriend to smell anything in their shower at home. Too shy, too afraid to break out of his rut. He made sure the tile floor was clean, rubbing around with a bit of shampoo to be sure, and then rinsed himself off. He turned the faucet to shut off the water and composed himself, shedding all the self-loathing despair, leaving only the nagging little knowledge that he would be right back here in twenty-four hours.

Five minutes in the full-body dryer left his beige fur fluffy. He turned around to give his tail a few extra minutes, while he brushed the rest of his body fur out, thinking of nothing in particular. And he dressed for work, as he did every day, and walked out of the locker room.

Only today, as he was walking out, he noticed an older coyote glaring at him. And Marty, in his "Steel Body Staff" tank top, started walking purposefully toward Tobias as the lemur crossed the main floor of the gym.

Tobias felt his stomach sink. Keep calm, it's probably not what you think. He just wants to ask you about doing more sessions. But although Marty did occasionally approach him to ask about that, the fox's dark muzzle was serious now, his eyes not sparkling.

"Hey, Tobias," Marty said. Before Tobias could respond, he said, "Mind stepping over into the office for a second?"

Marty always called him "Tobe." Tobias fought the pressure in his throat and nodded, following the fox across the floor. He looked morosely at the big glass windows. Maybe a car would careen out of control into one of them. Or maybe a political riot would break out, though admittedly even in his home country that only happened every twenty years or so, and here in Riviera they were going on fifty years since the last one.

The gym remained intact as Marty gestured him to one of the stiff office-supply chairs and seated himself on the other side of the desk. The fox's ears were back, and he didn't look at Tobias as he took a breath. "So, look, do you know what this is about?"

Tobias shook his head without even thinking about it. That was another strange thing about this country: if Marty'd just clapped him on the shoulder and said, "Hey, quit beating off in the shower, okay?" it would have been a lot easier. But the fox's sympathetic shame on Tobias's part just made Tobias feel it more acutely.

Marty took another breath. His paw rested on a binder on the desk, and his eyes kept flicking to the computer screen. The spine on the binder was angled so Tobias could just barely read the title: "Steel Body Fitness Member Conduct Rules." He spent a moment thinking about why a public gym needed an inch-thick stack of paper telling people how to behave in public before realizing with a guilty start that it was because of people like him.

"There's some stuff that you can't do in the showers," the fox said, without looking at him. "Listen, I get the whole gym thing, y'know. But please just wait 'til you get home." And that wasn't so bad, not by itself, until he went on. "A couple of the other members have complained."

Tobias opened his mouth to reply, but his mind jumped ahead to the fact that not only Marty, but other people—the older coyote who'd given him the stink-eye on his way out today, probably—had seen him. And that meant that they probably knew how unfulfilling his relationship was and therefore how much of a failure he himself was. None of this registered consciously, but overwhelmed him in a hot rush. "S-sorry," he choked out, squeezing his eyes shut and pressing a paw to his face.

"Hey...hey." Marty's voice had lost the clinical detachment and regained its warmth. He was kneeling beside Tobias's chair a moment later, the warmth of his body and his smell at once reassuring and a reminder of humiliation.

"I'm okay," Tobias said in a small voice.

Marty rested a paw on his knee. "It's no big deal," he said. "Look, we catch guys every other week. I just have to give you a warning not to do it again. It's no big deal," he repeated.

"I know," Tobias said, struggling to get himself under control. "Sorry. I w-won't do it again."

Marty lifted his paw. "Anything you want to talk about?"

"No! I'm fine." Tobias rubbed the fur around his eyes. "I'll be fine."

Any more sympathy from Marty might be too much. Fortunately, the fox stood up and leaned against the desk. When Tobias raised his head, he was looking into a calm smile. The sparkle had returned, at least a little, to the fox's dark eyes. "Hey, do you work nearby? You said something about Crick Co.?"

Tobias nodded. "Down on High, just off 890."

Marty walked back around the desk. "That Victorino's Pizza is around there, isn't it? I like their thin-crust. I might head over there for lunch once I get out of here. Around one."

"I won't do it again, Marty," Tobias said. "I promise." He stood with one more long sniff and waited to see if the fox would say anything else, but Marty just waved. Tobias hurried out of the office.

All the way to work, he regretted moving to Riviera. Back home, things were simpler. People just talked, and the things you didn't talk about, you didn't talk about. You didn't allude to them with your ears down as if they were a piece of garbage. And back home, he had family and friends—well, not so many since he'd moved to the New World.

At least here, if he didn't have friends other than Dylan, he had a comfortable routine. When the questions got to be too loud, he could just lower his head and lose himself in his life. Such as it was. He nodded to his co-workers and settled himself into his cubicle, but when he called up the article he was supposed to review, he just stared without seeing the words. The morning's humiliation, on top of what he'd come to view as the wreck of his life, gnawed at him. How would the raccoon in the next cube react if Tobias asked him for relationship advice over morning coffee? For that matter, what kind of relationship was the raccoon even in? Tobias didn't know whether he was married or dating, gay or straight.

The bat-eared fox who worked on the other side of him, she was married. He heard her talking to her husband on the phone, and she had to leave to pick up kids about once a week. But he couldn't talk to her. He shook his head and tried to read through the article again, but he kept having to remind himself that he couldn't talk to anyone, didn't want to talk to anyone.

He'd only gotten through half the article when he realized he was starving. Guiltily, he looked up and saw that it was one o'clock already. He'd have to do better this afternoon, but he needed food now.

So he wandered down to the street, and stopped outside Victorino's Pizza. He needed someone to talk to more than he needed food, but could he bring himself to talk to Marty? He stared in the door at the slices of pizza, and then at the sandwich shop next door. It'd be easy to go have a sandwich, keep an eye on the street, and if Marty showed up, he could make a decision then. It'd be easier to keep his head down.

Or he could just make the decision now. He was tired of not talking. He'd been not talking for months, years. And he didn't have to talk to Marty, not if he didn't feel like it. But as he inhaled the aroma of cooking dough and tomato sauce, letting the door swing shut behind him, he rather thought he would.

* * *

"So how long have you been in Riviera?"

Marty'd strolled in at quarter past and sat down at Tobias's table just as naturally as if he'd made an appointment, two slices of Hawaiian pizza on his plate. And his first question hadn't been what Tobias was expecting.

The lemur found it easier to answer because it was so impersonal, unrelated to everything else that had happened. "Eight years last March."

Marty nodded, munching his pizza. "Did you move here for someone?"

"No." He said it automatically and then felt ashamed. He took the scrap of crust he had left and chewed on it.

"I did." Tobias looked up at the cross fox's wry smile. Marty nodded once. "Grew up in the south on a farm. Went to the big city every month. Clubbing, drinking, having fun. Met a lion there." He leaned back and took a breath, gesturing with the paw that held the slice of pizza. "He was exotic, he was beautiful, and he was into me. Told me if I came to Riviera with him, he'd take care of me."

He took another bite. Tobias leaned forward. "I guess he didn't?"

Marty chewed, taking his time. "He did, for a while," he said, once he'd swallowed. "Then I got boring."

"I'm sorry," Tobias said.

Marty waved him off. "It was a few years ago. I decided to stick around, joined the gym, started training there last year. You were one of my first trainees, did you know that?"

Tobias grinned, spontaneously. The fox was wearing a tight t-shirt that mashed down his fur in muscular contours. It was hard to imagine that he hadn't been always a trainer at the gym. "You never told me."

"You remember what you said when I asked you why you joined the gym?"

Tobias nodded. "I just wanted to get in shape." But the question recalled to him that Dylan had joined with him, making his smile falter.

Marty pointed a finger at him. "Exactly. Done a good job of that, too. You want to hear a secret, though?" He took another bite of pizza and chewed as Tobias nodded. "That's not the real answer. Everyone comes to the gym to get in shape. What we don't ask people is why they want to get in shape."

"Oh." Tobias's ears drooped. He waited for the question to come, but Marty just finished off the first slice of pizza. He didn't say anything else until he'd taken a drink, and then he smiled.

"So what do you do at Crick?"

"Quality assurance," Tobias said. "I review the scientific reports before they go out."

"Wow, you're a scientist?"

"Not really." Tobias smiled, Dylan receding from his mind. "I had some science training but I never finished my degree. I mostly proof them to make sure all the tables match the numbers and the names are all spelled right, stuff like that."

"What happens if you mess up?"

"Nothing, really. Nobody reads them. We just release them to make sure people remember our name. Kinda pathetic." The fox's dark muzzle was welcoming, smiling. Tobias ventured a question. "Do you do the training full-time?"

Marty shook his head. "Part time, and I do odd jobs for a carpenter when he needs me. But it pays the rent."

By the time Tobias had to go back to work, to his astonishment, the subject of him being caught at the gym hadn't even come up. But as they got up, Marty eyed the menu. "There's a lot of good-looking pizzas here," he said. "Might come back here for lunch. I train Monday-Wednesday-Friday."

Tobias smiled and clasped the fox's offered paw. "Maybe I'll see you," he said.

He found himself smiling as he walked back up to work.

* * *

When he got home, Dylan was at the game console playing Streets of War 3. "Hey," he said as Tobias closed the door. "How was your day?"

Tobias said, "Pretty good" before remembering that he'd been warned at the gym for masturbating in the shower.

"Cool. Want to grab some Chinese when I finish this level?"

"Sure," he said, heading into the bedroom to drop his stuff off. He looked down at the bed and then out at Dylan, and walked slowly back out. "Dylan?"

"Just a sec." The panther kept shooting down terrorists, peeking out of windows and hiding behind barricades.

"What's going on?" Tobias's good mood was gone. He could barely remember what it had been like talking to Marty, making a friend.

"Uh...I'm trying to clear Manchester of terrorists."

"No, I mean..." He glanced back at the bed again. "Is everything okay?"

Dylan killed two terrorist weasels and paused the game. "Fine," he said, but after eight years Tobias knew the guarded look, the half-back ears, and the twitch in the panther's tail that he could never quite disguise, that meant he was tense about something. And he didn't want to talk about it.

Because it doesn't feel fine to me, Tobias wanted to say, but Dylan's expression discouraged him. "All right," he said. "I'll call ahead for the Chinese."

The Chinese food was good, but once it was gone, Dylan went back to his computer. Tobias took over the video game console, and then went to bed, pressing his face into the pillow and wondering if anything would ever change.

In the morning, he almost did opt to sit for two hours in a coffee shop. But then he thought, if I stop going to the gym now, I'll never go back. That prospect filled him with a strange hollowness. So he walked in again, ran on the treadmill, and when he was done, stepped into the shower and did nothing but wash.

Walking out, to the older coyote's narrowed eyes, Tobias gave an innocent smile, bouncing his ringed tail behind him. The smile persisted most of the way to work, and when he went to lunch, even though he didn't go to Victorino's, he got a warm feeling when he walked by it.

And on Friday, when he did go to Victorino's, Marty was already there, relaxing in a corner booth. Tobias picked up two slices of plain cheese and went to sit with him.

"How's work?" Marty started, and they talked about people at the gym and scientific reports, until it was time for Tobias to go. Marty clasped his paw when they stood and said, "Have a nice weekend."

And the first thing he asked on Monday was, "How was the weekend?"

"We went to dinner and saw a movie. I played some video games," Tobias said. "How about you?"

"Did some carpentry work. Helped build a table. Went out to a club, got laid."

He said it casually, the slice of alfredo pizza halfway to his muzzle, but his eyes watched Tobias keenly. Tobias forced himself to be casual as well, chewing the rest of his pepperoni and swallowing before saying, "Oh yeah?"

Marty dipped his muzzle in a nod, ears flicking. "You ever go to clubs?"

"Not really my scene." Tobias shook his head, staring down at his pizza.

"Well, I admit the guy wasn't all that hot stuff, but it's a good way to relax once in a while." When Tobias looked up, Marty'd put the pizza down. "I mean, works for me."

"I dunno. My boyfriend's not really into that."

"What do you guys do together?"

"Oh, we play video games sometimes. We used to, anyway. Now we mostly watch movies and TV. Sometimes at the same time."

"What video games?"

And they talked about video games, and left the subject of Dylan for that day.

It was sausage and mushroom pizza on Wednesday, and only a couple bites into his slice, Tobias took a breath and looked across the plastic table at the fox. "It's been a while since things were really good with me and Dylan," he said, and then stopped.

Marty just nodded his long muzzle, ears perking slightly. "What changed?"

Tobias put the pizza down. "I don't know," he said. "It must be something I did, but..."

When he didn't go on, Marty raised an eyebrow. "You haven't talked about it?"

"I try." Tobias rested a paw on the table and looked at his fingers tapping the plastic. "But he just...doesn't talk."

"At all?"

Tobias sighed. "When my father threw me out, y'know, he said, 'If you won't carry on the family, you are no longer part of it.' And that was it. There was nothing to talk about."

"Tobe, that's not really a model you want your boyfriends to follow. Don't go Oedipal."

"Edible?"

Marty grinned. "Don't look for your father in your boyfriend."

Tobias sighed. "We like the same games, movies...relationships are so hard."

Marty shoved the remaining slice of pizza into his muzzle. "Mmm. 'S'why I don't bother with'em. You got friends to do all that stuff with, and you can always find people to do the..."

Tobias looked curiously at Marty, who paused and then went on. "The everything else." He waved a paw. "I get on by myself pretty good. Not saying that's what you should do, just saying that works for me. So how about you come out to a club Friday night?"

"I, uh, what?" Tobias flicked his ears up, wondering if he'd missed a linking sentence somewhere.

"You know, dancing, drinking, bright lights, lots of hot guys?"

"Oh, it's not really my thing." Tobias nibbled on his crust.

"Ah, you've tried it already."

He put the crust down and took a drink. Marty waited. "Well. No."

"Look, I'm not saying you have to hook up or anything. It's a great way to burn calories. More fun than the treadmill."

"I'd have to ask."

Marty brushed crumbs from his whiskers, his smile broader. "So ask."

* * *

Of course, it wasn't that easy. Thursday night, Tobias realized he wasn't going to have much more chance to ask Dylan if he wanted to go Friday, so as he was getting ready for bed, he rehearsed what he was going to say in his mind. For all that helped; it still came out awkward as he said it.

"Hey, I met this guy at the gym, and he wants to take me to a club tomorrow night. If that's okay."

Dylan looked up from the computer. "What club?"

"I...don't know. I mean, he didn't specify."

Dylan tilted his head, ears flicking. "You don't have to ask me. If you want to go, go."

Impulsively, Tobias said, "You want to come?"

The panther shook his head slowly. "I got stuff to do here. Not really into the loud music and stuff, you know."

"Okay." Tobias paused. "I might...I might be out pretty late."

"Okay. You want me to wait up?"

"Oh, no. Well, I mean, if you want..." He trailed off. He wanted to say, "what for?" but that seemed rude, and Dylan was just being pleasant.

The panther shrugged. "If I'm up, I guess." He turned back to his computer, and Tobias thought that was it, but a couple minutes later, Dylan said, "I didn't know you were into dancing."

"Oh, yeah." Tobias looked up from his game. "Used to do it back home."

"You had clubs in Terrian?"

Dylan still wasn't looking at him, but Tobias shook his head anyway. "No, just with the family, you know? All of us together."

"Mm." Dylan's tail twitched. Tobias waited for him to say something, and finally he did. "Let me know how it is."

Tobias sighed. "Yeah," he said. "I will."

There wasn't an easy way to bring up the possibility of doing more than dancing, so Tobias just told himself that he wasn't intending to "hook up," though it was hard to stop his daydreams all through Friday. And when he met Marty outside Splitz, the music loud enough that it was hard to talk even in the street, he couldn't take his eyes from the dark-shouldered fox's light white vest, open to show off his fluffy chest ruff, and the tight black shorts, cut high enough that Tobias could see the bottom of a little triangle of white fur on the inner thigh.

"You wear more clothes than that to the gym," he couldn't help saying as they stood in line.

Marty grinned. "If you want to come back, I'll have to take you shopping."

Tobias fingered his t-shirt, looked down at the jeans. "Is this bad?"

"Nah, if you're not looking to hook up. You'll get pretty warm, so just remember to drink a lot of water. But you should be doing that anyway."

The bouncer, a six-and-a-half foot tall tiger, watched the gum-chewing vixen at the entrance take their money and smear something invisible on their wrist fur. Marty was already bouncing on the balls of his feet, his tail switching in time to the music as they walked in. Tobias's long tail, too, undulated in time with the music, creating waves along it that distracted Marty as he turned to ask Tobias something.

"That's cool," he said, snaking his arms to try to imitate the motion.

Tobias stopped. He looked around, but didn't see anyone else in the club who had as long a tail. All the other dancers just seemed to be hopping and bouncing, with short, fluffy tails. Marty's was longer than anyone else's—no, wait, there was a cougar, but he was facing Tobias, his tail hidden from view.

"Hey," Marty said, now hopping from one foot to the other and clapping his paws together. "First rule of the club is don't worry what other people think of you. Unless you're trying to hook up, but you're not, so what do you care? Just let yourself go. Come on, I'll help."

Still bouncing, he dragged Tobias over to the bar, bathed in purple light, where a white ferret's glowing fur showed Tobias that the light was probably a UV. "Two Steamboats," Marty said to the ferret, holding up two fingers.

The ferret gave him a thumbs-up and continued serving the pair of bears standing beside them. Marty closed his eyes briefly, swinging his hips and still clapping his paws. "What's a Steamboat?" Tobias asked.

"Come on, feel the beat," Marty said. "You'll like the Steamboat. It's fruity."

Tobias took a breath. Back home, growing up, they used to dance a lot, but the dances people were doing here were different. They were more jerky, except for a few who were dancing fluidly with glowing wristbands. He started tapping his foot to the throbbing beat, and let his body sway ever so gently from side to side.

If he just focused on the beat, he could almost imagine his father pounding on the porch, his brother and the families next door dancing off the Sunday pot luck. He hadn't thought of home in years, mostly because of the way he'd left it, and remembering the feeling of dancing brought back a startling liberty with it. He curled his tail around the bar rail, and then uncurled it, letting it sway back and forth. Both feet got into it, and just then, the glowing white ferret plunked down two glasses on the bar.

"I got this one," Marty said, "you get the next."

"Deal." Tobias clinked his glass against Marty's and brought it to his nose while the fox drank. He caught the flavor of banana, strongly, over the familiar smell of rum. Orange and cherry followed them when he took a gulp, and then the rum overwhelmed them all. "Wow," he said, looking down.

Marty'd already finished his. "No hurry," he said, "but finish up so we can go dance."

Tobias looked again at the drink and then at the fox. He gave him a quick grin and brought the glass to his mouth.

The dance floor was a wild mass of chaos, a hundred different kinds of musk and flashing lights of every color. Marty let go of Tobias's paw at what seemed like a random spot on the floor and started swinging his hips again, more aggressively than he had at the bar. Tobias looked around and saw as many different dance styles as people, and almost as many different kinds of dress. Next to them were two female pine martens, spandex tops stretched tightly across their ample chests, with matching hip-huggers shimmering under the rainbow lights. They slapped paws while dancing, as if their matching outfits weren't enough to show they were together. To his other side, a white tiger, almost a photo-negative of Dylan, was dancing so jerkily that Tobias thought at first he must be completely drunk, until he pulled out a phone and tapped out a text message with more coordination than any drunk person could manage. The phone wasn't the only conspicuous bulge in his shorts when he slid it back in place.

"Hey." Marty punched him on the shoulder. "You can look, just don't stare." He had to yell over the music. "Have fun dancing."

"Right." Tobias felt a warmth in his cheeks and a different warmth in his stomach, where the drink was sitting very comfortably. The former faded while the other spread to his legs and arms, and since nobody seemed to notice he was staring or even care what he was doing, he started to dance. "Hey," he called to Marty, and waved at his nose. "Don't the smells bother you?"

Marty's smile widened. He just curled his tongue around his lips and lifted his muzzle, inhaling visibly. Tobias laughed. It didn't bother him, but he wondered what the fox and his sensitive nose made of it. He must like it, because he looked very much in his element.

Once it was clear Tobias was having fun, he expected Marty to move away and circulate, but the fox seemed happy staying where he was. Other dancers flowed around them, but Tobias didn't stare overtly, except at the striking arctic fox, moving with serpentine grace, whose only concession to propriety was a small gold pouch that strained to keep his maleness concealed. Tobias couldn't help staring at his abs and legs, rippling under short shaved fur, but it didn't seem to matter, because the fox was traveling in a small cloud of staring dancers, male and female both. Tobias turned back to Marty and saw the fox grinning. "Don't worry," Marty shouted over the music. "Nobody else can look like that."

"Too flashy for me," Tobias responded, but that wasn't true for everyone. In the short time he was near them, Tobias saw a black panther and a large tigress both dance their way up to the white fox, gain his attention for a few seconds, and then get left behind as he danced on. He shook his head and grinned, clapping his paws together to the beat and hopping more vigorously, more carefree in the certainty that nobody within twenty feet of the arctic fox was looking at anyone else.

"You look fine," Marty said. Tobias gave the dark-maned fox a thumbs-up to show that he appreciated the reassurance. Marty himself looked pretty good. He too shaved close on his arms and stomach (though not as close as the arctic fox), but left his shoulders and the mane on the back of his neck long and fluffy. Tobias wondered why he hadn't noticed the fox's rear before, or the way his hips moved invitingly, or why he hadn't appreciated the power in those paws when Marty'd helped him with his exercises months ago.

Somewhere in between his second and third Steamboat, Tobias realized that he was going to go home with Marty and have sex. The realization was as liberating as the passage of the arctic fox had been to his dancing—with the outcome of the night settled, he didn't have to worry about it. He could just let himself go. The memories of home faded, the dance floor and club becoming its own experience, allowing Tobias to get lost in the music. After his fourth drink, his body felt tingly, aching for a touch, so he rubbed his paws along his sides. And that felt good, so he rubbed them down his thighs, too. Marty was echoing his dancing, and perhaps the music had slowed, or Tobias's perceptions had speeded up, because the fox seemed to be swaying rather than swinging, stepping rather than hopping.

"Another one?" Tobias yelled, pointing at the bar.

Marty shook his head and pointed at the exit. Tobias's tail shivered, his heart skipping a beat. The warmth of four drinks all poured into his groin. He nodded.

They made their way through the crowd of dancers, out into the dark street. Marty was panting heavily, and Tobias could feel the stickiness of sweat all through his fur. "You're lucky," Marty gasped. "God, can't close my mouth." His tongue was dripping.

"Good," Tobias said, and before he could change his mind, he stepped up to Marty and kissed him.

He'd grabbed the fox's muzzle and planted his mouth across the open lips, and Marty responded immediately. He tasted like orange and cherry, and rum, and fox. Different from Dylan, warmer and more exotic. And when he pulled the fox to him, he felt the hardness of his arousal, something else he hadn't felt for years. Marty's paws slid down and cupped Tobias's rear, tongue flicking against the lemur's. Tobias's heart raced. His tail swung around to brush the back of Marty's legs.

Then the fox pulled away and took a step back, resting a paw on Tobias's shoulder. He smacked his lips. "Hey," he said, his voice muffled by the residue of the club music in Tobias's ears. "Let's get you something to drink."

That wasn't quite the response Tobias had expected. He paused and then nodded, curling his tail down by his legs. He wasn't staggering, he noticed, so he wasn't that drunk. Sure, he was drunk, but the world wasn't spinning, and all in all, it just felt very pleasant and free. Marty's rejection, though, had started to let nagging worries creep in. He started to apologize, but Marty was smiling and walking along with a springy step, so there didn't seem to be a need for it.

Marty led him to a gas station, where he grabbed a couple huge bottles of Powerade and handed one to Tobias. "Tastes like crap, but it's good for you," he said. "Hangover's worse if you've been dancing." He downed a good quarter of his bottle in one long drink, and when he set it down, he wasn't panting so hard. "Hate it when my mouth's all sweaty."

Tobias took a drink, and it really did feel good, even though the night air was cooling him down considerably. His groin still felt hot. "It wasn't so bad," he said boldly.

Marty's ears flicked. "You have a good time tonight?"

"Yeah." Tobias took another drink.

"Good." Marty clapped him on the shoulder. "Come on, I'll walk you to the bus."

"No, I drove." Tobias slapped his pocket for the car keys.

Marty shook his head. "You ain't driving like that."

"I'm fine," Tobias insisted.

"Do I have to take your keys?"

"Okay." Tobias leaned closer. "How close is your place?"

Marty laughed. "You clear this with your boyfriend?"

"It's none of his business," Tobias said. "If he wanted me, he could touch me once in a while."

He was surprised at how easily the words came out. Marty's eyes softened. "Come on, there's a diner not too far. Let's get some coffee."

Okay, so maybe he wasn't going to have sex with Marty tonight. But this might actually be better. "Hell yes," Tobias said.

The diner was called "Grant's," and it smelled like all 24-hour diners smelled, of eggs and toast with an undertone of deli meat. They sat away from the few other patrons, shared a plate of fries with coffee, and Tobias told Marty about Dylan. How things had been so good when he'd moved from the tropical country of Terrian; how Dylan had been there for him, filling the void left by his family; how they'd slowly settled into a rut and slowly just stopped having sex.

"How long?"

"Oh..." Tobias counted backwards in his head. "Three years? There was one night when we tried, but he wasn't really into it." God, he'd almost forgotten about that night. It had been so awkward, and afterwards he'd felt so ashamed of pressuring Dylan that he'd lain awake the rest of the night. Now, with the buzz of alcohol in his mind, it seemed as though it had happened to someone else.

"Years?" Marty's ears went flat. "Oh, Tobe. That's not right."

"That's why I was going to the gym," Tobias said, emboldened by the four Steamboats.

"'Coming' in the gym was the problem."

It took Tobias a second to realize that Marty was making a joke. The humor broke through the absurdity of it, making him grin, which made Marty smile in return. "I know, it was stupid, I just..."

"Nah, to be honest, I figured. I mean, there must be something going on at home. Either that or you're just so turned on by muscles that you couldn't hold it in, but you don't really seem like that type."

"I like some muscles." Tobias ignored the stare from the jaguar two tables over and looked pointedly at Marty's shoulder.

"Is your boyfriend in shape?"

He waved a paw. "He stopped going to the gym years ago." But the mention of Dylan brought back some tension, killing the relaxation the alcohol had brought. Or maybe that was the coffee. He wanted another drink from the bar, but all he had was the coffee, so he took another drink.

Marty lifted his coffee cup as well. "Why don't you just DTMFA?"

"Sorry?"

"Dump the motherfucker already."

Tobias inhaled the smell of his coffee. It was weak and crappy, but right now it was just perfect. "Because...well, where would I go?"

Marty shrugged. "Anywhere's better than nowhere, right?"

"Well..." Tobias looked out the window at the street. It was one in the morning, and still people were walking by: a bear couple, a porcupine. "It's not that bad. I mean, he was cool with me going out tonight. We both like video games and stuff. If we could just get the sex thing sorted out."

Marty rubbed his muzzle. "You think he'd be okay with you messing around with other people?"

"What, like cheating on him?"

The fox's dark shoulders shrugged. "If you ask him first, is it cheating?"

"I don't know..."

"If you're not getting what you want from him, he can't expect you to just go without, can he?"

Of course, that was exactly what Dylan had been doing. Or had he? "He's not like that." Tobias looked into Marty's eyes. "I mean, he was willing to try, but it was just so...ugh."

"He doesn't have to say it out loud," Marty said. "He can make it uncomfortable for you. And it sounds like he is."

"Yeah, but he doesn't mean it...I don't think." Under Marty's gaze, Tobias rubbed the black mask over his eyes and sighed.

"I'm not coming on to you," Marty said. "I told you, I'm not into the whole relationship thing. But I hate to see a friend unhappy. Haven't any of your other friends told you that?"

"Most of my other friends are Dylan's friends," Tobias said. "I can't really talk to them about him."

Marty exhaled and leaned across the table. "At least," he said, "you should talk to him. Don't let him shut you down. He owes you that."

* * *

Between the coffee and the Powerade, and the time elapsed, Tobias wasn't even buzzed any more when he walked in the door of their apartment at quarter to three in the morning. He realized as he saw the blue glow of Dylan's computer screen that he had no idea when Dylan regularly went to bed any more. Had the panther just stayed up for him or not? He wasn't anywhere to be seen.

Tobias locked the door behind him and stood looking at the empty living room. Maybe Dylan was out, had taken advantage of Tobias's absence to go to a friend's house for a movie night. Or maybe he'd run out for a quick fast food fix, which was more likely since he'd left his computer on.

The toilet flushed. Or, Tobias thought, maybe he was just using the bathroom. He waited in the living room as Dylan came down the hall, ears and muzzle up. "Thought I heard the door," he said. "How was it?"

"Pretty good." Tobias stifled a yawn. "I'm gonna head to bed. You?"

Dylan's eyes slid away from his. He gestured at the computer. "I'm kinda in the middle of something."

Tobias sighed. "Okay." He walked slowly toward the hallway, then stopped and turned around. "How about if I stay up for a bit?"

Dylan was already seated at his desk. He shrugged. "Sure."

"I mean," Tobias said, "can we talk for a bit?"

He saw the panther's shoulders slump. Dylan spun his chair around and settled his paws in his lap, his tail curled around the base of his chair. "What's up?"

Tobias flopped down in the small loveseat, draping his tail along the cushions and his arm over the armrest. "Are you bored with me?"

Dylan dropped his head. "No," he said.

Tobias waited for more, but the panther stayed silent. "Because, I mean, you haven't touched me in like, ages."

"I know."

The silence between them took an effort to break, like getting up out of a warm, comfortable bed. "So what happened?"

"I'm sorry," Dylan said, slumped over in his chair.

I should never have started this, Tobias thought. I should've just told Marty I'd already talked it over. Wouldn't everyone be happier that way? I could be lying in bed with him right now. Or I could be walking home with the memory of him. Why am I dragging poor Dylan through all this? He started to turn away, and then remembered Marty's injunction. One last try, Tobias thought. "I just want to know if it's something I did," he said.

That didn't come out quite as he'd intended, but it did at least provoke a response. Dylan shook his head. "It's not you. It's me."

Tobias had seen enough TV to be wary of that one. "What do you mean, it's you?"

"It's just me, okay? It's my problem."

"Are you breaking up with me?"

Now Dylan lifted his head. "No! Wh—do you want to break up?"

He was staring, close to tears now. Tobias felt answering tears in his throat. "No. I mean, not if you don't want to."

Dylan shook his head, lowering it again. "You seemed so understanding about it... I thought you'd have said something. I could tell you weren't doing anything on your own."

Not here, at least. Tobias looked away from Dylan, to the curtains drawn over the window. He thought about Marty again, about the fox's tongue dancing with his own, the warm heat of his arousal. He shifted his weight on the cushion. "If I were doing something...somewhere else? Would you want to know?"

This silence wasn't a comfortable chair. This was the mother of all awkward silences. Dylan cleared his throat and started to talk, then stopped again. "I don't know," he said.

"Would you care?"

"Sure." He replied quickly that time, making Tobias perk his ears up. Dylan looked at him. "I mean, I want you to be happy."

Tobias leaned back into the loveseat, exhaling. He let the silence wash over them, and then stood. "Okay," he said. "Look, if you want to come to bed, we don't have to do anything. Maybe just curl up together?"

Dylan nodded. "Let me just shut this down."

In bed, the panther comfortably next to him, Tobias relaxed and looked up at the ceiling. His tail rested over Dylan's stomach, their paws just touching. And he didn't have to worry about what Dylan wanted, and he didn't have to worry about when and where he was going to get off.

He saw Dylan's nose twitch. The panther took a breath. "If you're doing...something...somewhere else."

Tobias waited. Dylan's tail brushed his. "God," Dylan said, "this is so stupid. I wish..." He stopped again.

There was nothing Tobias could say that would help. He stayed quiet, letting Dylan work it out in his head. "If you're happy," he said, "with me..."

Tobias held his breath. Dylan exhaled. "If you're gonna stay here...with me...then I don't wanna know what else you have to do to be happy."

Staring at the ceiling, Tobias breathed out slowly. He nodded, and squeezed his boyfriend's paw, and then he closed his eyes.

"Ailoura" was written for Once Upon a Galaxy, *edited by Wil McCarthy, Martin H. Greenberg & John Helfers (DAW Books, September 2002). The instructions to the authors of that original-fiction anthology were to write, as Di Filippo has put it, "the restaging of fairy tales in SF terms." Di Filippo chose the tale of "Puss in Boots". The dying old miller with three sons has become the ultra-rich patriarch Vomach Stoessl of Stoessel House on the planet Chalk. The anonymous youngest son has become Geisen Stoessl, his father's favorite who is not penniless because his father had only a cat to leave him, but because he has been cheated out of his heritage by his greedy half-brothers. The enigmatic Puss who comes to Geisen's aid is Ailoura, his former nursemaid, a cat-derived "bestient" servant whom he has always treated as an equal. Di Filippo shows admirable originality by making Geisen and Ailoura equal partners in their carefully-crafted revenge, instead of letting the son fade to insignificance while the cat does all the work; and in having Geisen, posing as the long-absent heir of ancient "Carrabas" House, reject rather than wed the equivalent of the King's daughter.*

Ailoura

Paul Di Filippo

The small aircraft swiftly bisected the cloudless chartreuse sky. Invisible encrypted transmissions raced ahead of it. Clearance returned immediately from the distant, turreted manse–Stoessl House, looming in the otherwise empty riven landscape like some precipice-perching raptor. The ever-unsleeping family marchwarden obligingly shut down the manse's defenses, allowing an approach and landing. Within minutes, Geisen Stoessl had docked his small deltoid zipflyte on one of the tenth-floor platforms of Stoessl House, cantilevered over the flood-sculpted, candy-colored arroyos of the Subliminal Desert.

Geisen unseamed the canopy and leaped easily out onto the broad sintered terrace, unpeopled at this tragic, necessary, hopeful moment. Still clad in his dusty expeditionary clothes, goggles slung around his neck, Geisen resembled a living marble version of some young roughneck godling. Slim, wiry, and alert, with his laughter-creased, soil-powdered face now set in solemn lines absurdly counterpointed by a mask of clean skin around his recently shielded green eyes, Geisen paused a moment to brush from his protective suit the heaviest evidence of his recent wildcat digging in the Lustrous Wastes. Satisfied that he had made some small improvement in his appearance upon this weighty occasion, he advanced toward the portal leading inside. But before he could actuate the door, it opened from within.

Framed in the door stood a lanky, robe-draped bestient: Vicuna, his mother's most valued servant. Set squarely in Vicuna's wedge-shaped hirsute face, the haughty maid's broad velveteen nose wrinkled imperiously in disgust at Geisen's appearance, but the moreauvian refrained from voicing her disapproval of that matter in favor of other upbraidings.

"You arrive barely in time, Gep Stoessl. Your father approaches the limits of artificial maintenance, and is due to be reborn any minute. Your mother and brothers already anxiously occupy the Natal Chambers."

Following the inhumanly articulated servant into Stoessl House, Geisen answered, "I'm aware of all that, Vicuna. But traveling halfway around Chalk can't be accomplished in an instant."

"It was your choice to absent yourself during this crucial time."

"Why crucial? This will be Vomacht's third reincarnation. Presumably this one will go as smoothly as the first two."

"So one would hope."

Geisen tried to puzzle out the subtext of Vicuna's ambiguous comment, but could emerge with no clue regarding the current state of the generally complicated affairs within Stoessl House. He had obviously been away too long–too busy enjoying his own lonely but satisfying prospecting trips on behalf of the family enterprise–to be able to grasp the daily political machinations of his relatives.

Vicuna conducted Geisen to the nearest squeezer, and they promptly dropped down fifteen stories, far below the bedrock in which Stoessl House was rooted. On this secure level, the monitoring marchwarden hunkered down in its cozy low-Kelvin isolation, meaningful matrices of B-E condensates. Here also were the family's Natal Chambers. At these doors blazoned with sacred icons Vicuna left Geisen with a humid snort signifying that her distasteful attendence on the latecomer was complete.

Taking a fortifying breath, Geisen entered the rooms.

Roseate illumination symbolic of new creation softened all within: the complicated apparatus of rebirth as well as the sharp features of his mother, Woda, and the doughy countenances of his two brothers, Gitten and Grafton. Nearly invisible in the background, various bestient bodyguards hulked, inconspicuous yet vigilant.

Woda spoke first. "Well, how very generous of the prodigal to honor us with his unfortunately mandated presence."

Gitten snickered, and Grafton chimed in, pompously ironical: "Exquisitely gracious behavior, and so very typical of our little sibling, I'm sure."

Tethered to various life-support devices, Vomacht Stoessl–unconscious, naked and recumbent on a padded pallet alongside his mindless new body–said nothing. Both he and his clone had their heads wrapped in organic warty sheets of modified Stroonian brain parasite, an organism long-ago co-opted for mankind's ambitious and ceaselessly searching program of life extension. Linked via a thick living interparasitical tendril to its younger doppelganger, the withered form of the current

Vomacht, having reached the limits of rejuvenation, contrasted strongly with the virginal, soul-less vessel.

During Vomacht Stoessl's first lifetime, from 239 to 357 PS, he had sired no children. His second span of existence (357 to 495 PS) saw the birth of Gitten and Grafton, separated by some sixty years and both sired on Woda. Toward the end of his third, current lifetime (495 to 675 PS), a mere thirty years ago, he had fathered Geisen upon a mystery woman whom Geisen had never known. Vanished and unwedded, his mother– or some other over-solicitous guardian–had denied Geisen her name or image. Still, Vomacht had generously attended to all the legalities granting Geisen full parity with his half-brothers. Needless to say, little cordiality existed between the older members of the family and the young interloper.

     Geisen made the proper obeisances at several altars before responding to the taunts of his stepmother and stepbrothers. "I did not dictate the terms governing Gep Stoessl's latest reincarnation. They came directly from him. If any of you objected, you should have made your grievances known to him face to face. I myself am honored that he chose me to initiate the transferance of his mind and soul. I regret only that I was not able to attend him during his final moments of awareness in this old body."

     Gitten, the middle brother, tittered, and said, "The hand that cradles the rocks will now rock the cradle."

     Geisen looked down at his dirty hands, hopelessly engrained with the soils and stonedusts of Chalk. He resisted an impulse to hide them in his pockets. "There is nothing shameful about my fondness for fieldwork. Lolling about in luxury does not suit me. And I did not hear any of you complaining when the Eventyr Lode which I discovered came online and began to swell the family coffers."

     Woda intervened with her traditional maternal acerbity. "Enough bickering. Let us acknowledge that no possible arrangement of this day's events would have pleased everyone. The quicker we perform this vital ritual, the quicker we can all return to our duties and pleasures, and the sooner Vomacht's firm hand will regrasp the controls of our business. Geisen, I believe you know what to do."

     "I studied the proper Books of Phowa enroute."

     Grafton said, "Always the grind. Whenever do you enjoy yourself, little brother?"

     Geisen advanced confidently to the mechanisms that reared at the head of the pallets. "In the proper time and place, Grafton. But I realize that to you, such words imply every minute of your life." The young man turned his attention to the controls before him, forestalling further tart banter.

271

The tethered and trained Stroonian lifeforms had been previously starved to near hibernation, in preparation for their sacred duty. A clear cylinder of pink nutrient fluid laced with instructive protein sequences hung from an ornate tripod. The fluid would flow through twin IV lines, once the parasites were hooked up, enlivening their quiescent metabolisms and directing their proper functioning.

Murmuring the requisite holy phrases, Geisen plugged an IV line into each enshrouding creature. He tapped the proper dosage rate into the separate flow-pumps. Then, solemnly capturing the eyes of the onlookers, he activated the pumps.

Almost immediately the parasites began to flex and labor, humping and contorting as they drove an infinity of fractally miniscule auto-anesthetizing tendrils into both full and vacant brains in preparation for the transfer of the vital engrams that comprised a human soul.

But within minutes, it was plain to the observers that something was very wrong. The original Vomacht Stoessl began to writhe in evident pain, ripping away from his life-supports.

The all-observant marchwarden triggered alarms. Human and bestient technicians burst into the room. Grafton and Gitten and Woda rushed to the pumps to stop the process. But they were too late. In an instant, both membrane-wrapped skulls collapsed to degenerate chunky slush that plopped to the floor from beneath the suddenly destructive cauls.

The room fell silent. Grafton tilted one of the pumps at an angle so that all the witnesses could see the glowing red numerals.

"He quadrupled the proper volume of nutrient, driving the Stroonians hyperactive. This is murder!"

"Secure him from any escape!" Woda commanded.

Instantly Geisen's arms were pinioned by two burly bestient guards. He opened his mouth to protest, but the sight of his headless father choked off all words.

* * *

Gep Vomacht Stoessl's large private study was decorated with ancient relics of his birthworld, Lucerno: the empty, age-brittle coral armature of a deceased personal exoskeleton; a row of printed books bound in sloth-hide; a corroded auroch-flaying knife large as a canoe paddle. In the wake of their owner's death, the talismans seemed drained of mana.

Geisen sighed, and slumped down hopelessly in the comfortable chair positioned on the far side of the antique desk that had originated on the Crafters' planet, Hulbrouck V. On the far side of the nacreous expanse sat his complacently smirking half-brother, Grafton. Just days ago, Geisen knew, his father had hauled himself out of his sickbed for one last appearance at this favorite desk, where he had dictated the terms of his third reincarnation to the recording marchwarden. Geisen had played the affecting scene several times enroute from the Lustrous Wastes, noting how, despite his enervated condition, his father spoke with his wonted authority, specifically requesting that Geisen administer the paternal rebirthing procedure.

And now that unique individual—distant and enigmatic as he had been to Geisen throughout the latter's relatively short life—the man who had founded Stoessl House and its fortunes, the man to whom they all owed their luxurious independent lifestyles, was irretrievably gone from this plane of existence.

The human soul could exist only in organic substrates. Intelligent as they might be, condensate-dwelling entities such as the marchwarden exhibited a lesser existential complexity. Impossible to make any kind of static "backup" copy of the human essence, even in the proverbial bottled brain, since Stroonian transcription was fatal to the original. No, if destructive failure occured during a rebirth, that individual was no more forever.

Grafton interpreted Geisen's sigh as indicative of a need to unburden himself of some secret. "Speak freely, little brother. Ease your soul of guilt. We are completely alone. Not even the marchwarden is listening."

Geisen sat up alertly. "How have you accomplished such a thing? The marchwarden is deemed to be incorruptible, and its duties include constant surveillance of the interior of our home."

Somewhat flustered, Grafton tried to dissemble. "Oh, no, you're quite mistaken. It was always possible to disable the marchwarden selectively. A standard menu option—"

Geisen leaped to his feet, causing Grafton to rear back. "I see it all now! This whole murder, and my seeming complicity, was planned from the start! My father's last testament—faked! The flow codes to the pumps—overriden! My role—stooge and dupe!"

Recovering himself, Grafton managed with soothing motions and noises to induce a fuming Geisen to be seated again. The older man came around to perch on a corner of the desk. He leaned over closer to Geisen and, in a smooth voice, made his own shockingly unrepentant confession.

"Very astute. Too bad for you that you did not see the trap early enough to avoid it. Yes, Vomacht's permanent death and your hand in it were all neatly arranged—by mother, Gitten and myself. It had to be. You see, Vomacht had become irrationally surly and obnoxious toward us, his true and loving first family. He threatened to remove all our stipends and entitlements and authority, once he occupied his strong new body. But those demented codicils were edited from the version of his speech that you saw, as was his insane proclamation naming you sole factotum of the family business. All of Stoessl Strangelet Mining and its affiliates was to be made your fiefdom. Imagine! A young desert rat at the helm of our venerable corporation!"

Geisen strove to digest all this sudden information. Practical considerations warred with his emotions. Finally he could only ask, "What of Vomacht's desire for me to initiate his soul-transfer?"

"Ah, that was authentic. And it served as the perfect bait to draw you back, as well as the peg on which we could hang a murder plot and charge."

Geisen drew himself up proudly. "You realize that these accusations of deliberate homicide against me will not stand up a minute in court. With what you've told me, I'll certainly be able to dig up plenty of evidence to the contrary."

Smiling like a carrion lizard from the Cerise Ergstrand, Grafton countered, "Oh, will you, now? From your jail cell, without any outside help? Accused murderers cannot profit from the results of their actions. You will have no access to family funds other than your small personal accounts while incarcerated, nor any real partisans, due to your stubbornly asocial existence of many years. The might of the family, including testimony from the grieving widow, will be ranked against you. How do you rate your chances for exculpation under those circumstances?"

Reduced to grim silence, Geisen bunched his muscles prior to launching himself in a futile attack on his brother. But Grafton held up a warning hand first.

"There is an agreeable alternative. We really do not care to bring this matter to court. There is, after all, still a chance of one percent or less that you might win the case. And legal matters are so tedious and time-consuming, interferring with more pleasurable pursuits. In fact, notice of Gep Stoessl's death has not yet been released to either the news media or to Chalk's authorities. And if we secure your cooperation, the aftermath of this tragic 'accident' will take a very different form than criminal charges. Upon getting your binding assent to a certain trivial document, you will be free to pursue your own life unencumbered by any obligations to Stoessl House or its residents."

Grafton handed his brother a hardcopy of several pages. Geisen perused it swiftly and intently, then looked up at Grafton with high astonishment.

"This document strips me of all my share of the family fortunes, and binds me from any future role in the estate. Basically, I am utterly disenfranchised and disinherited, cast out penniless."

"A fair enough summation. Oh, we might give you a small grubstake when you leave. Say—your zipflyte, a few hundred esscues, and a bestient servant or two. Just enough to pursue the kind of itinerant lifestyle you so evidently prefer."

Geisen pondered but a moment. "All attempts to brand me a patricide will be dropped?"

Grafton shrugged. "What would be the point of whipping a helpless, poverty-stricken nonentity?"

Geisen stood up. "Reactivate the marchwarden. I am ready to comply with your terms."

* * *

Gep Bloedwyn Vermeule, of Vermeule House, today wore her long blonde braids arranged in a recomplicated nest, piled high atop her charming young head and sown with delicate fairylights that blinked in time with various of her body-rhythms. Entering the formal reception hall of Stoessl House, she marched confidently down the tiles between ranks of silent bestient guards, the long train dependent from her form-fitting scarlet sandworm-fabric gown held an inch above the floor by tiny enwoven agravitic units. She came to a stop some meters away from the man who awaited her with a nervously expectant smile on his rugged face.

Geisen's voice quaked at first, despite his best resolve. "Bloedwyn, my sweetling, you look more alluring than an oasis to a parched man."

The pinlights in the girl's hair raced in chaotic patterns for a moment, then settled down to a stable configurations that somehow radiated a frostiness belied by her neutral facial expression. Her voice, chorded suggestively low and husky by fashionable implants, quavered not at all.

"Gep Stoessl, I hardly know how to approach you. So much has changed since we last trysted."

Throwing decorum to the wind, Geisen closed the gap between them and swept his betrothed up in his arms. The sensation Geisen enjoyed was rather like that derived from hugging a wooden effigy. Nonetheless, he persisted in his attempts to restore their old relations.

"Only superficial matters have changed, my dear! True, as you have no doubt heard by now, I am no longer a scion of Stoessl House. But my heart, mind and soul remain devoted to you! Can I not assume the same constancy applies to your inner being?"

Bloedwyn slipped out of Geisen's embrace. "How could you assume anything, since I myself do not know how I feel? All these developments have been so sudden and mysterious! Your father's cruelly permanent death, your own capricious and senseless abandonment of your share of his estate— How can I make sense of any of it? What of all our wonderful dreams?"

Geisen gripped Bloedwyn's supple hide-mailed upper arms with perhaps too much fervor, judging from her wince. He released her, then spoke. "All our bright plans for the future will come to pass! Just give me some time to regain my footing in the world. One day I will be at liberty to explain everything to you. But until then, I ask your trust and faith. Surely you must share my confidence in my character, in my undiminished capabilities?"

Bloedwyn averted her tranquil blue-eyed gaze from Geisen's imploring green eyes, and he slumped in despair, knowing himself lost. She stepped back a few paces and, with voice steeled, made a formal declaration she had evidently rehearsed prior to this moment.

"The Vermuele marchwarden has already communicated the abrogation of our pending matrimonial agreement to your house's governor. I think such an impartial yet decisive move is all for the best, Geisen. We are both young, with many lives before us. It would be senseless to found such a potentially interminable relationship on such shaky footing. Let us both go ahead—separately—into the days to come, with our extinct love a fond memory."

Again, as at the moment of his father's death, Geisen found himself rendered speechless at a crucial juncture, unable to plead his case any further. He watched in stunned disbelief as Bloedwyn turned gracefully around and walked out of his life, her fluttering scaly train visible some seconds after the rest of her had vanished.

* * *

The cluttered, steamy, noisy kitchens of Stoessl House exhibited an orderly chaos proportionate to the magnitude of the preparations underway. The planned rebirth dinner for the paterfamilias had been hastily converted to a memorial banquet, once the proper, little-used protocols had been found in a metaphorically dusty lobe of the marchwarden's memory. Now scores of miscegenous bestients under the supervision of the lone human chef, Stine Pursiful, scraped, sliced, chopped, diced, cored, deveined, scrubbed, layered, basted, glazed, microwaved and pressure-treated various foodstuffs, assembling the imported luxury ingredients into the elaborate fare that would furnish out the solemn buffet for family and friends and business connections of the deceased.

Geisen entered the aromatic atmosphere of the kitchens with a scowl on his face and a bitterness in his throat and heart. Pursiful spotted the young man and, with a fair share of courtesy and deference, considering the circumstances, stepped forward to inquire of his needs. But Geisen rudely brushed the slim punctilious chef aside, and stalked toward the shelves that held various MREs. With blunt motions, he began to shovel the nutri-packets into a dusty shoulderbag that had plainly seen many an expedition into Chalk's treasure-filled deserts.

A small timid bestient belonging to one of the muskrat-hyrax clades hopped over to the shelves where Geisen fiercely rummaged. Nearsighted, the be-aproned moreauvian strained on tiptoe to identify something on a higher shelf.

With one heavy boot, Geisen kicked the servant out of his way, sending the creature squeaking and sliding across the slops-strewn floor. But before the man could return to his rough provisioning, he was stopped by a voice familiar as his skin.

"I raised you to show more respect to all the Implicate's creatures than you just exhibited, Gep Stoessl. Or if I did not, then I deserve immediately to visit the Unborn's Lowest Abbatoir for my criminal negligence."

Geisen turned, the bile in his craw and soul melting to a habitual affection tinged with many memories of juvenile guilt.

Brindled arms folded across her queerly configured chest, Ailoura the bestient stood a head shorter than Geisen, compact and well-muscled. Her heritage mingled from a thousand feline and quasi-feline strains from a dozen planets, she resembled no single cat species morphed to human status, but rather all cats everywhere, blended and thus ennobled. Rounded ears perched high atop her densely pelted skull. Vertically slitted eyes and patch of wet leathery nose contrasted with a more-human-seeming mouth and chin. Now anger and disappointment molded her face into a mask almost frightening, her fierce expression magnifed by a glint of sharp tooth peeking from beneath a curled lip.

Geisen noted instantly, with a small shock, the newest touches of gray in Ailoura's tortoiseshell fur. These tokens of aging softened his heart even further. He made the second-most-serious conciliatory bow from the Dakini Rituals toward his old nurse. Straightening, Geisen watched with relief as the anger flowed out of her face and stance, to be replaced by concern and solicitude.

"Now," Ailoura demanded, in the same tone with which she had often demanded that little Geisen brush his teeth or do his schoolwork, "what is all this nonsense I hear about your voluntary disinheritance and departure?"

Geisen motioned Ailoura into a secluded corner of the kitchens and revealed everything to her. His account prompted low growls from the bestient that escaped despite her angrily compressed lips. Geisen finished resignedly by saying, "And so, helpless to contest this injustice, I leave now to seek my fortune elsewhere, perhaps even on another world."

Ailoura pondered a moment. "You say that your brother offered you a servant from our house?"

"Yes. But I don't intend to take him up on that promise. Having another mouth to feed would just hinder me."

Placing one mitteny yet deft hand on his chest, Ailoura said, "Take me, Gep Stoessl."

Geisen experienced a moment of confusion. "But Ailoura—your job of raising me is long past. I am very grateful for the loving care you gave unstintingly to a motherless lad, the guidance and direction you imparted, the indulgent playtimes we enjoyed. Your teachings left me with a wise set of principles, an admirable will and optimism, and a firm moral center—despite the evidence of my thoughtless transgression a moment ago. But your guardian duties lie in the past. And besides, why would you want to leave the comforts and security of Stoessl House?"

"Look at me closely, Gep Stoessl. I wear now the tabards of the scullery crew. My luck in finding you here is due only to this very demotion. And from here the slide to utter inutility is swift and short—despite my remaining vigor and craft. Will you leave me here to face my sorry fate? Or will you allow me to cast my fate with that of the boy I raised from kittenhood?"

Geisen thought a moment. "Some companionship would indeed be welcome. And I don't suppose I could find a more intimate ally."

Ailoura grinned. "Or a slyer one."

"Very well. You may accompany me. But on one condition."

"Yes, Gep Stoessl?"

"Cease calling me 'Gep.' Such formalities were once unknown between us."

Ailoura smiled. "Agreed, little Gei-gei."

The man winced. "No need to retrogress quite that far. Now, let us return to raiding my family's larder."

"Be sure to take some of that fine fish, if you please, Geisen."

* * *

No one knew the origin of the tame strangelets that seeded Chalk's strata. But everyone knew of the immense wealth these cloistered anomalies conferred.

Normal matter was composed of quarks in only two flavors: up and down. But strange-flavor quarks also existed, and the exotic substances formed by these strange quarks in combination with the more domestic flavors were, unconfined, as deadly as the more familiar antimatter. Bringing normal matter into contact with a naked strangelet resulted in the conversion of the feedstock into energy. Owning a strangelet was akin to owning a pet black hole, and just as useful for various purposes, such as powering star cruisers.

Humanity could create strangelets, but only at immense costs per unit. And naked strangelets had to be confined in electromagnetic or gravitic bottles during active use. They could also be quarantined for semi-permanent storage in stasis fields. Such was the case with the buried strangelets of Chalk.

Small spherical mirrored nodules–"marbles," in the jargon of Chalk's prospectors–could be found in various recent sedimentary layers of the planet's crust, distributed according to no rational plan. Discovery of the marbles had inaugurated the reign of the various Houses on Chalk.

An early scientific expedition from Preceptimax University to the Shulamith Wadi stumbled upon the strangelets initially. Preceptor Fairservis, the curious discoverer of the first marble, had realized he was dealing with a stasis-bound object and had unluckily managed to open it. The quantum genie inside had promptly eaten the hapless fellow who freed it, along with nine-tenths of the expedition, before beginning a sure but slow descent toward the core of Chalk. Luckily an emergency response team swiftly dispatched by the planetary authorities had managed to activate a new entrapping marble big as a small city, its lower hemisphere underground, thus trapping the rogue.

After this incident, the formerly disdained deserts of Chalk had experienced a landrush unparalleled in the galaxy. Soon the entire planet was divided into domains–many consisting of noncontiguous properties–each owned by one House or another. Prospecting began in earnest then. But the practice remained more an art than a science, as the marbles remained stealthy to conventional detectors. Intuition, geological knowledge of strata and sheer luck proved the determining factors in the individual fortunes of the Houses.

How the strangelets–plainly artifactual–came to be buried beneath Chalk's soils and hardpan remained a mystery. No evidence of native intelligent inhabitants existed on the planet prior to the arrival of humanity.

Had a cloud of strangelets been swept up out of space as Chalk made her eternal orbits? Perhaps. Or had alien visitors planted the strangelets for obscure reasons of their own? An equally plausible theory.

Whatever the obscure history of the strangelets, their current utility was beyond argument.

They made many people rich.

And some people murderous.

* * *

In the shadow of the Tasso Escarpments, adjacent to the Glabrous Drifts, Carrabas House sat desolate and melancholy, tenanted only by glass-tailed lizards and stilt-crabs, its poverty-overtaken heirs dispersed anonymously across the galaxy after a series of unwise investments, followed by the unpredictable yet inevitable exhaustion of their marble-bearing properties—a day against which Vomacht Stoessl had more providently hedged his own family's fortunes.

Geisen's zipflyte crunched to a landing on one of the manse's grit-blown terraces, beside a gaping portico. The craft's doors swung open and pilot and passenger emerged. Ailoura now wore a set of utilitarian roughneck's clothing, tailored for her bestient physique and matching the outfit worn by her former charge, right down to their boots. Strapped to her waist was an antique yet lovingly maintained variable sword, its terminal bead currently dull and inactive.

"No one will trouble us here," Geisen said with confidence. "And we'll have a roof of sorts over our head while we plot our next steps. As I recall from a visit some years ago, the west wing was the least damaged."

As Geisen began to haul supplies—a heater-cum-stove, sleeping bags and pads, water-condensers—from their craft, Ailoura inhaled deeply the dry tangy air, her nose wrinkling expressively, then exhaled with zest. "Ah, freedom after so many years! It tastes brave, young Geisen!" Her claws slipped from their sheaths as she flexed her pads. She unclipped her sword and flicked it on, the seemingly untethered bead floating outward from the pommel a meter or so.

"You finish the monkey work. I'll clear the rats from our quarters," promised Ailoura, then bounded off before Geisen could stop her. Watching her unfettered tail disappear down a hall and around a corner, Geisen smiled, recalling childhood games of strength and skill where she had allowed him what he now realized were easy triumphs.

After no small time, Ailoura returned, licking her greasy lips.

"All ready for our habitation, Geisen-kitten."

"Very good. If the bold warrior will deign to lend a paw...?"

Soon the pair had established housekeeping in a spacious, weatherproof ground floor room (with several handy exits), where a single leering windowframe was easily covered by a sheet of translucent plastic. After distributing their goods and sweeping the floor clean of loess drifts, Geisen and Ailoura took a meal as their reward, the first of many such rude campfire repasts to come.

As they relaxed afterward, Geisen making notes with his stylus in a small pocket diary and Ailoura dragging her left paw continually over one ear, a querulous voice sounded from thin air.

"Who disturbs my weary peace?"

Instantly on their feet, standing back to back, the newcomers looked warily about. Ailoura snarled until Geisen hushed her. Seeing no one, Geisen at last inquired, "Who speaks?"

"I am the Carrabas marchwarden."

The man and bestient relaxed a trifle. "Impossible," said Geisen. "How do you derive your energy after all these years of abandonment and desuetude?"

The marchwarden chuckled with a trace of pride. "Long ago, without any human consent or prompting, while Carrabas House still flourished, I sunk a thermal tap downward hundreds of kilometers. The backup energy thus supplied is not much, compared with my old capacities, but has proven enough for sheer survival, albeit with much dormancy."

Ailoura hung her quiet sword back on her belt. "How have you kept sane since then, marchwarden?"

"Who says I have?"

* * *

Coming to terms with the semi-deranged Carrabas marchwarden required delicate negotiations. The protective majordomo simultaneously resented the trespassers—who did not share the honored Carrabas family lineage—yet on some different level welcomed their company and the satisfying chance to perform some of its programmed functions for them. Alternating ogreish threats with embarassingly humble supplications, the marchwarden needed to hear just the right mix of defiance and thanks from the squatters to fully come over as their ally. Luckily, Ailoura, employing diplomatic wiles honed by decades of bestient subservience, perfectly supplemented Geisen's rather gruff and patronizing attitude. Eventually, the ghost of Carrabas House accepted them.

"I am afraid I can contribute little enough to your comfort, Gep Carrabas." During the negotiations, the marchwarden had somehow self-deludingly concluded that Geisen was indeed part of the lost lineage. "Some water, certainly, from my active conduits. But no other necessities such as heat or food, or any luxuries either. Alas, the days of my glory are long gone!"

"Are you still in touch with your peers?" asked Ailoura.

"Why, yes. The other Houses have not forgotten me. Many are sympathetic, though a few are haughty and indifferent."

Geisen shook his head in bemusement. "First I learn that the protective omniscience of the marchwardens may be circumvented. Next, that they keep up a private traffic and society. I begin to wonder who is the master and who is the servant in our global system?"

"Leave these conundrums to the preceptors, Geisen. This unexpected mode of contact might come in handy for us some day."

The marchwarden's voice sounded ennervated. "Will you require any more of me? I have overtaxed my energies, and need to shut down for a time."

"Please restore yourself fully."

Left alone, Geisen and Ailoura simultaneously realized how late the hour was and how tired they were. They bedded down in warm bodyquilts, and Geisen swiftly drifted off to sleep to the old tune of Ailoura's drowsy purring.

* * *

In the chilly viridian morning, over fish and kava, cat and man held a war council.

Geisen led with a bold assertion that nonetheless concealed a note of despair and resignation.

"Given your evident hunting prowess, Ailoura, and my knowledge of the land, I estimate that we can take half a dozen sandworms from those unclaimed public territories proven empty of stranglets, during the course of as many months. We'll peddle the skins for enough to get us both off-planet. I understand that lush homesteads are going begging on Nibbriglung. All that the extensive water meadows there require is a thorough de-snailing before they're producing golden rice by the bushel—"

Ailoura's green eyes, so like Geisen's own, flashed with cool fire. "Insipidity! Toothlessness!" she hissed. "Turn farmer? Grub among the waterweeds like some *platypus*? Run away from those who killed your sire and cheated you out of your inheritance? I didn't raise such an unimaginative, unambitious coward, did I?"

Geisen sipped his drink to avoid making a hasty affronted rejoinder, then calmly said, "What do you recommend then? I gave my legally binding promise not to contest any of the unfair terms laid down by my family, in return for freedom from prosecution. What choices does such a renunciation leave me? Shall you and I go live in the shabby slums that slump at the feet of the Houses? Or turn thief and raider and prey upon lonely mining encampments? Or shall we become freelance prospectors? I'd be good at the latter job, true, but bargaining with the Houses concerning hard-won information about their own properties is humiliating, and promises only slim returns. They hold all the high cards, and the supplicant offers only a mere savings of time."

"You're onto a true scent with this last idea. But not quite the paltry scheme you envision. What I propose is that we swindle those who swindled you. We won't gain back your whole patrimony, but you'll surely acquire greater sustaining riches than you would by flensing worms or flailing rice."

"Speak on."

"The first step involves a theft. But after that, only chicanery. To begin, we'll need a small lot of strangelets, enough to salt a claim everyone thought exhausted."

Geisen considered, buffing his raspy chin with his knuckles. "The morality is dubious. Still—I found a smallish deposit of marbles on Stoessl property during my aborted trip, and never managed to report it. They were in a floodplain hard by the Nakhoda Range, newly exposed and ripe for the plucking without any large-scale mining activity that would attract satellite surveillance."

"Perfect! We'll use their own goods to con the ratlings! But once we have this grubstake, we'll need a proxy to deal with the Houses. Your own face and reputation must remain concealed until all deals are sealed airtight. Do you have knowledge of any such suitable foil?"

Geisen began to laugh. "Do I? Only the perfect rogue for the job!"

Ailoura came cleanly to her feet, although she could not repress a small grunt at an arthritic twinge provoked by a night on the hard floor. "Let us collect the strangelets first, and then enlist his help. With luck, we'll be sleeping on feathers and dining off golden plates in a few short weeks."

The sad and spectral voice of the abandoned marchwarden sounded. "Good morning, Gep Carrabas. I regret keenly my own serious incapacities as a host. But I have managed to heat up several liters of water for a bath, if such a service appeals."

* * *

The eccentric caravan of Marco Bozzarias and his mistress Pigafetta had emerged from its minting pools as a top-of-the-line Baba Yar model of the year 650 PS. Capacious and agile, larded with amenities, the moderately intelligent stilt-walking cabin had been designed to protect its inhabitants from climactic extremes in unswaying comfort while carrying them sure-footedly over the roughest terrain. But plainly, for one reason or another (most likely poverty) Bozzarias had neglected the caravan's maintenance over the twenty-five years of its working life.

Raised now for privacy above the sands where Geisen's zipflyte rested, the vehicle-cum-residence canted several degrees, imparting a funhouse quality to its interior. Swellings at its many knee joints indicated a lack of proper nutrients. Additionally, the cabin itself had been miscegenously patched with so many different materials—plastic, sandworm hide, canvas, chitin—that it more closely resembled a heap of debris than a deliberately designed domicile.

The caravan's owner, contrastingly, boasted an immaculate and stylish appearance. To judge by his handsome, mustachioed looks, the middle-aged Bozzarias was more stagedoor idler than cactus hugger, displaying his trim figure proudly beneath crimson ripstop trews and utility vest over bare hirsute chest. Despite this urban promenader's facade, Bozzarias held a respectable record as a freelance prospector, having pinpointed for their owners several strangelet lodes of note, including the fabled Gosnold Pocket. For these services, he had been recompensed by the tight-fisted landowners only a nearly invisible percentage of the eventual wealth claimed from the finds. Despite his current friendly grin, it would be impossible for Bozzarias not to harbor decades-worth of spite and jealousy.

Pigafetta, Bozzarias's bestient paramour, was a voluptuous, pink-skinned geisha clad in blue and green silks. Carrying perhaps a tad too much weight—hardly surprising, given her particular gattaca —Pigafetta radiated a slack and greasy carnality utterly at odds with Ailoura's crisp and dry efficiency. When the visitors had entered the cabin, before either of the humans could intervene, Geisen and Bozzarias had been treated to an instant but decisive bloodless catfight that had settled the pecking order between the moreauvians.

Now, while Pigafetta sulked winsomely in a canted corner amid her cushions, the furry female victor consulted with the two men around a small table across which lay spilled the stolen strangelets, corralled from rolling by a line of empty liquor bottles.

Bozzarias poked at one of the deceptive marbles with seeming disinterest, while his dark eyes glittered with avarice. "Let me recapitulate. We represent to various buyers that these quantum baubles are merely the camel's nose showing beneath the tent of unconsidered wealth. A newly discovered lode on the Carrabas properties, of which you, Gep Carrabas"– Bozzarias leered at Geisen–"are the rightful heir. We rook the fools for all we can get, then hie ourselves elsewhere, beyond their injured squawks and retributions. Am I correct in all particulars?"

Ailoura spoke first. "Yes, substantially."

"And what would my share of the take be? To depart forever my cherished Chalk would require a huge stake–"

"Don't try to make your life here sound glamorous or even tolerable, Marco," Geisen said. "Everyone knows you're in debt up to your nose, and haven't had a strike in over a year. It's about time for you to change venues anyway. The days of the freelancer on Chalk are nearly over."

Bozzarias sighed dramatically, picking up a reflective marble and admiring himself in it. "I suppose you speak the truth–as it is commonly perceived. But a man of my talents can carve himself a niche anywhere. And Pigafetta *has* been begging me of late to launch her on a virtual career–"

"In other words," Ailoura interrupted, "you intend to pimp her as a porn star. Well, you'll need to relocate to a mediapoietic world then for sure. May we assume you'll become part of our scheme?"

Bozzarias set the marble down and said, "My pay?"

"Two strangelets from this very stock."

With the speed of a glass-tailed lizard Bozzarias scooped up and pocketed two spheres before the generous offer could be rescinded. "Done! Now, if you two will excuse me, I'll need to rehearse my role before we begin this deception."

Ailoura smiled, a disconcerting sight to those unfamiliar with her tender side. "Not quite so fast, Gep Bozzarias. If you'll just submit a moment–"

Before Bozzarias could protest, Ailoura had sprayed him about the head and shoulders with the contents of a pressurized can conjured from her pack.

"What! Pixy dust! This is a gross insult!"

Geisen adjusted the controls of his pocket diary. On the small screen appeared a jumbled, jittering image of the caravan's interior. As the self-assembling pixy dust cohered around Bozzarias's eyes and ears, the image stabilized to reflect the prospector's visual point-of-view. Echoes of their speech emerged from the diary's speaker.

"As you well know," Ailoura advised, "the pixy dust is ineradicable and self-repairing. Only the ciphers we hold can deactivate it. Until then, all you see and hear will be shared with us. We intend to monitor you around the clock. And the diary's input is being shared with the Carrabas marchwarden, who has been told to watch for any traitorous actions on your part. That entity, by the way, is a little deranged, and might leap to conclusions about any actions that even verge on treachery. Oh, you'll also find that your left ear hosts a channel for our remote, ah, verbal advice. It would behoove you to follow our directions, since the dust is quite capable of liquefying your eyeballs upon command."

Seemingly inclined to protest further, Bozzarias suddenly thought better of dissenting. With a disspirited wave and nod, he signalled his acquiesence in their plans, becoming quietly businesslike.

"And to what Houses shall I offer this putative wealth?"

Geisen smiled. "To every House at first—except Stoessl."

"I see. Quite clever."

After Bozzarias had caused his caravan to kneel to the earth, he bade his new partners a desultory goodbye. But at the last minute, as Ailoura was stepping into the zipflyte, Bozzarias snagged Geisen by the sleeve and whispered in his ear.

"I'd trade that rude servant in for a mindless pleasure model, my friend, were I you. She's much too tricky for comfort."

"But Marco—that's exactly why I cherish her."

* * *

Three weeks after first employing the wily Bozzarias in their scam, Geisen and Ailoura sat in their primitive quarters at Carrabas House, huddled nervously around Geisen's diary, awaiting transmission of the meeting they had long anticipated. The diary's screen revealed the familiar landscape around Stoessl House as seen from the windows of the speeding zipflyte carrying their agent to his appointment with Woda, Gitten and Grafton.

During the past weeks, Ailoura's plot had matured, succeeding beyond their highest expectations.

Representing himself as the agent for a mysteriously returned heir of the long-abandoned Carrabas estate—a fellow who prefered anonymity for the moment—Bozzarias had visited all the biggest and most influential Houses—excluding the Stoessls—with his sample strangelets. A major new find had been described, with its coordinates freely given and inspections invited. The visiting teams of geologists reported what appeared to be a rich new lode, deceived by Geisen's expert saltings. And no single house dared attempt a midnight raid on the unprotected new strike, given the vigilance of all the others.

The cooperation and willing playacting of the Carrabas marchwarden had been essential. First, once its existence was revealed, the discarded entity's very survival became a seven-day wonder, compelling a willing suspension of disbelief in all the lies that followed. Confirming the mystery man as a true Carrabas, the marchwarden also added its jiggered testimony to verify the discovery.

Bozzarias had informed the greedily gaping families that the returned Carrabas scion had no desire to play an active role in mining and selling his strangelets. The whole estate–with many more potential strangelet nodes– would be sold to the highest bidder.

Offers began to pour in, steadily escalating. These included feverish bids from the Stoessls, which were rejected without comment. Finally, after such highhanded treatment, the offended clan demanded to know why they were being excluded from the auction. Bozzarias responded that he would convey that information only in a private meeting.

To this climactic interrogation the wily rogue now flew.

Geisen turned away from the monotonous video on his diary and asked Ailoura a question he had long contemplated but always foreborne from voicing.

"Ailoura, what can you tell me of my mother?"

The cat-woman assumed a reflective expression that cloaked more emotions than it revealed. Her whiskers twitched. "Why do you ask such an irrelevant question at this crucial juncture, Gei-gei?"

"I don't know. I've often pondered the matter. Maybe I'm fearful that if our plan explodes in our faces, this might be my final opportunity to learn anything."

Ailoura paused a long while before answering. "I was intimately familiar with the one who bore you. I think her intentions were honorable. I know she loved you dearly. She always wanted to make herself known to you, but circumstances beyond her control did not permit such an honest relationship."

Geisen contemplated this information. Something told him he would get no more from the close-mouthed bestient.

To disrupt the solemn mood, Ailoura reached over to ruffle Geisen's hair. "Enough of the useless past. Didn't anyone ever tell you that curiosity killed the cat? Now, pay attention! Our Judas goat has landed–"

* * *

Ursine yet doughy, unctuous yet fleering, Grafton clapped Bozzarias's shoulder heartily and ushered the foppish man to a seat in Vomacht's study. Behind the dead padrone's desk sat his widow, Woda, all motile maquillage and mimicked mourning. Her teeth sported a fashionable gilt. Gitten lounged on the arm of a sofa, plainly bored and resentful, toying with a handheld hologame like some sullen adolescent.

After offering drinks—Bozzarias requested and received the finest vintage of sparkling wine available on Chalk—Grafton drove straight to the heart of the matter.

"Gep Bozzarias, I demand to know why Stoessl House has been denied a chance to bid on the Carrabas estate."

Bozzarias drained his glass and dabbed at his lips with his jabot before replying. "The reason is simple, Gep Stoessl, yet of such delicacy that you would not have cared to have me state it before your peers. Thus this private encounter."

"Go on."

"My employer, Timor Carrabas, you must learn, is a man of punctilio and politesse. Having abandoned Chalk many generations ago, Carrabas House still honors and maintains the old ways prevalent during that golden age. They have not fallen into the lax and immoral fashions of the present, and absolutely contemn such behavior."

Grafton stiffened. "To what do you refer? Stoessl House is guilty of no such infringements on custom."

"That is not how my employer perceives affairs. After all, what is the very first thing he hears upon returning to his ancestral homeworld? Disturbing rumors of patricide, fraternal infighting and excommunication, all of which emanate from Stoessl House and Stoessl House alone. Leery of stepping beneath the shadow of such a cloud, he could not ethically undertake any dealings with your clan."

Fuming, Grafton started to rebut these charges, but Woda intervened. "Gep Bozzarias, all mandated investigations into the death of my beloved Vomacht resulted in one uncontested conclusion: pump failure produced a kind of alien hyperglycemia that drove the Stroonians insane. No human culpability or intent to harm was ever established."

Bozzarias held his glass up for a refill and obtained one. "Why, then, were all the bestient witnesses to the incident terminally disposed of? What motivated the abdication of your youngest scion? Giger, I believe he was named?"

Trying to be helpful, Gitten jumped into the conversation. "Oh, we use up bestients at a frightful rate! If they're not dying from floggings, they're collapsing from overuse in the mines and brothels. Such a flawed product line, these moreauvians. Why, if they were robots, they'd never pass consumer-lab testing. As for Geisen—that's the boy's name—well, he simply got fed up with our civilized lifestyle. He always did prefer the barbaric outback existence. No doubt he's enjoying himself right now, wallowing in some muddy oasis with a sandworm concubine."

Grafton cut off his brother's tittering with a savage glance. "Gep Bozzarias, I'm certain that if your employer were to meet us, he'd find we are worthy of making an offer on his properties. In fact, he could avoid all the fuss and bother of a full-fledged auction, since I'm prepared right now to trump the highest bid he's yet received. Will you convey to him my invitation to enjoy the hospitality of Stoessl House?"

Bozzarias closed his eyes ruminatively, as if harkening to some inner voice of conscience, then answered, "Yes, I can do that much. And with some small encouragement, I would exert all my powers of persuasiveness—"

Woda spoke. "Why, where did this small but heavy bag of Tancredi moonstones come from? It certainly doesn't belong to us. Gep Bozzarias—would you do me the immense favor of tracking down the rightful owner of these misplaced gems?"

Bozzaris stood and bowed, then accepted the bribe. "My pleasure, madame. I can practically guarantee that Stoessl House will soon receive its just reward."

* * *

"Sandworm concubine!" Geisen appeared ready to hurl his eavesdropping device to the hard floor, but restrained himself. "How I'd like to smash their lying mouths in!"

Ailoura grinned. "You must show more restraint than that, Geisen, expecially when you come face to face with the scoundrels. Take consolation from the fact that mere physical retribution would hurt them far less than the loss of money and face we will inflict."

"Still, there's a certain satisfaction in feeling the impact of fist on flesh."

"My kind calls it 'the joy when teeth meet bone,' so I fully comprehend. Just not this time. Understood?"

Geisen impulsively hugged the old cat. "Still teaching me, Ailoura?"

"Until I die, I suppose."

* * *

"You are appallingly obese, Geisen. Your form recalls nothing of the slim blade who cut such wide swaths among the girls of the various Houses before his engagement."

"And your polecat coloration, fair Ailoura, along with those tinted lenses and tooth-caps, speak not of a bold mouser, but of a scavenger through garbage tips."

Regarding each other with satisfaction, Ailoura and Geisen thus approved of their disguises.

With the aid of Bozzarias, who had purchased for them various sophisticated, semi-living prosthetics, dyes and offworld clothing, the man and his servant—Timor Carrabas and Hepzibah—resembled no one ever seen before on Chalk. His pasty face rouged, Geisen wobbled as he waddled, breathing stertorously, while the limping Ailoura diffused a moderately repulsive scent calculated to keep the curious at a certain remove.

The Carrabas marchwarden now spoke, a touch of excitement in its artificial voice. "I have just notified my Stoessl House counterpart that you are departing within the hour. You will be expected in time for essences and banquet, with a half-hour allotted to freshen up and settle into your guest rooms."

"Very good. Rehearse the rest of the plan to me."

"Once the funds are transferred from Stoessl House to me, I will in turn upload them to the Bourse on Feuilles Mortes under the name of Geisen Stoessl, where they will be immune from attachment. I will then retreat to my soul-canister, readying it for removal by your agent, Bozzarias, who will bring it to the spacefield—specifically the terminal hosting Gravkosmos Interstellar. Beyond that point, I cannot be of service until I am haptically enabled once more."

"You have the scheme perfectly. Now we thank you, and leave with the promise that we shall talk again in the near future, in a more pleasant place."

"Goodbye, Gep Carrabas, and good luck."

Within a short time the hired zipflyte arrived. (It would hardly do for the eminent Timor Carrabas to appear in Geisen's battered craft, which had, in point of fact, already been sold to raise additional funds to aid their subterfuge.) After clambering clumsily onboard, the schemers settled themselves in the spacious rear seat while the chauffeur—a neat-plumaged and discreet raptor-derived bestient—lifted off and flew at a swift clip toward Stoessl House.

Ailoura's comment about Geisen's attractiveness to his female peers had set an unhealed sore spot within him aching. "Do you imagine,

Hepzibah, that other local luminaries might attend this evening's dinner party? I had in mind a certain Gep Bloedwyn Vermeule."

"I suspect she will. The Stoessls and the Vermeules have bonds and alliances dating back centuries."

Geisen mused dreamily. "I wonder if she will be as beautiful and sensitive and angelic as I have heard tell she is."

Ailoura began to hack from deep in her throat. Recovering, she apologized, "Excuse me, Gep Carrabas. Something unpleasant in my throat. No doubt a simple hairball."

Geisen did not look amused. "You cannot deny reports of the lady's beauty, Hepzibah."

"Beauty is as beauty does, master."

* * *

The largest ballroom in Stoessl House had been extravagantly bedecked for the arrival of Timor Carrabas. Living luminescent lianas in dozens of neon tones festooned the heavy-beamed rafters. Decorator dust migrated invisibly about the chamber, cohering at random into wallscreens showing various entertaining videos from the mediapoietic worlds. Responsive carpets the texture of moss crept warily along the tesselated floor, consuming any spilled food and drink wasted from the large collation spread out across a servitor-staffed table long as a playing field. (House chef Stine Pursiful oversaw all with a meticulous eye, his upraised ladle serving as baton of command. After some argument among the family members and chef, a buffet had been chosen over a sit-down meal, as being more informal, relaxed and conducive to easy dealings.) The floor space was thronged with over a hundred gaily caparisoned representatives of the Houses most closely allied to the Stoessls, some dancing in stately pavanes to the music from the throats of the octet of avian bestients perched on their multi-branched stand. But despite the many diversions of music, food, drink and chatter, all eyes had strayed ineluctably to the form of the mysterious Timor Carrabas when he entered, and from time to time thereafter.

Beneath his prosthetics, Geisen now sweated copiously, both from nervousness and the heat. Luckily, his disguising adjuncts quite capably metabolized this betraying moisture before it ever reached his clothing.

The initial meeting with his brothers and stepmother had gone well. Hands were shaken all around without anyone suspecting that the flabby hand of Timor Carrabas concealed a slimmer one that ached to deliver vengeful blows.

Geisen could see immediately that since Vomacht's death, Grafton had easily assumed the role of head of household, with Woda patently the power behind the throne and Gitten content to act the wastrel princeling.

"So, Gep Carrabas," Grafton oleaginously purred, "now you finally perceive with your own eyes that we Stoessls are no monsters. It's never wise to give gossip any credence."

Gitten said, "But gossip is the only kind of talk that makes life worth liv—oof!"

Woda took a second step forward, relieving the painful pressure she had inflicted on her younger son's foot. "Excuse my clumsiness, Gep Carrabas, in my eagerness to enhance my proximity to a living reminder of the fine old ways of Chalk. I'm sure you can teach us much about how our forefathers lived. Despite personal longevity, we have lost the institutional rigor your clan has reputedly preserved."

In his device-modulated, rather fulsome voice, Geisen answered, "I am always happy to share my treasures with others, be they spiritual or material."

Grafton brightened. "This expansiveness bodes well for our later negotiations, Gep Carrabas. I must say that your attitude is not exactly as your servant Bozzarias conveyed."

Geisen made a dismissive wave. "Simply a local hireling who was not truly privy to my thoughts. But he has the virtue of following my bidding without the need to know any of my ulterior motivations." Geisen felt relieved to have planted that line to protect Bozzarias in the nasty wake of the successful conclusion of their thimblerigging. "Here is my real counselor. Hepzibah, step forward."

Ailoura moved within the circle of speakers, her unnaturally flared and pungent striped musteline tail waving perilously close to the humans. "At your service, Gep."

The Stoessls involuntarily cringed away from the unpleasant odor wafting from Ailoura, then restrained their impolite reaction.

"Ah, quite an, ah, impressive moreauvian. Positively, um, redolent of the ribosartor's art. Perhaps your, erm, advisor would care to dine with others of her kind."

"Hepzibah, you are dismissed until I need you."

"As you wish."

Soon Geisen was swept up in a round of introductions to people he had known all his life. Eventually he reached the food, and fell to eating rather too greedily. After weeks spent subsisting on MREs alone, he could hardly restrain himself. And his glutton's disguise allowed all excess. Let the other guests gape at his immoderate behavior. They were constrained by their own greed for his putative fortune from saying a word.

After satisfying his hunger, Geisen finally looked up from his empty plate.

There stood Bloedwyn Vermeule.

Geisen's ex-fiancee had never shone more alluringly. Threaded with invisible flexing pseudo-myofibrils, her long unfettered hair waved in continual delicate movement, as if she were a mermaid underwater. She wore a gown tonight loomed from golden spidersilk. Her lips were verdigris, matched by her nails and eye-shadow.

Geisen hastily dabbed at his own lips with his napkin, and was mortified to see the clean cloth come away with enough stains to represent a child's immoderate battle with an entire chocolate cake.

"Oh, Gep Carrabas, I hope I am not interrupting your gustatory pleasures."

"Nuh–no, young lady, not at all. I am fully sated. And you are?"

"Gep Bloedwyn Vermeule. You may call me by my first name, if you grant me the same privilege."

"But naturally."

"May I offer an alternative pleasure, Timor, in the form of a dance? Assuming your satiation does not extend to *all* recreations."

"Certainly. If you'll make allowances in advance for my clumsiness."

Bloedwyn allowed the tip of her tongue delicately to traverse her patina'd lips. "As the Dompatta says, 'An earnest rider compensates for a balky steed.'"

This bit of familiar gospel had never sounded so lascivious. Geisen was shocked at this unexpected temptress behavior from his ex-fiancee. But before he could react with real or mock indignation, Bloedwyn had whirled him out onto the floor.

They essayed several complicated dances before Geisen, pleading fatigue, could convince his partner to call a halt to the activity.

"Let us recover ourselves in solitude on the terrace," Bloedwyn said, and conducted Geisen by the arm through a pressure curtain and onto an unlit open-air patio. Alone in the shadows, they took up positions braced against a balustrade. The view of the moon-drenched arroyos below occupied them in silence for a time. Then Bloedwyn spoke huskily.

"You exude a foreign, experienced sensuality, Timor, to which I find myself vulnerable. Perhaps you would indulge my weakness with an assignation tonight, in a private chamber of Stoessl House known to me? After any important business dealing are successfully concluded, of course."

Geisen seethed inwardly, but managed to control his voice. "I am flattered that you find a seasoned fellow of my girth so attractive, Bloedwyn. But I do not wish to cause any intermural incidents. Surely you are affianced to someone, a young lad both bold and wiry, jealous and strong."

"Pah! I do not care for young men, they are all chowderheads! Pawing, puling, insensitive, shallow and vain, to a man! I was betrothed to one such, but luckily he revealed his true colors and I was able to cast him aside like the churl he proved to be."

Now Geisen felt only miserable self-pity. He could summon no words, and Bloedwyn took his silence for assent. She planted a kiss on his cheek, then whispered directly into his ear. "Here's a map to the boudoir where I'll be waiting. Simply take the east squeezer down three levels, then follow the hot dust." She pressed a slip of paper into his hand, supplementing her message with extra pressure in his palm, then sashayed away like a tainted sylph.

Geisen spent half-an-hour with his mind roiling before he regained the confidence to return to the party.

Before too long, Grafton corralled him.

"Are you enjoying yourself, Timor? The food agrees? The essences elevate? The ladies are pliant? Haw! But perhaps we should turn our mind to business now, before we both grow too muzzy-headed. After conducting our dull commerce, we can cut loose."

"I am ready. Let me summon my aide."

"That skun— That is, if you absolutely insist. But surely our marchwarden can offer any support services you need. Notarization, citation of past deeds, and so forth."

"No. I rely on Hepzibah implicitly."

Grafton partially suppressed a frown. "Very well then."

Once Ailoura arrived from the servants' table, the trio headed toward Vomacht's old study. Geisen had to remind himself not to turn down any "unknown" corridor before Grafton himself did.

Seated in the very room where he had been fleeced of his patrimony and threatened with false charges of murder, Geisen listened with half an ear while Grafton outlined the terms of the prospective sale: all the Carrabas properties and whatever wealth of strangelets they contained, in exchange for a sum greater than the Gross Planetary Product of many smaller worlds.

Ailoura attended more carefully to the contract, even pointing out to Geisen a buried clause that would have made payment contingent on the first month's production from the new fields. After some arguing, the conspirators succeeded in having the objectionable codicil removed. The transfer of funds would be complete and instantaneous.

When Grafton had finally finished explaining the conditions, Geisen roused himself. He found it easy to sound bored with the whole deal, since his elaborate scam, at its moment of triumph, afforded him surprisingly little vengeful pleasure.

"All the details seem perfectly managed, Gep Stoessl, with that one small change of ours included. I have but one question. How do I know that the black sheep of your House, Geisen, will not contest our agreement? He seems a contrary sort, from what I've heard, and I would hate to be involved in judicial proceedings, should he get a whim in his head."

Grafton settled back in his chair with a broad smile. "Fear not, Timor! That wild hair will get up no one's arse! Geisen has been effectively rendered powerless. As was only proper and correct, I assure you, for he was not a true Stoessl at all."

Geisen's heart skipped a cycle. "Oh? How so?"

"The lad was a chimera! A product of the ribosartors! Old Vomacht was unsatisfied with the vagaries of honest mating that had produced Gitten and myself from the noble stock of our mother. Traditional methods of reproduction had not delivered him a suitable toady. So he resolved to craft a better heir. He used most of his own germ plasm as foundation, but supplemented his nucleotides with dozens of other snippets. Why, that hybrid boy even carried bestient genes. Rat and weasel, I'm willing to bet! Haw! No, Geisen had no place in our family."

"And his mother?"

"Once the egg was crafted and fertilized, Vomacht implanted it in a host bitch. One of our own bestients. I misapprehend her name now, after all these years. Amorica, Orella, something of that nature. I never really paid attention to her fate after she delivered her human whelp. I have more important properties to look after. No doubt she ended up on the offal heap, like all the rest of her kind."

A red curtain drifting across Geisen's vision failed to occlude the shape of the massive auroch-flaying blade hanging on the wall. One swift leap and it would be in his hands. Then Grafton would know sweet murderous pain, and Geisen's bitter heart would applaud–

Standing beside Geisen, Ailoura let slip the quietest cough.

Geisen looked into her face.

A lone tear crept from the corner of one feline eye.

Geisen gathered himself and stood up, unspeaking.

Grafton grew a trifle alarmed. "Is there anything the matter, Gep Carrabas?"

"No, Gep Stoessl, not at all. Merely that old hurts pain me, and I would fain relieve them. Let us close our deal. I am content."

* * *

The starliner carrying Geisen, Ailoura and the stasis-bound Carrabas marchwarden to a new life sped through the interstices of the cosmos, powered perhaps by a strangelet mined from Stoessl lands. In one of the lounges, the man and his cat nursed drinks and snacks, admiring the exotic variety of their fellow passengers and reveling in their hard-won liberty and security.

"Where from here—son?" asked Ailoura with a hint of unwonted shyness.

Geisen smiled. "Why, wherever we wish, mother dear."

"Rowr! A world with plenty of fish then, for me!"

It has been a tenet of the Roman Catholic Church for centuries – millennia – that animals do not have souls. Almost from the moment that Furry fans have started writing fiction, they have speculated on what the Church's – and the public's – position would be as to whether artificially-intelligent animals would have souls. Kritzer's "St. Ailbe's Hall" is one of the best of these.

Naomi Kritzer has been a published author for the past dozen years. She has written five novels, all from Bantam Spectra, and eleven short stories, most published in Realms of Fantasy *magazine. She has had poetry published while living in Nepal.*

St. Ailbe's Hall

Naomi Kritzer

There was a Siberian husky in the last pew of St. Mary's. It was standing on its hind legs, holding a hymnal and singing, so Father Andrew knew that it must be an enhanced dog, but in church for heaven's sake. There were parishioners who owned enhanced dogs but today was not the Blessing of the Animals, so what was it doing here? Father Andrew realized abruptly that the hymn had ended several seconds ago, and he'd been staring at the dog. He hastily opened the missal and started the opening prayer.

During the first reading, he looked at the back pew again. After a few minutes of covert study, he recognized the young woman beside the dog as Lisa Erickson. Lisa had been confirmed during Father Andrew's first year at St. Mary's; she'd left Willmar for college six years ago. Her parents had complained to Father Andrew that Lisa had drifted away from the Church while at college. He'd heard that she'd moved back to the farm after her parents died. But what was the dog doing with her?

The rest of the church noticed the dog during the Sign of Peace; Father Andrew stifled a smile as he watched people saying "Peace be with you" while craning their necks to stare. It took longer than usual for everyone to sit back down.

After the Mass, Father Andrew stood just inside the shade of the door to greet his parishioners. Lisa came out with the dog. "Remember me, Father?" she asked. She had a button saying "AWARE" pinned to her sundress.

"I sure do, Lisa," he said.

"This is Jasper," Lisa said, and prodded the dog towards him. "She'd like to meet you."

Father Andrew was uncomfortable with the idea of enhanced animals. The Pope had condemned the manipulation of God's creation, and the results of the manipulation made Andrew nervous. Still, he forced himself to make eye contact with the dog, wondering what exactly Lisa expected from him. Jasper's eyes looked neither like the eyes of Caramel, Andrew's emphatically unenhanced pet mutt, nor like human eyes. She came up to about his chest, and her coat was brown and black. She ducked her head slightly; behind her, he could see that her tail was waving, very gently, like a fan.

Rote training took over: "It's a pleasure to meet you," he said, and extended his hand.

The dog clasped his hand in hers; the enhancements had included an opposable thumb. Her hands were almost human, except for the fur. "It's a pleasure to meet you, too," Jasper said. Her voice was low and a little raspy.

"I hope we'll see you here again next week," Father Andrew said, and Jasper's strange eyes brightened; he could see her tail quicken.

There was a startled murmur from the other churchgoers, and Lisa stepped forward quickly to clasp Jasper's elbow. "You will," Lisa said.

Lisa and Jasper headed away towards the parking lot, the rest of the churchgoers staring after them.

"I didn't know that they were allowed in churches," one of the men said as Lisa and Jasper disappeared around the corner. He was looking at Father Andrew.

Father Andrew had been staring after Lisa and Jasper, but now he turned back. "I don't believe there's a rule against it," he said, and ducked his head to shake hands with a child.

When everyone had left, Father Andrew closed up the church, hung up his vestments, and walked back to the Rectory. Across the street from the church, there was a yellow lab picking up litter outside of the bar. Father Andrew studied the dog as he passed by. The yellow lab never looked up from her task. Her tail waved lazily as she worked. She was retrieving, Andrew supposed. No wonder she was happy.

When genetic technologists had enhanced dogs, they'd left a lot of the breed traits intact. Enhanced retrievers liked to retrieve, picking up litter, harvesting crops, finding misplaced items in grocery store shelves. Airports had crews of Border collies directing people to gates and baggage claims. Swimming pools used Newfoundlands as lifeguards.

Andrew wondered why you'd enhance a Siberian husky. Jasper was bipedal and she didn't look like she'd pull a sled very well. And what on earth was she doing with Lisa? He unlocked the Rectory; Caramel bounded to the door to meet him, skinny tail whipping back and forth.

"Down," he said, and patted Caramel on his side. "Good boy."

Andrew got some leftover potato salad out of the refrigerator for lunch and took it into his study, padding across the carpet in his bare feet.

He kept the blinds drawn against the July sun, and the study was cool and dim. He sat down at his net terminal and flipped it on; sure enough, he had a letter from Leo. Leo was a Jesuit theologian who lived in Rome; Andrew had met him at a conference. After an interesting conversation, they had exchanged email addresses. Andrew had heard from Leo almost daily since then.

Andrew scrolled quickly through Leo's message, and then hit Reply.

> Leo -
> You're not going to believe what someone brought to Mass this morning. One of those enhanced dogs! Maybe the girl who did it had her dates mixed up and thought that today was the Blessing of the Animals, but I doubt it. It was pretty clear she was trying to make a point. She brought the dog up to me after the Mass to introduce her. So now I've shaken hands with a dog. Come to think of it, I've trained Caramel to do that, but this one didn't then roll over and beg for a treat...
> - Andrew

The phone rang. Andrew saved the message and picked up, hitting the display key on the terminal so he could see his caller. "Hello," he said.

"Hello, Father." The caller was Jerry, one of the older men of the Parish. Jerry still had his tie on from church; his voice was even stiffer than his collar. "Er, I'm calling about the dog."

"Yes?" There wasn't much point in pretending he needed to ask which dog.

"I'd appreciate it if you could talk to the young lady about appropriate behavior in church." Jerry's voice had taken on a bit of an edge, and Andrew felt himself bristle slightly. Jerry's eyes narrowed and he added, "My wife, she's allergic to dogs. We had to leave early today, she was starting to sneeze."

Jerry and his wife nearly always left Mass early, as soon as communion was done. Andrew smiled as sincerely as he could. "I tell you what, Jerry. There are almost always plenty of seats up front. Why don't you and your wife sit up there next Sunday? It's a big church, and I'm sure that if the dog comes again, it won't bother you."

Jerry muttered something inaudible and closed the connection abruptly.

Andrew turned back to his email message to Leo. He read through it, then deleted what he'd written and retyped it:

Leo -

You're not going to believe what came to Mass this morning. One of those enhanced dogs! I recognized the parishioner who brought the dog. Lisa grew up in the parish, though she's been somewhat less than a twice-a-year Catholic since her confirmation. Anyway, I spent most of the Mass trying not to stare.

- Andrew

The phone rang again. This time it was Carolyn, a woman in her early thirties with three young children. She'd called from her kitchen; behind her, Andrew could see her nanny-dog feeding Carolyn's children their lunch.

"Hello, Father," Carolyn said. "I was just calling to tell you that I think it was just awful of Lisa to drag her dog along to church this morning. Some people just have no idea how to behave, don't you think?"

"I was a bit surprised," Andrew said.

"I just wanted to let you know, if you'd like someone to go talk to her, to let her know that this is just not okay, if you know what I mean, I've talked to my neighbor Marie and we'd be happy to go talk to her for you, you know—"

"That really won't be necessary," Andrew said.

"So you'll talk to her yourself? Oh good. I think it will have a lot more effect coming from you, and Marie agrees with me, that it would really be best if you talked to her—"

"Carolyn," he said.

"Yes, Father?"

"Why do you have such strong feelings about this? Especially when you have a nanny-dog yourself."

Carolyn's face twisted into something ugly. "Dogs don't belong in church," she said.

* * *

Leo -

This is really becoming the controversy du jour, amigo. Two phone calls so far; it'll be ringing off the wall once everyone's had lunch and a chance to think things over. Everyone seems to want a "No Dogs Allowed" sign on the door. So far I've just been noncommittal and as soothing as possible, but it's clear

I'm going to have to make some sort of decision here. What
do you think?
- Andrew

Andrew sent the message just as the phone rang again. He picked up
the receiver to speak voice-only; if it was about something other than the
dog, he could always switch the screen on. "Father Andrew?" a woman's
voice said. For a moment he thought it was Lisa calling, but the voice had
an oily sheen of self-satisfaction that didn't fit his image of her.
"Speaking," he said.
"I thought you might like to know why that girl brought the dog to
church today." The caller did not identify herself, and the edge in her voice
sharpened into something almost gleeful. "Lisa is in one of those Animal
Liberationist groups. You know, Free the Horses and all that."
"Really," Andrew said. There was a long pause, and he hoped that his
caller was winding herself up in frustration at not being able to see his face.
"I just thought you might like to know," the caller said again. "That's
why she brought the dog – her kind think the dogs are people in fur coats,
you know? Why shouldn't they go to church?"
"Ah," Andrew said. He remembered Lisa's button, AWARE. He
remembered suddenly what AWARE stood for: Activists Working for
Animal Rights and Emancipation. He'd seen a brochure a few months ago.
"I just thought you'd–"
"–like to know. Yes. Was there anything else?"
The caller hung up without saying goodbye.
Andrew decided to get out of the house before the phone rang again.
He needed a chance to think about this before he had to make a decision.
Running, he'd go running.
Father Andrew's doctor had suggested for the last five years that he take
up some other form of exercise, swimming perhaps, or biking. Something
easier on the knees. Andrew had tried biking; he even purchased one of
those silly rowing machines, which he ended up using as a place to drape his
clothes. There was just something about running that nothing else could
substitute for. To satisfy his doctor, he dropped the idea of a marathon, and
he simply endured the knee pain.
Andrew changed into running clothes, locked up the Rectory, and
stretched his muscles as quickly as he could. If he had to run, his doctor
had suggested last time, at least he could use the high school track, instead
of running on the sidewalk. Today, though, Andrew ran along the tree-
lined residential streets of Willmar. Running in circles on a track would
feel too much like he wasn't getting anywhere.

So. Lisa considered the dog equal to a person. Andrew found himself remembering Jasper's strange eyes; she certainly wasn't just a dog, like Caramel was. He had never spent that much time around enhanced animals. No, that wasn't really true. They were everywhere these days. Last year at the Blessing of the Animals he'd blessed as many nanny-dogs as pets. He ate at the bar and grill across from the church, ignoring the enhanced yellow lab that swept the floors; last year when he was trying to take up swimming, he swam at a pool with a Newfoundland lifeguard. He'd spent plenty of time around enhanced dogs. He'd just never really looked at one before.

Still, what did Lisa hope to get out of bringing Jasper to church? Or— what did Jasper hope to get? Presumably if Lisa treated the dog as a person, she didn't make the dog go anywhere. Or maybe she did. Or maybe if Lisa wanted something, Jasper wanted it too. Enhanced dogs were designed to be eager to please.

He could, he supposed, simply ask Lisa.

The phone was ringing when he got back to the Rectory, but he ignored it. He stood in the shade of the maple tree in the yard, stretching his muscles and hoping no one would drop by to confront him about the dog in person. Once he'd showered and dressed, he picked up the phone while it wasn't ringing and called Lisa.

"Hello?" The face on the screen wasn't Lisa's. For one disconcerting moment, Andrew thought he'd dialed the wrong number when he realized that the funny wrinkled face staring at him belonged to a puppy.

"Hello, I'm Father Andrew from St. Mary's," he said. "Is Lisa there?"

The puppy wagged its tail. "I'll go find her," it said with an air of immense dignity that was somewhat spoiled by the tail. It hopped off the phone table and yelled, "Lisa!"

"Who is it?" Lisa's voice called back from another part of the house. Another puppy leapt up on the table, peering quizzically into the screen.

"It's Father Andrew from St. Mary's," the first puppy repeated carefully.

"Oh! Tell him I'll be right there."

The puppy jumped back onto the phone table. "Hey!" said the puppy who'd been peering at the screen. "I was up here."

"I was here first," said the puppy who'd answered the phone, forgetting all about the message. They'd degenerated into squabbling when Lisa came in.

"Cut it out, both of you. Down, off the table. I need to talk to Father Andrew." The puppies jumped down and rolled into a tussle in the corner.

"Sorry for the chaos," Lisa said with a nervous smile. "Was there something you needed?"

"How many enhanced dogs do you have?" Andrew asked, staring past her at the puppies, and at the enhanced Border collie that had just arrived to hustle them out of the way.

"I live with twenty-seven," Lisa said. "I don't have any."

Andrew winced. "Right," he said.

"Was that what you called to ask me?" Lisa said.

One of the puppies jumped back onto the phone table to stare at Andrew; its nose squeaked against the glass. "Actually, I was wondering if I could talk to you and Jasper again," Andrew said. The puppy stepped on the keyboard and nearly disconnected the call; Lisa picked up the fat little body and deposited it on the floor, ignoring the puppy's protests. "In person, maybe?"

A faint rueful smile crept into Lisa's eyes. "It is a little difficult using the phone with puppies around," she said. "Why don't you come out to my farm? I'm just south of town on Highway 5."

"Sounds great. This afternoon?"

"I'll be here," she said, and rang off.

As soon as he'd hung up the phone, it rang again, but he didn't answer. He knew he was neglecting his other duties, but they'd just have to wait, because it was clear that this could not.

Lisa's family's farm was about ten minutes outside of Willmar; a long unpaved driveway stretched from the road to the cluster of willow trees sheltering her house. He pulled up beside Lisa's oversized van and parked. The property included a house, barn, and shed; dogs poured from all three as he got out of his car. At the edge of the driveway, some of the puppies were swinging from the willow branches; one of them seemed to be wearing a cape.

Lisa had followed the dogs out and stood in the doorway of the house; a very small puppy snoozed in the crook of her arm. "Come on in," she called, and Andrew trudged past the dogs to the house; the screen door banged shut behind him.

All the furniture in the living room was covered in dog hair. Andrew sat down gingerly, thinking about dog hair all over his black trousers, but he felt like it would be rude to brush off the sofa first.

"Jessie is setting up a sprinkler outside for the puppies," Lisa said. She set the sleeping puppy down on an overstuffed chair, and poured iced tea into two heavy glasses, handing one to Andrew. "That should keep them out of the way. Jessie's a Border collie, and really good with the puppies. She was bred as a nanny-dog."

Andrew was going to ask about Jasper when he realized she hadn't been in the crowd outside. "Where's Jasper?" he asked.

"She should be back soon. She went running after Mass."

"Running?" Andrew said.

"Siberian huskies were bred to run. Jasper isn't really built for it. Huskies were meant to run on four legs, not two, but she loves running anyway."

"How did Jasper end up with you?" Andrew asked.

Lisa hesitated, taking a sip of iced tea. Outside, Andrew heard the water turn on; a puppy shrieked, "It's COLD. You didn't say it was going to be COLD," and Lisa stifled a smile. She set down her glass. "After I graduated from college, I was hired to oversee a work team of dogs at a recycling plant in Rochester."

Andrew tried to imagine Lisa in an overseer's uniform; he realized that he couldn't even imagine her at a regular job.

"I 'knew' what everyone else 'knows' about enhanced dogs. They were genetically altered to make them more intelligent, but it was really just a highly efficient form of breeding. They were intelligent, but they weren't human, so it was okay to buy them and sell them, so long as you fed them and gave them somewhere to sleep. After all, what were you supposed to do, give them a paycheck and let them go rent an apartment? They're just dogs." Lisa picked up her glass of iced tea and took a sip; her eyes met Andrew's over the rim. Andrew had expected steely eyes, rigid with determination. Lisa's eyes were defiant, but uncertain, and a little bit afraid.

"Most of the dogs at the plant were golden retrievers. The designers kept the sweet disposition and eagerness to please, so that the dogs would be happy so long as you said 'good dog' periodically. But Jasper was different."

Andrew heard the tick-tick-tick of dog's claws on a wood floor. He turned around; Jasper had returned. "I'm telling your story," Lisa said to her, a little abashed.

Jasper shrugged. "Keep going," she said. "It's as much your story as mine, anyway."

Lisa went on. "You can say that retrievers are happy doing whatever you tell them to, or that terriers are too dumb to know they're slaves, but you can't say either of those things about enhanced huskies. I could tell that Jasper wasn't happy. So I started keeping an eye on her. One day, when I got back from lunch, she was missing. I found her curled up under the basement stairwell, squinting in the dim light at the pages of a book. It took me a minute to realize what I was seeing. I'd always been told–"

"Dogs can't read," Andrew murmured.

"As soon as Jasper saw me, she threw the book down and jumped up, apologizing and begging me not to tell anyone. All I could think was, 'Dogs can't read, and where on earth did she learn?'"

Andrew looked at Jasper. "Where did you learn?"

"They let us watch TV sometimes," Jasper said. "I learned from a TV show."

"The book was mine," Lisa said. "Jasper had borrowed it to read."

"After she found out," Jasper said, "Lisa would bring books just to lend to me. I read them in the evenings."

Lisa looked over at Jasper with a gentle smile. "Her favorite was the one she called 'the one with the talking animals, and the Great Lion that everyone likes.'"

"C. S. Lewis," Andrew said. "*The Lion, the Witch, and the Wardrobe.*"

"You guessed it," Lisa said. "But she didn't understand a lot of it, so then I brought in a book of Bible stories for children. We spent months that way." Lisa took a sip of iced tea. "Then one day, I was running late, and one of the other overseers covered for me. When I arrived on the factory floor, the other overseer was beating Jasper. I snatched the whip out of his hand, and shouted, 'How dare you?' And then suddenly I realized that I was as guilty as he was. Even if I was kind to Jasper, I was still her master. Not her friend."

Jasper took over, her voice quiet. "Lisa went to the manager of the factory, and she bought me. She took me away from the recycling plant and told me that as far as she was concerned, I was free. I could go running whenever I felt like it, I could read all the books in the world, whatever I wanted." Jasper paused. "Of course, I've had to stay with Lisa. There's no law recognizing a free dog. But I don't mind staying with Lisa. She doesn't tell herself that I'm just an animal. She'd set me free if she could."

"How does St. Mary's fit in with all of this?" Andrew asked.

"Lisa brought me a Bible," Jasper said. "Once I understood what religion was, I realized that I wanted a part of it." Andrew met her eyes, and again he was struck by their strangeness. Jasper straightened her shoulders. "I want to be baptized," she said.

Andrew's iced tea glass, which was fortunately empty, slipped out of his hand and hit the floor with a clunk. "Baptized?" he said.

"That's right," Jasper said.

Andrew had almost reached the conclusion that he would welcome Jasper to church even if everyone else in the parish engaged in pointed sneezing fits, but baptism was something else entirely. "Do you even understand what that means?"

"Yes," Jasper said. "Baptism will bring me closer to God."

Andrew carefully picked up the glass he'd dropped. "I'll have to think about this," he said.

"In the meantime, may I continue to attend church?" Jasper asked. "That is why you came today, right? The other humans this morning were not happy."

Andrew stood up and handed the glass to Lisa. "That's their problem," he said. "I said I hoped I'd see you both again. I haven't changed my mind."

* * *

"The church's doors are open to all, Mrs. Petersen," Andrew said. It was Tuesday afternoon, and the flood of calls had finally started to slack off. Jasper had a handful of supporters who'd made their opinions known, but they were vastly outnumbered by the people who were horrified at the idea of praying beside a dog.

Mrs. Petersen glared at him from his screen. "It's not that I don't like enhanced dogs," she said. "I don't know what we'd do without our children's nanny-dog. But to take one to church … !"

"If Jasper wants to come to my church, she is welcome," Andrew said.

"I'm going to have to complain to the bishop," Mrs. Petersen said.

"That's your choice, of course," Andrew said, and hung up.

Andrew had sent the email to Leo as soon as he returned from Lisa's farm, even though Leo hadn't answered his first message yet. Baptism. Of a dog? His parishioners were outraged enough by the idea of a dog attending Mass, never mind participating in the sacraments. The message Andrew sent to Leo was one hundred lines long, closing with a question: "This is an absurd request. Why am I even considering this?"

Late Tuesday afternoon, he finally had a chance to read the reply.

> Andrew,
> Your final question is the easy one. You're considering it because you've looked into Jasper's eyes. I have to confess, though there are easily as many enhanced dogs in Italy as in America, I had always ignored them as blithely as you do. After I received your story, I found one of the dogs who sweeps the streets here in Rome and engaged him in conversation for a few minutes. You're right; they're definitely not "just animals." But the question becomes then, what are they? Doctrine tells us that animals have only temporary souls. They lack the immortal souls of human beings because in eternity, they would be unable to comprehend and contemplate the glory

of God. Animals are irrational and act entirely on instinct, whereas humans can resist our instinctual urges, and I have certainly seen instinctive behavior in the enhanced dogs I have observed. Finally, animals were not created in the image and likeness of God.

You'll want to talk to Bishop Gunderson, of course. But I don't see any way you can do it, even if you decide you want to. Not that you should stop the dog from coming to church. I think you've got that one right, at least. But I'm always in favor of unsettling the complacent, by whatever means seem most attractive.

- Leo

The phone was finally quiet, and Andrew went to pick up the paper mail. In addition to the usual junk mail, there was an envelope with no return address. He opened it immediately, expecting a prayer request. The paper inside was tightly folded; as he unfolded it, something fell out. He saw what it was when he bent down to pick it up, and felt ill.

Someone had used an image editing program to make a picture of Father Andrew engaging in... carnal relations with an enhanced dog. It was crudely done and wouldn't have fooled a first-grader, but the intent was not libel, it was threat. The picture showed gruesome bloody slashes across both his throat and the dog's. Just in case the message wasn't clear, the paper that had been wrapped around the picture spelled it out in block letters:

DOGS DON'T BELONG IN CHURCH YOU BITCH FUCKER. TELL IT AND THE GIRL TO FUCK OFF OR YOU'LL BE SORRY.

Father Andrew set both the letter and the picture down with a shudder, glancing involuntarily towards the window. No one was in sight, but he called Caramel inside and locked the door of the Rectory anyway. He turned off the ringer on the phone and went to his study to sit down.

His knees were aching again, so he stretched out his legs on his ottoman, putting a little pillow under his knees for support. He needed to call the bishop, and probably the police come to think of it, but definitely the bishop. Before he did that, though, he wanted to get his own thoughts in order.

Although C. S. Lewis had not been a Catholic, Andrew had a shelf in his study dedicated to Lewis's books. Including, of course, the Chronicles of Narnia, the one with the talking animals, and the Great Lion that everyone likes. He stood up with a groan, pulled *The Lion, the Witch, and the Wardrobe* off the shelf, and put his legs back on the ottoman.

Andrew had only intended to look up the parts with the Great Lion, Aslan, but as soon as Edmund stepped through the wardrobe, to sell his soul to the White Witch for a box of Turkish delight, Andrew was as hooked as he'd been when he read the story in elementary school. He finished the book in another three hours of nonstop reading. When he'd finished, he set it down and looked up at the crucifix on his wall. "The image and likeness of God," he said aloud.

> Yes, Leo, but what is the image and likeness of God? Does it mean opposable thumbs and a body without fur? We could make that in a test tube these days, starting with dog DNA, if we wanted to. Jasper became interested in religion after reading C. S. Lewis. In her eyes, God's "likeness" is that of a Great Lion. How sure are you that she's not right?
> - Andrew

At Andrew's insistence, Bishop Gunderson took Jasper's request seriously, although he was dubious. "I'll have to talk to Rome," he said after a long conversation. "This may take some time." He agreed to meet with Jasper and Lisa, and agreed that in the meantime, Jasper should be allowed to attend church. "It hardly seems as if it could hurt anything," he said.

Leo's response to Andrew's message was short and predictable: "C. S. Lewis. Bah. Bloody Anglican. You'll need a better argument than that to convince a Jesuit like me."

On Sunday, the church was packed to the walls. It wasn't even this crowded at Easter. Looking around, Andrew saw as many Lutherans as Catholics, there to gawk at the dog. Lisa and Jasper tried as hard as they could to ignore the crowd, despite open glares and whispered insults.

Andrew had decided that on this Sunday, subtlety would be wasted. During his homily, he spoke directly to the question that was on everyone's mind. "So far as we know, Christ embraced all who came seeking him. He ate with tax collectors; he defended prostitutes; he taught his followers that the hated Samaritans were their neighbors. Just as Christ turned no one away from his ministry, neither will St. Mary's turn anyone away from our ministry."

There was a rustle as people shifted in the pews, and a low rumble of whispered conversation. "Christ had words for people who would close doors on others," Andrew said, raising his voice. "'Woe to you, scribes and Pharisees, you hypocrites! You lock the kingdom of heaven before human beings. You do not enter yourselves, nor do you allow entrance to those trying to enter.'" The rumble increased in volume. "Let me say this as plainly as I can. This church's doors are open to anyone who comes here. Anyone. That is not going to change."

Andrew had expected someone to walk out, but no one did, not even the Lutherans. Some of the parishioners glared at him with steaming fury; others stared at the floor in what might have been shame. Lisa kept her face carefully expressionless, looking at him intently; Jasper fixed her eyes on the hymnal. They left quickly when the Mass was over; so did most of the others.

Andrew stayed up late that night, searching for theological texts that had some sort of bearing on this situation. At ten minutes to midnight, he was reciting the Evening Office in preparation for going to bed when he heard a knock at the door. He went downstairs and peered out through the peephole, but couldn't see anything. The knock came again, but at knee height. He opened the door, and a greyhound stood on his doorstep. It was clearly an enhanced dog, though it stood on four legs rather than two.

"Lisa sent me," the greyhound said. "She wants you to meet her three miles east of the farm, as soon as you can get there. She needs your help. It's really important."

"Let me get dressed," Andrew said. He let the greyhound inside, to wait in his hallway while he changed back into clothes and combed his hair. Caramel barked at the greyhound, then hid under the kitchen table. The greyhound rode in the car with Andrew to the meeting place. Lisa was waiting for them, on foot, with a collie that Andrew didn't recognize. Andrew pulled over and parked at the edge of the road, then got out and walked towards them.

"I'm so sorry to bother you, Father," Lisa said. "I know this really isn't very good timing, especially since people are so angry about Jasper, but I really didn't know who else to go to."

Andrew looked closely at Lisa. Her face was pale, and she'd clearly dressed quickly; her shirt was buttoned up wrong. "What can I do to help you?" he asked.

"This is Phoenix," Lisa said. "She's owned by a man who lives outside of town, not too far from me; he uses her as a servant and a field hand."

Andrew looked at Phoenix. Her long tail waved like a flag in a hesitant wind, but she avoided his eyes. Her long fur was matted.

"Her owner—" Lisa paused to wipe her eyes impatiently with her sleeve. "Whenever Phoenix makes a mistake, no matter how small, her owner beats her. This afternoon, she couldn't take it anymore and she bit him. Now he's going to kill her. Have her 'put down' is how he puts it. So she ran to my farm. She knew I'd try to protect her. But that's–" Lisa's voice gave out again. Andrew offered her tissues from his jacket pocket, but she shook her head. She took two deep breaths, then went on. "I can't protect her, Father. Everyone knows how I feel about enhanced dogs. Whenever anyone goes missing, my farm is the first place they look."

"You want me to hide her?" Andrew said.

"No," Lisa said. Her voice was calm again. "There's a safe house in Minneapolis. I need you to drive her there. Once she's out of the area, there are people who can arrange for false ownership papers. Please, Father. There's no one else up here who will do this, and I'm being watched too closely right now. If they come looking at my farm and the van is gone–"

"I'll do it," Andrew said. "Phoenix, go get in the back seat of my car and lie down on the back seat so that you can't be seen through the window."

Lisa gasped and then let out a long, shaky breath. "Thank you," she said. She scribbled down an address. "If it's safe to drop Phoenix off, they'll have a lamp burning in the upstairs window that looks like a single candle."

Andrew checked the address and put the paper in his pocket. "You didn't buy all your dogs, exactly, did you?"

Lisa gave him a wry smile, her eyes still a little watery. "No. Not exactly."

Andrew started the car and headed towards Minneapolis.

After five minutes of driving, his bravado started to fade. Andrew had never broken the law before, except for exceeding the speed limit. He tried to remember what the penalties were for Grand Theft Animal. There'd been a case in Brainerd recently. Someone got ten years, but that wasn't a first offense. If Andrew were caught, he'd probably get a suspended sentence. And he'd lose his parish. And Phoenix would die.

The drive to Minneapolis took two hours; Phoenix was silent the whole way. The house was easy to find on the grid of numbered streets east of Interstate 35W. Then he turned down the street the house was on – and saw blue and red flashing lights. Cops. He felt a surge of panic; from the back seat, Phoenix whined softly. Not daring to turn around, Andrew cruised slowly past the former safe house. The lights in the house were all on; he could hear the howl of an anguished enhanced dog inside. Phoenix whimpered again.

"We'll be okay, Phoenix," Andrew said as he passed the police car. He turned the corner and headed east. I'll think of something, he thought. God, help me out here.

Andrew wandered the streets of Minneapolis for the next two hours. Maybe, he thought, he'd see another house with the lamp in the window.

Maybe he could knock on the door and they'd say something like, "So, where's the dog who needs a safe house?" so he'd know it wasn't just an odd decorating choice. More than once, he thought about calling Lisa, but if she were really under suspicion for this sort of thing, her phone might well be wiretapped. The best he could do would be to drive Phoenix back to the Rectory and contact Lisa in the morning. Maybe she knew of another safe house. Maybe.

At four in the morning, Andrew pulled over near a park. "Wait here," he said to Phoenix, and went to kneel in the damp grass. The Irish Saint Brigid was the patron of fugitives; he petitioned her now. "I haven't done this before," he whispered. "I don't know what I'm supposed to do. Help me to get Phoenix somewhere safe."

He got back in the car. "Are you hungry?" he asked Phoenix.

"Yes, please," Phoenix said. Her voice was eager. Andrew drove to the university and found an all-night Chinese restaurant; he bought a bowl of noodles for himself and some egg rolls for Phoenix and took them out to the car. Phoenix got out and they sat side-by-side on the rear bumper of the car, eating their food.

On the other side of the parking lot, there was a shop with an illuminated painting in the window. Andrew squinted at it. It showed a man embracing what looked like a Siberian husky. He walked over to look closer, and realized that it was a wolf. The picture was labeled, "St. Ailbe, Patron of Wolves."

Andrew looked up at the name of the shop. The St. Ailbe and St. Brigid Wine and Cheese Shop. There was an apartment over the shop; looking up, he saw what looked like a single candle burning in the window.

"Phoenix!" he called excitedly. "Wait here. I'm going to go talk to someone."

The door to the stairs leading up had been propped open slightly; Andrew ran up the stairs and knocked on the door. After several minutes, a young man opened the door, dressed in boxer shorts and blinking a little in the hallway light. He squinted at Andrew. "Are you a priest?" he asked.

"Yeah," Andrew said, and realized that he didn't know what to ask. "I, uh, is this a safe house?"

The man blinked at Andrew groggily. "Are you the priest?" he asked.

"Yes. I mean, I don't know. I saw the light in your window. I'm here with a dog—"

That woke the man instantly. "A runaway? Where is she?"

"She's downstairs," Andrew said, with a rush of relief. "I'll get her."

"Hang on a sec," the man said. "Let me get my glasses. And some clothes."

Andrew fetched Phoenix and brought her up to the apartment. The man met them at the door, wearing jeans now, and wire-rimmed glasses. "I'm Tim," he said, and clasped Phoenix's hand. "You'll be safe here." There was another painting of St. Ailbe on the wall.

On his way out, Andrew leaned against the doorway, realizing suddenly how tired he was. "You can spend the night here, too," Tim said. "You don't look like you should be driving."

"If I'm not home in the morning, the police might realize I helped Phoenix," Andrew said. "That might put her in danger, or you."

Tim nodded.

Andrew turned to leave, then paused. "Who's Saint Ailbe?" he asked.

"He's Irish," Tim said. "A friend of Saint Patrick's. He was raised by wolves, and he was a good son according to legend. His foster-mother lived out her life in Ailbe's hall."

The sun was rising as Andrew reached the outskirts of Willmar. He realized with a pang that he'd never finished saying the Evening Office, and now it was time for the Morning one. He felt queasy, as he always did when he was up too late, and his eyes felt like they had gravel in them. Still as he watched the plains turn gold in the rising sun, he felt a strange quiet assurance that he had done the right thing.

* * *

Andrew badly needed his sleep the next night, but he was woken three times by late-night calls. One was an anonymous caller who snarled an obscenity and hung up. Andrew finally turned off his phone to get some sleep. Tuesday morning, he had more hate mail. Wednesday morning, he found that his tires had been slashed; he had to borrow a car to visit his parishioners in the hospital. At least no one seemed to connect him to the "theft" of Phoenix. Though, as she had predicted, Lisa's farm was searched.

In the dark hours of Thursday morning, Andrew woke to a crash and tinkling glass. Caramel started barking frantically. Andrew grabbed his glasses and his phone, dialing 911. "This is Father Andrew Pieri from St. Mary's," he said to the dispatcher. "I think someone just broke one of my windows." Outside, he heard the screech of tires on gravel as someone pulled away very quickly.

"The police are on their way," the dispatcher told him.

Andrew flipped on his bedroom light; it was 4:07 a.m. He pulled on his bathrobe and slippers and went downstairs. Caramel was still barking.

The shattered window was in his study. Andrew shut Caramel in the basement, to keep him away from the shards of glass. There was a brick on the floor; it had been thrown with a great deal of force, slamming past the drawn blinds to land in the middle of the room. Andrew went in; the glass crunched under his feet, grinding into the carpet fibers. He squatted down to pick up the brick, his knees cracking. There was a note wrapped around the brick. "BITCH LOVER," it said.

Andrew put the brick back where it had fallen, for the police officers, and went back out of the study to start a pot of coffee. He could hear the sirens, and wished that he had time to get dressed. In his collar, at least he looked like a man in control of his own life.

The police were not unsympathetic. "This is about the dog in the church, I assume?" one asked. Andrew nodded. "Too bad people feel like they need to attack you over this," the other said. Andrew wondered if that meant that the police felt that violence would be more appropriately directed towards Lisa.

The officers took photos of the damage, and put the note and the brick in evidence bags. Andrew gave them the other nasty letters he'd received, and they put those in evidence bags, as well. "We'll send someone around in the morning, to interview the neighbors," one said. "They might have seen something." They declined the offer of coffee.

Andrew poured himself a cup once the police officers had gone, then went to look at the study again. He'd have to clean up the glass before he could use the room again. He didn't look forward to getting the slivers out of the carpet, and his favorite chair. And his ottoman. And the pillow he used to prop up his knees. His wave of anger and resentment took him by surprise. He slammed the door of the study hard enough to make the house shake, and then let Caramel out of the basement.

Caramel followed him into the kitchen, flopping down at Andrew's feet and thwacking Andrew's calves with his long, skinny tail. Andrew put down his coffee and rested his forehead on his arms. He was tired of this. He missed his life. He'd taken controversial stands before, but nothing that people didn't expect from a priest. Nothing that generated this sort of hostility towards him.

Andrew sat up and bowed his head to pray, and suddenly felt horribly guilty. As persecution went, this was pretty trivial. What kind of wimp complained so bitterly about a few harassing phone calls and a broken window? The realization only made him feel worse.

He finished his coffee and went upstairs to shower and shave. Of course, he got soap in his eyes while washing his face, and then he cut himself shaving. He discovered that his favorite shirt was missing a button, and when he started to tie his shoes, his shoelace broke.

He forced himself to say the Morning Office, though Lauds – Praise to God – were hardly what he was in the mood for right now. The psalm for the morning was a Prayer in Time of Trouble: "Come quickly and hear me, O Lord, for my spirit is weakening." That was appropriate enough, but only made him feel guiltier for his whining.

When he'd finished the Office, he decided to check for email from Leo before he started cleaning. There was glass all over his chair, so he dragged in a chair from the kitchen, promising himself that he would clean up the glass as soon as he was done checking his mail. No mail was waiting, so he poured out this latest misfortune into a letter, telling Leo about the brick, the glass all over everything, the hurried police officers, even cutting himself shaving.

> Leo,
> I know that Christ said that we're blessed when we're persecuted in His name. But you know, this would be a lot easier if I knew that I was putting up with all this in His name, you know? I told you about that wonderful serene feeling I got on Monday morning, but that could just as easily have been sleep deprivation as transcendence. I want to know that I'm doing the right thing. I could put up with anything, if I knew that.
> - Andrew

To Andrew's surprise, the terminal beeped just moments after he sent his message off, with a reply. Leo must be at his own terminal right now. He opened the message quickly; it was very short.

> Andrew, my poor persecuted friend. Of course you want to know that you're doing the right thing. I know that the pure faith you felt at dawn on Monday seems so frail now, so fragile, but recall it as best as you can and trust in it. Most of the time we have to trust with so much less. And Andrew, don't worry about whining to God. You whine to me, and you know that God is more sympathetic than I am.
> - Leo

Andrew finished cleaning up the study at around ten in the morning; his phone rang just as he was going to open the door and let Caramel in again. He answered the call; it was Lisa. Her face was distraught.

"Jessie found something in the south pasture," she said. Her voice was shaking. "A leg-hold trap."

It took a moment for Andrew to understand what she was talking about. "A trap. Like, to trap animals?"

Lisa held it up where he could see it on the screen. It was an ugly thing, like a jaw with metal spikes for teeth designed to snap shut over a foot. "This could have killed one of the puppies. But it wasn't set for them. It was set for Jasper. She goes running in that pasture, and anyone who watched this farm would know it."

"Lisa, that's terrible. You have to call the police."

"I have. They came and took a report. I'm calling you because if someone would do this to us they may do something to you, too. I just wanted to tell you to be careful."

Andrew grimaced. "I got a brick through my window in the early hours of the morning."

"Do you know who did it?"

"No." Andrew paused for a moment, distracted by a puppy squabble behind Lisa. "How's Jasper?"

"As well as can be expected. She and the other adult dogs are out combing through the pastures, looking for any more surprises like this one. I don't know if they've found any." Lisa shook her head. "Father, could you come over today? I want to talk."

* * *

Andrew saw the dogs out in the fields as he pulled up the driveway. Lisa and the puppies met him at the door of the farmhouse. The puppies were restless from being trapped inside the house on a sunny day; one of the living room chairs had been tipped over, and the puppies were using it as a fort.

Lisa pulled chicken salad out of the refrigerator for lunch and sat down across from Andrew. Two puppies tore past them and up the stairs, shrieking insults at each other. Another trotted over to the table, standing up with his hands on Andrew's knee. "Can I have some of your chicken salad, mister?"

"Teddy, you've already had your lunch," Lisa said. "Go play."

"But I didn't get chicken salad," Teddy protested.

"You got chicken, just without mayonnaise. Mayonnaise isn't good for you."

Teddy turned back to Andrew. "Please?" he said, tipping his head to the side to lean it against Andrew's arm. "Pretty please with sugar on top? And whipped cream and a cherry?"

"If Lisa says no," Andrew said reluctantly, "then I don't think I'd better."

Lisa rolled her eyes. "Teddy, go play."

Pouting, Teddy trotted off to join the others playing under the overturned chair.

"So was there anything specific you wanted to talk about?" Andrew asked, when they'd finished their lunch.

"I guess... I've started worrying," Lisa said. "Taking Jasper to church seemed like such a fine, bold idea. A good statement. Now well, at least so far no one's been hurt. Maybe I should drop this."

"How does Jasper feel about it?" Andrew asked.

"She wants to keep going," Lisa said. "She likes you. She believes in this. But I think I could talk her out of it."

"Do you think that would be right?" Andrew asked.

"I don't know." Lisa stared down at the floor. "You know, to be perfectly honest, the main reason I wanted to bring Jasper to church, to make a big deal out of it, was to draw attention to the cause of enslaved animals. I mean, you know, if we could get the Catholic Church to say that enhanced animals have souls then it would be very difficult for people to continue to pretend that enslaving an enhanced dog is no different than keeping a plain dog as a pet."

Andrew shrugged. "You're probably right about that."

"I don't want you to think that was Jasper's motive, though," Lisa said. "She honestly does want to be baptized. She's totally sincere."

"But you aren't."

"It depends on what you mean by sincerity."

Andrew sighed. "This will be harder for you if you don't feel that you can trust in God," he said.

"Then you think we should keep on with this?"

"I think that Jasper has an immortal soul, just as you and I do. And that if she wants to be baptized and to receive the sacraments, then it would be a terrible injustice not to permit her that."

Lisa looked up again, meeting his eyes; for a moment, she stared into them deeply. "In that case, I won't give up," she said.

Lisa walked Andrew to his car. The dogs were returning; they didn't seem to have found any more traps. Hopefully they hadn't missed any. "Lisa, you know, the Church's doors are as open to you as they are to Jasper."

"I know," Lisa said. "Thank you."

* * *

"The enemy of the human race, who opposes all good deeds in order to bring men to destruction, beholding and envying this, invented a means never before heard of, by which he might hinder the preaching of God's word of Salvation to the people: he inspired his satellites who, to please him, have not hesitated to publish abroad that the Indians of the West and the South, and other people of whom We have recent knowledge should be treated as dumb brutes created for our service, pretending that they are incapable of receiving the Catholic faith." Pope Paul III wrote that, Leo, shortly after the discovery of the Americas. That was the hard position to take then, and this will be hard now. But it's the right thing to do.
- Andrew

Andrew, my friend, there are rumors flying in Rome about "that priest in America with the canine catechumen." Your bishop has consulted Rome, but I fear that others may not see it as you do. The Congregation for the Doctrine of the Faith will take into account not only the good of your friend Jasper, but the good of all the faithful. If we accept a dog, we will be mocked across the globe. You know that. Some people will leave the Church in disgust. You know that, too. The Holy Father can overrule the CDF, but he won't - we both know that. So, where does that leave you?
-Leo

Twisting in the wind, Andrew thought, reading the letter. Leo was right. In all likelihood the CDF would recommend against Jasper's baptism, though they were unlikely to ban her from attending church.

This past Sunday had been the craziest yet. There had been protestors outside the church – some objecting to Jasper's presence, others defending her right to be there. Three quarters of the people waving signs weren't Catholic, and nearly all of them were from out of town. The police had been there, but several fights had broken out anyway. The story had been broadcast on TV stations as far away as Chicago, though most were treating it as a joke.

At least it didn't sound like Rome was laughing.

Andrew typed in a quick reply:

Leo,

You talk about the good of all the faithful. Does it serve the faithful to allow them to continue in evil and sin? If the Church denies that enhanced dogs have immortal souls, this legitimizes those Catholics who participate in the enslavement of the enhanced dogs. This cannot be right.

- Andrew

Andrew sent the message and had started to turn on the ten o'clock news, to see if they'd done another story about Jasper, when the phone rang. It was Lisa; her face was stark, and she was not calling from home. "What's wrong?" he asked.

"Teddy's been poisoned," Lisa said. "Someone left poisoned meat out in our yard."

"Oh my God," Andrew said. "Is he—"

"We're at the vet hospital."

"I'm on my way."

The veterinary hospital was on the edge of town; it had a new wing for enhanced animals, with beds instead of cages. Lisa was in the waiting room, her entire clan of dogs with her, scattered across the vinyl chairs and chipped white tables. "Teddy will eat just about anything," Lisa said. Her face was white, but she wasn't crying. "The vet thinks he'll be all right."

Jessie was keeping the rest of the puppies from wandering out of the waiting room. "Why would anyone do this?" she asked Andrew. "How could a human be so cruel?" There was genuine bewilderment in her voice. Nanny-dogs were designed to love and trust humans; as much as Jessie had been through with her old family, this was the worst betrayal yet.

Jasper sat in a chair in the corner, her eyes closed. Dogs couldn't cry; they could howl, but a howling dog would have been asked to leave the hospital waiting room. A rosary hung limp from Jasper's hand. Andrew sat down beside her. "This is all my fault," Jasper said.

There was a general chorus of denials from the other dogs, and from Lisa. Andrew took Jasper's almost-human hand gently and stroked the fur of her wrist. "You didn't set the poison out, did you? Then this isn't your fault, Jasper; this is the fault of a horrible, evil human."

"If I hadn't come to St. Mary's—"

"You had every right to come to St. Mary's. You have every right to ask for baptism. Jasper, do you know anything about the early Christians?"

Jasper shook her head.

"For hundreds of years, Christianity was illegal and anyone who asked for baptism could be persecuted if they were caught. Sometimes their families suffered as well. That doesn't mean that those Christians were wrong for seeking baptism." Jasper was silent. "You have the courage of one of those early Christians, Jasper," Andrew said. "Most of us never have to." Andrew touched the fur on her shoulder. "Trust in God."

Jasper nodded and closed her eyes again. The rosary twitched in her hand.

One of the vets came out to the waiting room. "Lisa?" she said nervously. Lisa leapt to her feet; everyone else fell silent, turning to look at the vet. "Your puppy – um, Teddy – he'll be okay. We're going to hold him overnight just to be sure, but he should be fine."

The dogs, other than Jasper, were jubilant; Jasper and Lisa were just deeply relieved. Lisa signed some papers and paid for Teddy's stay. Outside, the dogs piled into Lisa's van. Lisa watched them for a moment, then looked at Andrew.

"Father, I want to reconcile. I want to return to the Church."

Andrew paused. "Now?"

"As soon as possible. Now, I guess. I – um, I promised God, in the waiting room, that if he spared Teddy I'd return."

Andrew sat down on the bumper of the van. "Well, I hear confessions on Saturday afternoons, or by appointment. This counts as an appointment, if you want to do it face-to-face."

Lisa shrugged. "It's not like you wouldn't know it was me in the confessional. Everyone tells me that they can smell dog the minute I walk into a room."

Andrew laughed at that. "I honestly hadn't noticed."

"Well." Lisa made the sign of the cross. "In the name of the Father, and of the Son, and of the Holy Spirit, Amen." She looked at Andrew. He nodded encouragingly. "Bless me, Father, for I have sinned. My last confession was five years ago." She paused again. "So, that's five Lenten seasons that I haven't gone to confession, and five years that I haven't gone to Mass, and five years that I haven't taken communion. Also, I messed around with a couple of the guys I dated in college, and I've been jealous of friends and impatient with strangers, and I wasn't always a good daughter to my parents. I've yelled at the dogs I promised myself I'd always treat as equals, yelled at them like children. Should I try to count the times I've done stuff? It's been so long..."

"Do you know why you left the Church?" Andrew asked.

"I guess I lost my faith," Lisa said. "Sometime early on in college. I kept going to church for a while, but I was just going through the motions. I still don't know if I believe in God or not."

"But you didn't let that stop you from praying for Teddy," Andrew said.

"Yeah, and I got what I asked for, didn't I? You'd think that would remove all my doubts, wouldn't you."

Andrew leaned back against the van, looking up at the sky. The stars were obscured by the floodlights of the parking lot. "At sunrise, the morning after I took Phoenix to the safe house, I had this one moment of perfect clarity, where I knew that I was doing the right thing. Then it passed. Since then whenever I've had doubts, I've tried to remember that moment, but it doesn't always help."

"But I've never had a moment like that," Lisa said. "If I had, I wouldn't have doubts."

"Yes, you would," Andrew said. "That's what I'm trying to tell you. God doesn't always knock you off your horse and shout at you to make a point. Usually, God whispers to us, and it's up to us to sort out God's voice from the static of everyday life."

Lisa was silent for a moment. Then she said, "So I guess I don't get to come back to the Church, since I still don't fully believe."

"No," Andrew said. "You believed enough in God to make the bargain—and to keep it. God loves you, doubts and all; He rejoices in every step you take towards Him, no matter how small it is. You get to come back to the Church, if you want to come back."

Lisa didn't answer; after a moment, Andrew looked at her face, and realized that she was struggling not to cry.

"You can say the act of contrition later," Andrew said. "For now why don't you go ahead and let yourself cry." He handed Lisa a tissue. She took it and burst into silent, wracking sobs. He pulled her head gently against his shoulder, letting her lean against him. When she had cried herself out, he steadied her, then cupped his hands around her head. "I absolve you from your sins in the name of the Father, and of the Son, and of the Holy Spirit." He made the sign of the cross. "Amen."

"Amen," Lisa whispered.

"Go in peace," Andrew said. "But call me tomorrow and let me know how Teddy's doing."

Back at the Rectory, Andrew logged on to check for mail from Leo. He had a letter, but it was very short.

Andrew,
Sorry, something's come up. I really can't discuss

Jasper's situation right now. We'll talk later.

- Leo

Andrew blinked at the letters on the screen. No matter how busy Leo was, he never let it keep him from his e-chats with Andrew. Andrew scrolled back through the old messages, wondering if he'd said something that annoyed Leo, or if there was some hint–

> The Congregation for the Doctrine of the Faith will take into account not only the good of your friend Jasper, but the good of all the faithful... The Holy Father can overrule the CDF, but he won't – we both know that.
> - Leo

Andrew sat up straight in his chair. Of course. Anyone involved with the CDF's deliberations on any subject was strictly barred from discussing it. Leo was a theologian, he had probably been brought in for his analysis of the situation, or maybe just because he knew Andrew. That meant the CDF was already discussing the situation. Maybe it would all be resolved soon, one way or another.

The phone rang. It was Lisa, voice only.

"Oh my God," she was saying, over and over. "I can't believe it, I can't believe it."

"Lisa," he said. "What's wrong? What's happened?"

"–the farm."

"I'm on my way," he said, hanging up and heading for the door.

It was humid and very dark outside. He had his windows rolled down, and he smelled what had happened even before he saw the flashing lights at the end of Lisa's driveway. Fire. Lisa stood with the dogs beside the barn. The house was charred to the foundations; a single upright beam still stood, a pillar of blackened timber. Along with the smoke, he could smell the gasoline that had been used to set the fire.

"No one was hurt," Lisa said, her voice toneless. "We were all at the vet hospital, because of Teddy."

The dogs huddled together, staring at the dying flames. There was an arson investigator on the scene; he wanted to talk to Lisa, so Andrew helped Jessie hustle the rest of the dogs into the barn, and sat down to comfort the puppies. They vied for the opportunity to sit in his lap; the ones with human-like hands wanted to exchange high-fives with him, like Jasper had told them Andrew did with the human children on Sundays.

Jasper sat close by, holding one of the puppies. "Tell us a story," the puppy in Jasper's lap said.

For a moment, the only stories that Andrew could think of involved early Christian martyrs. Then he remembered that his copy of *The Lion, the Witch, and the Wardrobe* was in his briefcase, in his car. He fetched it, along with his emergency flashlight, and sat down on the floor of the barn to read it to the puppies.

The barn was hot and humid; the air was still. The floor was concrete, and covered in swallow droppings. The puppies curled around each other in a heap at Andrew's feet, in the circle of light made by the flashlight. One by one, they fell asleep. As the last puppy stopped struggling to keep her eyes open, Andrew looked around. Jessie had fallen asleep hours ago. Lisa had come in at some point, and gone to sleep with her head resting on the haunch of the Newfoundland. Andrew had reached the point in the story where Aslan slipped away to allow himself to be sacrificed, in exchange for the life of the misguided Edmund. Now Andrew fell silent, wondering if anyone was still awake and listening. At the edge of the circle, someone's eyes glittered – Jasper.

"You know the rest of the story," Andrew said.

Jasper nodded. After a little while she said, "There is something I have always wondered about that book."

"Ask me. I'll try to answer," Andrew said.

"What exactly is Turkish delight?"

Andrew laughed a little. "It's a sort of candy. After I first read the book, I asked my parents for some. I figured it must be awfully good, for Edmund to sell his soul for it. Actually, it's kind of sticky, and too sweet. I didn't much care for it even when I was a kid."

Jasper came forward into the circle of light. "People have sold their souls for less," she said.

"True enough." Andrew watched as Jasper settled down protectively beside the puppies. "Jasper, I have a question for you," he said.

"Ask away."

"Why do you want to be baptized?"

Jasper was silent for a long time. "I know that Lisa supported the idea because she thought it would bring attention to the movement to free enhanced animals," she said. "I'm not as committed to the cause as Lisa is, though. If that were all I cared about, I'd have given up after that first Sunday." Jasper propped herself up on one elbow, and her tail thumped twice. "I want to be baptized because it is a prerequisite to taking communion."

There was a pause.

"I suppose you want to know why communion matters so much to me," Jasper said.

"It had crossed my mind," Andrew said.

"I believe in God," Jasper said. "At first, I believed because I was so relieved at the idea that I might have a Creator who truly loved me, unlike the humans who manipulated dog DNA and designed me before my birth. But then I came to value the love of God in itself." Her voice was deep and a little hoarse. "When I first became interested in religion, I assumed I'd never be allowed even into a church building. I read some books by religious people who kind of set out on their own and found God by themselves. But I'm not a saint – and I could barely understand what they wrote. To come to God, I would need an easier way. And in the Catholic Church, God gives Himself to us as food. Could any way be simpler?"

"Probably not," Andrew said.

"So," Jasper said. "That's why."

There was a long pause. Andrew was mentally composing his next letter to Leo. Some say that God made humans, but humans made the enhanced dogs, and that therefore they don't have immortal souls. But, consider. Jasper has the intellect to understand what God is; she has the desire to know God; she wants to obey God's will as best as she knows how. Would a merciful God deny Jasper His presence? Then Jasper spoke, breaking into his reverie. "Father, can I ask you a question?"

"Ask," he said.

"Do you think that the Church will let me be baptized?"

"It doesn't matter," he said. Jasper raised her head to peer at him questioningly. "It doesn't matter because I'm not going to wait for a yes or a no. I'm baptizing you tomorrow morning."

* * *

They drove over to St. Mary's at dawn – Lisa, Andrew, Jasper, and all the other dogs, since Lisa was afraid to leave anyone alone. To receive baptism, Jasper needed a sponsor who was an active Catholic; fortunately, with Lisa's return to the Church, she could sponsor Jasper.

Lisa parked outside the church, and Andrew hustled everyone inside as quickly as he could, then locked the door behind them. The puppies wandered around, gaping at the stained glass windows. Andrew vested as quickly as he could, then strode down the aisle to join Jasper and Lisa just inside the door.

Baptism was an intimate ritual; Andrew could smell Jasper's breath as he inhaled. He had expected her to smell fusty, like Caramel, but her breath was no sourer than any human's. It occurred to him that she probably brushed her teeth.

"Do you reject sin, so as to live in the freedom of God's children?" he asked her.

"I do," Jasper breathed. Her eyes glinted at the words God's children.

Andrew led Jasper through the rest of the baptismal vows, rejecting Satan and affirming the Apostle's Creed. Though smaller than Lisa, Jasper was still much too big to pick up and hold over the baptistery; he had Lisa place her right hand on Jasper's shoulder, and Jasper bowed her head as Andrew poured water over her. "Jasper, I baptize you in the name of the Father." He poured: the water beaded up against her thick fur, and ran down her face. "And of the Son." He poured again. "And of the Holy Spirit." He poured again.

The baptism done, he anointed her with holy chrism; the oil made her fur slick. "The God of power and Father of our Lord Jesus Christ has freed you from sin and brought you to new life through water and the Holy Spirit," Andrew said. And through fire and violence, and a stubborn lapsed Catholic, he thought. "He now anoints you with the chrism of salvation, so that, united with his people, you may remain forever a member of Christ who is Priest, Prophet, and King." United with his people. God, let it be so.

When the rite was done, Andrew gave Jasper a hug. "Welcome to the Church," he said.

Public weekday Mass would be held later that morning; Jasper would receive communion then. Lisa was still afraid to leave the other dogs alone, but the puppies definitely couldn't be trusted to behave in church, so Andrew arranged for them to stay at the Rectory. The puppies wanted breakfast, so he poured out bowls full of dry Raisin Bran. It was the only thing he had in quantity. The puppies ended up playing with the raisins, rather than eating them, but they seemed reasonably satisfied with their breakfast.

Andrew brought Jasper and Lisa back over to the church with him a half hour before Mass. They sat down in the front row, this time – Andrew wanted Jasper to receive communion before anyone else knew what was going on. He went back to vest again, then lurked where he could keep an eye on things. His palms were sweating; he wiped them on his alb.

When Andrew came out, he was relieved to see that only a handful of people were there. One of them was Carolyn, the woman who has thought it was so inappropriate to bring a dog to church. Well, it didn't matter. He started the Mass.

Andrew realized as he started the Consecration of the Eucharist that his voice was shaking. He closed his eyes for a moment, trying to steady his breathing. God, I trust in You, he thought, and felt better, but his voice continued to shake. His heart was pounding so hard that he could hear it in his ears. He raised the chalice, chanting the prayer of consecration.

When it was time for the parishioners to approach and receive communion, Jasper rose and started towards him as quickly as she could. There was a crash from the back of the church, the sound of a falling kneeler. "No! What are you doing?" Carolyn shouted. She stood in the aisle. The other parishioners froze where they stood, staring at Jasper.

"This is desecration," Carolyn said. "This is desecration of the Eucharist! Jesus said, 'It is not right to take the children's food and throw it to the dogs.'"

Jasper kept her eyes fixed on Father Andrew. Andrew met Carolyn's eyes, hearing his own voice echo in the church. "Jesus did say that," he said. "And the Canaanite woman said, 'Lord, even the dogs eat the scraps that fall from their master's table.' And Jesus praised her faith, and healed her daughter. For you see, Carolyn, in that story, we – the gentiles – were the dogs. The 'children' Jesus spoke of were the Jews. Christ came for all of us. Anyone who seeks, anyone who knocks. Jasper is seeking him, Carolyn. I hope that someday you will, too." He looked back at Jasper and raised the wafer. "The Body of Christ," he said.

Carolyn started forward; her voice went up to a shriek of rage. "If you do this, Father, there is no turning back. You will be on their side. Theirs. Do you understand me?"

"Then that's the side I need to be on," Andrew said. "Whatever the cost."

"Thanks be to God," Jasper whispered.

"No!" Carolyn shouted.

Andrew placed the Host in Jasper's mouth. Jasper crossed herself, and moved aside, bowing her head, waiting.

Andrew raised another communion wafer. "The Body of Christ," he said. Something wet splashed his vestments, and he realized that he was crying.

Carolyn turned on her heel and left the church. One by one, the others followed, except for Lisa.

Lisa moved to stand before him. "Thanks be to God," she said, and he placed the Host into her outstretched hand.

About the Authors

Brock Hoagland

The son of a career Air Force Officer, Brock Hoagland grew up in several states and three years in England. He served six years in the Navy and after working 31+ years in a power plant he retired to the Black Hills of SD. Brock spends his time serving two cats, planting fruit & nut trees, hunting & fishing and photographing wildlife & landscapes. The author of a number of furry stories and one novel, Brock now writes occasional non-furry fiction.

Michael H. Payne

Michael H. Payne's short fiction has appeared in places like *Asimov's SF* magazine, the Writers of the Future collections, and the upcoming Bronies anthology from Kazka Press. His novel *The Blood Jaguar*, originally published by Tor Books, is scheduled for rerelease in an illustrated edition from Sofawolf Press. The further adventures of Cluny the sorceress squirrel can be found in every issue of *Marion Zimmer Bradley's Sword & Sorceress* series beginning with volume 23.

M. C. A. Hogarth

M.C.A. Hogarth is the author of over fifty stories in the genres of science fiction, fantasy, romance and humor, and also writes a business column for creative professionals. She lives in Florida, where she is currently engaged in observing the growth of children, particularly her own.

Charles P. A. Melville

Charles "Chuck" P. A. Melville has been involved in various corners of furry fandom since the late 1980's, contributing to furry fanzines and APAs like *Rowrbrazzle*, *Ink Spots* and *Tales Of The Tai-Pan Universe*. He was also an editor at MU Press during the 90's when he helped to create and produce the Furkindred shared world, and editing titles like *Corum*, *Cyberkitties*, and *ZU*. Originally from upstate New York, he now lives in the great Northwest, where he works on his webcomics (*Mr. Cow*, *Champion Of Katara*, and *Felicia: Sorceress Of Katara*) and the occasional short story and novel.

About the Authors

<u>Kristin Fontaine</u>

Kristin Fontaine has been involved with *Tales of the Tai-Pan Universe* as a writer and editor since 1989. She enjoys the give-and-take of writing in a shared universe. Born in a small town in Wyoming, Kristin escaped to the grey skies and evergreen trees of the Pacific Northwest. In her spare time she battles the black spot on her roses and mutters to herself in Norwegian.

<u>Kyell Gold</u>

Kyell Gold is best known for his gay fiction using animal people to represent human archetypes. He has won the Annual Anthropomorphic Literature & Arts (Ursa Major) Award ten times for his novels and short stories, and the Rainbow Award twice (2009, Best Gay Novel and Best Fantasy Novel, for *Out of Position*). He has also been nominated for a WSFA Small Press Award ("Race to the Moon", 2009). His various online presences are linked from www.kyellgold.com. He lives in California with his husband, but can often be found at conventions around the country and internationally.

<u>Samuel C. Conway</u>

Samuel Conway is a chemist who holds a Ph.D. from Dartmouth and works in a laboratory in his native Pennsylvania. He is also the chairman of Anthrocon, the world's largest Furry convention, held annually in Pittsburgh, PA. Known as "Uncle Kage" to his fans, he is an experienced raconteur who has performed on stage all around the country and even in such far-flung places as Germany, Australia and the Czech Republic. He has been called by some an unofficial spokesperson for the Furry fandom since he has dedicated a good deal of time and energy to dispelling the myths and misconceptions surrounding the world of anthropomorphics. In what spare time he can find he likes to write and has published a number of stories in small-press titles, although he did break into the Big World in 1999 when his story "Tweaked in the Head" was included in *Flights of Fantasy*, an anthology of bird-related SF tales assembled by Mercedes Lackey. His favorite convention activity is meeting with friends in the bar, and if you're inclined to ask he has a preference for sweet rieslings (Germany's Mosel Valley or Washington's Columbia Valley, neither older than three years) although he'll always settle for a nice cheap white zinfandel out of a box with a plastic spigot on the bottom.

Paul Di Filippo

Paul Di Filippo sold his first story in 1977, and has since sold 200 more. They are accumulated in some thirteen collections, keeping company with his several novels. He lives in Providence, Rhode Island, with Deborah Newton, Brownie the cocker spaniel, and Penny Century the calico cat.

Naomi Kritzer

Naomi Kritzer's short stories have appeared in *The Magazine of Fantasy & Science Fiction*, *Realms of Fantasy*, and *Strange Horizons*, and are available in two e-book collections: *Gift of the Winter King and Other Stories*, and *Comrade Grandmother and Other Stories*. Naomi lives in Minneapolis with her husband and two daughters.

About the Artists

Blotch

The leopard known as Blotch is the collaboration between Teagan Gavet and Tess Garman, with one sketching and the other painting. They've worked together since 2006, creating illustrations, web comics and graphic novels. They won the Ursa Major Award for Best Anthropomorphic Published Illustration in 2007, 2008, and 2009, and you can find more of their combined work at www.screwbald.com

Vicky Wyman

Vicky Wyman: Creator of the *Xanadu* comic series. Professional artist since 1983, specializing in animal forms in ink, watercolor, acrylic, embroidery and sculpture. Cat-lover since birth.

Mike Raabe

Seattle native, Mike Raabe has been doodling professionally since 1993. He studied illustration at the New School of Visual Concepts in Seattle and digital graphics at Bellevue College. The past two-decades has seen his work utilized in collector card games, computer games, board games, role-playing games, comic books, storyboard work for television animation, commercial advertising, and in various publications. He also does a considerable amount of consulting and development work. At present he can be found working as the art director and graphic designer for Wattsalpoag Games. Mike lives in Bellevue, Washington, with his beautiful wife, Kristina.

About the Authors

C. D. Woodbury

C.D. Woodbury is a musician in Washington state who doesn't publicize much of his personal life and occasionally draws pictures and copy edits for his friends at the Tai-Pan Literary & Arts Project.

Cooner

A cartoonist, illustrator, animator, and digital artist, whatever is needed from day to day. Cooner is an artist known for his distinctive style and for his amazing con badges. Over the years, he has made badgesin branded wood, laser etched aluminum, and craved acrylic. You can see them and more available at http://cooner.johntoons.com/

Synnabar

S. M. Bittler (Synnabar) is a full-time graphic designer/illustrator by trade, though she draws for herself and others when she can. She loves to include elements and symbolism from various cultures in her art, and though she'll draw almost anything, her favorite subjects include prehistoric animals, mythical creatures, and big cats. She lives with her husband and daughter, does pyrography and beadwork when she's not drawing or reading, and thinks that life is best with birds and bunnies and books and sunshine. Never stop learning!

Heather Bruton

Heather is the Canadian artist who did the orignal Ursa Major bear artwork. Her amazing work can be found at the many conventions she attends and online at http://www.furaffinity.net/user/hbruton/

About the Editor

Fred Patten

Born 1940; began collecting s-f in 1953. He joined s-f fandom in 1960, comic-book fandom in 1962. Published fanzines since 1961. Co-founded anime fandom in 1977; anthropomorphics fandom in 1980. Was a charter member of *Rowrbrazzle* in 1984; attended the first furry convention in 1989. Has written furry comic books in the 1980s through the 2000s for Antarctic Press and Radio Comix, and over 700 s-f (including furry) book reviews for various publications. Proposed the Ursa Major Awards in 2000 and is still on its Anthropomorphic Literature and Arts Association (ALAA) administrative committee. Edited *Best in Show*, the first furry anthology in 2003. A member of the Furry Writers' Group and the Furry Hall of Fame.

About the Publisher

FurPlanet Productions

FurPlanet is a small press publisher serving the niche market that is furry fiction. We sell furry-themed books and comics published by us and most major publishers in the community. If you can't get to a furry convention where we are selling in the dealers room, visit *www.FurPlanet. com* to shop online.

Best Anthropomorphic Short Fiction Awards by Year

2001

"Beneath the Crystal Sea", by Brock Hoagland
(in *Tales of Perissa*, United Publications, July)

Also nominated were:
"Niner-Thirteen", by Jim Hayden
(in *Yarf!* #61, January)
"The Good Sport", by Bill Kieffer
(on *MetamorKeep.com*, March 29,)
"The Brave Little Cockroach", by Mark Mellon
(in *Anthrolations* #3, Sofawolf Press, January)
"Man In The Mirror", by Sly Squirrel
(*Cubist's Stories website*, October 17)

2002

"Familiars", by Michael H. Payne
(in *Sword and Sorceress XIX*, edited by Marion
Zimmer Bradley, DAW Books, January)

Also nominated were:
"Six", by Samuel C. Conway
(in *Anthrolations* #5, Sofawolf Press, July)
"Ailoura", by Paul Di Filippo
(in *Once Upon a Galaxy*, DAW Books, September)
"Milk Run", by Jim Hayden
(in *Yarf!* #65, July)
"A Prison of Clouds", by Tim Susman
(in *Breaking the Ice: Stories from New Tibet*, edited by Tim Susman,
Sofawolf Press, January)

2003

"In the Line of Duty", by M. C. A. Hogarth
(in *Anthrolations* #7, Sofawolf Press, November 2003)

Also nominated were:
"Doggy Love", by Scott Bradfield
(in *The Magazine of Fantasy & Science Fiction*, August)
"Kiss and Tell", by Gene Breshears
(in *Tales of the Tai-Pan Universe* #32, March)
"Law and Justice", by Michael H. Payne
(in *Black Gate: Adventures in Fantasy Literature* #5, Spring)
"Riding the Lady", by Charles P. A. Melville
(in *Tales of the Tai-Pan Universe* #33, July)

2004

"Felicia and the Tailcutter's Curse", by Charles P. A. Melville
(*Café Press*, June)

Also nominated were:
"Felicia and the Dreaded Book of Un", by Charles P. A Melville
(*Café Press*, February)
"Princess Bracelet Snap!", by Shannon Stuart
(*Fauxpaw Publications*, July)
"St. Ailbe's Hall", by Naomi Kritzer
(in *Strange Horizons*, January)
"Telephone Inspector Stagg!: The Gambit", by E. O. Costello
(on *Spontoon Island*, October)
"Three Ladies", by Michael H. Payne
(on *ClawandQuill.net*, October 17)

2005

"In His Own Country", by Kristin Fontaine
(in *Tales of the Tai-Pan Universe*, #39, July)

Also nominated were:
"Anyone for Venison?", by M. Mitchell Marmel and E.O. Costello
(on *Spontoon Island*, June)
"Chasing the Lady", by Mark Allen Davis
(in *Tales of the Tai-Pan Universe*, #38, June)
"Contrition: It's Not Just For Breakfast Anymore", by
M. Mitchell Marmel (on *Spontoon Island*, September)
"Let's Not Duello on the Subject", by M. Mitchell Marmel and
E.O. Costello (on *Spontoon Island*, December)
"Meet Jane Doe", by E.O. Costello
(on *Spontoon Island*, March)
"Morning Head", by E.O. Costello
(on *Spontoon Island*, March)

2006

"Jacks To Open", by Kyell Gold
(on *FurRag.com*, June)

Also nominated were:
"Monkey in the Middle", by Mark Allen Davis
(in *Tales of the Tai-pan Universe* #41, May)
"Helping Hands", by Equestrian Horse Wrangler
(in *Anthro* #5, May-June)
"Full Immersion", by Phil Geusz
(in *Anthro* #4, March-April)
"Felicia and the Wrath of the Elder Glops", by Charles P. A. Melville
(*Café Press*, August)
"Bob's Greezamus Carol", by C.D. Woodbury
(in *Tales of the Tai-Pan Universe* #42, December)

2007

"Don't Blink", by Kyell Gold
(in *Heat #4*, Sofawolf Press, July)

Also nominated were:
"A Non-Biodegradable Fox", by Ryan Campbell
(in *New Fables*, Summer 2007, Sofawolf Press, July)
"For Love or Family", by Kyell Gold
(in *The Prisoner's Release and Other Stories*, Sofawolf Press, January)
"Putting the Universe Back Together", by Charles P. A. Melville
(in *Tales of the Tai-Pan Universe #43*, August)
"Chrysanthemum and Cabbage", by Gerald Perkins
(in *Renard's Menagerie #4*, October)

2008

"In Between", by Kyell Gold
(In *Out of Position*, Sofawolf Press, January)

Also nominated were:
"It's a Beautiful World", by Kyell Gold
(in *Out of Position*, Sofawolf Press, January)
"Secrets", by Kyell Gold
(in *Out of Position*, Sofawolf Press, January)
"Third Date", by Kyell Gold
(in *Heat #5*, Sofawolf Press, May)
"Earth Rise", by Ivor W. Hartmann
(in *Something Wicked #7*, July)
"Candy and Music", by K. M. Hirosaki

(in *Heat #5*, Sofawolf Press, May)

2009

"Drifting", by Kyell Gold
(on *FurAffinity.net*, August)

Also nominated were:
"Moonthief", by Not Tube
(in *X*, edited by Kyell Gold, Sofawolf Press, July)
"Stop the World", by Kyell Gold
(in *Anthro #24*, July/August)
"Thou Shalt Not Make Wrongful Use of the Name of Thy Lord", by
Whyte Yote (in *X*, edited Kyell Gold, Sofawolf Press, July)
"Trading Wishes", by Kevin Frane
(on *FurAffinity.net*, November)

2010

"Bridges", by Kyell Gold
(Novella by *FurPlanet Productions*, February)

Also nominated were:
"False Dawn", by Kyell Gold
(on *FurAffinity.net*, February 11)
"Felis Ex Machina", by E.O. Costello
(on *Spontoon Island*, March)
"Gerty and the Doesn't-Smell-Like-a-Melon", by Mary E. Lowd
(*Golden Visions Magazine*, October)
"The Peculiar Quandary of Simon Canopus Artyle", by Kevin Frane
(Novella by *FurPlanet Productions*, June)

When the Ursa Major Awards were created in 2001, voting was by paper ballots sent to preregistered Confurence 2002 members and to those few fans who requested one. Barely a hundred ballots were returned. By 2010, the voting was online and fully automated. 1,372 Furry fans from Australia, Austria, Bulgaria, Canada, Eire, Germany, Italy, Laos, Mexico, New Zealand, the Philippines, Russia, Spain, Sweden, the U.K., and the U.S.A. logged onto www.ursamajorawards. org and voted; 222 more than 2009's total.